D[

Fate had left Clay
try. Yet he dared not
So Clay did the onl
leaned low over the stallion's neck and urged it on, applying
the reins and his feet. The fissure flashed toward them. He
tore his eyes off the yawning chasm and concentrated on the
far rim. Nothing but the far rim.

"Don't try it!" the officer yelled. "You'll be killed!"

The ragged edge rushed toward them. White Apache
stayed focused on the rim. He tensed as they crashed down.
His body was jolted by the heavy impact, but he held on.
For a few harrowing seconds the stallion scrambled wildly,
its rear legs fighting for purchase on the edge. Rocks and
dirt cascaded from under its flailing hooves to plummet into
the depths below. Then, to his horror, they began to go over
the side.

HANGED!

Grinning in triumph, Clay Taggart lunged, spearing the
Bowie at Marshal Crane's throat. Suddenly it felt as if an
invisible hammer slammed into his left shoulder. He was
flung over three feet and crashed onto his back; only then
did he hear the boom of a distant rifle and realize he had
been shot.

Crane wanted to howl for joy. Then he saw Taggart move.
Twisting, he renewed his attempt to draw his pistol.

Clay rose onto an elbow, warding off dizziness and
nausea. The slug had cored the fleshy part of his shoulder,
sparing the bone and veins. It hurt like hell. But compared
to the agony of being hanged, it was nothing. He started to
rise. The impact had jarred the Winchester from his hands,
but he still had the Bowie....

Other *White Apache* Double Editions:
BLOODBATH/BLOOD TREACHERY
WARRIOR BORN/QUICK KILLER
HANGMAN'S KNOT/WARPATH
BLOOD BOUNTY/THE TRACKERS

WHITE APACHE

DESERT FURY

⟵⟶

HANGED!

Jake McMasters

LEISURE BOOKS   NEW YORK CITY

To Judy, Joshua, and Shane.

A LEISURE BOOK®

February 1998

Published by

Dorchester Publishing Co., Inc.
276 Fifth Avenue
New York, NY 10001

ISBN 0-8439-4358-0

The name "Leisure Books" and the stylized "L" with design are trademarks of Dorchester Publishing Co., Inc.

Printed in the United States of America.

WHITE APACHE

DESERT FURY

HANGED!

DESERT FURY

Prologue

The man in the shack was nervous. He paced the rickety floor like a caged cougar, one hand resting on the butt of the Remington tucked into his waistband. Quite often he licked his lips and tugged at the corners of his mustache. Regularly he prowled to the two small windows and gazed out at the somber Illinois woods in which the shack was located.

The sun had set less than 10 minutes ago. Twilight still claimed the countryside but would soon give way to darkness. A short while ago the birds in the forest had been offering their farewell chorus to the dying day. Now the woodland lay as quiet as a cemetery, the trees devoured by lengthening shadows.

Suddenly the man stiffened. Faint footsteps could be heard on the narrow path that led to the front door. Whipping out the revolver, he leveled it at the latch. When, a few seconds later, a light rap sounded, he had to swallow twice before he could speak. "Who is it?"

"Who do you think?" came the haughty reply. "Let me in, Mr. Benson. It's a bit brisk out and I don't intend to catch my death of cold."

Benson was a thin man; his clothes hung on him like rags. Unconsciously, he smoothed his faded jacket as he stepped to the door and opened it a crack. "Is it really you, Mr. Randolph?" he asked, his voice cracking with emotion. "I honestly didn't think you would come."

William Randolph was not a man who suffered fools gladly. Sniffing in distaste at the foul odor that wafted from within, he gestured impatiently for the door to be opened all the way. "Of course it's really me," he snapped. "Who else would be insane enough to travel to this godforsaken spot to meet with you?" He regarded the shack as he might a pile of cow dung. "My job, sad to say, is not nearly as glamorous as most people believe it to be."

Charles Benson jerked the door wide and offered his hand. In his haste, he forgot about the Remington and nearly poked his visitor in the gut.

Randolph gave the pistol the same sort of severe look he had given the shack. "Is that absolutely necessary?"

"Sorry," Benson blurted, shoving the gun back into his belt. "I can't be too careful. There is a price on my head, you know."

"Unjustly so," Randolph said. "Or so you claim." Primly folding his slender hands at his waist, he slowly entered, being careful not to brush his immaculate suit against the jamb or the ramshackle furniture. His long nose crinkled. "Was it also necessary to pick this filthy hovel? I would have preferred a nice hotel in the center of the city."

Randolph sighed wistfully. "It has been a while since last I savored the wonderful nightlife Chicago has to offer."

"I wouldn't know about any of that," Benson said, poking his head outside. The trail was empty; the woods were as quiet as ever. Satisfied, he shut the door and moved to a pitiful excuse for a table where he took a seat. "I've been on the run so long that I can't remember the last time I was able to relax and enjoy myself."

"If you're fishing for sympathy, you won't get any from me," Randolph said. "Not until you've convinced me that you are not the callous murderer the law claims." He glanced at the two windows, then casually moved to a spot in the center of the gloomy room. "Before we go any further, I would like some light. I can't conduct a proper interview otherwise."

Benson shook his head. "That's not wise. No one knows I'm living here, and I don't intend to advertise the fact."

"My good sir," Randolph said formally, "be reasonable. There isn't another dwelling within half a mile. No one can see this place from the road, so you're perfectly safe."

"I'd still rather not."

"I must insist. If you refuse, I'm afraid I've come all the way from New York in vain. Our interview is off. Your sister will have wasted her time, and mine."

Uncertainty etched Benson's haggard features. He gnawed his lower lip for a full half a minute, then reluctantly crossed to a lantern on a peg and lit it.

"That's much better," William Randolph said happily. He stroked his neatly groomed sandy mustache and beard, then adjusted the fine, black bowler hat he wore. A long gold watch chain sparkled when he moved his coat aside to take a leather-bound tablet from a vest pocket.

"Wouldn't you like a seat?" Benson asked, gesturing at the other chair.

Randolph flipped a few pages, ignoring the question. "It was eight months ago that you beat your employer, Percy Wainright, to death with his own cane. A warrant was issued for your arrest but you fled New York City—"

"Can you blame me?" Benson interrupted. "Wainright's father has offered ten thousand dollars to the man who brings me in, dead or alive."

"What else did you expect? The man you murdered was the son of one of the richest, most powerful men in New York—"

Again Benson cut his visitor off. "Mr. Randolph, you work for the *New York Sun*. You have a reputation for being the best reporter in the city, maybe in the whole country. That's why my sister believed you when you looked her up and told her that you were willing to listen to my side of the story. She never would have set up this meeting otherwise." Benson paused. "You must know how the Wainrights made their money. They run the worst sweatshops in New York. They're vicious, evil—"

Randolph held up a hand. "Please. Everything they do is perfectly legal."

Benson could no longer contain himself. Livid, he sprang erect. "Legal?" he practically roared. "Was it legal of Percy to corner my sister in a storeroom? Was it legal for him to take vile liberties? He forced himself on her!"

"There's no proof of that," Randolph said, unruffled.

"He admitted it to me when I confronted him!"

Benson said. "He sat at his desk and laughed in my face, telling me there was nothing I could do, that it was her word against his, that if she pressed charges he would ruin her. He bragged that he would buy witnesses to prove she was a trollop!"

"So you flew into a rage and beat him to death," Randolph said. "How very unfortunate for Percy. But how fortunate for me."

Benson blinked a few times. "What do you mean?"

William Randolph took off his black bowler hat. The instant he did, a rifle barrel pushed aside the drab rags that had been tacked over the west window. Benson tried to pull the Remington, but he hardly touched it when a thunderous blast filled the cabin and the rear of his cranium exploded outward, showering the wall behind him with bits of brain, gore and blood. The fugitive was dead before his body fell to the floor.

Three brawny men bearing rifles rushed into the shack, They ringed the body. One knelt to verify that Benson was dead.

Presently, in strolled another man: a tall, elderly figure, his clothes the most expensive money could buy, his dark eyes smoldering with satanic glee. In his left hand was a smoking rifle which he gave to one of his subordinates. Going up to Randolph, he pulled out a thick wad of bills. "Here's your blood money, Bill. And I must say, you earned every penny. Everything went exactly as you said it would."

Randolph caressed the 10,000. "Thank you, Mr. Wainright. It's always a pleasure to be of service to a fine gentleman like yourself."

Wainright walked to the sprawled form, drew back a foot and kicked Benson in the groin. "That's for my son, you bastard."

9

Together, the reporter and the older man stepped outdoors. "Will you be returning to New York City in the morning?" Wainright asked.

"No, I'm off to Arizona after a stop in St. Louis," Randolph said.

"Arizona? Whatever for? It's a wasteland. I hear there's nothing out there but rattlesnakes and scorpions."

"There's also someone with a twenty-five thousand dollar price on his head, which I intend to collect."

"You've never failed yet." Wainright pulled up the collar of his coat to ward off the brisk breeze. "Who is this doomed soul, if I might ask?"

"They call him the White Apache."

Chapter One

Clay Taggart was a white man but he did not look like one. His raven hair had been cropped below the shoulders and tied with a headband, Apache style. His clothing consisted of a breechclout and knee-high moccasins. The sun had bronzed his skin to the point where, from a distance, he might easily be mistaken for a full-blooded warrior. Small wonder, then, that he was known far and wide as the White Apache. Or, as the Apaches themselves called him, *Lickoyee-shis-inday*.

Only his piercing, lake-blue eyes gave away Clay's true heritage. But with those eyes Clay could read in a glance more than most white men could decipher in a lifetime. Clay knew, for instance, that the three white men he was tracking had passed that way less than an hour ago, that soon he would overtake them and learn why they were so deep into the Chiricahua Mountains, where few whites ever came.

The remote range was part of a vast reservation set up by the government. It was supposed to belong to the Chiricahua for as long as the earth endured.

At least those were the terms under which the great leader Cochise had agreed to a treaty. Less than six months ago the great leader had gone to his grave believing that his people had a place where they could live for all time, a haven they could roam as they pleased. Recently, however, whites were violating the terms of the agreement without punishment. Prospectors sought gold among the high peaks. Trappers and hunters paid no heed to the boundaries. Settlers nibbled at the fringes.

At the rate things were going, Clay mused, it wouldn't be long before the treaty wasn't worth the paper it had been printed on— which was typical. Try as he might, he couldn't recollect a single treaty his former people had ever honored.

Shaking his head, Clay focused on the hoofprints in front of him. As the Good Book made plain, there was a time and a place for everything. And it would not be smart to let himself be distracted when he was so close to his quarry. If they spotted him, they'd likely set up an ambush.

The marks in the ground told Clay that two of the men rode stallions, the third a mare. From the boot tracks made when the men stopped to relieve themselves, Clay also knew that the man who rode in the lead all the time was a big, husky character. Another was skinny and bowlegged. The third wore old army boots with holes in the soles.

Clay had been out hunting when he came on their trail. That had been five hours ago, shortly after sunrise, and although his woman expected him back by noon, he was not about to give up

12

the chase. Learning the identity of the trio was more important than having fresh meat for the evening meal. Especially since there was a very good chance the men were after him.

Clay Taggart had the distinction of being the single most wanted hombre in the whole territory. Anyone wearing a tin star, the entire Fifth Cavalry, bounty hunters, scalp hunters, every type of human predator alive—they were all after his hide.

Their reasons varied. The lawmen wanted him on a trumped-up murder charge. The army was after him for riding with a notorious band of renegade Apaches. The bounty hunters and scalp hunters were more interested in the 25,000 dollars being offered for his head than they were in seeing justice served.

None of which mattered to the White Apache. Let them come, he told himself. Let them all come. He would send them packing as he had so many already. It was kill or be killed, and he had every intention of outlasting his many enemies.

Suddenly the canyon walls echoed to the whinny of a horse. White Apache promptly ducked behind a boulder and listened for the sound to be repeated so he could pinpoint the animal's position. After a bit he heard instead the clink of a shod hoof on stone. Then, faintly, there were voices.

It surprised him. White Apache had not expected to catch up to the riders quite so soon. Wary of a trap, he cat footed forward, blending into the terrain as his Apache mentors had taught him, using the available cover so masterfully that only another Apache could have spotted him.

Clay came to a bend and slowed. The voices were louder, but he still could not make out the words. Lowering onto his belly, he snaked to the corner.

The whites had stumbled on a spring. In the shade of the right-hand canyon wall they'd made camp. Wisely, they had tethered their mounts to picket pins near the water. Two of the animals were grazing on sparse grass, but the third, a big black stallion, pranced and tossed its head.

The three men were much as Clay had imagined them to be. A hulking specimen in a wide-brimmed hat sat with his back propped against a saddle. Strapped around the man's waist was an ivory-handled Colt. Sticking out of the top of a boot was the bone hilt of a large knife.

The second man was thin enough to be a broom handle. He fiddled with a coffeepot while feeding dry brush to a greedy fire. His hat was a Stetson, and he favored Mexican spurs with huge rowels.

Last, there was a grizzled old-timer in faded buckskins. This one carried a Spencer in the crook of an arm and wore army-issue boots. A former scout, by the looks of him.

Curious to hear what they were saying, Clay wormed his way around the bend, hugging the base of the towering stone wall. Whenever one of the trio glanced in his direction, he froze. Soon he was among boulders and could make better time. As silently as a specter he closed in on his quarry, stopping twenty feet out. The tantalizing aroma of coffee reminded him how long it had been since last he had any.

"—so good," the skinny one was saying. "We've come this far without the Chiricahua being any the wiser."

"Don't let it go to your head, Bodine," said the scout. "We've been lucky, is all."

The thin man snickered in contempt. "You're

getting a mite gun-shy in your old age, Plunkett.
Fess up. All these high-and-mighty Apaches just
ain't as tough as you made 'em out to be, are
they?"

Plunkett bristled at the suggestion of cowardice.
"Go to hell, you damned Johnny-come-lately! I
was fightin' these red devils since before you were
born, and I say we should thank our Maker that
they haven't made wolf meat of us yet." Glancing
at the giant, he said, "Tell this jackass, Quid. I
swear; he'll get us all killed if we're not careful."

The man named Quid was rummaging in his
saddlebags. He looked up, annoyed, and growled,
"If you ask me, the two of you don't behave no
better than a couple of ten year olds. If I'd known
that you were going to jabber like chipmunks the
whole time, I never would have let you boys throw
in with me."

Bodine averted his gaze, but Plunkett refused to
be cowed.

"That's not fair and you darn well know it," the
older man groused. "How many times have we
ridden together now? Nine? Ten? And have I ever
given you cause to complain before?" He did not
wait for an answer. "No, I haven't. It's this kid
you've brought along. He's enough to drive a body
to drink."

Quid produced a piece of jerky. Taking a large
bite, he smacked his lips, then said, "Simmer
down, Bob. You're right. You're a good man to
have around in a pinch or I wouldn't keep cutting
you in for a share of the money."

"And I'm the best tracker you'll find this side of
Tucson," Plunkett boasted. "All those years of eat-
in' lousy army grub paid off, I reckon."

Clay Taggart crept steadily nearer. He had to be
extra careful because the wind was blowing from

him to them and he didn't want their mounts to pick up his scent. The black stallion had already been agitated by something and would not stand still. Whenever it raised its head to test the breeze, Clay flattened.

Presently Clay drew within 20 feet of the shallow oval pool. Holding his Winchester in front of him, he slowly thumbed back the hammer. The three men were so busy jawing that none heard the telltale click.

"If you're so blamed good," Bodine challenged the old scout, "why is it that you can't find hide nor hair of this White Apache we're after?"

Plunkett muttered a few curses, then rasped, "It's not as if he's going to put up a sign tellin' us where to find him. He's like a ghost, that one. They say he doesn't leave any more trace of his comings and goings than a true Apache would."

"Excuses, excuses," Bodine said.

Quid stopped chewing. "You're pushing, Jess. We can't hold it against Bob if it's taking longer than we figured. I told you this wouldn't be easy, that it might take us a long time to find the turncoat. For one third of the reward money, I think you can afford to be patient."

Bodine laughed lightly. "Hell, for that much money, I'll wait until doomsday if need be."

Clay took that as his cue. Springing erect, he trained the Winchester on them and said, "I reckon it won't be quite that long, mister."

"*You!*" Plunkett cried.

To say they were flabbergasted would be an understatement. Bodine gawked, frozen in the act of reaching for a tin cup. The scout let his mouth drop, revealing a gap where three of his front teeth had been. Only Quid recovered right away and started to make a stab for his fancy pistol before he thought better of the notion.

"Shuck the hardware, gents," Clay directed. "Real slow, unless you're partial to being lead poisoned." Tensed to cut loose at the first wrong move, he watched them shed their revolvers. Quid lowered his bent leg to hide the knife in his boot but Clay wagged the Winchester. "That Kansas neck blister of yours, too, mister."

The big man reluctantly tossed the Bowie onto the pile.

All three of them had rifles, but only the scout had kept his handy. Motioning, Clay made Plunkett throw it to one side. Then he indicated a flat spot to the left of the pool. "Plant yourselves over there while I have a look at your war bags."

Bodine glowered. "You keep your hands off our personal effects, damn you!"

"Or what?" Clay could not resist taunting. "You'll talk me to death like you do your pards?" Accenting his order with a jab of the rifle, he let them seat themselves; then he hunkered and poked through their saddlebags.

Once, the mere thought of going through another man's plunder would have filled Clay Taggart with indignation. That was before his wealthy neighbor had framed him in order to steal his ranch out from under him. That was before he had been saved from a lynching by Delgadito and the renegades. And that was before he had learned every white man in Arizona had turned against him, even men he had once called friends, men who had shared drinks with him, won some of his money at cards, or been to his ranch.

Bitter experience had taught Clay Taggart to think as an Apache would. Now he regarded all whites as mortal enemies who would gun him down on sight. That made these men fair game, as well as everything they owned.

It was more than a matter of a simple lust for vengeance. Clay Taggart had taken to the Apache way of life heart and soul. He had remade himself in their image, becoming more Apache than white, and buried the part of him that had been caused so much torment under the hard exterior of an Apache warrior.

The unwritten Chiricahua creed had become the sole standard by which Clay Taggart lived: To kill without being killed, to steal without being caught.

So it was not Clay Taggart, rancher, who rummaged through the belongings of the bounty hunters. It was *Lickoyee-shis-inday*, an Apache warrior in spirit, if not by birthright. He cast useless articles aside: extra spurs and cinches, whang leather, a deck of playing cards, and spare clothes. Boxes of ammo, though, he stacked in a pile next to the guns. When he was all done, he stuffed the cartridges into an empty saddlebag and crammed the pistols into another.

Quid studied him the whole time. Plunkett played with his beard, his brow puckered. Bodine acted as if he had ants in his britches. Finally, the young cutthroat could not stand the suspense any longer.

"What do you aim to do with us, Taggart?"

White Apache glanced at them. "I haven't rightly made up my mind yet. You deserve to be skinned alive and staked out for the buzzards to eat."

"I'd like to see you try!" Bodine blustered.

Rising, White Apache picked up the Bowie. "Suit yourself," he said, and could not repress a grin when the skinny tough recoiled and raised a hand as if to ward off a blow.

Their leader unexpectedly smacked Bodine on the shoulder. "Damn, kid! Show some grit. I'm starting to think that bringing you along was a mistake. Can't you see this varmint is playing with us?"

Clay had noticed that Quid spoke with a distinct drawl of a sort he had heard before. "Texan?" he asked.

"Born and bred."

"You're a long way from home."

"Blame yourself."

"Me?"

Quid nodded. "You've become downright famous, mister. Word of the price on your head has spread clear to the Pecos, and beyond. That much money is mighty hard to resist. It's more than most folks earn in a lifetime." He shrugged. "You can't blame a man for trying."

"Yes, I can," Clay countered harshly. It had been troublesome enough when he had to contend with every local gun shark under the sun. To learn they were coming from far and wide to compete for the honor of filling him with holes made Clay realize, as nothing else could, that he would be a hunted man for as long as he lived. No matter how deeply into the mountains he retreated, or how far out into the desert he might go, there would always be greedy men willing to risk all they had for a chance at the 25,000. North of the border, south of the border, it made no difference. They would plague him to the very gates of hell, if need be.

Months ago, when Clay first started down his new path, he'd known that it would lead to more and more bloodshed as time went on. At that time he had vowed to blow out the lamps of each and every man who had unjustly lynched him, as well as take his revenge on the mastermind behind the necktie social. He had also given Delgadito his word to help the renegades in their relentless war on his former people, in return for their having saved his hide.

But Clay had never foreseen that he would become the object of the most relentless manhunt in the history of the territory. He had figured on being the hunter, not the one being hunted.

It angered Clay to think that men like Quid, Plunkett and Bodine would never permit him a moment's peace. It infuriated him that whites were sneaking onto the reservation, in defiance of the law, just for the privilege of bedding him down, permanently.

The treaty that Cochise and Jeffords had hammered out after so much effort, the precious treaty that let the Chiricahua continue living pretty much as they had since the dawn of their people, now stood in grave jeopardy because of *him*.

Just then the big bounty hunter known as Quid offered a crooked grin. "Tell you what, Taggart. How about if I give you my word that we'll leave this part of the country and never come back? Would you let us go?"

White Apache stalked up to them. The young one slid backward a few feet in blatant fear. The old one eyed him warily. Quid sat there with that brazen grin plastered on his face awaiting an answer.

"How stupid do you reckon I am?" White Apache asked Quid, then hit him. In a short, powerful stroke he slammed the stock of his rifle into the bounty hunter's face.

There was a loud crunch and a thud as Quid keeled onto his back. Both of his lips were smashed and two lower teeth were busted. Blood poured down over his chin. Dazed, he tossed his head as a great bull might, then raised a hand to his mouth. Sheer rage lit his dark eyes. Snarling, he heaved up off the ground and threw himself at Taggart.

White Apache was ready. Sidestepping the foolish rush, he drove the stock into Quid's gut, doubling the man in half, and followed through with a brutal arc to the temple that felled the bounty hunter like a poled ox.

The patter of onrushing footsteps warned White Apache of another attack. He had barely an instant in which to react. For most men, that would not have been enough; they would have gone done under Plunkett's flailing fists. But Clay Taggart's reflexes were not like those of most men. His had been honed to a razor's edge by experts in close combat. His were virtually the equal of the finest fighters on the continent, and they were certainly the equal of this occasion.

Lightning in motion, White Apace whirled and slammed the barrel across the scout's chest, knocking Plunkett head over heels. The man went down hard and made no move to stand.

Suddenly White Apache saw that Bodine was gone. He assumed the young killer was trying for the horses and shifted in that direction. Only he was wrong. White Apache whipped around at the very moment that Jess Bodine sprang at him with the Bowie he had dropped poised to strike. If not for the Winchester, White Apache would have died then and there. The big blade rang against the barrel as he jerked the rifle up. Pivoting, he dodged a wild slash that nearly opened his throat. Bodine closed in again.

White Apache simply leveled the Winchester and stroked the trigger at point-blank range.

The slug caught Bodine high in the chest and

catapulted him to the rear. He smacked onto his stomach in the dirt. Body convulsing, the bounty hunter tried to rise but could not. Uttering a strangled gasp, he died.

Clay Taggart surveyed his handiwork a few moments. Bending, he set to work preparing the big man and the scout. He finished mere seconds before Quid opened his eyes and sat up. The Texan started to rise, then caught himself.

"What the hell!"

Seated on a rock at the edge of the spring, Clay patted the mound of clothes, belts and boots beside him. "Are you looking for these, killer?"

Quid was livid. "You son of a bitch! What are you playing at? If you're going to shoot us, get it over with."

"I don't aim to waste another bullet on either of you," Clay revealed. Dipping his left hand into the cool water, he cupped it and took a loud sip.

Bob Plunkett stirred. Groaning, he slowly pushed up but froze halfway. "Damn!" he blurted. "I'm buck naked!" Shocked, he looked around and spotted the clothes. Insight dawned. He licked his thin lips. "The Apaches have taught you well, mister."

"Thank you," Clay said.

"You can't do this," Quid said without conviction. Squinting, he stared up at the burning sun, then at the stark canyon walls. "What chance would we have?"

"What chance were you going to give me?" Clay said. He jabbed a thumb to the west. "Tucson is that way. Start walking. With a little luck you might make it in two or three weeks."

The two bounty hunters slowly stood. Plunkett awkwardly covered himself as he shuffled off. Quid lingered to shake a fist and vowed, "Mark my words, hombre. I'll get even with you if it's the last thing I ever do."

Clay was in no mood to abide any sass. "Light a shuck before I see if your backside is bullet proof." Leaning back, he watched as they hurried to the bend, hopping and prancing like jackrabbits whenever their feet made contact with hot stone. Once they were gone, he collected their saddlebags and rounded up their horses.

Clay did not take Quid's threat seriously. If Apaches or wild animals failed to get the pair, the merciless land would eat them alive. He seriously doubted that Quid would ever be in a position to do him any harm.

Little did he know how very wrong he was.

Chapter Two

William Randolph did not think much of St. Louis. The city was too uncivilized for his tastes, too horribly uncouth. Filled with settlers about to head west, trappers, and buffalo men and frontiersmen of every kind in from the Plains, it had a raw, primitive air he positively loathed.

The reporter preferred the finer things in life. He could not say exactly when it had happened, but Randolph had developed a taste for the very best clothes, the very best food, in short, for the best of everything money could buy.

The process had been gradual. As a top journalist in New York City, it had been part of Randolph's job to seek out and interview the rich and the powerful, the cream of New York society.

Seeing how the elite lived, mingling with them at their favorite restaurants and their clubs, letting them treat him to the most expensive liquor and meals, Randolph had found himself growing passionately fond of the tapestries of wealth. Unfortunately, he was in a profession that seldom rewarded those who made their living at it with great wealth.

So Randolph had been faced with a problem: How was he to treat himself to all the wonderful goodies money could buy when he *had* no money?

The answer had come to him quite by accident.

Randolph had been assigned to cover the story of a man wanted for several vicious robberies. The fellow also happened to have a sizable price on his head. Randolph had made the rounds of the man's family and friends, as was customary, to gather background information.

Word got back to the robber, who then sent a message to Randolph offering to turn himself in if Randolph would guarantee his safe conduct. The police, it seemed, had been upset because the man had slain one of their own, a sin New York police never forgave. They would kill the suspect on sight.

At first, Randolph had gone along with the man's request. In good faith he had arranged to meet and promised to set up the surrender so the robber would not be harmed.

Then, over a glass of wine that very evening, Randolph had second thoughts. It occurred to him that the 7,000-dollar reward would go to waste since, technically, it was for the suspect's apprehension. There had also been the murky question of ethics. In his professional capacity, he did not have the right to claim the money.

So Randolph had compromised. He had contacted the merchants' association offering the reward and discreetly let them know that he could lead their men to the robber's hiding place if they were willing to slip him the money without anyone being the wiser. They had agreed, and the poor suspect had been killed "resisting." Meanwhile Randolph had started on a new phase of his journalistic career.

In three years Randolph had made more money than in all his previous years combined. His bank account had swollen to over 100,000 dollars, and still he craved more. His goal was to have a million to his name before he reached 60. And at the rate he was going, he would achieve it.

As the carriage Randolph had rented at a livery clattered along a rough country road on the outskirts of the city he despised, he consulted the tablet he was never without. On the first page were listed the names of those who would unwittingly contribute to his growing hoard. At the top, in bold print, was the name Clay Taggart.

The carriage took a turn too fast for Randolph's taste. Poking his head out, he said, "I want to reach my destination alive, driver, if that is at all possible."

Perched on the seat was a bearded rascal in clothes fit for burning. Cackling crazily, he lashed the team with the whip so they would go faster even as he answered, "Whatever you want, fancy pants."

Randolph stewed. The man's lack of respect was galling, another example of the rustic mentality of the common herd. He was glad that there would come a time when he no longer had to deal with people like that, when he could surround himself with those who appreciated their betters.

The land beyond the window held little interest for Randolph. It was verdant farmland, too flat and green for his taste. He glimpsed farmers toiling in their fields, and he branded them as dolts for being stupid enough to accept such a grueling life.

Why did people do it? Randolph wondered. Why did they break their backs year after year to eke out a living on paltry parcels of land? Of what real value were their crude little homes? Their packs of squalling brats? Their filthy pets? In his view their lives were a total waste.

A shout from the driver drew the reporter's gaze to a cutoff ahead.

"That's the Taggart place yonder, fancy pants. You're in luck. Somebody is home."

A dirt track led to a frame house that had seen better days. From a stone chimney curled smoke. In the yard grazed a mule and a half-dozen sheep and goats. Chickens pecked and scratched. In a fenced field to the west were eight or nine cows.

Randolph hated the farm on sight.

Most of the animals scattered as the carriage rattled up. The chickens squawked and fluttered about. Only the mule was unperturbed. It went on munching contentedly.

Whistling to himself, the driver hopped down and opened the door. "Here you are, fancy pants. And you're still alive, too. Ain't it a miracle?"

"Your employer will hear about your rude behavior," Randolph said sternly, alighting. "You are a menace to yourself and others, Mr.—" he tried to remember the man's name but couldn't.

"Fletcher. Ike Fletcher," the man informed him. Arching an eyebrow, Fletcher nudged Randolph with an elbow and said, "Is it me, or could you use a quart or two of prune juice? How a person can go through life with such a sour disposition is beyond me."

Irate, the reporter pushed on past and marched the length of a narrow gravel path to the front

27

porch. He was about to step up when the screen door creaked open to reveal a young woman in a homespun dress and an apron. Instead of the robust, rough-hewn matron Randolph had expected to meet, here was a dark-haired, delicate beauty whose face bore more lines than her age merited and whose lake-blue eyes mirrored an inner strength that seemed out of place in one so frail. She regarded him with fleeting interest, scanned the carriage, then smiled at Fletcher.

"It's been a coon's age, Ike. How are you?"

"Just fine, ma'am," the man dutifully replied, doffing his battered hat. "Yourself?"

"Making do." Those piercing eyes fixed on Randolph. "I'm Amelia Taggart. Who might you be, mister? Another bill collector?"

"No, not at all," the journalist assured her, inwardly delighted to learn she was strapped for money. Randolph introduced himself, adding, "I've traveled a considerable distance, at great personal expense, to talk to you. I do so hope you will extend me the courtesy of listening." Pausing, he said conspiratorially, "It's to your benefit, my dear. Yours, and that of your cousin, Clay."

"My cousin?" Amelia repeated in surprise. "Land's sake, I haven't seen Clay since we were sprouts. How is it that you know about him?"

"It's my business to know things," Randolph said suavely. "For instance, his father, Rafe Taggart, was your father's older brother. The two of them lived on adjoining farms back in Ohio before Rafe headed west to take up ranching. Your father, Cyrus, did the same a few years later but settled here instead of going on to the Arizona Territory."

Amelia had been wiping her slender hands on the apron. Stopping, she studied him anew.

"Goodness, you do know an awful lot about us. Everything you say is true. My pa took up roots here because ma grew sickly. He feared going on would kill her."

"How noble of him," William Randolph said. False flattery, he had learned, gave people the impression that he genuinely cared about them even though nothing could be further from the truth. It helped him win their trust, which was crucial in convincing them to agree to his proposals. "Your father must have been a fine man."

"That he was," Amelia said, saddening. "He lost his will to live when he heard about my older brother's death at Gettysburg."

Randolph consulted his notes. "That would be Thomas, correct? He was a captain, I believe."

"Yes." Amelia's eyes moistened, and for a few harrowing moments Randolph feared she would burst into tears. To her credit, she composed herself and pushed the door wider. "Where are my manners? Come on in, why don't you? I can make some tea, if you'd like. For you and Ike, both."

Fletcher heard and started up the path, but Randolph quickly said, "No tea for me, thanks. And if you don't mind, what I have to say is for your ears, and yours alone. It's a matter of the utmost importance. Life and death, you might say." Brushing the driver off with a wave, he strolled past the woman and at her bidding walked down a narrow hall to a spartan parlor. A frayed rug covered the center of the floor. To his right stood a settee, its arms and legs nicked and scraped. To his left were a rocking chair and a straight-backed chair, both well past their prime.

The more Randolph saw, the more excited he became. Clearly the woman was in dire need of money. He seated himself on the settee as she sank into the rocking chair. Her expression told him that she was puzzled, another factor in his favor. By keeping her guessing, he could manipulate her better, all part of his master strategy.

"It must be rough on you," Randolph fired his opening salvo, "trying to make ends meet all by yourself. It's hard enough for a husband and wife to run a farm smoothly."

"Don't I know it," Amelia Taggart said. "If I had a lick of common sense, I would have sold the place for what little I could get after my pa died and gone to live in the city." Pausing, she fondly gazed at the four walls. "But I couldn't bring myself to do it. This farm holds too many memories for me just to give up. That's not the Taggart way, as my pa used to say."

Randolph nodded in sympathy. "Wouldn't it be nice if you had a nest egg socked away to tide you over during the tough times?"

Her eyes narrowed suspiciously. "Why dream of things that can't be? Wishing is for those who don't have the gumption to go out and make things happen."

Randolph found her quaint sayings rather amusing. "More words of wisdom from your father?"

"He was big on proverbs. It came from his study of the Good Book."

"Cyrus was a religious man? That I didn't know," Randolph said absently, then tensed when her mouth pinched together.

"You make it sound as if being religious is like having a disease," Amelia said. "Don't tell me that you're one of those puny thinkers who believes that the sun and the stars and all the critters in creation sprung up by accident?"

Randolph hastily repaired the breech. "Not me,

madam, I can guarantee!" he lied. "My parents raised me to have a firm faith in our Maker." Deciding it prudent to move on to another subject, he said hastily, "I was quite serious about the nest egg. There is a way you might be able to acquire, say, four hundred dollars, and help your cousin at the same time."

"Four hundred?" Amelia exclaimed, then caught herself. "What do you mean help Clay? What kind of trouble is he in that he'd need my help?"

"You haven't heard?" Randolph said. "Doesn't St. Louis have a newspaper?"

"It has several, but I can't afford to subscribe," Amelia said frankly. "Since I don't get into the city all that often, I don't keep abreast of the news."

Randolph liked to flatter himself that he planned for every contingency. Reaching inside his jacket, he removed a folded page from a recent edition of the *New York Sun*. In the center of the page was an article, written by him, detailing the escapades of the so-called White Apache. Handing it to her without comment, he waited impatiently for her to finish. Her face went pale as she read, which pleased him immensely.

Coughing to clear his throat, Randolph said, "The account you hold is my summary of all the pertinent facts as they are known. Sad to say, but your cousin is the most wanted man in the Southwest. Unless he turns himself in, I'm afraid his end will be quite violent."

"Clay did all these things?" Amelia said in disbelief. "Butchered innocent people? Burned ranches to the ground?" She vigorously shook her head. "I can't believe it!"

"Newspapers don't lie," Randolph said in his most indignant tone. Then, softening so as not to offend her, he continued, "What matters is that there might be a way to save your cousin. When I was researching his background, I learned how close the two of you were when you were little. The odds are that he still has a soft spot in his heart for you." He leaned toward her. "If you were to go to Arizona, Miss Taggart, if you were to talk to him, perhaps you could persuade Clay to change his bloodthirsty ways before it's too late."

"Go to—" Amelia blurted, and broke off. "You can't be serious, Mr. Randolph."

"Never more so."

"Out of the question. I'm sorry to say, but I just couldn't afford to."

"What if I paid your expenses and saw to it that you were given an additional four hundred dollars, in advance, for your trouble? That would enable you to hire someone to take care of the farm in your absence."

"It would, yes," Amelia said, her confusion evident. "But what is in this for you? No offense, but I doubt you're doing this out of the goodness of your heart."

Randolph warned himself to be careful. She was more perceptive than he had bargained on, but he was still one step ahead of her. "I'll be honest with you. I'm not. I'm doing this for the copy it will generate."

"How's that?"

"Journalistic parlance, Miss Taggart. Or, to put it more simply, a sensational story like this can't help but boost the *Sun's* circulation. Not to mention the boon it will be to my career since I'll be with you every step of the way, recording all that takes place for posterity."

Amelia bobbed her head. "So that's your interest. I thank you for being so honest with me."

"The truth is my byword," Randolph said, keeping a straight face.

"Then I'll be honest with you. I'm tempted, but I just don't know if it's the wise thing to do."

"I'm in no hurry," Randolph fibbed again. "Take your time. Think it over. I'll be back in the morning for your decision. If you agree, we'll leave for Tucson as soon as you arrange things here. With my knack for finding the right people, it shouldn't take us long to set up a meeting with your cousin. You can take it from there."

"I wouldn't know what to say to him after all these years."

Randolph had her hooked, and he knew it. "Say whatever is in your heart. The important thing is that you'll have tried to get him to mend his ways."

Giddy with his victory, Randolph nearly ruined it by laughing out loud. With the woman's unsuspecting help, he would lure the White Apache into a trap and afterward claim the reward. The pathetic creature in front of him did not realize it, but her cousin was as good as dead.

After the reporter left, Amelia Taggart sat in the rocking chair staring blankly at the clipping in her lap. Her emotions were in a whirl, her mind half numb. She kept telling herself that she must have imagined the whole thing. Every time she did, she would touch the clipping to confirm the truth of William Randolph's visit.

Closing her eyes, Amelia leaned back and commenced rocking gently, her toes pushing against the floorboards. Whenever she was upset, whenever her troubles proved almost too much to bear, it helped to sit in the rocking chair and sort through her thoughts.

Cousin Clay. Her mind filled with images of

their childhood together, of the many happy hours they had spent roaming the woods and frolicking in the fields. They had been as close as brother and sister, inseparable until that awful day Rafe Taggart hauled his family off to the frontier to make a new life for them.

Frankly, Amelia never had understood why. There had been nothing wrong with the old life. As she recollected, they had never wanted for food, and they always had clothes on their backs and other essentials.

Once the Conestoga carrying her cousin had disappeared in the distance, Amelia had gone off behind the woodshed and bawled her heart out. For over a year she had missed Clay terribly. Then, as time passed, the ache had eased. She had thought about him less and less.

Amelia could not even remember exactly how old she had been when news reached them that Rafe had gone on to meet his Maker. She did recall wondering whether Clay would return to Ohio. Later, she learned that he took over the ranch near Tucson and was doing quite well.

Which made the account in the newspaper all the more bewildering. Why would a prosperous rancher give up everything he owned, everything his father had worked so hard to build up over the years, and turn renegade? The only explanation she could think of was that Clay had gone insane. But that was preposterous, she told herself. Clay had always been a sober, considerate person.

Amelia read the article again, lingering over the paragraph that mentioned Clay's attempted rape of a neighbor's wife, and how he shot a man who tried to stop him. The Clay she remembered would never do such a thing. He would never stoop so low as to force himself on a woman.

Or would he?

Amelia had to admit that people could change. And it had been ages since last she'd seen him. Perhaps he had taken a turn for the worse. Maybe he had fallen in with the wrong crowd and gone completely bad. It happened, even to the best-intentioned people.

For some reason Amelia thought of Frank and Jesse James. It was common knowledge that they were the sons of a Baptist minister, and after his death were reared by a kindly physician, yet they were both notorious killers and robbers.

Absently plucking at her apron, Amelia gazed out a side window. Whether Clay had turned vicious was not all that important. No matter what he was like, he was still her cousin. They were *kin*, and the Taggart clan had always looked out for its own. In the old days, at any rate.

The reporter had a point. She might well be the only one who could persuade Clay to mend his ways. Could she turn her back on him when he needed her the most? In her mind's eye she saw Clay's youthful features, just as they had been so many years ago; she heard his carefree laughter as they raced across a meadow to see who would reach the other side first.

Amelia Taggart smiled, a wistful sort of smile for her lost childhood, for simpler days when she had not had a single worry. Life had been perfect then. In the mornings she had milked the cows and done her other chores. In the afternoons, her parents had permitted her to go off and play. Always Clay had joined her, and hand in hand they had explored every square inch of the countryside.

The memories, although long neglected, were as fresh as on the day they occurred, as crystal clear as if Clay were right there in the parlor with her. A powerful yearning came over Amelia, a yearning to see him again, to recapture some of the wonderful feelings they had once shared.

Another motive was also involved. One Amelia would not admit to herself except in her most unguarded moments. One that had caused her to spend many an hour late at night weeping softly into her pillow. One that tore at her insides every time she was outside working and happened to see a happy family go by in a wagon, or when she spied loving couples out for Sunday rides on horseback.

Amelia Taggart was bitterly lonely. Working the farm by herself, day in and day out, she rarely saw other souls except for her neighbors and an occasional friend who stopped to visit. It had taught her that of all the burdens the human soul endured, loneliness was one of the worst.

She missed having the companionship of someone who cared. She missed having someone else in the house, someone to talk to, someone to joke with. She knew that she should seek out a suitor, but she had been too busy keeping the farm afloat to make the effort.

Once, her cousin Clay had cared. Once, they had been the best of friends. As Randolph had mentioned, Clay was probably still fond of her. It was yet another reason to seek him out.

Just like that, Amelia realized she had made up her mind without being aware of doing so. She would go to Arizona. For old time's sake, because they were kin, and to ease her sense of aching loneliness, if only for a short while, Amelia would seek Clay out and save him in spite of himself.

And because she was a Taggart, Amelia would let nothing stand in her way.

Chapter Three

His name was Ken Weber and he made his living
by hauling freight along the Tucson-Mesilla road.
Folks claimed he was plumb loco to take a job that
sent him daily through the heart of Apache territory, but Ken paid them no mind. For one thing,
the army kept the Apache pretty much in line. For
another, the freight company paid extra for anyone willing to make the run.

Ken Weber was no fool. He kept a Spencer
handy at all times and was always on the lookout
for renegades like Delgadito or the White Apache.

On this particular day, as the wagon rumbled
down a knoll onto a straight stretch flanked by
mesquite and cactus, Ken was about to reach for
his canteen to slake his parched throat when he
spotted something that moved off to the north.
Instantly, he scooped up the Spencer and cradled
it in his lap.

Ken was not about to stop. It was well known

that Apache were clever devils. They had all kinds
of tricks to lure a victim close. Clucking, he urged
the team on. The big wheels churned, raising
clouds of dust in his wake.

Due to the thick mesquite, Ken was unable to
see the spot clearly until he drew abreast of it. 60
yards away, in the center of a small clearing, lay
a sprawled human form. A naked man. Ken
placed a hand on his rifle. It was an Apache ruse,
he figured, but the heathens were in for a surprise.
He was too smart for them. Hiking the reins, he
went to lash the horses into a gallop.

Just then, the figure weakly lifted a hand. A feeble voice bawled, "Help us! For God's sake, mister!
We're white, just like you!"

Ken hesitated. The man spoke English, sure
enough, but so did a few Apache. And if it was a
white man, why was he in his birthday suit?

"*Please*! I'm, beggin' you!"

There was no denying the jasper was in earnest.
Ken brought the wagon to a lumbering halt,
looped the reins around the brake handle and
jumped down. His boots crunched as he warily
advanced. Mesquite soon hemmed him in, which
he didn't like one bit. Every shadow hid an
Apache, waiting for the right moment to pounce.

Still, Ken went on. Folks might say he was loco,
but no one had ever accused him of being a coward. Sweat streamed down his face into his bushy
beard as he paused to listen. Other than a low
groan from the man up ahead, who had collapsed,
and the buzz of a wandering insect, the chaparral
was deathly still.

Finger on the trigger, Ken moved to the edge of
the clearing and dropped to one knee. "Mister?"
he whispered. "Can you hear me?"

The man grunted, then looked up. A thatch of

gray hair crowned a weathered face burnt nearly black by the sun. His skin was blistered, his lips puffy and cracked. He had to try twice before he could speak. "Name's Plunkett. Me and my partner tangled with the White Apache—" He was going to say more but his head sagged.

Ken Weber surveyed the mesquite. The mention of the scourge of the territory had knotted his innards. He wanted nothing to do with the White Apache. Now here was a man who genuinely *was* loco. "Is he nearby?" he whispered.

Plunkett groaned once more. Laboriously propping his elbows under his chest, he rimmed his lips with his swollen tongue and croaked, "No, no." Mustering his strength, he said, "You're safe. It was up in the Chiricahua. He stripped us and made us hike on out."

Ken's eyes widened. "You've walked all this way?"

"Me and my partner."

The reminder brought Ken to his feet. "I don't see any—" he began, but stopped on spying another sprawled figure forty yards away. "Hang on, friend. I'll check on your pard, then fetch you some water."

The second man was much bigger. Muscles corded his back and shoulders. His skin was blistered so horribly that it had peeled in many spots, allowing the sun to burn the flesh underneath.

Ken doubted this second one was still alive. Hunkering, he gingerly touched the giant's arm. Suddenly the hulking ruin flared to life. Iron fingers clamped on his wrist and he was yanked down close to a face so bloated that it barely appeared human.

"Calm down, mister!" Ken said as the stranger started to twist his arm. "I'm here to help you."

"Who—" the man mumbled, blinking rapidly in the bright light.

"I'm a freighter, on my way to Tucson. I can take you there," Ken said, thinking that would convince the man to let go. But the big man showed no such inclination.

"Where am I?" he rasped.

"About halfway between the Dragoons and the San Pedro," Ken replied. "Your pard told me that you were left afoot in the Chiricahua. Beats me how you managed it. Most would have dropped dead long ago." When the man showed no reaction, Ken commenced prying the fingers off him.

"The San Pedro River?" the man repeated thickly. "We made it, then?"

"That you did," Ken confirmed. When the giant released him, he stood. "Lie still. I'll be back right quick." Ken started to leave but halted when the man muttered a few words. Apparently they were not addressed at him.

All he heard was "Taggart" and "kill."

Clay Taggart had been astride many a horse in his time, but few measured up to the hot blood of his newest mount. The black stallion proved a joy to ride. He could go all morning at a trot, give the stallion a short rest, and gallop half the afternoon without tuckering it out. Clay had never seen the like.

Within a week of acquiring the animal, Clay had grown so fond of it that he wouldn't think of parting with it for any reason. Prudently, he told no one. Not Marista, the Pima woman who shared his wickiup, nor Colletto, her son. And certainly not the other members of Delgadito's band.

Apaches never grew attached to horses. They saw no sense in becoming fond of something they were bound to eat sooner or later. For the simple truth was that horse meat was a staple of the Apache diet.

Many a time Clay had witnessed one of his warrior friends steal a magnificent horse in a raid, only to find it roasting over a fire a week or a month later. He had yet to see a horse last more then six months in their camp.

For a former rancher, the Apache attitude toward livestock had been one of the most difficult to accept. Clay could understand how they felt about his own kind, since white-eyes had stolen most of their land right out from under them. He could appreciate why they regarded all other people as enemies to be vanquished or driven off since the history of their tribe was one long string of bloody clashes. But their callous disregard for horses, even those that had served them in good stead, was an outlook he found impossible to share.

On a sunny day, about two weeks after he tangled with the three bounty hunters, White Apache rode along a high ridge several miles to the northwest of the sheltered canyon in which the renegades were camped. He was after antelope and hoped to come upon some in one of the low valleys that bordered the Chiricahua Mountains.

It was a hot day, so hot that even the lizards and snakes had sought shade during the inferno of early afternoon. Once, not all that long ago, White Apache would have done the same. That was before he had been taken under Delgadito's wing, so to speak, and taught how to survive in the wilderness, how to find food where no other white men could, how to locate water in the middle of the driest of deserts, and how to endure the blistering Arizona sun without complaint.

Presently a winding valley watered by a narrow stream unfolded below him. Sticking to whatever cover was handy, White Apache worked his way down the boulder-strewn slope to a stand of saplings near its base. The stream was a stone's throw away, so close he could smell the dank scent of the water. That, and something else.

White Apache stiffened as the acrid odor of fresh horse urine wafted to his sensitive nostrils. Scouring the cottonwoods that lined the serpentine waterway, he noticed a wide area where the grass lining the bank had been trampled. A few hoofprints were visible.

The tracks deserved to be investigated, but White Apache was not about to ride out into the open. Sliding from the stallion, he ground hitched it, then snaked through the saplings to a belt of grama grass, where he lowered onto his hands and knees. The grass was waist high and could have concealed an entire war party. Securely shrouded, he made a beeline for the stream, poking his head into the open within 10 feet of the flattened area.

Other than the fluttering of leaves, the cottonwoods were still.

White Apache boldly stepped from concealment, the Winchester pressed to his shoulder, hammer cocked. No shots greeted him. No shouts broke out.

Judging by the number of prints, the freshness of the impressed dirt, and the fact the horses had all been shod save one, White Apache deduced that a routine cavalry patrol out of Fort Bowie had stopped to rest there less than an hour ago. Stepping to a slender cottonwood, he leaned his rifle against another, coiled, and sprang as high as he could. Grabbing the trunk, he wrapped his arms and legs around it and shimmied as high as the thin bole allowed.

No troopers were evident, but White Apache did discover a small herd of antelope grazing a mile off. Descending, he hunted for a thin branch about the length of his arm, which he then stripped of leaves and offshoots. Then he set off on foot toward them, hunched at the waist so they would not catch sight of him. The barrel of his rifle parted the high stems of grass much as the prow of a ship cleaved ocean waves.

Within several hundred yards of his quarry, White Apache knelt and burrowed under the sand and grass with the ease of a gopher. Once he had a shallow hole excavated, he drew his Bowie knife, cut a strip from the bottom of his breechcloth, and tied it to the end of the branch.

Lying flat on his back, White Apache placed the rifle beside him. It took mere moments to scoop the loose dirt over his legs and torso. Perfectly concealed except for his left arm, he elevated the branch and slowly waved it back and forth. The strip flapped lightly.

Cuchillo Negro, one of the friendlier renegades, had taught Clay this trick, routinely used by Apache to kill antelope and sometimes deer.

Curiosity, the white-eyes liked to say, was the fatal flaw of felines. The same could be said of antelope. Clay had been dumbstruck the first time he had observed the ploy in operation. It had struck him as plain ridiculous. Antelope were among the wariest of animals, able to spot movement four miles off, ready to flee at the first hint of a predator in their vicinity, human or otherwise. None would be deceived by so obvious a tactic.

Yet, to Clay's astonishment, dozens of the animals had been drawn to the waving bit of cloth Cuchillo Negro had used to tempt them in close, drawn as inexorably as fish to a bright lure or deer to a salt lick.

Now White Apache turned his head, placing an ear to the ground. He heard them long before he saw them. The dull patter of their small hooves gave them away. Presently he glimpsed furtive four-legged shapes gliding cautiously toward the branch. He did not stop waving it. To break the motion, Cuchillo Negro had instructed him, would send the animals fleeing in panicked flight, and once they were on the move, it was next to impossible to bring one down.

Antelope were the fastest animals on the North American continent, among the fleetest in the world. Vaulting in 20-foot bounds, they could race along at over 60 miles an hour for minutes at a time. No horse could keep up. And trying to fix a bead on their bobbing forms was a study in frustration.

Suddenly a pronghorn buck made bold to approach. Its wide dark eyes were fixed on the flapping strip. As if mesmerized, it walked up and tilted its head to sniff.

White Apache had to strike before the befuddled animal registered his scent. He swung the stick away from the antelope, and when it started to lean forward, he let go and looped his left arm around its neck even as he speared the Bowie into its throat. Automatically, the buck bounded backward, or tried to, but White Apache held on, stabbing again and again, slicing the pronghorn's throat to ribbons in a span of seconds. Warm blood gushed down over his chin and poured down his chest. Sharp hooves scraped at his legs. In frenzied desperation the buck half dragged him

44

out of the hole. Still, White Apache held on. Then his forearms grew slick. He began to lose his hold. Just when he feared the animal would slip free and flee, it wheezed like a bellows, staggered, and fell on top of him.

White Apache heaved and rolled to the right. Experience had taught him that stricken antelope often thrashed madly about. In their wild convulsions they had been known to impale anyone rash enough to be within reach of their short but wicked black horns.

This particular buck sported a pair of 14 inchers, curved to the back and slightly inward. They had conical tips. About halfway up, each had a short, broad prong that jutted to the front, from which the name pronghorn was derived.

The rest of the herd was in full flight. White Apache watched them rapidly recede to the north while wiping blood from his body with clumps of grama grass. At his feet the buck kicked and flopped about until too weak to continue. Finally, it expired. White Apache slid the Bowie into the beaded sheath Marista had made for him, stooped, and hoisted the antelope onto his shoulders. It weighed in excess of 120 pounds, but he bore it effortlessly.

White Apache retrieved his rifle, faced westward, and made for the stand where he had left the stallion. The hunt had gone so well that he would be back at the wickiup before nightfall.

To the south a large red hawk soared high over the Chiricahua. White Apache felt the sun on his back and smiled. At that moment in time he felt more alive than he ever had as a rancher. His whole body pulsed with health and vigor. His muscles, once sinewy and lean, bulged with raw vitality.

Years ago, if anyone had come up to Clay and told him that one day he would be living the life of a renegade Apache and loving every minute of it, he would have branded the man plumb loco. Until Delgadito saved him from a strangulation jig, he had been much like every other white man in the territory, mistaking the Apache for vermin.

Clay chuckled. That old saw about walking a mile in the other fellow's boots, or in this case, moccasins, was as true as ever. Now that he saw the world through the eyes of a Chiricahua, he had a whole new outlook on life.

Deep in thought, White Apache reached the stream and started to wade across. A faint noise made him pivot to see behind him. For a moment he stood riveted in place, then he whirled and ran.

The soldiers had returned. Led by a saber-wielding officer, they had fanned out in a half-moon formation and advanced as quietly as possible. Their intent was transparent. Not knowing that Clay had a horse hidden nearby, they sought to take him alive by getting as close as they could and then encircling him before he could flee.

White Apache raced for the saplings, the antelope bouncing with every stride. The smart thing to do was to cast the buck aside so he could run even faster, but he stubbornly refused. He had gone to a lot of trouble to slay the animal. No matter what, he was bound and determined to hold on to it.

"After him, boys!" the officer bellowed. "Don't let him get away!"

At a gallop the troopers closed in. To a man they had their carbines out and ready for action. The young officer was slightly in the lead, his gleaming saber thrust in front of him, his features aglow with excitement.

. White Apache knew that the only reason they had not opened fire on sight was because they had no idea whether he was a renegade or a tame Apache. As yet they were not near enough to note his blue eyes. To them, he appeared to be a typical warrior, and so long as he held his fire, they would probably do the same.

As if to confirm his hunch, many of the troopers commenced whooping and hollering, treating the chase as some kind of game. They thought they had him at their mercy.

White Apache was going to prove them wrong. He gained the edge of the stand, spun, hoisted the Winchester overhead, and yipped at them in defiance. Then, weaving among the thin trees, he reached the stallion.

The big black had been agitated by all the racket and had started to run off but stepped on the dangling rein and been drawn up short. It snorted as Clay slung the buck up over its back. Gripping its mane, Clay swung up, cut to the south, and jabbed his heels into its flanks.

The stallion needed little encouragement. Spooked by the yells of the cavalrymen and the thunder of scores of hooves, it burst from the saplings at a full gallop.

Harsh shouts and lusty curses greeted White Apache's reappearance. He had to ride with his body partially twisted in order to hold on to the antelope, and he saw the surprise on the troopers' faces give way to anger. They did not like being outfoxed. With their officer goading them on, they swept toward him, converging into a compact column.

"Halt!" the officer roared. "In the name of the U.S. Government, I order you to stop where you are!"

White Apache grinned. The lieutenant had to be green indeed to think that he would obey. Flapping his legs, he spurred the stallion into a draw which shortly brought him out at the base of the ridge he had descended earlier. To attempt to scale the steep slope with the army so hard on his heels would invite disaster, so he hugged the bottom and bent low, the air fanning his cheeks, his long hair whipping.

The stallion ran with a smooth, steady gait, the equal of any thoroughbred. Clay marveled again at its speed and superb endurance. He had no worry of being caught. Already the troopers were rapidly falling behind.

Then White Apache swept around a bend, and suddenly in front of him loomed a spine of earth and rock too steep for any horse to climb. He had to swing wide to the right to go around. In the process, he lost ground. A lot of ground.

The young lieutenant angled to intercept him, saying, "We have him now, boys! Onward!"

It would have been so easy for White Apache to drop five or six of them then and there. Delgadito, Fiero or one of the other renegades would have. But Clay held his fire, telling himself that he would still not shoot unless they did.

White Apache came to the end of the spine. The big black skirted a boulder the size of a log cabin. Beyond it lay an open stretch where they could regain some of the lead they had lost. They fairly flew, Clay firming his hold on the antelope which had started to slip off.

Ahead, White Apache spied a long shadow which he assumed was cast by the ridge to his left. But as he streaked nearer, he realized it could not possibly be a shadow. The ridge was to the east; the sun was to the west. There was no logical explanation for the shadow being there. Or so he mistakenly believed until he covered another 50 yards and was close enough to see the presumed shadow for what it really was. His pulse quickened and his mouth went dry.

Long ago a wide fissure had rent the earth, forming a dark abyss. The width of the cleft was uneven. It narrowed and widened haphazardly. At its narrowest, though, the distance to the opposite rim was at least 15 to 20 feet.

There was no going around it. Slanting to either side would give the troopers the chance they needed to overtake him. He might reach the end of the fissure before they did, but by then they would be so close that it might occur to the young officer to drop the stallion with a well-placed shot.

Fate had left Clay a single option. It was sheer lunacy to try. Yet he dared not let the soldiers get their hands on him. Once they realized who he was, he'd be trussed up and taken back to Fort Bowie. Whether the army turned him over to the civilian authorities was irrelevant. The end result would be the same, namely, his neck stretched at the end of a long piece of hemp.

So Clay did the only thing he could do. Reluctantly, he shoved the antelope off, leaned low over the stallion's neck and urged it on, applying the reins and his feet. The fissure flashed toward them. He tore his eyes off of the yawning chasm and concentrated on the far rim. Nothing but the far rim.

"Don't try it!" the officer yelled. "You'll be killed!"

White Apache paid the man no heed. Unconsciously, he took a deep breath and held it as the stallion covered the final few yards. The big black leaped, arcing high into the air. Below them, the fissure dropped into the bowels of the earth. To fall meant certain doom.

The ragged edge rushed toward them. White Apache stayed focused on the rim. He tensed as they crashed down. His body was jolted by the heavy impact, but he held on. For a few harrowing seconds the stallion scrambled wildly, its rear legs fighting for purchase on the edge. Rocks and dirt cascaded from under its flailing hooves to plummet into the depths below. Then, to his horror, they began to go over the side.

Chapter Four

"You want to do *what*?"

William Randolph could not quite believe his ears. They had been in Phoenix less than 10 minutes, and had only just checked into the best hotel the primitive adobe trade center had to offer. His plan was to spend one night there and no more. He was about to go to arrange for their passage to Tucson when the Taggart woman walked up to him and made her preposterous request.

"I would like to see the governor," Amelia repeated, at a loss to understand why her benefactor was so upset. He need not go along if he did not want to, but she just had to see the honorable John N. Goodwin before she talked to Clay. Her cousin's life depended on it.

Randolph hesitated. For the life of him, he could not imagine what the woman was up to. But he was dead set against her going. In order for his plan to succeed, they must keep a low profile. The

51

fewer who knew about their arrangement, the less the likelihood of anyone putting two and two together after her cousin was killed. Recovering his composure, he inquired politely, "Might I ask why?"

Amelia almost told him. Something, a feeling deep inside, intuition perhaps, changed her mind as she opened her mouth. "I'd rather not say, Mr. Randolph. I must insist, though. You can go on about your business while I do what has to be done."

The reporter was mad enough to spit nails but he hid it well. He'd had plenty of practice on their journey west.

Of all the women William Randolph had ever met, Amelia Taggart had turned out to be the most exasperating. She was a willful woman who did as she damn well pleased whether he liked it or not.

The first time had been when he paid her the 400 dollars. He had brought cash but she insisted on being paid in gold coins. Just for her, he'd made an extra trip into St. Louis and visited a local bank.

The second time took place when they rode into the city to catch the stage. She had refused to leave until she bought a new outfit, and because she had dawdled, they had nearly been left behind.

In Denver, Randolph had arranged for a suite for the two of them. He saw no harm in sharing it since there were two bedrooms, at opposite ends. But Amelia had stubbornly refused to sleep under the same roof as him, saying it was not the ladylike thing to do. So he'd had to get her a separate room at an added expense.

There had been other incidents, minor affairs in themselves, but collectively they had aggravated him to no end. Randolph would never have tolerated her behavior if she were not so crucial to the success of his scheme.

"I'm deeply hurt that you don't trust me enough to confide in me," Randolph said, playing his part to the hilt. "But I will, of course, abide by your wishes." He bestowed his most charming smile on her. As always, it failed to elicit any response. "As for my other business, it can wait. Unless you have an objection, I would very much like to go with you."

Amelia saw no harm in it. "Very well. Let's get started."

Randolph was relieved. He had to learn what she was about and how it would effect his scheme. As they descended the plush stairs to the ornate lobby, he racked his brain for an argument he could use to convince her that it was best for everyone that they not go through with it. The best he could come up with was to remark casually, "You know, my dear, it might not be wise to draw too much attention to ourselves. There are many unscrupulous men in Arizona who would leap at the chance to claim the bounty on your cousin. If any of them should learn your identity, they might use you to get at him."

"Don't fret on that score," Amelia said, surprised that he would think she could be that stupid. "I don't aim to advertise the fact."

"Good," Randolph said. Another idea hit him and he said offhandedly, "I'll see about renting a carriage at a livery. It will take us a couple of days to reach Fort Whipple, where the governor lives." He paused masterfully. "I just hope the delay doesn't prevent us from reaching your cousin before something dreadful befalls him."

Amelia glanced at him. "Is that why you were

so upset?" she asked. "Mercy me! I wouldn't bother to go if we had to travel that far. I'm more eager than you are to see my cousin." They were passing the front desk. The clerk grinned and nodded at her, and Amelia smiled. It was the least she could do since he was the one who had inadvertently given her the idea.

"You've lost me," Randolph admitted.

"While you were checking us in, I overheard the desk clerk mention to someone else that the governor is in Phoenix at the moment," Amelia explained. "I realized that the Good Lord was blessing us with a golden opportunity."

"How so?"

"You'll see," Amelia said. She let him hail one of the carriages that always waited in front of the hotel. Once inside, Amelia made it a point to sit a discreet distance from him. Even though they had been together for almost two weeks, she could not warm to the man as she could to most folks. There was something about him that rubbed her the wrong way. She could not say exactly what. Perhaps it was his smug air, or the habit he had of being brusque with everyone except her.

"Do you know where the governor is staying?" Randolph asked the driver. Secretly, he hoped the desk clerk was wrong, or that the governor had already left.

"Sure do, mister," the man said. "Just down Central Avenue a ways. We'll be there in two shakes of a lamb's tail."

"How wonderful. Take us there." Randolph stared morosely out the window as they clattered along, blind to the bustle of activity around them as well as the scenic beauty of the nearby Phoenix Mountains. When the carriage stopped, he climbed out expecting to find a stately building worthy of housing a territorial governor. Instead, he set eyes on yet another modest adobe structure. "Are you sure this is the right place?" he asked irately.

The driver, a man who bore an uncanny resemblance to the cantankerous carriage driver in St. Louis, cocked an eye at the reporter and snorted like a buffalo. "Sure as I'm sitting here, mister. This is where John hangs his hat when he's in town."

"John?" Randolph said, appalled by such familiarity. "You call your governor by his first name?"

The driver found the question hilarious. Sobering, he said, "This is Arizona, not Washington, D.C. We're not much for being formal and standing on ceremony." He punctuated his statement with a well-aimed squirt of tobacco juice that narrowly missed Randolph's polished shoes. "Folks hereabouts don't cotton to those highfalutin top hats who think people ought to bow and scrape like slaves to their masters."

"I see," Randolph said, convinced that compared to Phoenix, St. Louis had actually been a cradle of decency and decorum. He helped Amelia down, then told the driver, "We shouldn't be long. Please wait for us."

"Sure thing. I've got nothing else to do but finish a checker game I was playing with a friend of mine."

Randolph did not care to hear it. "That's nice," he said to be civil and trailed Taggart to a small gate which opened onto a narrow walk. There were no guards, no police, no one to bar their way. It was too incredible for words.

Amelia squared her slender shoulders as she came to a door. Self-consciously, she smoothed her dress and adjusted her hat. She had never spoken to a governor before and fretted that she might be overreaching herself. The man probably had 101 important things to do, and here she was, about to bother him over a personal matter. But as her pa had always liked to say, she had it to do. Rapping lightly, she listened as footsteps resounded within.

The door swung inward. Framed in the doorway was a tall, wiry man whose kindly features somewhat eased Amelia's fears. "Yes?" he said.

Randolph stepped forward. Since he had vastly more experience in dealing with individuals of distinction, he addressed the manservant formally. "My good man, would you be so kind as to inform his excellency that William Randolph, star reporter for the *New York Sun*, and a friend, would very much like to take up a few moments of his time."

The man raked Randolph from head to toe with the kind of look a person might give one of the creatures certain astronomers claimed inhabited the planet Mars. "I *am* the governor," he said softly. "John Goodwin, at your service." He offered his hand.

Randolph was startled by the power in the man's callused grip. The driver had been right; this was no bureaucratic pencil pusher who fawned on ceremony.

Amelia swallowed as the governor took her fingers and gave them a light squeeze. Fanning the flames of her dwindling courage, she introduced herself, adding, "It's urgent that I speak to you, your honor."

Goodwin smiled. "I'm not a judge, Miss Taggart. There's no need for—" Unexpectedly, he broke off and started, as if he had been pricked by a pin.

"Pardon me. Did you say that your last name was *Taggart*?"

"Yes, sir. Clay Taggart is my cousin."

"Well, I'll be!" Gov. Goodwin declared. Catching himself, he beckoned. "Where are my manners? Come on in, both of you." He turned as an elderly Mexican woman appeared, and he spoke to her in Spanish. "I've asked Maria to bring us refreshments," he explained, then escorted them down a long, cool corridor to a spacious room containing a desk, bookshelves, several chairs and a table.

Randolph was gratified to note that the furniture was all mahogany. The man had some taste, after all. It peeved him, though, that Goodwin focused on the woman and hardly seemed to notice he was there.

"What may I do for you, Miss Taggart?"

Amelia formulated her thoughts carefully before answering. So much was riding on what she had to say that she wanted to get it just right. "It wouldn't take a genius to figure out that I'm here to see you about Clay," she began. "Only recently, when Mr. Randolph showed up on my doorstep, did I learn of all the horrible things my cousin has done. For that, I am truly sorry."

Gov. Goodwin made a tepee of his hands on top of his desk. "You have no call to apologize, ma'am. Your cousin is the one who is terrorizing the area."

"But he's blood kin, and blood, as they say, is thicker than water. I must bear some of the shame, even though I'm not the one who butchered all those poor people."

Randolph disliked being ignored, so he piped in with the query uppermost on his own mind, "As far as you know, sir, is Taggart still at large?"

"So far as I know," Gov. Goodwin said. "But you

must understand that it can take a long time for word to trickle to Phoenix or Fort Whipple from down Tucson way, and even longer from Fort Bowie."

Amelia was encouraged by the news. Her main fear during the trip west had been that Clay would be killed before she was able to track him down. "Mr. Randolph tells me that a large reward is being offered."

"Yes, ma'am. Twenty-five thousand dollars." Goodwin hesitated, then finished with, "Dead or alive."

"Is there anyone you know of who wants to bring Clay in alive?"

The governor leaned back, his brow puckered. "Since you're not one to mince words, Miss Taggart, neither will I. No, I doubt very much if there is a single soul in Arizona who would go to that much effort. I don't mean to upset you, but your cousin is the most hated man alive. Most of our citizens would as soon slit his throat as look at him."

"I expected as much," Amelia said. "Yet the very reason I am here is to try to talk Clay into turning himself in without more bloodshed."

"I wish you luck. Frankly, I think you're wasting your time. When did you last see your cousin?"

"We were about ten."

Gov. Goodwin let out a sigh. "Miss Taggart, please bear in mind that what I say next is meant to spare your feelings. You have come a long way with the very best of intentions, but I feel you are setting yourself up for a disappointment that will tear you in two." Bending, he opened a drawer and removed a stack of papers several inches thick. "Do you see these? Each and every one is a report of an atrocity committed by your cousin, both on our side of the border and down in Mexico. He has raided ranches, slaying whole families and burning the buildings to the ground. He has attacked wagon trains, random travelers, prospectors and cowboys, even cavalry patrols."

Amelia was staggered by the number. "I knew there were a lot, but that many?"

The governor tapped on the stack. "Granted, not half of these are confirmed accounts. Most are hearsay. Some, undoubtedly, were committed by other renegades and chalked up to your cousin. But the point I am trying to make is that the man you seek is not the little boy you once knew. He is a cold-hearted fiend who might well add you to his growing list of victims."

"I can't believe Clay would ever harm me."

"Are you being realistic?" Goodwin challenged her.

Amelia refused to be cowed. "I reckon I won't know until I meet him face-to-face." Straightening, she opted to get right to the point of her visit. "And that's where you come in, sir. I was hoping you could help me out in that regard."

Gov. Goodwin glanced at Randolph, who shrugged to show he was as much in the dark as the head of the territory. "Can you be more specific, ma'am?"

"I came here to ask if you would see fit to grant my cousin your protection if he turns himself in."

Goodwin was stupefied.

So was William Randolph. Never in a million years would he have suspected her true motive. It was so ludicrous, he reflected, that only a hick like her would have thought of it. Had he known, he would have kept her from coming at any cost.

"Hear me out," Amelia said, afraid that the governor would make her leave for having the audacity to impose upon him. "As you yourself just pointed out, the moment Clay shows his face he's liable to be gunned down. But not if I had a paper from you guaranteeing he would not be harmed."

"You can't be serious," Gov. Goodwin said.

"Never more so."

Randolph squirmed in his chair. A safe-conduct pass from the governor would spoil everything. It was the legal equivalent of temporary amnesty, and anyone who shot the White Apache might not be eligible to collect the reward.

Amelia could tell that the governor was against the idea, so she quickly pressed her point. "What have you got to lose, sir? The important thing is to put an end to the bloodshed, isn't it? Well, Clay will never turn himself in knowing that he'll be killed doing so. But he just might if I can persuade him that no one will lift a finger against him."

"Your cousin is no fool. Do you honestly think he'll go to all the trouble of surrendering, only to be hung?"

"No, but he'll do it if you give me your word that instead of hanging, he'll spend the rest of his life in prison."

"Miss Taggart, you ask too much."

"Do I?" Amelia persisted. "Even if it means saving countless lives?"

Their eyes met, and locked.

At the northern edge of the Chiricahua, a cleft in the earth nearly brought about what the good people of Arizona wanted more than anything else: the death of the White Apache. As the black stallion's flying hooves lost their purchase on the south rim, Clay Taggart and his mount started to go over the edge. Another few inches was all it would have taken. But at the very last moment, at

the brink of their destruction, the stallion frantically righted itself and bounded into the clear.

Clay laughed. The close call had set his pulse
pounding. Intoxicated by the heady excitement,
he galloped toward the foothills, swiveling to
check on his pursuers.

The troopers had halted at the fissure. Few
could hide their amazement at his deliverance.
The young officer peered into the murky abyss,
then looked at Clay. Rising in his stirrups, he
snapped his saber in a sincere salute.

It was a grand gesture, an acknowledgement of
Clay's courage and riding skill. Clay waved his
Winchester in return but decided that was not
enough. Slowing, he cupped a hand to his mouth
and shouted, "Better luck next time, blue bellies!
Give my regards to Col. Reynolds!"

They knew then. He had given his identity away
as surely as if he had hollered his name. They became excited, gesturing and jabbering, some
wheeling to the right and the left to go around the
fissure. The officer wisely stopped them since it
was plain they had no hope of catching him.

Clay knew he had made a mistake in revealing
who he was. The army had made his capture or
elimination a top priority. Once the officer in
charge at Fort Bowie, Col. Reynolds, heard the
lieutenant's report, a half dozen more patrols
would be sent into the area to hunt him down.
Delgadito's band would be forced to lie low.

Clay wasn't very worried. He doubted the troopers would locate the renegade sanctuary, hidden
in a remote valley known only to a handful of
Chiricahua, whose dislike of all whites prevented
them from revealing the secret.

Clay's only regret was the loss of the antelope.
Three days later, when he reached the hidden en-

trance to the valley, a pair of plump rabbits and a small doe were draped over the back of his horse.

A ribbon of a trail wound among massive boulders that were so high, they blotted out the sun. Clay threaded the stallion through, at times having to lift one leg or the other to avoid scraping them. Soon the trail broadened. He entered the verdant valley and reined up to scan the heights above.

There had been a time when Clay would not have spied the lookout, so expertly did the warrior blend into the background. Now, his keen eyes detected the outline of a human head screened by brown weeds. Clay hoisted his rifle in greeting.

Ponce, the youngest renegade, showed himself. In the Chiricahua tongue he called down, "It is good you have come back, *Lickoyee-shis-inday*. There has been trouble. Fiero and Delgadito have argued, and Fiero says he is leaving in the morning."

"Thank you for the warning," Clay responded in kind. Although he had the habit of accenting the wrong syllables on certain words, diligent effort on his part had resulted in a fluency in the Chiricahua language few whites could equal.

Clucking to the stallion, White Apache trotted toward cottonwoods that rimmed the spring which fed the valley. Presently he saw five wickiups. Figures moved about. Most were women. Mexican women.

It had been White Apache's idea to venture into Sonora and attack a large *conducta* for the purpose of obtaining wives for the four warriors.

His purpose had been twofold, companionship being the most obvious. Without women, the warriors had been growing more and more restless, and restless men were careless men.

Since Delgadito and the others were considered outcasts by the Chiricahua, and no Chiricahua women would have anything to do with them, stealing Mexican women had seemed the natural thing to do.

The Apache had been doing so for generations. They much preferred Mexican women to white women for the simple reason that white women seldom lasted long in captivity. Most would rather die than let a warrior take advantage of them. The few who submitted never wholeheartedly gave in and were always seeking an opportunity to escape. They were, in short, more trouble than they were worth.

Mexican women were different. It wasn't that they were more docile than their sisters to the north. Nor were they weaker in any respect. No, White Apache had come to understand that Mexican women made excellent Apache wives because of the raw terror the Apache inspired in them; they were too afraid to resist.

To understand, one had only to realize that decades of Apache raids into Mexico had instilled a fear so deep and widespread in the Mexican people, that the mere mention of an Apache band being on the prowl was enough to make them bolt their doors and windows until the peril had passed.

Where white women regarded Apache as plain vile savages, Mexican women had been raised to view Apache as savage demons, as virtual ghosts who flitted about the countryside with impunity, as supernatural fiends who delighted in carving the warm, beating hearts from living victims. Utter dread made Mexican women ideal captives.

The second reason White Apache had insisted on the raid had to do with Delgadito's desire to see the band grow. Few whites were aware that renegade bands invariably included women and children. No band without them ever lasted long. By taking the Mexican women as wives, Delgadito's band demonstrated to their reservation brothers that the band was prospering, that it was safe for others to bring their families and join the renegade cause.

So far, though, no one had done so. Clay reckoned that it would take a while yet before the band's numbers swelled. The way he saw it, a few more bold, successful raids would do the trick. Once word spread, warriors would come from far and wide to help drive the whites from their homeland. In the bargain, they would help him take his revenge on the vermin who had tried to string him up.

But now Clay's scheme was in jeopardy. If Fiero left, there would only be three of them. It might influence others not to join. Maybe the band would even fall apart. And if that happened, his carefully laid scheme to get revenge on the man who had stolen his ranch and the woman he loved would be ruined.

He could not let that happen.

Chapter Five

The five wickiups, made from brush and grass, layered over a framework of slender poles, were arranged in a circle in a clearing beside the spring. Seated outside one of them was Delgadito's woman, Alexandra, a big-chested woman who had crafted herself a baggy dress from deer hide. She was busy weaving a basket that would be used to store food.

Kneeling by the stream was the woman Cuchillo Negro had claimed. Florencio was her name, and of all the captives, she had adapted best to their new life. Already she had learned many Apache words and phrases, and before long she would be fluent enough to hold regular conversations.

Standing outside White Apache's dwelling were Marista, the Pima outcast who had become his mate, and Fiero's woman, Delores Garcia. Garcia had streaks of gray in her hair and was as thin as a rail, but she also had an inner toughness that made her a match for the hotheaded warrior who had stolen her.

Nearby, mending a broken bowstring was Coletto, Marista's son.

Marista glanced around as White Apache entered the clearing, her long raven hair glinting luxuriously in the sunlight. Her smile of welcome warmed his heart. In imperfect English she had learned from Dr. David Wooster of San Francisco, a physician who had once lived among her people, she said, "My heart be glad to see you safe, *Lick-oyee-shis-inday*."

Clay tossed the rabbits at her feet. "And I am happy to be back," he answered. Sliding down, he nodded at Coletto, who only smiled. The Pima boy had been trying his utmost to emulate the Chiricahua, and since it was unseemly for an Apache warrior to display strong affection in public, neither did he.

Delores Garcia spoke little Apache and less English. She did say, "Hello, White Apache."

"*Buenos tardes, senorita*," Clay said. His Spanish was limited, but he knew enough to say, "I hear your man wants to leave us."

"*Si*," Delores said, her disappointment as evident as her large hooked nose.

"*Por que?*"

"He says he is tired of hiding in these mountains. He says he wants to go kill white-eyes and *Nakai-yes*. He says Delgadito and you and the other men are content to live like women, but he is not. So we leave at first light."

"He is taking you with him?"

Delores gazed wistfully at the wickiups. An unattractive middle-aged widow, she had been wasting her life away in Mexico, where no man wanted her, at the time she had been abducted. She had been so grateful to Fiero for saving her from her lonely life of drudgery, that she actually liked being the firebrand's woman. "Where he goes, I go."

"Where is he?"

Marista nodded toward a knoll to the north. "They try make Fiero stay."

Without another word, White Apache hurried off. He heard no voices and figured that he had arrived too late to join in, but on reaching the top, he found the three warriors seated there, Fiero glowering at Delgadito and Cuchillo Negro while the latter two stared at the temperamental warrior in frank annoyance.

Delgadito was an exceptionally tall, superbly muscled warrior. His black hair was bound at the forehead by a strip of cloth. He had a wide, smooth brow, riveting eyes, and a thin, tight— some might have said cruel—mouth. A long-sleeved shirt covered his chest. He also wore a breechcloth and high moccasins typical of his people.

Cuchillo Negro was shorter and stockier, but his style of dress was identical. His name meant black knife. He had earned it years ago after slaying a formidable *nakai-yes*, or Mexican, in a hand-to-hand knife fight. Afterward, Cuchillo Negro had claimed the man's black-handled blade as his own. As a result of that clash and many others, he was generally believed to be the best knife fighter in the entire Chiricahua tribe.

Fiero lived up to his name. He was almost as tall as Delgadito but much more broad through the chest. And where Delgadito was sinewy, Fiero, rare for an Apache, bulged with rippling muscles. His dark eyes were set uncommonly close together. On his forehead, he bore a scar in the shape of a lightning bolt, the legacy of a fight with scalp hunters.

"*Lickoyee-shis-inday*, he said in greeting. "You have come in time to hear my decision."

White Apache sank cross-legged to the ground and rested his .44-40 across his legs. "I have already heard. You are leaving. I will be sorry to see you go."

Fiero was puzzled. He had counted on White Apache being upset, on his white-eye brother making a plea for him to stay. "You do not care?"

"My people have a saying," White Apache said, and translated it as best the Chiricahua tongue allowed. "A true man does what he has to do. If you are tired of fighting to free your people, that is your choice. I hope you will be happy living as a reservation Apache."

The insult was almost more than Fiero could bear. Flushing scarlet, he said, "I will never live as a reservation cur! I would rather die first!"

Countless disagreements had taught White Apache to pick his words carefully when dealing with the firebrand. Pretending to take no notice of Fiero's agitation, he said, "I see. You plan to go live down in Mexico. That is very smart. You will be safer there. Perhaps we will come and visit you when time allows."

For anyone to imply that Fiero valued his personal safety over all else was a slight on his manhood. When charging enemies, he was always foremost. In battle, he was always in the thick of the fight. Every Chiricahua, male or female, knew there was none braver than Fiero. "You saved my life once," he said, "or I would shoot you."

"What have I done?" White Apache asked, feigning innocence.

"I go to hunt the white-eyes, to slay them as they

have slain my people, to show them that so long as a single Chiricahua refuses to give up, they have not won."

White Apache was in no rush to respond. The more Fiero stewed and the more flustered he became, the easier it would be to bend the warrior to his will. "How strange. We all want the same thing, and in numbers there is strength. You know this, yet you want to desert us."

Cuchillo Negro had to look away so Fiero would not see the laughter in his eyes. The cleverest of the band, he could see what their white friend was up to. It was yet another example of why he believed White Apache made a better leader than Delgadito.

The warrior in question also saw through Clay Taggart's tactic, but he was nowhere near as pleased. Of late, the members of the band relied more on Clay Taggart's judgment than his own, which disturbed him greatly. He was the one who had organized the band. He was the one who had been its leader until Sonoran scalp hunters nearly wiped them out. Now, for all intents and purposes, White Apache was in charge. It should not be.

"I desert no one," Fiero was saying. "I go to do that which we agreed to do: fight white-eyes. It is the rest of you who have forgotten why we joined together. It is the rest of you who are content to sit around like women, telling stories and sharpening your knives when you should be sticking them in the bellies of our enemies."

White Apache brandished his Bowie, tilting the blade so it mirrored the bright sun. "I, too, want to bury my blade in my enemies. That is why I head south tomorrow on a raid." He glanced at Black Knife. "Will you join me, Cuchillo Negro?"

"Yes, *Lickoyee-shis-inday*."

"And you, Delgadito?"

The former leader struggled to hide his resentment. "Yes," he said.

"And Ponce will come, too," White Apache said. He faced the firebrand and sighed. "Which means you are the only one who will not be going. We will miss you. But we know you do what is best for you."

Fiero's mouth creased in a rare smile. He did not really want to leave. By claiming he would, his purpose had been to force the others into agreeing to another raid. And here *Lickoyee-shis-inday* had played right into his hands! Filled with glee at how clever he had been, he said, "When my brothers need me, am I not always there? If you go on a raid, I will be at your side."

"You will stay with the band, then?" White Apache asked.

"I will stay." Fiero rose. "I go to tell my woman before she packs all we have."

As the hothead departed, Delgadito plucked a stem of grass and placed it between his lips. "You have done well, *Lickoyee-shis-inday*," he complimented his adversary. "Let us hope that Fiero never learns how you have tricked him all these times." Rising, he likewise departed.

Clay did not open his mouth again until he saw Delgadito reach the wickiups. "Do you think that was a threat?" he asked his friend.

"What do you think?" Cuchillo Negro rejoined. "I have warned you before not to trust him. His knife, like Fiero's and yours, thirsts for blood." The warrior paused. "Your blood, *Lickoyee-shis-inday*."

* * *

At that very moment, Benjamin Quid stood at the bar of his favorite water hole in Tucson and glumly lifted a glass. The coffin varnish burned a patch down his throat to his stomach, but he did not enjoy it as much as he normally would.

Quid had not enjoyed much of anything since tangling with the White Apache. During the grueling trek through the parched wilderness, all he could think of was one day soon savoring sweet revenge.

The humiliation burned within him, festering, growing more and more as the days went by. Now his every waking moment was soured by the realization that Clay Taggart had gotten the better of him. No one had ever done that before. It rankled, as nothing else ever had. It made him constantly bitter, toward himself and the world in general.

If it was the last thing he ever did, Quid resolved while downing more whiskey, he would pay the renegade son of a bitch back. He didn't know how. He didn't know when. But he wouldn't rest until he had.

As Quid lifted the bottle to pour more red-eye, he happened to glance out the window and spy the steeple atop one of Tucson's churches, several blocks distant. Without giving any thought to what he was doing, he said under his breath, "I'd be willing to give my soul to the devil for a chance to get back at that bastard!"

Hardly were the words out of the bounty hunter's mouth than a grizzled figure in buckskins stepped through the door and hastened over to him.

Bob Plunkett had fared better than Quid during their ordeal. A lot of it had to do with the old scout being as hard as rawhide and as mean as a riled grizzly.

Plunkett's mean streak was the reason he had lost his job as an army scout back in Texas. A captain had caught him with a young Kiowa girl, taken one look at her bound, bleeding form, and hauled Plunkett up before the commanding officer at Fort Richardson.

Quid knew that the old man had saved their lives. Had Plunkett not spotted the freighter, they would have died out in the mesquite. It was yet another thorn in his side, because it made him beholden to the scout. And Quid hated owing any man. "What do you want?" he demanded gruffly.

"I have some news you might like to hear," Plunkett said. He had ridden with the big bounty hunter long enough to know how moody Quid could be when under the influence of bug juice. But since he had made more money in the few years they had been partnered up than in all the years he had worked for the army, Plunkett took the foul moods in stride.

"Go away," Quid said. "I still have half of this bottle to finish, and I don't want to be disturbed until I'm done."

Plunkett did not budge. "Not even if it concerns the White Apache?"

Quid squinted at the old coot. "Don't tell me someone else has claimed the bounty?"

The scout leaned on the bar, then glanced both ways to ensure no one else was close enough to overhear. He didn't want to risk his secret becoming common knowledge. They weren't the only ones after Clay Taggart. "No, nothing like that," he said quietly.

"Then what?" Quid snapped, wishing Plunkett would go away and leave him alone so he could drink himself into a stupor as he had done every day since they arrived in Tucson. It helped ease the gnawing rage that was eating him alive.

Plunkett leaned closer, smirking in anticipation of his pard's reaction.

"Well?" Quid goaded. "Get on with it."

"You'll never guess who just checked into the very hotel we're stayin' at," the scout said to draw out the suspense. He was enjoying himself immensely.

Quid came close to losing his patience. "Who?" he asked testily, not really caring. Tired of Plunkett's silliness, he raised the glass one more time.

"Clay Taggart's cousin."

The bounty hunter went as rigid as a board. Then, aglow with an inner fire, he whirled and smacked the glass on the counter so hard that half the whiskey spilled. "The hell you say!" he exclaimed.

Plunkett scanned the other patrons, a few of whom had looked up at Quid's outburst. "Keep your voice down," he said, "unless you want the whole blamed town to find out."

"Are you sure about this?" Quid asked. "So far as anyone knows, he doesn't have any kin."

Dropping his voice to a whisper, the scout said, "I was in the lobby, watchin' for this girl who goes by every day about this time, when in walked a dude and a pretty filly." Plunkett snickered. "You should see the dude! The yack is wearin' a suit so stiff, the clothes could stand up without him in 'em. He struts around like one of them peacocks, talkin' down his nose at anyone and everyone. I'd sure like to—"

Quid did not give a royal damn about the dandy. Grabbing the scout's arm, he growled, "The filly, Bob. I want to hear about the filly."

Plunkett shrugged free. To have others touch him was distasteful, even his few friends. "All right, simmer down." Again he checked the nearest patrons. None showed any interest. "So there I was, starin' out the window, when I heard the woman tell the desk clerk that her name was Amelia Taggart. The clerk looked as if he were going to choke. He asked if she were any relation to Clay Taggart, and she up and admitted that she's his cousin, come all the way from St. Louis to see him."

"I'll be damned," Quid said, astounded by their stroke of luck.

"I felt the same way," Plunkett said. "I was hopin' to learn more, but the dude whisked her up the stairs before the clerk could ask more questions. I got the idea that the dude wasn't too happy about her spoutin' off like she'd done."

Quid immediately thought of the other bounty hunters after Taggart's hide. "The clerk will probably spread it around, and by nightfall the whole town will know."

"Maybe not. No sooner did the dude take the filly to her room than he was back again. I heard him ask the clerk not to let the cat out of the bag. A few bills exchanged hands. The dude hinted there would be more if they could get out of Tucson without anyone being the wiser."

"Smart man, this dude."

"I wonder what they're up to?" Plunkett said.

"Let's find out."

Quid paid the barkeep and strolled out into the blazing sun. Pulling his new hat low, he turned to the left and almost bumped into a sturdily built man ambling along the boardwalk.

It was the town marshal.

Marshal Tom Crane had a reputation for being

tough. Rumor had it that when bucked, he could turn downright vicious—which had made Quid all the more suspicious when, after hearing of their recent plight, the lawdog had come by the sawbone's office to ask how they were faring and to wish them well.

Now Crane hooked the thumb of his right hand in his gun belt next to the well-worn butt of his Colt, idly stroked his waxed mustache with his left, and said, "Howdy, gents. I see you're both feeling a lot better."

"That we are," Plunkett said.

Quid merely nodded. He had a hunch that there was more to the lawman's seeming friendliness than Crane let on, although what it might be, he couldn't say. On the sly he had asked around, but the only interesting fact he had gleaned was that Crane was in the pocket of a wealthy local rancher named Miles Gillett, the same Gillett who had kindly offered to foot the bill for the clothes Plunkett and he were wearing.

What made it more interesting was that Miles Gillett happened to be the husband of the woman Clay Taggart supposedly tried to rape before being forced to flee into the mountains, where he somehow hooked up with renegade Apache. And it had been one of Gillett's men who Taggart gunned down while escaping.

Quid liked to flatter himself that he knew human nature inside and out. Having lived most of his life on the thin edge that separated the law abiding from the lawless, he could smell something crooked a mile away. And his inner nose told him that the business with Gillett's wife and Taggart reeked to high heaven.

"I see you got yourselves new outfits," the marshal was saying. "What did you do? Rob the bank?" A hint of a grin curled his neatly trimmed mustache, but there was no humor in it, no warmth. It was the grin of a wolf before it attacked.

"Not hardly," Plunkett said. "An hombre named Gillett sent word that we were free to help ourselves to whatever we needed from Anderson's General Store and Feed. I reckon he heard about our fix and took pity on us."

"Mr. Gillett did that?" Marshal Crane said, and suddenly he was as friendly as could be, clapping the scout on the back as if they were the best of acquaintances. "Well, that's Miles for you. There isn't a more decent man in the territory. The salt of the earth, he is."

Quid decided to pry without being obvious. "I sent him a note saying how grateful we were, but Gillett never answered it."

"He's a busy man," Crane said. "Or didn't you know that he owns the largest ranch in these parts?"

"So I heard tell," Quid said. Acting casual, he added, "Weren't Gillett and Clay Taggart neighbors at one time?"

The lawman nodded. "That they were, until the turncoat bastard tried to rape Gillett's wife." His features clouded. "Who would have thought that Taggart would hook up with Delgadito's bunch? For the life of me, I can't figure out how it came about. Delgadito hates whites."

Quid already knew all there was worth knowing about the renegades. He was more interested in something else. "What happened to Taggart's ranch after he turned bad?"

Crane stroked his mustache again. "Miles bought it for pennies on the dollar." He snickered. "I'd say that served Taggart right after all the grief he caused Mr. Gillett, wouldn't you?"

"There is justice in the world, after all," Quid said, masking his true feelings. Suddenly he saw the whole affair in an entirely new light. Any man who could keep a vicious lawdog like Tom Crane on a tight leash had to be even more vicious himself. Which meant that Miles Gillett was not quite the saint Crane made the man out to be.

If Quid was right, it explained a lot. Gillett might have set Taggart up to get his greedy hands on Taggart's land. No wonder Clay Taggart had crossed the line. To confirm his hunch, he said, "Is there any truth to the reports I've heard that the White Apache likes to raid ranches around Tucson? It might help me track him down, if so."

Marshal Crane spat in the dust. "It's true, unfortunately. A rancher named Prost and another, Jacoby, were dragged from their beds in the middle of the night and murdered."

Quid was going to ask if they were friends of Gillett's, but the lawman abruptly touched his hat brim and tromped off.

"I've got work to do, gents. Be seeing you around."

Bob Plunkett was glad to see the lawman go. Eager to get to the hotel and learn why Taggart's cousin was in Tucson, he turned to hurry off. To his utter surprise, the very man they needed to talk to was walking toward them. "It's him!"

"Who?" Quid asked, still watching Crane.

"Who else? The dude."

William Randolph had his hands clasped behind his back and his head bowed. He was beginning to think that trying to claim the bounty on the White Apache was the biggest mistake he had ever made. Nothing had gone right. Amelia had persuaded Gov. Goodwin to issue a safe-conduct pass. Once it was in Taggart's hands, killing him would be out of the question.

The reporter refused to concede defeat. He had too much time and money invested in the venture to back down. Somehow, he mused, there had to be a way to thwart the governor's intervention.

The solution hit him like a ton of bricks. Stopping short, Randolph smiled. It was so simple! All he had to do was arrange for Taggart to be slain *before* Amelia made contact. The reward would still be in effect. He would get his hands on the $25,000, after all.

But how to go about it? Randolph wondered. Where was he going to find someone deadly enough to do the job on such short notice? He had hoped to stall the woman long enough for him discreetly to seek a likely prospect, but she was determined to leave in the morning.

Just then a shadow fell across him. Randolph stopped and looked up into the flinty face of a broad-shouldered man in a wide-brimmed black hat. The stranger wore an ivory-handled Colt on one hip and a large knife in a leather sheath on the other.

"We need to palaver, mister," the hardcase declared. "And I won't take no for an answer."

William Randolph smiled. Something told him that his prayers had just been answered.

Chapter Six

The renegades had been traveling south for six straight days when they came upon tracks made by three heavily laden wagons and a half-dozen riders winding along the border of the Chiricahua reservation. The tracks led farther south, toward Mexico.

Since the wagons avoided the only road in the area, and since the party always made camp in out of the way places where they were unlikely to be noticed by roving cavalry patrols, Clay deduced that the wagons belonged to one of the many bands of smugglers operating in the region.

It was no secret that a thriving illegal trade flourished between criminal elements in southern Arizona and northern Mexico. Rifles, pistols and ammunition were routinely smuggled across the border, as were cattle, horses and other livestock.

Years ago, before the coming of the whites, the Spanish had seen fit to enslave members of various Indian tribes. Men, women, even children had been marched south in chains and made to work in mines or labor on vast haciendas. They were treated like animals, given barely enough food to survive and worked to the point of exhaustion day in and day out. Not surprisingly, few of the Indians lasted very long.

The American Government had tried to put a stop to the slave trade. But the cavalry could not be everywhere at once. The border was so long, the region so remote, that those who operated outside the law continued to do so with virtual impunity.

Clay Taggart was glad they had stumbled on smugglers and not unsuspecting families on the move. Although raiding was part and parcel of the Apache way of life, and killing without being killed was one of the highest Apache virtues, he balked at the notion of wiping out innocent pilgrims.

The band stuck to the trail like a pack of wolves on the scent of a deer herd. As was the Chiricahua custom when on raids, the warriors were on foot.

From early childhood Apache males trained as long-distance runners. Boys were routinely made to cover four-mile courses over rough country. On hot days they had to do it carrying a mouthful of water which they could neither swallow nor spit out. Gradually over the years, the distance was increased. By the time Apache males were full grown, they could travel 75 miles over scorched desert in a single day and be no worse the wear for their ordeal.

Clay Taggart was not yet the equal of his fellow renegades, but he could go farther on foot, and faster, than any white man in the territory. On this particular sunny day he loped at the head of the

Chiricahua, who were strung out in single file behind him. As was always the case when on the go, no one spoke. The hardy warriors jogged in stoic silence, their churning legs eating up the miles with deceptive ease.

To the northwest, two days' travel by horseback, was Fort Bowie. Together with Fort Apache, located farther north, the post was a bastion of American military might in the southeast corner of Arizona. Troopers out of Fort Bowie routinely patrolled the border, so Clay was on the lookout for them. He did not care to be taken by surprise, as he had been after slaying the antelope.

Of the five members of the band, only Clay wore a hat. Apaches, by and large, shunned headgear, except for headbands of various colors. Clay's hat was brown. It sported a wide brim that shaded his eyes from the sun. Weeks ago, for the sheer hell of it, Clay had stuck a feather in the crown.

Fiero often remarked that the hat looked ridiculous, but Clay refused to stop wearing it on raids. It had become his trademark, serving to identify him to any who might spot them.

Clay wanted to be recognized. He wanted those who had ruined his life to know that he was very much alive. He wanted them to quake with fear, never knowing when he might show up on their doorstep to exact vengeance for the wrongs they had done him.

It was an hour before sunset when a telltale plume of dust marked the position of the small caravan. White Apache slowed, signaled to the others, and veered into high rocks to the east of the rutted track. He soon came within sight of the wagons and riders.

Most were Mexicans, distinguished by their sombreros and flared pants. Armed to the proverbial teeth, three riders were in front of the wagons, three behind. Bandoliers crisscrossed their chests. Double cartridge belts encircled their waists. Each man had two pistols in side holsters and a third wedged under the front of his belt. Each man carried either a Henry, a Spencer, or a Winchester. These were men who knew what they were doing. They would not be easy to take by surprise.

A pair of men rode on each of the last two wagons. One man handled the mule team while the other, bristling with hardware, kept watch.

White Apache was most interested in the lead wagon—and not because of the beefy, greasy half-breed armed with four pistols and a brass-frame Henry who was riding guard. His gaze was drawn to the long-haired driver, a Mexican woman who was dressed like a man and had a sawed-off shotgun propped between her legs.

Clay had heard of her. Anglos called her Sonora Sally. Mexicans knew her as *Hechicera Rojo*, the Red Witch. She was a wily smuggler who had been working the illicit border trade for the better part of a decade. Only once had she been caught, on the Mexican side. Saloon gossip had it that she had bribed her way out of jail and disappeared. Her men were all confirmed killers, *pistoleros* with no scruples. Rumor had it that she kept them in line by offering them shares in her operation, as well as letting them take turns sampling her feminine charms.

Every lawman in Arizona would have given their right arm for a crack at her. The army had posted circulars, asking anyone with information on her whereabouts to come forward.

But the White Apache had found her first. From a high roost he spied on them, debating what to do. The wagons were bound to contain a lot of plunder. The big question was whether it was plunder the Apache could use, or whether they would be risking their lives for useless dry goods.

Then there was Sonora Sally to consider. Clay had an aversion to killing women, even a woman who made her living on the wrong side of the law. He attempted to come up with an excuse to let the smugglers go on their way unmolested.

The wagons rattled steadily southward. Now and then an outrider would go up to one of them and help himself to a dipper of water from a side-mounted barrel.

White Apache and the Chiricahua shadowed the smugglers until sunset. As the light dwindled, Sonora Sally guided her team into a gully; the others followed suit, and within no time they had a fire going and were treating themselves to coffee and beans.

When Clay was positive the gang had settled down for the night, he withdrew from his vantage point, silently signaling to the warriors as he did. They all joined him except for Ponce. The young warrior was left to keep watch.

Presently White Apache and the three Apache warriors were gathered under a rock overhang, squatting in a circle. Fiero spoke first. Simmering with excitement, he declared, "I say we attack before dawn. Most of the *Nakai-yes* will be asleep. We can kill half of them before the rest know what is happening. It will be easy."

"You always want to attack," White Apache pointed out, eliciting a grin from Cuchillo Negro. "But we must ask ourselves whether it would be worth it. What do we stand to gain?"

"Rifles, ammunition, horses," Fiero ticked them off.

"We have enough horses. We have plenty of guns from previous raids. And we have collected enough ammunition for an army." White Apache held his ground.

The hothead did not like it when someone disputed him. "So? Are you becoming lazy, *Lickoyee-shis-inday*? Since when is a warrior content with what he has? Have you forgotten that we are Apache? The *Shis-Inday* are warriors, before all else. We have always been so. We will always be so. My father, his father, and my father's father all lived by their quickness and their wits. We must do the same."

It was a valid point that White Apache could not dispute, so he did not even try. It would have done no good, anyway. Once Fiero made up his mind, changing it was like changing the course of a river—next to impossible unless you were the Almighty. He turned to Delgadito for support. "What do you say?"

The renegade leader thought it folly to go up against so many guns. In the old days, before *Lickoyee-shis-inday* usurped his position, he would have dismissed it as too reckless. But he had been working on a plan to win back the trust of the other warriors, and to that end, he had to side with them against *Lickoyee-shis-inday* whenever possible. So he answered, "Fiero's thoughts are mine. We have been idle too long. If we do this the right way, we will not lose anyone."

"And you?" White Apache asked Black Knife.

Cuchillo Negro had always been the most cautious member of the band. He always counseled against doing anything rash. This time was no different. "I once heard Cochise say that a wise warrior knows when to fight, and when not to. There is little to gain by attacking these *Nakai-yes*. I say we keep hunting. Something better will come along."

The wrangling would have gone on indefinitely had Ponce not materialized out of the shadows. "Come quickly," the young warrior urged.

"What has happened?" White Apache asked.

"You must see for yourselves."

Into the darkness they melted, spectral figures who made no more noise than real ghosts would. Invisible to the smugglers below, they laid flat along the gully rim.

Clay was taken aback to see that a girl of 10 or 12 had joined the smugglers. It was an Indian girl, of all people, clothed in a store-bought dress, the cheap kind sold at trading posts. He was going to ask Ponce where she had come from when she rose from near the fire and hobbled over to Sonora Sally and several *pistoleros*. Around her ankles were shackles. The chain was so short, she could not take full strides without falling on her face.

"She is a Mimbre," Fiero said.

White Apache did not know how the warrior could tell, but he took Fiero's word for it. All four of the warriors had keener eyesight than he did. At times, he had to marvel at their ability to distinguish objects so far off that he was hard-pressed to make the objects out.

Of the various Apache tribes, the Mimbres were more closely allied with the Chiricahua than any other. In part, it stemmed from the deep personal friendship Cochise had shared with Mangus Colorado, the former head of the Mimbres. In part, too, because the two tribes lived close to one another, so close that the borders of their recognized territories overlapped.

The girl in the gully was carrying a tin cup of coffee. She bent to hand it to Sonora Sally, and tripped. The hot brew splashed on the smuggler's neck. Sally shot to her feet with a howl, cuffed the girl so hard that she fell onto her side, then lustily cursed the child in Spanish.

White Apache sensed a change come over his companions. Not one moved. Not one uttered a sound. Yet they were different. Their forms gave the illusion of being chiseled in stone, as if they had tensed from head to toe. They were human panthers, anxious to rip and rend.

Sonora Sally stopped swearing and stomped to a wagon. From it she pulled what appeared to be a coil of rope. A sharp flick of her arm revealed the truth. A bullwhip unfurled with a crack, inches from the prone Mimbre. The girl crawled backward to get out of reach, but hampered by the leg irons she could not crawl fast enough. Sonora Sally stalked her. The whip arced again, its tip biting into the girl's shoulder, ripping the material and the soft flesh underneath.

"You will learn to be careful, savage!" the smuggler railed. "Or I will peel your hide piece by piece until there is nothing left."

Clay doubted the Indian girl understood. The child covered her face with her arms and rolled onto her stomach, but that did not stop the whip from raining down over and over, its searing tip cutting her arms, her legs, her feet. Blood trickled from the wounds, coating her wrists and lower legs.

The girl never let out a peep. Teeth clenched, she bore the torment with the fortitude of an Apache adult. When Sonora Sally finally tired and lowered her arm, the Mimbre brazenly sat up and stared defiantly at her. Two men promptly seized her.

Sally walked forward, coiling the whip. When

she was close enough, she swung, smashing the girl across the mouth with the heavy handle. The Mimbre was rocked by the blow. Another caused her knees to buckle. A third, delivered to her stomach, doubled her over, at which point the *pistoleros* let her drop.

Fiero's blood pulsed in his veins. It was all he could do to keep from charging down into the camp. "Now what do you say, *Lickoyee-shis-inday*?" he whispered.

White Apache did not have to say anything. They all knew what had to be done.

The girl lay still for the longest while, until Sonora Sally, or the Red Witch, as Clay was now inclined to think of her, walked over and kicked the Mimbre in the back. When the girl did not rise quickly enough to suit her, the Witch grabbed her by the hair and jerked her upright.

"That one is mine," Fiero whispered.

The captive was made to wait hand and foot on the men, serving them coffee, spreading out their blankets and doing other chores. She was poked, prodded and slapped. Through it all, she held her bloodied head high.

"If she were a little older, I would take her to be my woman," Ponce said.

The young warrior was the only member of the band who did not have a mate. The woman he had kidnapped from the *conducta* had later escaped. Shortly before that, a Chiricahua maiden for whom he cared, Firefly, had been brutally butchered by an army scout. Ponce was profoundly lonely but he would never let on as much.

White Apache slid back from the edge. Grunting to alert the others, he rose, but stayed low so the smugglers would not glimpse him. One by one, the Apache dogged his footsteps. When they were far enough from the gully to speak openly, he swung around and bluntly declared, "We will kill them all. It is agreed?"

"*Tats-an*," Fiero said vehemently.

"As for the *ish-tia-nay*, one of us must take her to her people when it is over," White Apache noted.

"*Shee-dah*," Ponce volunteered.

White Apache bent his neck to study the sky. Scattered pale clouds scuttled across the heavens, dominated by a sliver of moon. It would pose no problem to men trained from childhood to blend into the terrain as if they were part of it. "We must attack the *kunh-gan-hay* from both sides of the gully at once. Delgadito and Ponce from the east, the rest of us from the west."

Clay did not mention that he felt it best to have Fiero near him so he could keep an eye on the firebrand. The others would not do anything rash. Fiero—was Fiero.

"What will be the signal?" Delgadito posed the most important question.

"When you see me go over the rim."

Fiero grinned like a kid who had been granted his heart's desire. "At last, a battle! *Nah-kee-sah-tah* to *asht-lay*. I like those odds!"

12 to five? Only Fiero would, White Apache mused, as they soundlessly fanned out to take their positions. He returned to the same vantage point as before.

The smugglers were relaxing after their long day of arduous travel. Several played cards. Others had a game of dice going. The Red Witch huddled with a husky *pistolero* who could not keep his hands off her shapely body.

Left alone, the Mimbre squatted by the fire. She was the perfect picture of misery. But she did not cry; she did not so much as sniffle.

Clay admired the girl's grit. He scanned the smugglers again, seeking evidence of liquor. It would help immensely if some of the *pistoleros* were too drunk to offer much resistance, but evidently their boss kept them on a tight rein. Coffee was drunk in large quantities, but nothing else.

Shifting, White Apache sought sign of his companions. To the north, Ponce and Delgadito were working their way along the rim toward the far side. Fiero lay at the base of a boulder 30 feet away. Of Cuchillo Negro, no trace could be seen.

There was nothing else for Clay to do but wait. Crossing his arms, he rested his chin on a wrist and made himself comfortable.

The smugglers talked in low tones. Every so often one would laugh or curse. Toward midnight most of them turned in, sprawling out under the stars. The Mimbre girl was shoved into a wagon. The Red Witch and her husky friend entered another and vanished under a blanket. One man was left to stand guard. He roved the perimeter for a while, then tired and sat on a flat rock near the fire, warming his hands.

Time passed. The wagon into which the Red Witch and her admirer had gone commenced to squeak and jiggle, proving the rumors to be true. At least it was a common enough occurrence that the guard did not even look up and none of the sleepers awoke.

White Apache found himself growing drowsy sometime around two in the morning. He drew back from the edge and stood. Pacing, he shook his arms and turned his head back and forth to get his blood flowing.

Although Clay tried his utmost to emulate the Chiricahua, he could not yet go for days at a time without sleep, as they could. Delgadito had revealed that training along those lines started when Apache boys were about 10 years old. They would be encouraged to stay up later and later, until they could go a whole night without rest. Later, they would go two nights. It was all part of their everyday practice for when they would be old enough to go on raids. Clay had gone two nights once, and been so tired on the morning of the third day that he had slept fourteen straight hours without stirring. Delgadito had laughed, joking how Clay had the stamina of a five year old and needed the rest of a person over 80.

Of course, that had been back in the days when Clay and Delgadito were the best of friends. Or so Clay had believed until Cuchillo Negro secretly let him know that he was a pawn in Delgadito's grand scheme to regain a position of prominence in the tribe.

Since then, thanks to a series of quirks of fate, Clay had been the one who grew in influence while Delgadito's standing among his fellows had waned. Clay knew that Delgadito resented it. Every time one of the others looked to Clay for advice, Delgadito stewed.

By unspoken agreement, Clay Taggart now found himself the leader of the band. More and more, important decisions were left to him. It had been his idea, for instance, to steal women for wives. He had been the one to lead the last few raids, and no one had seen fit to object.

Not even Delgadito, which troubled Clay. The warrior was not one to stand by and do nothing while someone else usurped his position. Yet Delgadito had lifted neither his voice nor a finger in protest. It made Clay suspect that the crafty renegade was up to something, that Delgadito had a plan to turn the tables somewhere down the line. Probably when Clay least expected.

Clay shrugged. If it was meant to be, so be it. He had no choice but to go on with things as they were and hope to hell he did not wind up with cold steel buried between his ribs one dark night.

Unknown to the Chiricahua, Clay has his own plan. He had to keep the band together at all costs, so that one day soon he could launch a campaign of terror against those who had wronged him. Before it was over, Arizona soil would run red with the blood of his enemies.

More time went by. White Apache lay back down. By the position of the constellations he knew that dawn was approximately an hour off.

It was time.

There had been three changes of guard overnight. A wiry Mexican whose spurs jangled as he walked was at that moment making a circuit of the wagons and the stock. A Spencer slanted across his left shoulder, he whistled softly, not paying much attention to his surroundings.

Exactly as the White Apache had counted on. Holding the Winchester close to his side, he crept to the very brink. The unwary smuggler, shuffling slowly, passed beneath him and began to loop to the east.

White Apache went over the edge. Body flat, wriggling like an oversized serpent, he wormed onto the brush-littered slope and headed toward the bottom of the gully. He had to exercise the utmost care. The incline was littered with small stones, and in spots the earth itself was loose. Dislodging either would alert the man on guard.

A bush barred his path. White Apache made like an eel, slanting to the right to go around it. He paused to lift his head high enough to see the Mexican. The man had slowed and was searching in his pockets, possibly for the makings of a cigarette.

White Apache slid lower. He was so intent on not making any noise that he did not give much notice to the weeds to his right. If he had, he might have seen some of them quiver, as if to the passage of a slender form. If he had, he would not have been taken by surprise when a clump of stems unexpectedly parted and the blunt snout of a roving rattlesnake poked out.

Its forked tongue flicking, the deadly reptile slithered into the open, straight toward Clay Taggart.

Chapter Seven

William Randolph had tossed and turned most of the night. Sleeping outdoors, in his estimation, was a barbaric practice, fit for country bumpkins and simple savages, but certainly not for a man of culture and refinement. Lying on the ground was torture compared to the wonderfully soft king-size bed he customarily slept in back in New York.

Even having three blankets under him and two on top did not help. Each morning he got up to find bruises everywhere. His skin was just too delicate for him to live primitively for any length of time. Yet that was exactly what he had been doing for the better part of a week.

The reporter frowned and sat up. Since he couldn't sleep, he might as well rise and get a pot of coffee brewing. Sunrise could not be far off, and a piping hot cup of Arbuckle's would go a long way toward restoring his spirits.

Stretching, Randolph surveyed the camp. Ten

feet away slept the accursed woman, a blanket pulled clear up to her chin. In repose her features were angelic, almost beautiful, and for a moment he almost forgot all the trouble she had given him. Almost, but not quite.

Randolph smirked. Little did she know that he had outsmarted her, that her plea to Gov. Goodwin had been wasted effort. The governor's safe-conduct pass would not save her precious cousin now.

One of the three men hired in Tucson to accompany Randolph and Amelia was over by the horses, keeping watch. Smoke curled from a pipe in his mouth.

The reporter regarded the trio as typical border ruffians. Their clothes were largely unkempt, their chins coated with rough stubble. Their sole redeeming grace was Quid's assurance that all three were proficient gunmen and knew how to live off the land.

Randolph knelt next to the smoldering embers of their campfire and added fuel to rekindle it. He had to hand it to Benjamin Quid. The bounty hunter had proved to be as good as his word.

The day they met, across from the Park Theatre in Tucson, Randolph had sensed a kindred soul. Like him, Quid worshiped the almighty dollar. Like him, Quid would do anything to fill his pockets. And like him, Quid could be as devious as a fox when it came to getting his way.

Once Randolph had heard the bounty hunter's tale of being made a fool of by the White Apache, Randolph knew he had his man. He had made his pitch and been overjoyed when Quid readily agreed to a 60-40 split. Quid's partner, Plunkett, had complained that he thought their cut should be more until Randolph pointed out that he was the only one who could get Amelia to do as they wanted, and without her unwitting help, they had no means of luring Clay Taggart into a trap.

For over an hour that day, Randolph and the two bounty hunters had sat in a murky corner of the saloon, plotting. Quid had agreed to find several reliable men to accompany Amelia and him. Since the bounty hunter knew the region fairly well, Quid had also suggested an ideal spot for the ambush.

Now, after almost a week of travel, Randolph and Amelia were nearing that spot, a place known as Devil's Canyon situated deep in the Dragoon Mountains. Why it was called Devil's Canyon, no one seemed to know. The important thing was there was only one way in or out.

Quid and Plunkett and two men with them had been shadowing Randolph and Amelia since they left Tucson. The bounty hunters would lie in wait at the canyon mouth, and when Clay Taggart rode into their sights, they would cut him to ribbons in a hail of lead.

The White Apache would be gunned down before he could reach his cousin. Amelia would never get to give him the safe-conduct pass, so the bounty would still be in force when he was slain.

Randolph chuckled to himself. He had the plan worked out to the letter. Nothing could go wrong.

At that moment, the loud crackle of a branch catching flame brought Amelia Taggart out of a troubled sleep. She had been having a horrible dream in which Clay was being led up a gallows to a waiting noose. A huge throng ringed the scaffold. In a panic, she had tried to push through them to get to him, but no one would move aside to let her pass. His head had been stuck into the noose and the hangman had tightened it around his throat. Then, just as the hooded figure was about to throw the lever that would drop the trap door and send Clay to his doom, her cousin had looked up, gazed smack into her eyes and asked sadly, "How could you, Amelia? How could you?"

Amelia had long believed that dreams were important. Some were windows to a person's innermost thoughts; others were omens of things to come. Whichever the case in this instance, his question haunted her as she rose and ran a hand through her tangled hair.

Randolph had not yet noticed her. He was grinning, as if at a secret joke.

It puzzled Amelia. He had been acting strangely ever since her visit with the governor. For a while he had been in a funk, hardly speaking unless spoken to, giving her the impression that she had done something wrong.

On reaching Tucson, the newsman's attitude had changed again. Suddenly he had been all smiles, as considerate as could be.

Amelia did not know what to make of his peculiar behavior. Her intuition warned that he was up to something, yet what it might be eluded her.

Had the dream been an omen in that regard? Amelia pondered. Or was it a reflection on her efforts? Gov. Goodwin had promised to do all in his power to ensure Clay spent the rest of his life in prison instead of being hanged, but maybe the governor's influence would do no good. Maybe Clay would go to the gallows, and it would all be her fault.

Amelia walked past the two gunmen who were still asleep. "Good morning, Mr. Randolph," she said softly, so as not to awaken them.

Randolph was so startled, he jumped. Sheepishly, he replied, "Good morning to you, Miss Taggart. I trust you slept well?"

"Not really, no."

"It's the excitement of soon seeing your cousin again after so many years," Randolph said. "Just think. By this time tomorrow we'll be at Devil's Canyon. Then all we have to do is make camp and wait for Clay to show up."

In a leather case beside Amelia's saddle were the circulars her benefactor had made up before they left Tucson. Amelia regarded it thoughtfully. "Do you really think it will work? What if he doesn't see them?"

Randolph added a handful of twigs to the growing flames. "I've been assured that word of mouth spreads news fast in this region. Sooner or later your cousin will learn of your whereabouts. He'll come. Trust me."

"But what if it's too late? What if we've left?"

Randolph humored her. "My dear, we have enough provisions to last us a month, which is more than enough time." He stared at the man smoking a pipe. "My only worry is that your cousin might not come alone. Mr. Stirco and his friends are fine shots, but there are only three of them."

"Clay would never let me come to any harm. And I won't let him or his Apache friends hurt you, not after all you've done on his behalf."

"How sweet of you," Randolph said, amused by the delicious irony. Upending the dregs in the coffeepot, he made for the shallow stream they had been following for the past two days.

A pink tinge adorned the eastern horizon, and somewhere far off birds were chirping.

Randolph had to concede a certain humble charm to the wilderness. The stark mountains, the vista of rolling slopes and gorges and ravines, had

a crudely majestic air about them. In a limited
way, so did the sea of boulders and sand and blistered earth. When he got home, he would tell all
his friends that Arizona was an interesting place
to visit, but no one in their right mind would ever
want to live there.

Amelia sat on a log to warm herself. The other
gunmen were stirring. Soon they would be on
their way again, another day spent in the saddle
under the broiling sun. She didn't mind. She was
growing to love this rugged land with its crags and
buttes and mesas, with its beautiful canyons, its
picturesque chaparral, its forests of stately ponderosa pines. Arizona Territory stirred her soul as
Ohio and Missouri never had. It helped her to
understand why her cousin had stayed.

If only he hadn't turned renegade.

What could he possibly hope to gain, other than
an early grave?

Clay Taggart might have been inclined to agree.
He froze as the sidewinder slithered toward him.
Suddenly it coiled and reared, its head less than
two feet from his neck. He held himself still as the
snake swayed and rattled its tail.

The Mexican on guard heard. Spinning, the
man leveled his rifle and cocked his head, at-
tempting to pinpoint exactly where the sound
came from.

Out of the corner of an eye, White Apache
watched the rattlesnake. He tensed his arms to
roll aside if it came at him even though his reflexes
were no match for the reptile's flashing speed. Its
tongue darted in his direction, again and again.
Its tail rose, rattling louder. He could see the tips
of its fangs through its parted lips.

White Apache also saw the guard coming toward the west slope. It wouldn't take the man long to notice him, lying in an open spot as he was. He had to crawl into the weeds, but any movement, however slight, might provoke the rattlesnake into attacking.

The sidewinder slid closer. Moving slowly, almost hypnotically, it lowered its head and crawled to within inches of Clay's throat, which was no more than a hand's width above the ground. It stopped rattling.

Clay's skin prickled. He broke out in a cold sweat. A bite in the arm or the leg he could deal with, and possibly survive. No one, though, ever lived after being bitten in the neck. The venom would reach his heart in seconds. Paralysis would set in within the first minute. Within three, he would be in convulsions. Within five, he would be dead.

The guard, almost at the bottom, was scouring the slope, lower down.

White Apache lost sight of the sidewinder's head. He felt something tickle his throat, and moments later the head appeared on his right side, moving slowly away. The snake brushed him several times. In each instance he erupted in goose bumps. Soon the tail slid out from under him, but he stayed where he was until the rattler entered a patch of dry brush.

None too soon.

The Mexican had started to climb. He was slightly north of White Apache's position, slinking toward a rock outcropping.

Drawing his Bowie, White Apache angled to intercept the man. A silent kill was called for. And a swift one. There was no telling how soon the other smugglers would wake up.

Abruptly, the guard halted and pivoted.

Jake McMasters

White Apache was screened by sparse brush. In broad daylight he would have been spotted. At night, shrouded in shadow, he was safe. Or so he thought until the Mexican hiked the Spencer and peered right at him. Quickly, he reversed his grip on the Bowie so that he held it by the flat of the blade. The guard took a stride. Then another.

Higher up, a pebble rattled.

Instinctively, the Mexican swung toward the sound, and as he did, White Apache reared onto his knees, flung back his right arm and hurled the heavy Bowie with all the skill and strength at his command.

The range was only 10 feet. The big knife was a blur. Flying end over end, it reached the guard as the man turned back. There was a spongy *thunk*. The Bowie sliced through the man's shirt and flesh, sinking to the hilt. A gurgle of shock burst from the Mexican, who dropped the Spencer, grabbed the knife and pulled. The knife came partway out, no more. Blood gushed as the guard staggered, opening his mouth to warn his friends.

White Apache shot to his feet and sprinted toward the man to shut him up. It was hopeless, though. He could never reach him in time.

Someone else did. A brawny arm looped around the guard's neck from the rear. A long butcher knife speared into his ribs three times in swift succession. At the last stroke, the Mexican gave up the ghost, crumpling in a miserable heap.

Fiero, bloody knife in hand, grinned broadly at White Apache. The warrior was in his element. He lived for the intoxicating thrill of combat, for the tingling joy that slaying enemies brought him. Even by Chiricahua standards, Fiero was bloodthirsty. He would be the first to admit as much. He would also admit that he liked being the way he was, and he had no intention of ever changing.

White Apache rushed over to reclaim the Bowie. Fiero said nothing, just melted into the grass. In moments White Apache was doing the same. He glided rapidly to the gully floor, verified that none of the horses or mules had caught the scent of fresh blood, then scrambled under the nearest wagon. It happened to be the same one the Red Witch and her lover had climbed into.

Some of the smugglers were snoring. Others slept quietly, blissfully ignorant of the bronzed death descending upon them.

White Apache, Bowie in hand, crawled to the inner wheel. Beyond it lay a half-breed, one arm crooked over his face. Setting down the Winchester, White Apache inched around the wheel's rim. He was almost close enough for a killing stroke when the breed's arm moved.

The man was awake. He saw White Apache. From his mouth ripped the terrified cry, "Apache! Apache! *Cuidado, amigos! Cuidado!*"

All hell broke loose. Smugglers sprang from their blankets, some fumbling for rifles, others drawing pistols. The half-breed pushed erect but only got to one knee before White Apache was on him. A revolver glinted. It went off almost in White Apache's ear as the Bowie lanced into the cutthroat's abdomen above the belt. The man gasped, grunted, and folded over.

White Apache drew back the Bowie to finish his victim off, but suddenly guns were firing all over the place. Slugs smashed into the wagon, into the spokes of the wheel, into the ground around him. Diving under the wagon, he snatched the Winchester on the fly and rolled out the other side as war whoops rent the air.

Dashing to the front of the wagon, White

Apache drew abreast of the seat just as the husky *pistolero* emerged. The man's shirt was missing, his pants half buttoned. He held a nickel-plated Remington, but he was looking toward the center of the camp, not down at his very feet.

White Apache slanted the Winchester and stroked the trigger. The .44-40 boomed and bucked, the slug catching the smuggler low in the torso. The impact flung the man from the wagon and he hit the ground hard, headfirst.

In the wagon a pistol cracked. A bullet bit into the seat so close to White Apache's face that flying slivers stung his cheek. He ducked, responded in kind. Working the lever of his rifle, he raced toward the next wagon, the one containing the Mimbre girl.

Ponce beat him there. The young warrior materialized out of nowhere, vaulted onto the seat and ducked under the canvas cover. In moments he reappeared, the girl held close to his chest. As he stepped to the end of the seat and coiled to jump, a smuggler raced up with a sawed-off Loomis shotgun. At that range, the scattergun would blow holes the size of melons in the pair.

White Apache was not about to let that happen. Snapping a shot from the waist, he hit the smuggler above the ear. The powerful .44-40 slug exploded out the other side of the man's cranium, showering brains, blood and bits of bone over the ground. The shotgun went off, but into the wagon, not into the warrior and the maiden.

Ponce acknowledged their being spared with a nod. In a lithe bound he gained the sanctuary of the darkness and vanished into it, taking the girl to safety.

Elsewhere, the raging clash had reached a crescendo. Guns blasted nonstop. Men swore in Spanish and in English. Some screamed. A stricken man wailed like a banshee. Six of the smugglers were down. The rest had sought cover under or behind wagons.

White Apache sprang for the wagon in front of him as rounds peppered the ground and leaden hornets buzzed through the air. Gaining momentary safety, he crouched, then peeked out. He saw one of the Mexicans slinking toward the panicked, milling horses and went to take a shot, but the man sank from sight in some high weeds.

Suddenly there was a lull as both sides reloaded. In the all too brief silence, White Apache could hear ringing in his ears. And one thing more. From the wagon which held the Red Witch came a faint ripping noise. A knife blade had been shoved through the canvas. As the gunfire resumed, the canvas parted. Out poked the head of the Red Witch. In a twinkling, she was wriggling through the opening she had made.

White Apache raised the Winchester. He had her dead to rights, but as he fixed a bead on her chest, a dusky figure appeared for a heartbeat in the brush near her wagon. It was a figure he recognized. Lowering the rifle, he let her slip to the ground and flee up the gully. She was almost out of sight when Fiero rose from concealment, knife in hand, and cat footed after her.

Turning his attention back to the smugglers, White Apache saw one go down with a neat hole in the center of his chest. The shot had come from the east rim, from Delgadito. White Apache added his rifle to the fray and winged a man crouched behind a wheel.

Off to the left, in a cluster of boulders, another rifle cracked. That had to be Cuchillo Negro, White Apache knew. Between the three of them, they had the smugglers pinned down in a cross fire. Since he doubted the Mexicans were willing to stay where they were and be picked off one by one, he foresaw them making a break for the horses at any moment.

It came seconds later. At a yip from a burly man in a sombrero, those smugglers able to do so surged to their feet and dashed toward their stock. They fired as rapidly as they could work their rifles, and in no time a wreath of gunsmoke engulfed them, concealing them as effectively as a thick fog.

White Apache spied a pair of legs, aimed twelve inches above them and fired twice. A body dropped, the smuggler twitching and kicking.

Delgadito and Cuchillo Negro were also pouring fire into the gunsmoke. Flashes from within it testified to the wild shooting of the Mexicans.

A horse whinnied in agony. Then a second. White Apache realized the Chiricahua were to blame. As a former rancher, as a man who had been raised around horses and thought more highly of them than he did of most people, he was appalled that they should needlessly suffer. But there was nothing he could do about it. The Apache were not about to stop firing so long as a single enemy stood. Also, to them a horse was just a horse. They harbored no sentimental feelings toward any animal.

Hooves drummed. A man riding bareback galloped out of the gunsmoke, leaning low over his mount's neck, a smoking pistol in his left hand. He fired at the rim, trying to keep Delgadito pinned down so he could make his escape.

Delgadito was not to be denied. His hatred of the *Nakai-yes* would not allow him to let a single one get away. It had been Sonoran bounty hunters who had massacred his wife, relatives and friends. All those he cared for, all those who had looked up to him as their leader, all those who had relied on him to keep them safe, had been exterminated like rabid dogs by ruthless Mexican butchers.

So it was no small wonder Delgadito risked exposing himself so he would have a clearer shot at the fleeing rider. He tracked the rolling gait of the man's bay, adjusted his aim accordingly, and snapped off a shot when the Mexican was almost out of sight. The smuggler flung his arms out, pitched backward and crashed into mesquite.

White Apache noticed that no more shots came from the boulders where Cuchillo Negro had been concealed, and he worried that something had happened to his friend. He started to back up and go around the wagon when a wounded smuggler across the clearing rose on one knee and snapped a shot at him. White Apache ducked as the lead bit into the wood above him. Thinking to return the favor, he straightened.

But the smuggler was already being taken care of. Like a panther out of the night, Cuchillo Negro pounced, bearing the man to the earth. A black-handled knife flashed once, twice, three times. Then, as swiftly as he had struck, Cuchillo Negro melted into the darkness again.

Five smugglers were still alive. Two, both severely wounded, were under the farthest wagon. The rest were among the prancing horses, striving desperately to climb on and get out of there.

White Apache left the sanctuary of the wagon bed, circling to the right to get closer to the men trying to ride off. The wounded ones were not going anywhere and could be finished off at the band's leisure. He passed the wagon the Red Witch had been in, paused and sought a target.

Before he could stroke the trigger, a steely hand clamped on his left ankle, and his leg was yanked out from under him, toppling him onto his back.

It was the half-breed White Apache had stabbed in the abdomen, a man White Apache assumed to be dead. Very much alive, on his knees next to the wagon tongue, his shirt and hands coated with blood, the man swept a dagger on high and closed in for the kill.

Chapter Eight

White Apache's rifle was across his chest. He did not have time to point it and fire. Instead he lashed the stock at the smuggler's head. He missed, but he thwarted the man's initial attempt to stab him. Flinging himself to the left, he heard the knife thud into the dirt. White Apache pushed to his knees as the breed came at him a third time. In the nick of time he blocked a swing that would have imbedded the dagger in his neck. He drove the rifle barrel into the man's gut. It doubled the smuggler over, but before White Apache could press his advantage, the man grasped the Winchester and threw all his weight into shoving White Apache onto the ground.

Locked together, they grappled. White Apache had to let go of his rifle to seize the breed's knife arm as it swept toward him. The tip of the blade was inches from his left eye. He strained to throw the smuggler off, but failed. Desperation lent the

man inhuman brawn. Just keeping the knife at
bay took every bit of might White Apache possessed. The smuggler, his lips curled, growled like
a wild beast.

They rolled to the right. They rolled to the left.
White Apache rammed a knee into the other's
crotch but it did not have an effect. The smuggler
tried the same with him. Twisting, White Apache
bore the brunt on his thigh. Exquisite pain racked
him, and for a moment he thought he would lose
his grip on his foe's wrist and be stabbed. Firming
his hold, he struggled to his knees, pulling the
man up with him.

They were in the open now, and one of the men
under the wagon across the clearing took a shot
at White Apache. The zing of the slug galvanized
him into a lunge to his left, onto his shoulder.

In a deft move, the half-breed shifted his weight
and executed a partial flip so that he wound up on
top. Using both arms, he threw everything he had
into a supreme effort to bury his slim blade.

The tip edged toward White Apache's face. His
muscles bulged with effort but he could not hold
the blade back. He felt the razor point prick his
cheek, felt a tiny trickle of blood. Suddenly arching his legs up and around, White Apache locked
his ankles around the breed's thick neck, then
wrenched his hips to one side.

It worked. The smuggler was flung to the dirt.
He rose quickly, though, even though his exertion
was causing his stomach wound to bleed more
profusely than ever. Most men would have keeled
over long ago. But not this one. He was as tough
as rawhide, as vicious as a loco wolf.

White Apache dodged a thrust to the chest,
swiveled and evaded a slash at his throat. Hurling
himself to the rear to gain room to move, he drew

the Colt as he landed flat. His thumb jerked the hammer and he fired his first shot as the smuggler reared, fired his second as the smuggler lunged, fired his third when the man was so close that he could see beads of sweat on the breed's brow and fired his fourth and final shot with his barrel pressed against the cutthroat's chest. The man collapsed on top of him.

White Apache exhaled and tossed the body off. Staying low, he reloaded the pistol, his fingers flying. Holstering it, he snaked to his rifle.

The fight was winding down. Only one of the wounded men under the wagon still lived. Over at the horses, two men were on their feet but one limped badly. A number of horses had broken loose and run off. Those that remained continued to mill every which way, neighing stridently all the while, raising a cloud of dust which mingled with the gun smoke to form a choking layer that blinded smugglers and mounts alike.

White Apache caught sight of Delgadito working his way down from the rim toward the animals and turned to concentrate on the smuggler under the opposite wagon. The man was on his belly behind the body of his fallen *amigo*, reloading a Spencer. White Apache could not get a clear shot.

Dashing to the right, into the brush, White Apache hunkered and surveyed the campsite to ensure no others were alive. He wanted no more nasty surprises like the half-breed. Other than a convulsing Mexican, none of the prone forms moved. Satisfied, he stalked the wounded man, using patches of weed and brush to his advantage. In the process he drew near the horses, but he counted on the last two smugglers being too busy trying to catch a horse to spot him.

The smuggler with the Spencer suddenly crawled to the north, staying under the middle of the wagon bed where it was darkest.

If White Apache had stayed by the Red Witch's wagon, he would have had a perfect shot. As it was, one of the wheels and the dead man's legs blocked his view.

Among the horses and mules, a Mexican fell. The other one gave up striving to mount and fled on foot.

Delgadito gave chase.

That freed White Apache to rise and sprint toward the wagon that shielded the last of their adversaries. It seemed lunacy, rushing into the open, but there was a method to his apparent madness. On the run, he jumped up and caught hold of the top of the rear loading gate as a shot blistered the fringe on his left moccasin. Springing up and over, he landed atop a pile of long crates that filled the bed.

Under the wagon, the smuggler cursed.

White Apache moved toward the front. He hoped to do so without being detected but the boards under the crates squeaked. Stopping in the center, he pulled the Bowie and quickly slashed the canvas on both sides. Now all he had to do was wait. Eventually the smuggler would attempt to sneak off, and he would be ready.

Resting on his knees, White Apache sheathed the knife, then pried the slit on the right open. Nothing moved. He did the same on the left. The cutthroat was not there. Nor was there any movement to the front or the back. The man still had to be underneath the wagon.

Somewhere down the gully a rifle boomed. A revolver cracked twice in reply. Again the rifle blasted, and this time it was punctuated by a short shriek which faded to a gurgling whine.

Delgadito, White Apache figured, had caught up with the man who had fled on foot. He pressed an eye to the right-hand slit once more. Then to the left-hand opening. Nothing. The smuggler under the wagon was taking his sweet time. White Apache wondered if the man was too weak from his wound to run for it.

Then there was a thump, as if something had bumped the bottom of the bed. White Apache peeked out the right-hand cut and saw the Mexican heading north, up the gully. One of the smuggler's shoulders drooped at an unnatural angle, suggesting his collar bone had been shattered. But that did not impair his legs, and he bounded like a terrified jackrabbit for the safety of the same boulders Cuchillo Negro had hidden behind a short while ago.

Sticking the Winchester's muzzle through the rent, White Apache fixed a hasty bead and fired. At the selfsame instant, another rifle thundered. Twin slugs slammed into the cutthroat's back. The smuggler hurtled forward as if swatted by a giant invisible hand and smashed onto his stomach near one of the boulders. His arms waving feebly, he grabbed hold of it and laboriously pulled himself to his knees. As he tried to rise higher, the other rifle cracked once more. The smuggler sank onto his belly, leaving a wide crimson smear on the boulder.

White Apache moved to the front of the wagon. Cuchillo Negro was 10 feet away, adding cartridges to his rifle. The warrior noticed him and nodded.

"*Yusn* was with us, *Lickoyee-shis-inday*."

To the east, the sky was brightening rapidly. Soon the sun would appear. White Apache went to climb down, then thought better of the idea. Moving to the crates, he carefully pried at the top of one with his Bowie until he had a crack wide enough to expose the contents. Inside were Spencer carbines, new models in perfect condition. Based on the number of crates, White Apache calculated there were enough to arm a small army. It spawned an idea, which for the time being he kept to himself.

Delgadito was approaching as White Apache emerged. Delgadito nodded once, curtly, then held out the gun belt and pistol that had belonged to the smuggler he had slain. "We will have no shortage of guns now," he said.

"Your words are more true than you imagine." White Apache indicated the wagon. "Look in there."

As Delgadito went to comply, a piercing whoop split the crisp morning air. Strolling toward them was Fiero. The firebrand had painted his cheeks, forehead and chest with bands of bright, fresh blood. An arrogant grin plastered his face as he came to a halt and extended his left hand for them to see the object he held. "I made her eat her own breasts before I was done."

It was the Red Witch's scalp, blood dripping from the thin strip of flesh to which the hair was attached. White Apache was surprised. Unlike Indians who lived on the Plains, Apache rarely took scalps. They did not decorate their lodges with such grisly trophies or adorn coup sticks with them, as was the custom among the Sioux and Cheyenne.

"What do you plan to do with it?" White Apache asked.

"I will give it to the Mimbre so she will have

something to remember this day by. Where is she?"

Just then, Ponce and the girl came around the northernmost wagon. He still carried her, her head resting on his shoulder. "We are here," he announced, accenting the "we."

White Apache crossed to meet them. "How badly is she hurt?"

"See for yourself."

The young warrior gently set the girl down. Up close, her bruises and welts were legion. A score of cuts from the whip marked her body. Dried blood caked her in spots.

White Apache saw that he had been mistaken. She was older than he had thought, perhaps fifteen or sixteen, but small for her age. Her doe eyes fixed on Ponce and would not leave his face.

Fiero came over. "Here girl," he said gruffly. "When you hear someone say that the *Shis-Inday* can be friends with the *Nakai-yes* or the white-eyes, hold this. It will remind you of how wrong they are."

Without looking directly at him, the girl took the gift. "Thank you," she said softly.

"Do you have a name?" Fiero inquired.

"*Nah-tanh.*"

It meant Corn Flower. For the girl to have her own name was unique. Long ago White Apache had learned that many Apache women did not. They were known simple as *ish-tai-nay*, or woman.

Fiero studied her. "You are brave for your age, *Nah-tanh*. You should have a man who is just as brave, or more so." He thumped on his chest. "I am that man. Among the Chiricahua, none have more courage. Ask any of my people." Fiero held himself straight and proud. "I offer you the honor of being my woman. I already have one, but I am a good hunter, a fine provider. You will never go hungry, never want for clothes. What do you say?"

Clay Taggart could scarcely believe his ears. The hapless girl had been through sheer hell. She was battered and bloody and weak. She was on the brink of exhaustion, alone among strangers, many miles from her family, her home. Yet the firebrand had the raw nerve to ask her to be his mate. Clay didn't like it one bit.

Neither did Ponce. The young warrior stepped protectively in front of her, planting his legs wide. "If she wants a man, she should take someone closer to her age," he boldly declared.

Fiero did not bat an eye. "What does age have to do with it? I am strong; I am healthy, and I know how to please women. She should be flattered that I give her the chance to share my wickiup."

Everyone there could tell that Ponce was about to say something Fiero would resent. White Apache grew alarmed. An insulted warrior had the right to issue a formal challenge, and should Fiero see fit to do so, the band would be shy one young warrior in very short order.

Moving up to Ponce before he could speak, White Apache put a friendly hand on the warrior's shoulder and said, "Corn Flower has had a very rough time. She can give Fiero an answer after she rests. Find a quiet spot where she can sleep undisturbed."

No warrior ever had to take an order from another. Every Apache was his own free man, to do as he pleased when he pleased. Ponce could have refused. He could have made an issue of Fiero's offer. He certainly wanted to. About to push *Lickoyee-shis-inday* aside, something about the look White Apache gave him, stopped him. Glancing at Cuchillo Negro, he saw the same look. The magnitude of the mistake he had been about to make slowly dawned. "I will do as you want, White Apache," he said, gratefully.

Clay turned to Fiero, afraid the hothead would insist Corn Flower decide right that moment. To his relief, the temperamental warrior moved toward the littered bodies, saying, "I am going to skin one of them."

"Skin one?" White Apache said, shocked. The renegades were guilty of many atrocities, but never before had one taken off the hide of another. "Why would you want to do such a thing?"

"I got the idea from a Comanche I killed many winters ago," Fiero explained, bending to examine a thickset Mexican. "He had a pouch made from human skin. I was young and did not think to keep it." He ripped the smuggler's shirt, then rolled the corpse over and poked the dead man's back. "I was stupid. It was a fine pouch, and I have wanted one like it ever since."

"Help yourself," White Apache said, for want of anything better to say. The notion repulsed him, but not as much as it should have—which bothered him a little. It seemed that the longer he stayed with the renegades, the less the constant brutality upset him. Acts that once would have churned his stomach, he now took in stride.

Before a golden crown rimmed the horizon, the smugglers had been stripped of their weapons. The rifles, revolvers, derringers, knives, daggers and dirks were piled in the wagon containing the Spencers. In the other wagons White Apache found ordinary trade goods, including a score of thick blankets the women would like.

Delgadito and Cuchillo Negro rounded up as

many horses and mules as they could find: 18, all tolled. Ropes were looped around the necks of each to form a long string.

Fiero peeled a large square of skin off the back of a half-breed. Going to a horse accidentally shot during the battle, he cracked its skull with a heavy boulder. From the cranial cavity he extracted the brains, scooping them out with his hand. These he rubbed onto both sides of the skin to keep it soft and supple until he was ready to fashion his pouch.

Treating hides with brains was a common Indian practice. Women belonging to certain Plains tribes simmered brains in water to dissolve them to the consistency of a thin paste, then rubbed the paste onto pelts.

White Apache made coffee. The warriors gathered around. A dispute broke out over whether to hide the Spencers and other weapons somewhere nearby and come back for them later or whether to head for their sanctuary in the Dragoons right away. Fiero wanted to go on raiding. But White Apache, Cuchillo Negro and Delgadito insisted it was wiser to take their plunder while they could. Reluctantly, Fiero agreed.

That left the matter of the Mimbre. Ponce had been absent the whole time, so he was not there to hear Fiero say, "It will be nice to have a strong girl like her to do my cooking and sewing. She will last many years."

Cuchillo Negro was about to take a swallow, but stopped. "You count your horses before they are stolen. Maybe she will not want to live with you."

"What woman would not?"

White Apache smothered a laugh by pretending to cough. In all his born days, he had never met anyone so outright cocksure as Fiero. Then a sobering thought hit him, and the mirth promptly died. He was wrong. He did know someone as smug, someone even more cruelly arrogant.

Miles Gillett, the man who had stolen Clay's woman and his land, was a lot like Fiero. Both men did as they damn well wanted without any regard for the feelings of others. But where Fiero assumed his belligerence by virtue of his very nature, Miles Gillett cultivated being vicious as some people might cultivate the social graces. Gillett worked at it day and night.

Clay had never liked the man, from the very first day they met. Right away he'd recognized that Gillett believed himself to be superior to everyone else. The man treated one and all with cold disdain. And when he wanted something, he had no qualms whatsoever about crushing anyone who stood in his way.

Some men craved power like others craved liquor or sweets. They could not get enough of it. Miles Gillett, one of the wealthiest ranchers in the entire territory, with one of the biggest spreads west of the Mississippi, was never satisfied with what he had. He always craved more, more, more.

Clay often wondered how many other men Gillett had ruined over the years. There must have been dozens, yet Gillett had never been caught doing anything illegal. With his money and influence, Gillett could always cover his tracks. In Clay's case, Gillett had set him up as a murderer, then sicced the long arm of the law on him to finish him off. All nice and legal-like.

Gillett was pure evil, through and through. He liked to squash people as if they were bugs. There was no reasoning with him, no convincing him that any course other than the one he had picked was the right one.

The only way to stop a man like that, Clay mused, was to kill him. Staring at the wagon that contained the Spencers, Clay realized that fate had played into his hands. If things went as he wanted, within a year Miles Gillett and all those who had done him wrong would be pushing up grama grass.

The voices of his companions brought an end to White Apache's reverie. Taking a sip of coffee, he listened to Cuchillo Negro address Fiero.

"We have been friends for many winters, have we not?"

"This is so," Fiero answered.

"Our arrows have flown side by side toward our enemies, have they not?"

Furrows lined Fiero's forehead. He had never been a deep thinker and he did not like it when other men tried to tie him up in knots of words. Unsure of the point Black Knife was trying to make, he became wary. "Yes."

"We have hunted together, feasted together, drank *twilt-kah-yee* together."

"Yes, yes," Fiero said impatiently. "So?"

"So it would sadden me if my brother were not able to accept the decision the *ninya* is going to make."

Fiero still did not see the point. "Can my brother see into her mind that he knows what she will say before she says it?"

Cuchillo Negro was slow to answer. As always when dealing with Fiero, words had to be most carefully chosen. "The minds of women are closed to men. That is why women are one of the great mysteries of life." He paused. "But a man can learn to read the trail of a woman's thoughts much as he reads the trail of an animal he hunts. The words they say, the looks they give, the way they hold their bodies, it can tell a man many things."

"And you think the *ish-tia-nay* will not want to share my wickiup?"

"I know she will not."

Fiero gave a toss of his shoulder. "So be it. Does my brother think so little of me that he imagines I would grow upset over something a female does?"

"My brother must admit that he is always ready to stand up for what he believes to be his. *Gian-nah-tah*."

"If the girl is not smart enough to know a good thing when it is offered to her, I will not object."

"Even if she decides that she wants someone else instead of you?"

"Who could she—" Fiero began, then stopped, the answer coming to him in a flash of insight. He remembered how the *ninya* had rested her head on Ponce's shoulder, how Ponce had hovered over the virgin as if she were something precious to him. He saw the others staring at him, saw the troubled expression *Lickoyee-shis-inday* wore, and discerned the truth. They were worried he would slay Ponce over the girl.

Inwardly, Fiero was amused. Sometimes his fellow warriors were like women themselves, getting upset over things over which they had no control. A warrior had the right to issue a formal challenge whenever he felt he had been slighted by another. But in this case Ponce had done nothing to merit it. And in any event, he was not about to stoop so low as to fight over a woman. "Let the *ninya* decide as she wishes. It is of no concern to me."

White Apache was relieved. Thanks to Cuchillo Negro, an explosive situation had been defused. Their next order of business was to get the Spencers and the stolen stock to their safe haven.

They headed out at noon, White Apache handling the wagon. The Chiricahua were all on horseback. Cuchillo Negro and Delgadito roved far ahead, on the lookout for cavalry patrols or other threats. Fiero rode well to the rear to keep an eye on their back trail. The string of extra horses and mules were left in the care of Ponce and Corn Flower.

For four uneventful days the renegades forged steadily northward. Twice they saw smoke from campfires in the distance and made wide detours to avoid being seen. Presently they reached the Tucson-Mesilla road. It was late in the afternoon.

White Apache did want to cross in broad daylight since the road was heavily traveled. Hidden in a dry wash a few hundred yards to the south, he sat in the shade of the wagon with Ponce and the girl and waited for the sun to go down.

Delgadito appeared, riding slowly, something clutched in his left hand. "Cuchillo Negro keeps watch," he said in thickly accented English. Of the four Chiricahua, he was the only one who spoke the white man's tongue. He had a long way to go before he would be fluent, and he practiced every chance he got. "A few white-eyes go by. No bluecoats." Holding out the item he held, he asked, "What does the talking paper say?"

White Apache stood. It was a circular. Quite often the band came on similar small posters, either tacked to trees along roads or placed at springs and other stopover points where travelers were bound to see them. Many were about him, about the bounty on his head, or else warnings to be on the lookout for his band.

Clay took one look at this one and felt his innards turn to ice.

Chapter Nine

"Why the hell do we have to go so damn slow?" Travis Belcher wanted to know. "I swear to God, this heat is killing me."

Benjamin Quid shifted in the saddle to fix the young gun shark with a withering look. "The heat will have to wait its turn if you don't quit your bellyaching. How many times do I have to tell you that we can't let the woman catch sight of us?"

Belcher rolled his eyes but had the good sense not to argue. Behind him rode another man killer Quid had hired in Tucson, a pudgy leather slapper who went by the handle of Fergy, short for Ferguson.

Quid faced front. Half a mile ahead was the slender column of dust being raised by William Randolph's bunch. He slowed even more, unwilling to risk getting too close. The dull clank of a horseshoe on stone sounded to his right as Bob Plunkett came up alongside of him.

"Mind if we jaw a spell, pard?" the old scout asked.

"What's on your mind?"

Plunkett also marked the position of the dust. It tickled him to think that before too long they would do what the army, the law and every other bounty hunter in the territory had been unable to do for months on end: make wolf meat of the White Apache. Speaking low, so the new gunnies would not overhear, he said, "I want the truth, Ben. Are you really fixin' to share the bounty with that damned clotheshorse from New York City?"

Quid wasn't surprised by the question. No one knew him better than the scout. "What do you think?" he said.

"I reckon you'll play along with the jackass until Clay Taggart is lyin' dead at your feet. Then the dude is in for a big shock. Him and the woman, both."

"And they're not the only ones," Quid said, referring to the five men he had hired in Tucson. To his way of thinking, Belcher and Fergy, as well as the three riding with Randolph and Amelia Taggart, were expendable. He had brought them along in case the White Apache did not come to Devil's Canyon alone. Once they had served their purpose, he'd pay them off in lead.

Quid saw no earthly reason to cut them in for part of the bounty. After all he had gone through, he deserved a full half share. He was tempted to dispose of Plunkett, too, but the old man's tracking skills would come in mighty handy later on when they went after other outlaws.

The scout had an idea that brought a grin of anticipation to his lips. "If you want, I'll take care of the female. It's been a while since I carved one up. I can use the practice."

"Suit yourself," Quid said testily, his conscience pricked. Amelia Taggart was a decent woman. If there were some way to spare her, he would, but he had to face facts. She wasn't about to keep quiet. She'd go straight to the governor and tell how her cousin was lured into a trap, how the reporter and the others met their end. No, he couldn't let that happen. She had to die.

Bob Plunkett studied the landmarks ahead. "We'll be there before dark, I reckon."

The big bounty hunter nodded. "As I recollect, the trail to the top is on the north side."

"It is," the scout confirmed. He scratched his stubble, then sniffed his armpits. "A fella sure does get whiffy in this desert country, don't he? Keeps up, I might have to take my annual bath ten months early." He meant it as a joke.

For as long as Plunkett could remember, he had been taking one bath and one bath only each and every year. Everyone knew that too many were bad for a person's health. As his great-grandmother had warned him when he was knee-high to a calf, "Too much washin' makes a body sickly and weak. If the Good Lord had meant for us to spend all our time soakin' in water, he would've gave us gills."

Quid checked behind them. It never paid to grow careless in Apache country, and Devil's Canyon was right at the edge of the Chiricahua homeland.

"What do you aim to do with your share of the bounty?" Plunkett asked idly.

"I haven't given it much thought," Quid said. "Maybe go to Denver. I hear the doves there are as thick as fleas on an old coon dog."

"You can have your tainted whores," Plunkett said. "Me, I'm partial to young females as pure as driven snow." He smacked his lips. "That Taggart woman is a mite older than I like, but I can make do." Leaning toward Quid, he said softly, "Do you want to hear what I have in mind?"

"I'd rather not. I just had a piece of jerky, and I want it to stay in my stomach."

The scout thought that hilarious.

To the east, Amelia Taggart looked up as a gust of hot wind fanned her hair. "Did you hear that?" she asked.

William Randolph sat slumped in the saddle in front of her. The insufferable heat was taking its toll; his body felt as if he had spent most of the day baking in an oven. Licking his parched lips, he wiped a hand across his perspiring brow and turned. "Hear what, my dear?" he said, in keeping with his act of being her good friend.

"I don't know for sure," Amelia said. It had sounded like distant laughter, but it might just as well have been her ears playing tricks on her. The blazing sun befuddled her senses to the point where half the time she rode along in a dazed stupor.

"I heard nothing," Randolph assured her.

A dozen yards in front of them was Stirco. To their rear were Wilson and Carver. The gunmen were supposed to stay alert, but the inferno had taken its toll on them as well. Carver dozed. Wilson looked ready to collapse.

The reporter took a handkerchief from a pocket and wiped his face and neck. He would have given anything for a bucket of ice. Or, better yet, a dip in the Hudson. A nice, leisurely swim, late at night, just as he had done so many times as a boy. It had been ages since he last recalled those carefree days. The mere thought of being enveloped from head to toe in cold water was invigorating, but only for a few seconds. Imagination could not compete with reality.

Randolph started to lift the canteen that was dangling from his saddle horn by a leather strap. He didn't count on anyone noticing, but he was mistaken.

"I'd save that water if I were you, sir," Stirco said.

The reporter hesitated. He wanted a drink so badly, he could barely stand it. Without one, he feared he might keel over.

"Remember my orders," Stirco said. "I'm to make sure you get to Devil's Canyon with your hide intact. So far as we know, a spring is there. But if it's dried up since anyone last paid the place a visit, we'll need every drop of water we have to make it back out."

Amelia Taggart had been listening with half an ear. She was more interested in the stark mountains before them, so it took a few moments for the gunman's words to register. Perking up, she said, "His orders? What does he mean by that, Mr. Randolph? You're the one in charge."

Randolph mentally cursed Stirco for being so careless. "Of course I am," he replied suavely. "I was the one he referred to. He was simply reminding me of instructions I gave him before we left Tucson."

"Oh," Amelia said, not completely convinced. It had struck her as strange back in Tucson when Randolph had let her know that he was going to go find suitable men to take along, and not 15 minutes later he had been back, saying he had come across three who fit the bill quite by chance. Later, as they prepared to leave town, she could not help but notice the many smirks the trio bestowed upon her, as well as their constant whispering. It confirmed her ever growing suspicion that William Randolph was up to something. Amelia had tried telling herself that she was making the proverbial mountain out of a molehill, that there must be innocent explanations for everything the reporter had done, but she could deceive herself no longer. The nearer they drew to their destination, the more worried Amelia became because any plot Randolph was hatching had to involve Clay.

Amelia had thought that by obtaining a safe-conduct pass for her cousin, she could keep him from harm. Now, she was not so sure. There might be a way to get around it.

The big question Amelia had to answer was why. What did Randolph hope to gain? He had claimed that his sole interest in helping her was to write a series of articles for the *New York Sun*, and she had taken him at his word. But what if he had lied? What if he wasn't after a great story, as he put it. What if he were after the reward money?

Amelia looked at him, at his expensive hat and suit and his fancy shoes. Randolph had shown her that he liked to live well. He always wanted to stay at the best hotels, to eat at the best restaurants, to dress in the finest clothes money could buy. And money didn't grow on trees.

She should have seen it sooner, Amelia chided herself. In her eagerness to see Clay again, in her rush to help him, she let herself be blind to the dozens of little clues which should have alerted her that all was not as it seemed. Had she seen the truth sooner, she could have called the whole thing off.

Now it was too late to turn back. In a short while they would be at the site Randolph had picked.

For all she knew, Clay had already come across one of the 40 or 50 circulars they had posted on their long trek from Tucson. At that very moment he might be on his way to see her.

Astride a sorrel, Clay Taggart sped like the wind to the northeast, toward Devil's Canyon. He flew past manzanitas, past mesquite, past cactus, and hardly noticed them. He spooked deer, lizards and birds, but paid them no heed. In his mind all he could see was the circular Delgadito had found:

CLAY TAGGART
OTHERWISE KNOWN AS THE WHITE
APACHE. YOUR COUSIN AMELIA WANTS
YOU TO MEET HER AT DEVIL'S CANYON
WITHIN 30 DAYS OF THE DATE ON THIS
CIRCULAR. SEE THE LIGHT OF REASON.
END THE BLOODSHED. DO WHAT IS
RIGHT AND HEAR HER OUT. WHAT HAVE
YOU GOT TO LOSE?

Clay posed the query aloud as he skirted a saguaro. "What have I got to lose?" The answer was as plain as the nose on his face: his life. On first reading the message, he had been partial to the notion that the invite had been concocted to draw him into an ambush. But the more he had thought about it, the more he decided that it couldn't be.

No one in Arizona, absolutely no one at all, knew about his cousin. He had never mentioned her to a living soul, never even talked about his childhood.

Why should he? It was painful for him to dwell on their wonderful friendship. Those had been some of the happiest years of his life, and recollecting them sparked anew the gut-wrenching hurt he had felt the day they parted company. For weeks afterward Clay had held a grudge against his pa.

In time, however, the hurt had faded. To keep it from cropping up again, he had shut Amelia from his mind.

Now she was back, and Clay was at a loss to know what to do. Seeing her was the first step, but then what? Why was she there? What did she hope to accomplish? The circular had said to "see the light of reason," to "end the bloodshed." What the hell did that mean? he mused. Was she going to try and convince him to turn himself in?

There were so many questions and so few answers.

Rather than wear himself out trying to solve the mystery, Clay buckled down to the task of covering as much ground as he could before sunset. By pushing hard, but not hard enough to ride the sorrel into the ground, he stood to reach the rendezvous site in three days. Each one would be an eternity of suspense.

Clay found himself reliving his childhood, recalling the joyful times he'd shared with Amelia, dredging up memories long forgotten.

It was a grave lapse in judgment. A man wanted by every lawdog in the territory, a man every Arizonan would like to see come down with hemp fever and do a strangulation jig, could not afford to let his guard down. Yet that is exactly what Clay Taggart did. He trotted on across the broad expanse of chaparral, so deep in thought that he was unaware others were nearby until a rifle retort rang out and the whine of lead off a rock made him snap around.

A bunch of cowboys swept toward him, several tugging long guns from saddle scabbards. A lanky scarecrow already had his out. Clay counted, seven, eight, nine, then another shot came closer than the first and he poked his heels into the sorrel and lit a shuck. Yips and hollers mixed with more shots, none of which scored.

Clay called himself an idiot and a lot of other names besides. Lead flew fast and furious around him, growing closer as the hands got the range. He did not return fire. To hit anything from horseback he had to slow down, and the moment he did, the punchers would pick him off.

He tried to recollect if a remote ranch was in the vicinity. It was so far out in the sticks that the hillbilly brush hands thirsting for his blood were probably lucky to strike town once a month. The men who worked for such outfits were always fiercely loyal to the brand. To them, he was an Apache, an enemy, a threat to their employer and his cattle. They'd chase him clear to Canada, if need be. He had to shake them, and quickly, before one made a lucky shot or the sorrel played out.

To the northwest beckoned a wall of mesquite, bristling with thorns. No ranny worthy of the name would take a horse in there. Clay counted on that as he reined to the left and lowered his chest to the sorrel's broad back.

Nine guns were booming in a thunderous din. Some of the shots came much too close for comfort. One nicked the sorrel's shoulder. Clay twisted and fired twice, wasting ammo in the hope of forcing the cowboys to fall back, but he might as well have used a slingshot. Those punchers did not wear all that hardware for bluff or ballast. They were not about to quit.

Clay sought an opening in the thorn wall. There had to be one, but none was evident. Cutting to the right, he paralleled the mesquite, the sorrel raising enough dust to make it hard for the cowboys to get a clear shot. They were fanning out, paralleling *him* to prevent him from doubling back on them or outdistancing them. Each was a seasoned cowman. They knew how to herd any critter alive, including the two-legged variety, into a tight corner, how to box in their quarry so that escape was impossible.

The sorrel ran superbly but it wasn't the black stallion. Clay could see that already two of the cowboys had looped around ahead of him and were angling to cut him off. Once that happened it was all over. He might blast his way past them, but they would delay him long enough for the rest to surround him and turn his body into a sieve.

Then a gap appeared in the mesquite. Not knowing if it was a trail or a blind alley, Clay swerved the sorrel into it. On either side the branches were so close that the thorns would rip his legs to shreds if he did not clamp them tightly to his mount. He had to straighten to see where he was going, and in doing so exposed his head and shoulders to his pursuers. A gunpowder litany rocked the chaparral. Something snatched at his hat but it stayed on.

The gap widened slightly. It angled to the north. Clay made the turn, discovered a godsend in the form of a long, straight stretch and whipped the reins against the sorrel's neck.

Clay had hoped that the cowboys would not plunge into the maze of thorns, but a glance back revealed that they wanted him so badly that four of them were willing to risk life and limb, as well as the welfare of their mounts, to catch him. Four had followed him in. The rest were spreading to the right and left, seeking a way around so they could cut him off before he found a way out.

Clay might have outsmarted himself. Unless he gained open ground before the punchers headed him off, he would be trapped. It would only be a matter of time before they put windows in his skull.

A few of the cowhands still fired every so often but most were waiting for clear shots.

Clay came to another bend. At a trot he rushed around it—and saw a wall of mesquite blocking his path. He hauled hard on the reins, bringing the sorrel to a sliding stop. In a spray of dust they halted mere inches from the barrier. He was trapped! The only way to go was back the way he had come.

Or was it?

To Clay's left was a narrow opening. Quickly dismounting, holding the reins, he stepped closer. It was a path leading deeper into the labyrinth, but it was barely wide enough for the sorrel. If it narrowed farther in, he would be as good as dead. Since he had no choice, he took it.

On foot, leading the sorrel, Clay threaded a serpentine course into the heart of the mesquite. Very soon he lost track of exactly where he was in relation to the point where he had entered. He had no idea whether he could find his way out again.

The only advantage was that now the mesquite was high enough to hide them. He paused to listen, to pinpoint the positions of his enemies, just as a gruff voice rang out.

"Where the hell did he go? I can't see him!"

"Me neither, Charley."

"Just keep lookin', boys. That red bastard is in here somewhere, and we're agoin' to blow out his lamp!"

Clay went on. Yet another turn loomed ahead.

He took it slowly, half afraid the trail would end at another thorn wall. It did peter out, all right, but at a small circular area bare of growth, a clearing eight feet in diameter. A brainstorm came to him.

Guiding the sorrel to the middle, White Apache stooped, bent one of its front legs back as far as it would go, then gripped the bridle and let his body go slack so that the animal's neck bore most of his weight. The sorrel resisted, but only for a few moments. Giving in to the inevitable, the horse slowly sank down, and he let go of its leg. Taking a seat beside it, he stroked the animal's neck.

Now all he could do was bide his time.

The cowboys were a persistent bunch. For hours they roved the mesquite, those on the outside circling around and around, those on the inside searching every twisting trail. They yelled back and forth a lot. As time dragged on, their confidence was replaced by baffled anger.

The sun was low in the sky when the man remarked for all to hear, "We should have found the mangy son of a bitch by now! I say we mosey on before it gets dark."

"We keep looking," someone responded curtly.

"Be reasonable, Baker," the first man said. "The big sugar is expectin' us back by nightfall. If we ain't there, he'll throw a fit. And I'd rather be stomped by an ornery bull than face our boss when his dander is up."

"He'll understand, Grimes," Baker said. "Apaches killed his wife, remember? We're under standing orders to kill every one of the vermin we see."

"Well, we won't be killin' this one," Grimes insisted. "Don't ask me how, but he's done givin' us the slip."

"That's an Apache for you," said a third man.

"They're as slippery as a passel of eels."

The hunt went on, but not for much longer. Baker finally called out, "Enough is enough, boys. I reckon Grimes has a point. We're wasting our time. Let's light a shuck for the ranch."

Clay Taggart sighed gratefully. He thought he would soon be on his way again, until a cowhand hollered.

"Baker! I can't find the trail that brought me in here! How the dickens am I supposed to get out?"

"What do you use for brains, Haverman?" Baker answered. "Didn't you keep track of where you were going?"

"Not exactly."

Several of the cowboys laughed. Baker swore, then said, "Backtrack yourself, then. That shouldn't be too hard."

"I can't. I got so twisted around, it wouldn't do me any good."

Someone chortled. "Leave it to Haverman! That boy don't have the brains God gave a yucca!"

"Can anyone see him?" Baker shouted.

Apparently no one could. Haverman was too far in. Clay Taggart heard the man, though, moving slowly toward him. The dull clump of hooves grew louder. Suddenly the puncher yelled excitedly.

"Baker! The rest of you! I found some tracks, but I don't think they're mine. They must belong to the Apache!"

"Damn!" Baker replied. "Take it slow, boy! If he's still in there, he knows right where you are."

"I ain't scared of no red heathen."

White Apache clenched his rifle. He had no desire to kill the young cowhand. He would rather the man turned back and left him alone. Then hooves drummed, and a lanky figure materialized on top of a bay. Haverman rushed around the last bend, spotted him and raised a pistol. White Apache fired just once.

For a few moments, silence greeted the blast. Baker called Haverman's name. Others joined in. When the cowboy did not answer, curses turned the air blue. Finally Baker quieted them and said, "The stinking Apache got him! But he's not going to get away with it! Grimes! Dixon! Pedro! Fan out! We're going to flush the scum out!"

"How?" a puncher asked.

"How else? We'll set this patch of mesquite on fire!"

Chapter Ten

Another day was drawing to a close. Deep in the winding recesses of Devil's Canyon, the shadows lengthened quickly once the sun dipped below the rim of the towering rock walls.

Amelia Taggart did not like it there. She tried telling herself that it was because the narrow canyon gave her a constant feeling of being hemmed in. But she was so inherently honest that she could not deceive herself for long. The real reason had nothing to do with the canyon and everything to do with one of the gunmen.

The hawkish gunman called Stirco had been eyeing her on the sly. Amelia had not noticed it until a few hours ago. By sheer chance she had happened to glance out of the corner of her eye and noticed the man giving her the sort of hungry look men normally reserved for fallen doves out strutting their physical wares. It had angered her but she had not made an issue of his rude behavior. She felt confident he would not try anything, not with Randolph and the other men there.

Then it occurred to Amelia that the other gunmen were Stirco's friends. And William Randolph did not impress her as being able to fend off a riled rabbit, let alone a frontier tough. Whether Randolph was morally stalwart enough even to try to defend a lady's honor was debatable. If Stirco tried to take liberties, she might need to fend for herself. Isolated as they were, outnumbered as she was, the outcome was a foregone conclusion.

Amelia shut the worry from her mind. As her pa had always liked to say, she would cross that bridge when she came to it. In the meantime, she had Clay to think of. Now that they had reached the rendezvous site, the prospect of seeing him again was imminent. She needed to work out ahead of time what she was going to say. She had to find the right words to persuade him to forsake the blood-stained path he had chosen and to give himself up.

Devil's Canyon ended at a high cliff. Massive boulders dotted its base and lined the bottom of the south wall. Among them, hidden from view until a person was right on it, was a clear, cold spring. Fully 10 feet across, it formed a waist-high pool.

They had only been there an hour or so. All of them had drunk their full, and the horses had been watered. Amelia sat on a small boulder, her hands folded in her lap, and scanned the ramparts on both sides. Preoccupied with thoughts of Clay, she did not hear the reporter come up.

"What are you looking at?" William Randolph demanded. Now that his plan had reached the critical point, he was growing more and more nervous. It bothered him to see her studying the heights. Quid and Plunkett were up there lying in wait. They were supposed to be near the canyon entrance, well out of sight, but Randolph would not risk her accidentally spotting them.

"Nothing much," Amelia said, puzzled by his strained tone and anxious manner.

"Oh, I thought you might have seen something," Randolph said and promptly regretted being so stupid. It would not do to have her suspect that he was in league with the men who would soon slay her cousin.

Amelia jumped to the obvious conclusion. "Are you worried about the renegades?"

They were the last thing on Randolph's mind, but he nodded and said, "Who wouldn't be?" Not caring to sound like a coward, he added, "Not for my own sake, you understand, but for yours. I've heard stories. Apache do terrible things to their captives. Why, even if they let you live, you'd be forced to take up with a buck."

"I'd kill myself before I would let any man violate me," Amelia declared loud enough for Stirco and the others to hear.

"I hope it won't come to that," Randolph said, and he was sincere. He had never meant for the woman to come to any harm. Walking off, he stared back down the dark canyon. How soon would it be, he wondered, before Clay Taggart showed up? He scoured the sheer sides, hoping Benjamin Quid was right about there only being one way in. If not, the consequences were too horrible to contemplate.

Amelia watched the reporter, seeking clues to confirm her suspicion that he was up to something. The feeling of someone watching her caused her to shift. She caught Stirco in the act of brazenly ogling her figure. To show her annoyance, she glared. To her dismay, he smiled, as if being a lecher were a joke, and casually turned back to the task of getting their fire started.

Amelia almost marched over to confront him. She would not tolerate being treated as if she were a common prostitute. Some women might enjoy it, but she wasn't one of them. Her folks had raised her to take pride in herself, and never to let anyone besmirch her dignity.

For the moment, Amelia did nothing. As the Good Book put it, there was a time and a place for everything, and Amelia judged it to be the wrong time to turn Stirco and his companions openly against her. Not when Clay might arrive at any time. They had been told about the safe-conduct pass so they would not take it into their heads to shoot him on sight. But she would not put it past them to do so anyway, especially if they held a grudge against her.

Amelia placed a hand on the small handbag she had toted from St. Louis. In it were her few cosmetics, for she was not one of those women who lavished powder and rouge and such on her face. Also in it was something that had belonged to her pa, something she had not parted with once since the long journey began, something no one else knew she carried, not even Randolph. It was an old, single-shot pocket pistol manufactured by Henry Derringer. A .41 caliber, it happened to be the exact same model used by John Wilkes Booth to assassinate Pres. Abraham Lincoln.

It reassured Amelia to know she could defend herself if attacked. Stirco and his ilk were bigger and stronger than she was, but any advantage their size gave them was more than offset by the gun. Few bad men would tempt fate by going up against a loaded revolver in the hands of someone determined to use it. That was one of the reason the framers of the Constitution included the right to bear arms as the Second Amendment.

Amelia did not see anything wrong with guns. They were tools, nothing more. Tools she had been around all her life. Her father and brother had used rifles regularly to hunt game. Her brother had been fond of a nickel-plated Remington he took with him when he signed on to fight for the Union cause. Many times she had taken a rifle and gone into the woods after game for the supper pot. So she had no qualms about using the pistol in her bag. Let Stirco or anyone else try something, and she would blow a hole in them the size of her fist.

William Randolph saw the woman smile and assumed she was thinking about her impending reunion with her cousin. It made him smile. She was so gullible, it was pathetic. Soon Clay Taggart would be dead, and all her good intentions would never bring him back to life again.

It had been preordained, William told himself, from the moment he put the White Apache at the top of his list. He had manipulated her from the beginning, and he would go on doing so after her cousin was dead.

In that great, complex chess game of life, William Randolph flattered himself that he had no equals. As Miss Amelia Taggart would shortly find out the hard way.

The instant the young cowhand named Haverman toppled from the saddle, White Apache leaped and caught hold of the bay's bridle before it could run off. Holding fast, he spoke softly to the horse to calm it, while stroking its neck.

White Apache heard the cowboys shout back

and forth. He heard the foreman, Baker, say that they were going to set the mesquite ablaze.

"Are you loco?" one of the others demanded. "We do that, we're liable to burn half the countryside."

"Like hell," Baker insisted. "This here stand is sitting all by its lonesome in the middle of nowhere. We can burn it down without having to worry about setting fire to anything else."

"It doesn't seem safe to me," said someone else.

Baker was not about to budge. "We're not letting the savage get away, and that's final. We owe Haverman at least that much. Now do as I tell you without kicking like a bay steer."

White Apache heard the thud of hooves on all sides. Rising onto his toes, he saw riders to the north, south, east and west. It gave him some notion of how large an area the mesquite covered, about four or five acres. He hunkered before any of the hands spotted him.

Then, for the longest, nerve-racking while, all was quiet. The sun, a blazing skillet, rested on the rim of the earth. It began to sink lower although not fast enough to suit White Apache. He wanted to make his bid for escape under the cover of encroaching darkness.

Suddenly the sorrel raised its head and sniffed loudly. A few seconds later the bay did the same, then nickered. White Apache tilted his head back, inhaled, and smelled the unmistakable acrid scent of smoke. The mesquite had been set ablaze.

Since the wind was blowing from the northwest, White Apache figured the flames would eat toward him from that direction.

On the bay was Haverman's lariat. Helping himself to it, Clay Taggart slid the loop over the bay's neck. With the rope in one hand, and the sorrel's reins as well as the Winchester in the other, he started to retrace his steps, bearing to the south at every junction. It was slow going since he had to keep low. Every now and then he rose high enough to scan the mesquite, and it was one of those times that he spied flames to the north. A little farther on, Clay looked again. Now there were flames to the east and west, as well.

The cowboys had set the mesquite on fire at all four points of the compass. The flames were rapidly converging, and once they linked up, he would be completely encircled.

White Apache could no longer afford the luxury of caution. Climbing onto the sorrel, he went faster, sticking to a southerly bearing. Soon he realized that the wind had shifted, as it often did at that time of the day. Now it pushed the flames from the southwest and they were advancing at an alarming rate, devouring the mesquite as a starved man might devour a plate of prime beef.

The smoke grew thicker. It swirled above the stand, settling when the wind briefly died now and again, hugging the top of the growth like a gray blanket. A roiling cloud of it swept toward White Apache. He held his breath just in time. In moments he was shrouded from head to toe in a swirling fog that stung his eyes and filled his nostrils even though he wasn't breathing. The horses snorted and pranced.

White Apache could not see the trail ahead, and had to slow to a crawl. He swatted at the smoke before his eyes but it did no good.

For over two minutes White Apache blundered on. Cupping a hand over his mouth, he took short breaths. He failed to pay attention to where he was going and unknowingly veered to the left. Thorns bit into his leg so he veered to the right, to where he thought the middle of the trail should be. In all the smoke, he misjudged and more thorns pricked his right leg.

The sorrel whinnied, its side pierced by a score of razor-thin barbs.

"Hey, did you hear that?" a cowboy called.

"I sure did!" answered another. "Keep your eyes peeled, boys! It won't be long before he makes a break for it!"

Clay would have liked to, but he was more lost than ever. He couldn't see his hand at arm's length, let alone the way out. Unwilling to give up, he nudged the sorrel. Behind him, the bay balked, and he had to tug on the rope to keep the animal going.

It seemed to him that the smoke was growing thicker. Presently the crackle of flames and flashes of orange and red alerted him to a burning column of mesquite directly in front of him.

White Apache looked to the right and the left. Any side trails he might take were obscured by the smoke. He had to find one, and quickly, or he would be roasted alive.

There wasn't enough room to turn around, so, slipping from the saddle, White Apache led the horses forward, a halting step at a time. Flames flared to his left. More blossomed to his right. The heat blistered him worse than the desert sun at midday. The air grew stifling, so much so that his lungs ached for a fresh breath.

A wave of intense heat stopped White Apache dead. Weakness claimed him. His knees buckled. He caught himself before he fell, clung to the sorrel, and was about to attempt to swing the animal around when he glimpsed what seemed to be an opening almost at his right elbow. He was unable to tell if it was another trail. Desperate, he stepped into the gap, shielding his face with his forearm. Crackling fingers of hissing fire had engulfed the brush all around him.

White Apache shuffled forward. There was a trail, sure enough, a narrow one that twisted and turned every which way. Whether it would take him away from the fire or deeper into it, he couldn't say. Since it was the only trail he was likely to find, he had to take it.

Both horses shied, almost yanking White Apache off his feet. Holding tight, he dug in his heels and advanced. The trail narrowed. Thorns hemmed him in so close that he could not extend an arm to either side. He dreaded that he had reached the end of his rope, that the trail would end and he would be trapped by the flames.

To the east a cowboy shouted. To the north someone responded. White Apache could not hear the words above the roar of the fire. Bending at the waist, he rounded a corner. A blast of flame gusted across the path. He threw himself backward but was too slow to avoid suffering a singed arm. Forgetting himself in his pain, he inhaled.

Searing agony lanced through White Apache's chest. Staggering, he erupted in a coughing fit which would not end. Every breath he took only made it worse, thanks to the soup-thick smoke. Falling to his knees, he doubled over, and by chance discovered a thin amount of untainted air close to the ground. He breathed greedily. When his lungs stopped hurting and his eyes stopped watering, he hurried on.

Flames writhed everywhere, transforming the chaparral into a living hell. White Apache had to fight the horses for every step he took. They were close to panic, the bay in particular.

"I can't see a damn thing!" one of the cowboys bellowed.

Neither could Clay. He bumped into a flaming limb, backpedaled, and went around another bend. The smoke thinned slightly. He thought that he saw an opening and broke into a brisk jog. In several strides he was in a large clearing, where he paused to take stock of the situation.

From out of the smoke solidified a figure on horseback. It was a puncher, and it was hard to say which of them was more surprised. The cowboy cursed and clawed for a pistol. White Apache snapped up the Winchester, his finger curling on the trigger. The barrel spat lead, which slammed into the man's sternum, ripped him from his horse and flung him into the gray veil.

White Apache was dumfounded that one of the punchers had ventured into the burning mesquite after him. The man had to have been loco, he mused. Then a powerful gust of wind parted the smoke, and where White Apache had expected to see more mesquite, he saw open prairie. It took a few moments for the reality to set in. He was out of the maze! He was in the clear! Now all he had to do was mount up and get the hell out of there.

But it wasn't quite that simple. To the right a cowboy hollered, "What were those shots about? Decker, was that you?"

Hooves thudded, coming closer. White Apache gripped the sorrel's mane and swung up.

"Decker? Where are you?"

To avoid another clash, Clay reined to the left and made off through the smoke at a walk so as not to make too much noise. His hopes were dashed when a pair of cowboys abruptly appeared in front of him. They were scanning the mesquite. One held a carbine, the other had a hand resting on the butt of a Colt. Both saw him at the same instant and went to bring their guns into play.

White Apache was already in motion. A jab of his heels sparked the sorrel into a gallop. He raced between the pair, the sorrel slamming into their mounts and barreling past. As he swept by, White Apache clubbed the puncher on the right with his Winchester while, at the same time, kicking out with his left leg and knocking the other man from the saddle.

A cloud of smoke sheathed White Apache as shots rang out. Lead buzzed on both sides. He did not return fire. Escaping was more important than slaying the punchers.

Fiero would not have thought so. For that matter, all the Chiricahua would have used the cover provided by the smoke to kill as many white-eyes as they could. It gave Clay Taggart a fleeting moment of doubt. How could he claim to be one of the renegades when, unlike them, he was willing to let their sworn enemies live?

The sound of pursuit derailed Clay's train of thought. Slanting to the right, he burst from the smoke into fresh air. The sun had set. Twilight claimed the landscape. He cut to the northeast, his original bearing, and rode full out, looking back every few seconds to see if any of the cowhands had spotted him.

They had. A lean brush hand trotted into view, yipped and gave chase. Seconds later another joined the first. They covered about 50 yards when a second pair showed up. The quartet applied their spurs with gusto.

Still holding the lead rope, White Apache went faster. A few shots zinged his way, but for the most part the cowboys concentrated on overtaking him.

They were superb horsemen, mounted on animals as fine as any anywhere. They could ride rings around most men. Their confidence showed in the set of their features and their whoops of excitement. They believed the outcome was inevitable.

But they did not know that the man they were after was not a full-blooded Apache. They had no idea that their quarry had once been a cowboy, just like them. That he had worked a ranch from dawn until well past dusk, day in and day out, year after year, doing most of the work from horseback. He was one of them, or had been, a kindred spirit in a very real sense. But to the riding skills and savvy he had learned as a rancher had been added the exceptional abilities of his Chiricahua mentors.

So after a mile, the cowboys were no closer than they had been when they first gave chase. They looked at one another but did not quit. It went against their grain. Besides, their quarry was leading a second horse, and that was bound to slow the first one down, eventually.

Clay Taggart knew that, too. Which was why he monitored the sorrel closely, and when it showed signs of being winded, when it started to flag, he would be ready to make his move.

Clay had brought the bay along for a reason. It was his ace in the hole. He slowed just a little and began to coil the rope, pulling the bay toward him. Soon it was galloping at his side.

For half a mile more Clay sped along through the gathering darkness. When next he checked over his shoulder, the four cowboys were vague shapes at the limit of his vision. Their mounts, like the sorrel, would be growing tired. It was time to play his trump card.

Clay tugged on the rope to draw the bay a little

closer still. Every inch counted. Switching the Winchester from his right hand to his left, he coiled his legs up under him so that he balanced on the sorrel's back on his heels. Tensing, he pushed off and leaped to the right, sailing in a tight arc that brought him down squarely atop the bay. He flung his legs wide to fork leather.

All should have gone well. Clay had timed his jump perfectly. But at the very instant he sprang, the horses came to a knoll and flew up the steep slope. It put the bay's back at a sharp angle. Instead of alighting in the center of the saddle, as Clay had counted on, he came down on the cantle. Pain speared his groin and shot up his spine. He began to slip to the left. Lunging, he grabbed at the saddle horn, but he missed it because the horse had hit a rut and stumbled. It threw him backward, over the cowboy's bedroll. For several harrowing heartbeats he swayed, about to pitch off the animal's rump. His flailing fingers found the cantle. He held on for dear life.

The bay righted itself. Clay was thrown forward. This time he caught hold of the horn and was not about to let go. Exerting every muscle in his right arm, he hauled himself up and over the bedroll and the cantle. At last his legs draped over the saddle. His feet found the stirrups and slipped into them. Leaning down, he snagged the dangling reins.

It felt strange to have a saddle under him again, after so many months of riding bareback. It brought back memories Clay would rather not dwell on. Gaining the top of the knoll, he looked back. The cowboys were closer, but they were in for a big surprise.

The sorrel, now riderless, was beginning to slow. Clay swatted it with the Winchester and it angled to the north at a trot. Perhaps it would lure the cowboys off. If not, Clay wasn't worried. The bay was fresher than their horses. It would rapidly outdistance them.

True to his prediction, five minutes later there was no sign of his pursuers. Clay Taggart, the White Apache, streaked across the vast Arizona wilderness under a myriad of sparkling stars, a brisk north wind fanning his face, fondness for his cousin fanning the flames of his heart. He was hell-bent for leather to reach Devil's Canyon as soon as possible. He couldn't wait to see Amelia again. But if she wasn't there, if it was a trap, those responsible were going to pay—in blood.

Chapter Eleven

Morning dawned crisp and clear. Benjamin Quid, perched on the north rim of Devil's Canyon, where he could see the canyon mouth and the approaches to it, shifted position to relieve a cramp in his calf. He had been standing watch since three in the morning, and he was tired.

Quid leaned against a boulder and took the makings for a cigarette from his shirt pocket. Once he had it lit, he puffed slowly, savoring the taste. He was not concerned about the smoke giving his position away. In the first place, he doubted that Clay Taggart would show up for days. In the second, he was so high up, Taggart would need to have the eyes of an eagle to spot the few wispy tendrils that rose above the boulder.

Quid was not going to make the mistake so many did and make Taggart out to be more than the man was. Because of the many tall tales about the White Apache's bloody exploits, folks had taken to regarding Taggart as some sort of human demon. Some claimed he was a ghost who could appear and disappear at will. A few asserted that he was damned near invincible, that Apache magic had rendered him bullet proof.

It was all nonsense, of course. Taggart was clever and had more lives than a cat, but he had no superhuman powers. The only reason the turncoat had gotten the better of Quid the first time they tangled was due to Plunkett's carelessness. The old scout had assured Quid that there had not been another living soul within miles of the spring. Since Plunkett had never been wrong before, Quid had accepted his word and let down his guard.

Never again. Quid had learned his lesson. Or, rather, *relearned* it. Early on in the bounty business he had found that a manhunter had to be cat eyed all the time or he wouldn't last long. Especially if, like Quid, the bounty hunter only went after those who had the highest bounties on their heads—usually, hard cases wanted for murder or other violent crimes, men who would kill anyone who tried to take them in.

Quid had claimed over 20 bounties. Never once had any of the men he sought beaten him at his own game—until Clay Taggart, that is.

Quid tingled at the thought of having the bastard lined up in his rifle sights. Only taking the body back to Tucson for one and all to see would erase the shame of their first encounter. In the bargain he might earn some spare change by charging admission, as was often done with notorious outlaws. Plenty of people would be willing to part with two bits for the privilege of boasting that they had seen the White Apache's corpse. Quid might even sell snips of Taggart's hair and offer them for 50 cents each.

"Is that smoke worth your life, Ben?"

Quid had not heard Plunkett come up on him, and started. "Damn," he growled, embarrassed that he had been taken unawares. "Don't sneak up on a man like that or you're liable to eat lead."

Plunkett moved to the edge to survey the canyon. "You've never fought Apache like I have, or you'd know they're two-legged bloodhounds. A buck could smell that cigarette of yours from a mile off."

"Spare me another tall tale," Quid said. Defiantly, he took a long drag and blew a small cloud into the air.

The scout glanced at his partner. It was rare for the big man to speak so harshly to him. "What's gotten into your craw?"

"Nothing," Quid lied.

Plunkett was too shrewd to be fooled. "Seems to me that you're lettin' this White Apache get under your skin. So what if he licked us once? This time we have an edge." Hunkering, he plucked the dry stem of a withered plant and stuck it between his front teeth. "It ain't like you to get all flustered. Keep it up and you'll worry me."

"I'm not flustered!" Quid snapped. "It's just that I want him dead so badly, I can damned near taste it."

"Which is just as bad, I reckon," Plunkett said. "Revenge makes a man reckless. A person in our line of work has to keep their wits about 'em at all times. So don't let Taggart drive you to the wall."

Quid did not like being lectured. "Don't worry about me, old man. When the time comes, I'll be ready." To avoid any more talk on the subject, he stalked off, along the rim. It was 75 yards from the spot they had selected for the ambush to the first bend in the canyon. Over a quarter of a mile past the bend lay the spring where Taggart's cousin waited.

Nothing moved down there. Yet. Quid walked to where the pudgy gunman, Fergy, knelt in a wide cleft. In his current frame of mind, if he had caught Fergy sleeping, there would have been hell to pay. But the gunman was awake, fiddling with a spur.

Looking up, Fergy said, "Anything wrong, boss?"

"No." Quid paused to gaze out over the foothills that led up to the canyon, and the plain beyond. "Bob just relieved me. I'll send Belcher up to spell you in a few minutes."

Fergy grinned. "It won't be long until Taggart shows, will it? I can't wait to get my hands on my share. It's more money than I've ever had at one time in my whole life."

Quid stared at the unsuspecting gunny. Little did Fergy realize that Belcher and he would never spend a cent of the reward. He turned to go.

"I've been meaning to ask you a favor," Fergy said.

The big man faced him.

"You're a fair hombre to work for. If you ever need an extra gun again, I hope you'll keep me in mind."

"I can always use a good man. Survive this," Quid said soberly, "and we'll see."

"Don't you worry. The White Apache isn't about to blow out my lamp if I can help it."

Nodding, Quid headed for their camp. A prick of conscience troubled him but he shrugged it off. He couldn't let feelings get in his way, not where money was concerned. That wouldn't be professional.

* * *

Amelia Taggart awoke with a start. For a while she lay staring at the top of her tent and wondering what had awakened her so rudely. She did not recall having a nightmare. Then, as she was about to close her eyes and snatch a little more sleep, her intuition flared. She experienced the most peculiar feeling that someone was watching her.

Rolling toward the front, Amelia was shocked to see the flap fluttering, as if it had just been closed. Yet that couldn't be. She had tied it shut prior to retiring.

Rising to her knees, a blanket held tightly around her shoulders, Amelia scooted over. She gripped the edge and pulled. To her horror, the flap swung freely. The tie string was on the ground.

At a loss to understand how her bow knot had come undone, Amelia examined the tie. Her consternation grew when she discovered the cord had been cut. Someone had slipped a hand under the bottom of the flap and silently sliced it while she slept.

Amelia parted the flap enough to see the camp. There was no sign of Randolph, but the three gunmen were up and about. Wilson was toting water from the spring. Carver tended the horses. Nearest the tent, preparing coffee at the fire, was Stirco. The man glanced at the tent, saw her and smirked.

What gall! Amelia thought to herself. Infuriated, she closed the flap and swiftly donned her everyday dress, as she called it. Clutching her handbag, she stepped out into the bright morning sunshine.

The canyon was deathly still, unlike her farm where birds would be chirping, chickens clucking, and sheep bleating. How she missed it!

At that moment, William Randolph emerged

from his tent, yawning and scratching his chin. In his opinion it was an ungodly hour to be getting up. But he was so excited by the possibility of Clay Taggart soon appearing that he had not slept well at all. The early morning commotion outside his tent had not helped in that regard.

Frontier types, Randolph had learned, invariably rose with the sun, or before, and for the life of him, he could not comprehend how they did it. His best guess was that they did not need as much sleep as he did because their doltish minds did not use as much energy during the day.

Randolph noticed the woman. He forced a smile. "Good morning, Miss Taggart. You're up earlier than usual, aren't you?"

Amelia did not reply. She had eyes only for Stirco. Marching up to him, she slipped a hand into her bag and palmed the pocket pistol. Boldly, she declared, "If you ever do that again, you will be sorry."

The gunman acted surprised. "What are you talking about, ma'am? All I'm doing is fixing coffee."

"You know very well what I am referring to," Amelia said, her anger fueled by his denial. "I am a lady, not a fallen dove. You will accord me the respect I deserve or suffer accordingly."

William Randolph had never heard the woman speak so harshly to anyone. "What's going on?" he asked. "What is this all about?"

"Ask the lecher," Amelia said. Pivoting on a heel, she walked to the spring to wash up. Wilson doffed his hat to her, so she acknowledged the greeting with a nod. Moving around to the far side of the pool, she sat and dipped her hand in the cool water.

Inwardly, Amelia seethed. It was the old Taggart temper, the one great weakness of the Taggart clan. Her pa had it; her brother had it; and she had it. So too, she figured, did her cousin Clay.

The Taggarts had always been slow to come to a boil, but once they did, they were capable of exploding in the most savage violence. She could still recall the time a drunk made an improper remark to her mother. Her father had beaten the scoundrel within an inch of his life.

Splashing her face and neck, Amelia fought to calm herself. By letting Stirco rile her, she was lowering herself to his crude level. She could only pray that her warning had served its purpose. If not, the man would rue the day they met.

Amelia gazed wistfully up the canyon, wondering where her cousin might be, and if he were aware of the circulars yet. She imagined him flying to her side, as anxious to see her again as she was to see him.

Clay Taggart had ridden all night long. He had pushed the bay mercilessly, something he would never have done during his years of ranching. Now, the day less than an hour old, he had about ridden the animal into the ground. It was caked with lather, wheezing like a stricken ox. He knew that he should stop, that it dearly needed rest, but he did not slacken his pace.

An internal urge spurred Clay on, an impulse to reach his cousin swiftly. He could not say what caused it. Maybe it was the bond they once shared. Maybe it was the fact that his cousin cared enough to go to all this trouble to see him. Maybe it was simply their being kin.

Kin. The word echoed in the caverns of Clay's mind, reminding him that the Taggart clan had always been tight knit, until the day his pa up and herded his family westward. He sometimes gave thought to how much different his life would have been had his pa stayed back East.

It was strange, Clay reflected, how life worked out. A man never really knew from one minute to the next what fate had in store for him. It might be glory. It might be ruin. Or it might be an average life with few peaks and valleys. His main wish was that his life would end in a blaze of gunfire and not in a pathetic whimper.

A sudden lurch by the bay brought Clay back to the present. The bay was staggering on its last legs. Clay reined up and dismounted. Nickering, the horse shook itself, tried to go on, but faltered. Slowly, frothing at the mouth, it oozed to the ground.

White Apache cocked the Winchester, then pressed the muzzle to the animal's head. The bay was of no further use to him. A true Apache would shoot it and be done with it. His finger tightened on the trigger, but not enough for the hammer to strike the cartridge.

The bay looked at him, eyes wide in fright, as if sensing impending doom.

It was Clay Taggart, not the White Apache, who lowered the .44-40. It was Clay Taggart, not the White Apache, who stripped off the saddle and blanket. And it was Clay Taggart, not the White Apache, who gave the horse a quick rubdown before turning and jogging to the northeast.

But once the bay was out of sight, it was the White Apache, not Clay Taggart, who ate up the miles at a pace few white men could match. It was the White Apache, not Clay Taggart, whose whipcord frame was unaffected by the blazing sun. It was the White Apache, not Clay Taggart, who took a two-hour nap shortly before sunset, then resumed his trek as refreshed as if he had slept the whole night through.

Thanks to his Chiricahua friends, *Lickoyee-shisinday* knew many of the shortcuts only the Indians knew. So it was that he came within sight of the mouth of Devil's Canyon at approximately four o'clock the next morning.

Clay was so eager to see Amelia that he almost entered the canyon without first making sure he was not walking into a trap. Well shy of the entrance, he halted in the shadow of a rock slab. He had only been in the canyon once before, when the band had stopped at the spring on their way back to the Dragoons after a raid into Mexico. It was, as he recollected, long and narrow, ideal for a bushwhacking.

White Apache studied the canyon floor, the sheer walls, the remote, jagged heights. For over an hour he scrutinized every nook and cranny. When he had satisfied himself that no enemies were lying in wait, he rose. And as he did, on the north rim, a red pinpoint of light sparked briefly.

White Apache froze. Someone was up there. Someone smoking a cigarette. It had to be a white man keeping a watch on the canyon mouth. Conflicting emotions tore at him. White Apache tried telling himself that the man must be a lookout, nothing more. Yet if the circulars had been legitimate, there would be no need for anyone to be up there, no need at all.

The only other explanation filled White Apache with boiling rage. Whirling, he dog trotted to the north, never once exposing himself. Soon he was past the high wall. On the far side a series of slopes seemed to rear to the very sky. He prowled their base, sniffing and listening. Forty yards in, the wind brought him the scent of horses and the faint smell of woodsmoke.

White Apache climbed. His moccasins made no noise. His form was a flitting shadow, in one spot one second, in another spot the next. Many times he went to ground to test the air with his finely honed senses.

Soon White Apache came on an old game trail bearing recent horse tracks. He took it to make better time. In due course he saw a pile of dung. Squatting, White Apache picked up a piece and rubbed it between his fingers. The degree of dryness told him that the pile had been lying there for two to three days.

Above him, someone coughed.

It was faint, but White Apache instantly gauged the general area from which it came. Becoming one with the shadows, he cat footed higher. Loose earth and small stones that might slide out from under him were diligently avoided. When he halted to test the air, as he often did, he crouched and mimicked the shapes of nearby boulders or brush.

It was one of the oldest Apache tricks, the keys to their uncanny ability to sneak up on victims without being spotted.

From an early age boys were versed in the craft. They were taught how to blend into the background by assuming the guise of whatever might be around them at the time. They might, for example, kneel and curl in half, tucking their heads flush to the ground, so that their silhouette resembled that of nearby boulders. Or they might sit with their back to their prey and hold their arms and legs so that their limbs resembled those of a small tree or shrub. The possibilities were limited only by their cleverness.

White Apache had spent many hours honing his skill. He had a long way to go before he would equal the Chiricahua, but he was good enough to fool most any white-eye or Mexican.

On this particular morning, White Apache came to the crest of a rocky spine. Rolling into a ball, he inched up alongside a pair of small boulders. Below him unfolded a basin. In it were camped four white men. Only two were present, but there were four horses tethered close by, and four saddles ringed the small campfire.

One man hunkered by the fire, sipping coffee. The other was asleep, snoring lightly.

White Apache noticed that neither wore a uniform or a badge. The man by the fire, whose face was shrouded by a low hat brim, looked up. White Apache stiffened. Recognition shot through him. It was the old scout, one of the three bounty hunters he had tangled with before. He searched his memory for the name: Plunkett, that was it.

The scout glanced at the sleeper and frowned. "Belcher, you'd best get your lazy ass up and go spell Quid. I've already relieved Fergy."

The snoring choked off. The man under the blankets cracked an eye, then yawned. "Five more minutes. That's all I want."

Bob Plunkett did not hide his contempt. In his opinion, Belcher was next to worthless. Of all the men they had hired on in Tucson, the skinny gunman was the laziest. Belcher never showed up to relieve anyone on time, yet griped to high heaven if his own relief showed up so much as a minute late. Griping, sad to say, was the one thing Belcher did well. He griped about doing his fair share of the cooking; he griped about taking a turn tending the horses; he griped about practically everything under the sun.

"Don't say I didn't warn you," the scout now warned. "Quid ain't going to like havin' to wait again. He's liable to bust your skull this time."

"He doesn't scare me," Belcher said.

"Only because you don't have any brains." Plunkett went to swallow more coffee when a feeling came over him that he was being watched. He swiveled toward the canyon, thinking that Quid had returned to beat the stuffing out of Belcher. But no one was there. Mystified, he studied the north basin rim and saw nothing to account for his feeling. He looked at the horses. None showed any alarm.

Shrugging, Plunkett tilted the tin cup to his lips. Liquid splashed his neck, and he felt a slight tingling sensation. Thinking that he had stupidly missed his mouth, he wiped his throat with the back of his hand. Abruptly, the tingle changed to a searing pain, just as he raised his hand high enough to see that the warm liquid clinging to it was not coffee. It was blood. His blood.

Bob Plunkett dropped the cup and started to rise. Opening his mouth to shout a warning, he stabbed a hand at his pistol.

White Apache was faster. He clamped a hand over the white-eye's mouth, seized the scout's gun arm and held Plunkett in an iron grip. The man thrashed and fought to break free. A crimson geyser spewed from the throat White Apache had slit with a single lightning stroke. Gradually, the older man weakened. Soon Plunkett's knees buckled. White Apache eased the scout to the ground, then pinned him until the body stopped convulsing.

Bowie in hand, White Apache stepped to the skinny gunman. Crouching low, he held the bloody blade over Belcher's face. A red drop slid off the cold steel, dripping onto the end of the man's nose.

The gunman snorted but did not open his eyes.

White Apache let another drop fall.

This time Belcher swiped a hand at the air, as if to ward off an annoying insect. He snorted and tossed.

Moving the blade over the man's right eye, White Apache angled it so that the next drop fell onto the eyelid.

"What the hell?" Belcher blurted, sitting up.

White Apache pounced. Slamming into the gunman's chest, he knocked Belcher flat again even as he drove the Bowie between two ribs. Belcher arched and went to scream. Instantly White Apache stifled the outcry, then savagely speared the Bowie into the gunman four more times as hard as he could. Belcher died wearing a look of dumb astonishment.

Like a tawny panther rising from its prey, White Apache stood and turned toward the canyon. Raw rage coursed through his veins. Two more men were out there somewhere. Two bounty hunters, scum who had somehow learned about his cousin and made up those fake circulars to lure him into a trap.

They were going to pay.

Chapter Twelve

Amelia Taggart was up before the sun. Taking her handbag and a towel, she slipped from her tent. The camp was quiet. None of the men were up and about yet except Wilson, whose turn it was to keep guard. He sat by the fire, his back to her, his chin bowed, dozing.

Amelia smiled. It was just as she had planned. She needed some time to herself, and there would be no better opportunity. Hastening to the spring, she went around to the far side where the shadows were deepest.

Here, Amelia hesitated. She craved a quick bath. Not since Tucson had she washed herself thoroughly, and she was tired of feeling grungy and sweaty all the time. A short dip was all she needed to be fresh and clean, at least until the sun came up and the temperature soared once again.

Amelia glanced at the gap in the boulders through which she had come. No one had followed her. But she could not help worrying about Stirco. The man had avoided her after she confronted him, but several times she had caught him giving her those same hungry looks. Given the chance, she was sure he would try something. It was up to her to deny him the chance.

After listening for footsteps, Amelia set the items she carried on a flat rock and swiftly stripped off her dress. Again she hesitated, reluctant to finish undressing for fear of being discovered. But not for long. The tranquil pool was so inviting that she shed her underthings in record time and slipped over the edge. The water was wonderfully, deliciously cool. She sank lower, kneeling, submerging herself to her chin.

No sounds came from the camp. Amelia smiled, leaned her head back and shut her eyes. The peace, the quiet and the water combined to lull Amelia into feeling momentarily secure. Leaning her head back on the rim, she closed her eyes and willed herself to relax.

Minutes went by. Amelia, savoring the exquisite sensation, did not stir. She wished that she were alone so she could stay there for hours. She promised herself that when they returned to Tucson, she would have a tub of cold water brought to her room and spend half a day in it. It wouldn't matter one whit if she resembled a prune when she was done.

Then the sole of a boot scuffed the ground. Amelia straightened. Her worst fear had been realized. Framed in the gap, leering at her, was Stirco.

"Well, well. This must be my lucky day."

"Go away," Amelia commanded.

Ignoring her, Stirco took a step toward the pool. "And if I don't, lady?"

"I will yell for Mr. Randolph."

The gunman chuckled. "Is that supposed to scare me off? Hell, that jackass couldn't beat a chipmunk in a fight. He's as useless a man as I've ever come across."

Amelia raised an arm to the rim. In doing so she exposed part of her right breast, but it could not be helped. Resting her hand near the flat rock on which her handbag sat, she made one last appeal. "This is your last warning, Mr. Stirco. I am a Taggart. I will not let you do what you have in mind."

"What are you fixing to do? Splash me?" Laughing merrily, Stirco came straight toward her.

Benjamin Quid glimpsed the crown of the sun on the eastern horizon and fumed. He should have been relieved by Belcher half an hour ago. Knowing the troublemaker as well as he did, Quid doubted that the bastard had even climbed out from under the blankets yet.

Quid was tired of waiting. He decided to go teach the no-account yack a lesson, but first he had to let Fergy know. Striding from concealment, he hiked along the edge. Far below, the canyon floor was empty.

As Quid passed a large boulder, he saw Fergy's brown hat near the top of the same cleft the pudgy gunman always hid in. Ferguson appeared to be slumped over, sleeping.

"What the hell is this?" Quid growled. "Can't anyone around here do their job right?"

The gunman from Tucson did not answer, did not even move. Angered, Quid went up and gave Fergy a rough shove. "Wake up. Damn your hide—" he began.

The big man's anger evaporated at the sight of a spreading crimson stain on Ferguson's shirt and the wide, blank eyes that were fixed on him. The gunman had been stabbed, not once but many times, in an attack so swift and vicious that Quid, 25 feet away, had not heard a thing.

"It's your turn next, bounty hunter."

The words cut Benjamin Quid to the quick. They came from behind him. There was no need for Quid to ask who it was. He knew. The White Apache had gotten the better of him a second time. It was unthinkable. It was unbearable. Firming his grip on his rifle, he tensed and whirled, hoping against hope that he could still win, that he could gun down the turncoat before the renegade did the same to him.

White Apache, though, had no intention of using his rifle or pistol. He wanted to slay the bounty hunter in personal combat, man to man. He wanted to see the look in Quid's eyes at the moment of death, to feel the life drain from Quid's body. This was the man who had duped him. This was the man who had falsely gotten his hopes up, who had stirred cherished memories which had twisted his soul into an agonized knot.

Perched on top of the large boulder, White Apache clenched his Bowie, then sprang. Quid looked up and tried to sweep the rifle higher. White Apache was on him in a flash, bowling the bounty hunter over. The Winchester clattered at their feet as they crashed into the cleft on top of Ferguson.

White Apache thrust at Quid's neck, but the big man twisted to one side, a hand dropping to his boot. Quid's Bowie flashed. Their blades met, rang, then met again. White Apache did not back up to gain more room. He was not giving any ground this day. Like a Viking of old, he was in the grip of a berserk blood lust. His sole thought was to slay the bounty hunter at any cost. Stabbing high and low, he waded in.

Quid was hard-pressed to ward off the rain of blows. The cleft was wide but not wide enough for them to move freely. His sole hope lay in getting out of there. Backpedaling as far as he could, he ducked under a slice that would have nearly decapitated him. His left hand brushed the ground. As he rose, he flung dirt at Clay Taggart's face.

White Apache dodged aside, but not quite quickly enough. His right eye seared with pain, then clouded with tears as he blinked rapidly to clear it. For a few seconds he was riveted in place.

Quid saw his chance. Pivoting, he leaped for the top, scrambling up and over. He still had his Colt. Switching the Bowie to his left hand, he drew the revolver. It was time to put an end to the White Apache's life once and for all.

Only White Apache had other ideas. In a powerful bound he cleared the top. The Colt leveled toward his chest as he flicked the Bowie, once.

Benjamin Quid saw a scarlet geyser burst from his wrist. He attempted to squeeze the trigger but his finger would not do as he wanted. His right hand had gone completely numb. Parrying another thrust with his Bowie, he retreated. Unwittingly, he backed into the boulder and could go no further.

White Apache leaped. His free hand caught Quid's left wrist. The bounty hunter managed to block his next swing. Spinning, White Apache hooked a foot behind Quid's legs and shoved. His intent was to push Quid down so that he could pin him and finish him off at leisure.

The bounty hunter guessed as much. So as he fell, he hurled himself backward, out of reach. A look of surprise came over Clay Taggart's face as his flailing left arm, which should have found purchase under him, cleaved empty air. His body, instead of hitting the ground, angled downward.

In a state of shock, Quid realized that Taggart's surprise had nothing to do with his agility and everything to do with the fact that in throwing himself to the rear, he had forgotten that his back was to the edge of the precipice.

The bounty hunter plummeted, headfirst. He tried to scream, but his vocal chords were paralyzed. He saw the boulders below rush up to meet him with incredible swiftness. His last thought before he struck was that he had gone after one bounty too many.

White Apache looked down from the lofty rampart at the pile of pulverized bone and pulped flesh, then sighed. It was over. All four of them were dead. Now he could go about his business and rejoin the Chiricahua.

At that juncture, from deep within the canyon, echoed a shot.

William Randolph also heard it. Seated in his tent with a small mirror on his lap, he was clipping his mustache with tiny scissors when the crack of a pistol made him jerk around. By accident, he snipped his nose, and almost shrieked in torment.

Outside, someone cursed. Feet pounded.

Randolph jumped up. His first thought was that Apache had found them. Dashing to the flap, he peered out and saw Wilson and Carver racing toward the spring. They both stopped short when Stirco stumbled into the open, a hand pressed to his right shoulder.

"She shot me!" Stirco raged. "The bitch up and shot me!"

Randolph wasn't sure if he had heard correctly. The man couldn't possibly be referring to Amelia Taggart, could he? Randolph shoved the flap and hurried toward the trio. "What was that? Who shot you, my good fellow?"

Stirco, doubled over, moist blood staining his shirt, nearly fell. His companions caught him, then steered him toward the fire. He glanced up, his flushed features contorted in spite. "Who the hell do you think, you idiot! That she cat!"

"Miss Taggart?" Randolph said in confusion. "Why on earth would she put a bullet in you?"

"She's a Taggart, isn't she?" Stirco snarled through clenched teeth. "What more of a reason does she need?"

The reporter stood by helplessly while Carver and Wilson lowered Stirco onto his back. The latter opened Stirco's shirt, revealing that the slug had not only left a hole the size of a walnut but also shattered Stirco's collarbone.

"I can't believe she would do such a thing," Randolph said.

"Are you calling me a liar?" Stirco declared.

Rather than face the gunman's wrath, Randolph hurried to the gap and strode on through. He was so startled to see Amelia seated in the pool that he halted in amazement before noticing the cocked pistol she held. "Miss Taggart!" was all he could think of to say.

Amelia held the pistol as steady as a rock, but inwardly her emotions seethed. Not with regret over having shot a man, but with elation at how easy it had been to squeeze the trigger. She had warned Stirco. She had aimed the Derringer and given him one last chance to leave. Yet all he had done was laugh and keep on coming. Well, he wasn't laughing now.

"Miss Taggart?" Randolph repeated. "What is the meaning of all this?"

"I want some privacy," Amelia said. She was not about to launch into a full explanation, not when she was sitting there with no clothes on. "Mr. Stirco was unwilling to respect that. I hope you will."

Randolph could not take his eyes off the pistol. "Most certainly, madam." Backing out, he gave a little bow. "Never let it be said that I'm not a gentleman. We can discuss this at your leisure."

Finally alone, Amelia sagged. Her arms commenced to shake so violently that she had to set the pocket pistol down for fear of dropping it in the water. Clasping her arms to her chest, she huddled in the water, shivering not from fear but from excitement. It was a heady, intoxicating feeling, and she wondered if her cousin felt the same when he raided ranches and attacked wagon trains.

For the longest while Amelia did not move. She struggled to come to grips with what she had just done, and with herself. *Thou shalt not kill*, the Good Book said. Yet look at what she had done, and she felt good about it!

Off by the campfire an argument broke out. Amelia heard Stirco mention her name and swear lustily. He went on and on about how he was going to pay her back. The reporter said something she did not quite catch. Whatever it was, Stirco cursed louder.

For the rest of her life, Amelia Taggart would never forget what happened next. There were nine tightly spaced shots, one right after the other, *bam-bam-bam-bam-bam-bam-bam-bam-bam*. Rifle shots from high up on the north wall of the canyon. After the fourth a horse whinnied stridently and continued to do so until the very last blast. Then an unnerving silence fell.

Bewildered, Amelia strained to hear more. Something wheezed noisily, but other than that, the canyon might as well have been a graveyard. Stepping from the pool, she hastily dressed, not bothering to dry herself first. "Mr. Randolph?" she called softly. "Are you all right?"

The reporter did not reply. Clutching the pistol, Amelia sidled to the opening and saw a widening puddle of blood.

The bodies of the four men ringed the fire. All had the tops of their heads blown off, and their blood was flowing into a shallow depression. Beyond them, sprawled in a row, were the horses. One still lived, but its brains seeped from the exit wound.

Dumfounded, Amelia scanned the lofty rim. Nothing moved. No one was up there. Whoever was responsible had not seen her and gone on.

In a burst of insight, Amelia Taggart realized who it must have been. Taking a few steps, she cupped a hand to her mouth and screamed at the top of her lungs, "Clay! Clay! It's me, Amelia! Don't go! Please! We need to talk!"

Her only answer was the wail of the wind.

Epilogue

Ken Weber, the freighter, was making his first trip from Tucson to Mesilla since the day he stumbled on the two bounty hunters. He had a wad of tobacco in his mouth and a silver flask in his shirt pocket, the two essentials he could never be without on a long run. A low hill rose before him and he lifted his whip to spur the team along.

Suddenly Ken froze. He gawked. He came close to pinching himself to see if he were truly awake. For shuffling toward him down the middle of the road was a woman, a bedraggled mess of a female wearing a torn dress caked thick with dust, her hair in tangles. Dry tears smeared the dirt on her face. So shocking was the apparition that he brought the wagon to a lurching halt.

Bewildered, Ken gazed out over the empty expanse of baked country the woman must have crossed to get there. "Ma'am?" he said as she plodded toward him. "You look as if you could use some help."

The woman made no reply. Eyes fixed dead ahead, her limbs moving woodenly, she came to the team and halted. One of the mules nudged her but she never so much as blinked.

"Ma'am?" Ken said. Setting the brake, he climbed down. She did not look at him when he reached her. She did not react when he gently touched her elbow. "Can you talk, ma'am? Who are you? How did you get here?"

The woman simply stood there, arms limp, her eyes dull and glassy.

A shiver ran down Ken's spine. As carefully as he could, he guided her to the wagon and boosted her onto the seat. She never let out a peep, never moved or showed she was alive in any way. Roosting beside her, he got the wagon going again, swinging it in a wide circle that brought them back to the road with the team pointed due west instead of east.

"I'm taking you to Tucson, ma'am," Ken informed her. "My boss will throw a fit, me losing time and all, but it can't be helped."

As still as a statue, the woman stared blankly into space.

Ken Weber had seen poor souls like her before, unfortunates whose brains had been fried to a crisp by the desert sun. They were never the same again. The walking dead, a pard of his had called them.

Another shiver chilled the freighter as he cracked his long whip and headed for Tucson as if all the demons of hell were nipping at his heels.

HANGED!

Chapter One

A warm wind fanned the craggy features of Samuel T. Walker as he rode toward his ranch house. It was twilight, and he was looking forward to the thick steak and potatoes his Mexican cook Pedro would have ready for him shortly after he strode in the door. Pedro was a fine cook, almost as skilled with a frying pan as Walker's dear departed wife Charlotte.

Walker thought of her gentle, loving nature and the amazing fact that she had loved him above all other men. A familiar lump formed in his throat. It had been three years since his darling Charlotte had gone to meet her Maker, yet a day did not go by that he did not think of her.

"Lord, I miss that woman," Walker said softly to himself, and he was startled by his lapse. In his opinion, it didn't do for a grown man to talk to himself. Sure, city-bred folks did it all the time, but they had puny thinkers. Any man worthy of the handle never went around babbling to himself.

Walker rubbed the stubble on his chin. Three days had gone by since he had taken a razor to his skin. He was toying with the notion of growing a beard. Twice in the past few months he had started to do so, but then he would recall that Charlotte had never liked facial hair. She'd claimed it itched when they were intimate, and he would shave it off. Maybe this time he would have the courage to grow a beard.

The trail Walker followed was one he had taken countless times. Mesquite flanked it on both sides. Ahead was a bend; beyond lay a small hill. From the top, he would look down on his house, barn, and corral, and he'd feel the same pride he always felt. The Bar W was one of the most prosperous spreads in the territory, thanks to years of sweat and toil.

Walker's dun suddenly raised its head and nickered. Walker promptly placed a hand on the smooth butt of the Colt on his right hip. It didn't pay for a man to be careless, even in the vicinity of Tucson. The damned Apaches could strike anywhere, anytime.

As the dun rounded the bend, Walker saw a pair of mounted figures a dozen yards farther on. Automatically, his hand tightened on the Colt, but then he saw that they were white men, not renegades. His first thought was that they must be two of his hands on their way out to pull night-herd duty. But when he looked closer, he recognized his nearest neighbor and the marshal of Tucson.

Surprised, Walker rode to within six feet of them,

then reined up. "Howdy, Miles," he said, touching the brim of his hat. "What brings you over here at this time of the day?"

Miles Gillett was a big man, broad at the shoulders and also at the hips. He was immensely powerful, his body rippling with iron sinew. His strength helped to explain why he so seldom carried a gun. When he had a dispute with someone, he preferred to resort to his massive fists.

He lifted one of his ham-size hands and said in greeting, "Hello, Sam. I reckon you know why I've come."

"Again?" Walker said in disbelief. "How many times do I have to tell you the same thing? I'm not about to sell—not today, not tomorrow, not ever. Charlotte and I worked too long and hard to make this place a success for me to part with it at any price."

Gillett kept his face a blank slate so his neighbor wouldn't suspect his true feelings. "I'm awful sorry to hear that, Sam. I've made it as plain as can be that I aim to have the Bar W, no matter what."

Amused, Walker grinned. "You just can't take no for an answer, can you? I suppose I should have expected as much. How long have we known each other, Miles? Twenty, twenty-five years? If anyone should know how mulish you can be, it's me."

Plastering a smile on his great moon of a face, Gillett sighed and rested his hands on his saddle horn. "Sam, please, for the last time. I'm willing to pay twenty thousand dollars more than I offered you last week."

Walker whistled. "That's mighty generous of you, I'll admit. With that much money, I could go anywhere I want and live out my days in the lap of luxury. But my answer is still the same: I won't sell. Sorry."

"So am I." Gazing out over the Bar W, Gillett went on. "I need you to understand so you won't think badly of me afterward. You have to realize that my dream has always been to own the largest spread around."

Samuel Walker could not help laughing. "In case no one has told you, Miles, you already own the biggest damn ranch in the entire Arizona Territory."

"That's not enough."

"Oh?"

"No. Before I'm done, I'm going to have the largest spread anywhere. Not just in Arizona. Not just west of the Mississippi. But the biggest damn ranch that ever existed." Gillett's dark eyes sparkled. "Actually, the Triangle G will be more than a ranch, Sam. It will be an empire."

Walker could not believe his ears. "I never knew you felt this way, Miles. But I don't think you're being very realistic. To own a spread like that, you'd have to buy up half the land in these parts. And I know for a fact that a lot of ranchers will be just like me and refuse to sell."

Gillett was so caught up in the vision of his sprawling dominion that he said absently, "Taggart wouldn't sell either, and look at where it got him."

"Clay Taggart?" Walker said, puzzled by the reference.

Taggart had owned a small spread between Gillett's and his. Some time back, the man had tried to rape Gillett's lovely wife Lily and killed a puncher who had gone to her aid. Taggart had been forced to flee into the mountains, and the next Walker heard, he had taken up with a band of renegade bucks from off the Chiricahua Reservation. Folks called him the White Apache.

That turn of events had shocked Walker almost as much as the death of his wife. He'd known Clay well, or at least he'd believed he had. The two of them had shared bottles of coffin varnish on occasion, and they'd played poker together in Tucson from time to time. He'd always rated Taggart as an upstanding, hardworking hombre, just like himself.

Not all that long ago, Walker had learned that Gillett had bought Taggart's ranch for pennies on the dollar shortly after the trouble began. He had not thought much of that news at the time, although he did recollect Clay saying once that Gillett had been badgering him to sell out.

With those memories fresh in his mind; Walker asked, "What does Taggart have to do with this?"

Miles Gillett regretted what he was about to do. He truly did. But he had reached the limits of his patience. Walker left him no other choice. "I wanted his place, but he wouldn't cooperate. So I took steps to guarantee he couldn't stand in my way."

"Steps?" Walker said. "I don't understand."

"Must I spell it out for you?" Gillett asked. He could tell by his neighbor's expression that the older man was thoroughly confused. "Very well. Taggart never tried to rape my wife. I trumped up the charge so he would be the guest of honor at a necktie social."

"You wanted him to be hanged?" Walker said.

Gillett nodded, then frowned. "How was I to know he'd get away and join Delgadito's cutthroats? I sent a posse after him. Crane and the rest lynched him over in the Dragoons, but somehow he survived. I swear, that bastard has more lives than a damn cat!"

Walker glanced at Marshal Tom Crane. Until that moment, he had not paid much attention to the lawman's brooding presence. Truth was, Walker had never much liked the man. There was something about Crane's wolfish features, flinty eyes, and long, waxed mustache that made him appear sinister.

Walker had always felt that Crane was no good. A rumor he had heard tended to confirm that suspicion. According to a story making the rounds of Tucson's saloons, the lawman routinely pistol-whipped drunks who passed out in the street just to teach them not to make a nuisance of themselves. No self-respecting tin star would ever do such a thing.

"It's only a matter of time before Taggart makes a mistake," Gillett said. "Sooner or later, I'll make him pay for all the grief he's caused me."

"What about the grief you've caused him?" Walker said, practically exploding. "You've made him an outcast, Miles! You've turned every white man in Arizona against him! You've ruined Clay's life just so you could get your hands on his land!"

"That's about the size of it." Gillett wasn't worried about confessing his crimes to Walker. No one else would ever discover the truth.

"How could you?" Walker glared at Crane and added, "And how could you be a party to this crime?

HANGED!

You're supposed to uphold the law, for God's sake, not break it!"

For the first time Tom Crane spoke, his voice deep and raspy. "Whatever Mr. Gillett wants, he gets."

Walker studied the two of them a moment. Then he jammed his hat back on and said, "So that's the way it is, Miles? Crane is in your hip pocket? Well, the two of you won't get away with this! At the crack of dawn, I'm leaving to pay the governor a visit. Once he hears what you've done, there will be a full investigation. I wouldn't be surprised if the both of you end up behind bars. And it will serve you right!"

Miles Gillett smiled again, this time the smile was genuine. He never ceased to be amazed at how stupid other people could be. "Sam, what makes you think I'm going to let you go to Fort Whipple to see Gov. Goodwin?"

His words were spoken lightly, with a tinge of silken sarcasm. Yet they seared through Sam Walker like a branding iron. Abruptly, he realized that Marshal Crane's right hand rested on a pistol. Gillett's smile took on a whole new meaning.

"You can't be saying what I think you're saying," Walker said.

"Why not?" Gillett asked. "Folks are getting butchered by Apaches all the time."

Walker broke out in a cold sweat. "Someone will suspect," he said, wishing he sounded more confident.

The man who craved an empire shook his ponderous head. "Wishful thinking on your part, old friend. By the time Tom is done carving you up, it will look just like the handiwork of the White

11

Apache and the red vermin he rides with." Twisting, Gillett reached into a saddlebag. "One of my hands found this a while back and gave it to my wife. Recognize it?"

Walker did. It was the broken end of an iron-tipped arrow, the kind used by Apaches. His mouth went dry. He had to cough before he could speak. "So what if you make wolf meat of me? You still won't get my spread. I have a will, Miles. Everything I own goes to my brother in Ohio."

Gillett slipped his other hand into the same saddlebag and pulled out a sheath of folded papers. "This the one you're talking about, Sam?" After unfolding the document, he said, " 'I, Samuel Thaddeus Walker, being of sound mind and body—' "

"That can't be my will!" Walker said. "Mine is in my lawyer's safe up in Tucson!"

"Is it?" Kneeing his sorrel closer, Gillett offered the document. "Here. Check for yourself."

Walker snatched the papers and ran his eyes down the first page, then the next. Everything appeared to be in order. Stunned, he flipped to the very last page and found his signature next to the official seal.

"Your lawyer Emmet Floyd is a fine attorney," Gillett said, savoring Walker's confusion. "But he's just like any other law wrangler. He'll do anything for money."

Walker's mind was in a whirl. He began to realize that this man—a man he had known for over two decades, a man he had been proud to call a friend, a man who had been his dinner guest more times than either could remember, a man he had helped during good times and bad—was fixing to kill him.

"You'll still never get away with killing me," Walker said. "Even without the will, my brother will put in a claim to my spread. He's aware I've left it to him."

"Is he also aware that you recently made out a new will leaving everything to me?" Gillett asked smugly.

"I did no such thing!"

Miles Gillett reached under his jacket and pulled out another legal document. "You know that, and I know that. But anyone else who reads the new will Floyd prepared is going to be convinced otherwise."

Bending, Walker tried to snatch the document from Gillett's grasp, but the big man was too fast for him. "I never signed it! No judge will say it's genuine!"

Laughter burst from the wealthy rancher. "Do you have any idea how easy it is to forge a signature? A little practice and practically anyone can do it." Opening the document, he showed a signature that was a perfect copy of Walker's narrow scrawl. "Lily did this one herself. She's quite talented in that regard."

"Your wife?" Walker knew a stacked deck when he ran up against one. He glanced at Marshal Crane, certain the crooked lawman would make his play at any moment.

"She works with me on everything I do," Gillett said.

"It was her idea to frame Taggart by claiming he tried to rape her."

"Poor Clay."

"If you want to feel sorry for someone, feel sorry for yourself," Gillett said.

Without warning, Gillett struck. Exhibiting the speed of a rattler combined with the raw brute force of a bull buffalo, he backhanded Walker across the chin. His knobby knuckles made a resounding crack as they connected with the older man's jawbone.

Sam Walker never saw the blow coming. Still watching Tom Crane, he was catapulted backward over his bedroll. The blow jolted him to his core, stunning him so badly that he had no idea he had left the saddle until he thudded to earth. Dazed, he struggled to sit up. Walker was keenly aware that he was a dead man if he did not get out of there quickly.

Slowly, almost reluctantly, Miles Gillett climbed from the sorrel. "I wish it hadn't come to this, Sam. I truly do. It would have been so much nicer, so much easier all around, if you had agreed to my terms."

Out of the corner of an eye, Walker glimpsed a heavy boot streaking toward his midsection. He tried to dodge aside, but his sluggish brain didn't relay the message to his body soon enough. Lancing agony speared through him. He collapsed onto his hands and knees and sputtered for air, sure every rib on his right side had been shattered.

"You're awful quiet all of a sudden," Miles Gillett said while circling like a vulture.

Walker, balling a fist, focused intently, then threw everything he had into a punch to the wealthy rancher's gut. To Walker's dismay, Gillett blocked the blow with astounding ease. Even worse, his arm was clamped in a vise of steel. Gillett's leg, the size of a tree trunk, whipped upward.

HANGED!

There was a loud snap, and Walker nearly cried out in anguish. Overcome by agony, he pitched onto his chest. "You broke my arm. Damn your hide!"

"You brought this on yourself," Gillett said. "It's what you get for being so pigheaded."

Rough hands gripped Walker from behind and he was hauled to his feet. He knew it had to be Marshal Crane who held him because Gillett stood before him. His six-gun was snatched from its holster, then flung aside.

"I apologize for having to rough you up first." Miles Gillett winked. "But you know how vicious Apaches can be."

Setting himself, Gillett let his fists fly. The first blow filled Walker with more torment than he had ever felt. The next rocked him on his bootheels, and he would have fallen if not for the lawman supporting him. The third punch was the worst. Walker's insides churned so violently that he expected to be sick. After that punch, his senses swam. His body was a mass of pain from his head to his toes. He wanted to curse Gillett to high heaven, but he needed all his strength to catch his breath.

After a while, Marshal Crane let go of Walker. The older rancher sagged to his knees, blood pouring from his ruptured nose and battered mouth. Mustering the feeble energy left to him, he said, "May the two of you rot in hell!"

"You first, old friend," Gillett said, then nodded at the marshal.

Crane stepped in front of Walker, holding an Arkansas toothpick. The slim blade glinted dully in the fading light as he wagged it near Walker's eyes. The marshall's thick mustache curled upward. "Remember that time one of your cowhand's was caught by Nana's pack of wolves?"

A grisly image popped into Walker's mind. An image of a young man stripped naked and staked out under the burning sun, his eyes gone, his fingers and toes missing, his private parts crammed down his throat. Walker nearly gagged.

"I figured you would." Marshal Crane laughed. Then the knife descended.

Samuel T. Walker wanted to scream, but his vocal chords were the first thing Crane cut. All Walker could do was suffer in silence. And suffer he did. He suffered so intensely that his very soul shriveled. He was profoundly grateful when, at long last, with the name of his precious Charlotte on his lips, he passed into eternity.

Three hours later Marshal Tom Crane entered Tucson from the northwest. He had circled completely around the town to avoid any suspicion, not that anyone would ever link him to Sam Walker's death. He just didn't believe in taking chances.

Crane could feel the wad of bills Gillett had given him in his pants pocket. Another thousand could be added to the nest egg he was squirreling away. Five more years, Crane figured, and he'd have enough to buy a small place out in California, where he'd spend the rest of his days fishing and loafing.

Crane had been to California once, during the rush of '49. He'd been impressed by the climate and the friendly people. Even though his father had dragged him back to Arizona after failing to strike it rich, his childhood memories stuck with him.

HANGED!

One day he was going there again. Provided he lived long enough, of course.

A stiff wind from the northwest stirred dust in the street as Crane rode up to the hitching post in front of the marshal's office and dismounted. Looping the reins, he strode inside, his spur jangling.

Slumped behind the desk was Deputy Weaver, a bean pole of a man who was almost as slow with his wits as he was with a gun. Crane had hired Weaver because he did as he was told without asking questions.

Slamming the door, Crane grinned. Weaver shot to his feet and made a clumsy stab for the Remington at his side. "Sleeping on the job again, I see? Looks like I'll have to dock you another hour this week."

Shem Weaver blinked. "Marshal! I thought you said that you wouldn't be back until mornin'."

"I wrapped up the business I was on sooner than I expected," Crane said, stepping around the desk and shooing the bean pole away so he could sit. "Anything happen while I was gone?"

"Not much," Weaver said. "I let old Anders out of the cell once he sobered up, just like you told me to do. The owner of the Acme came by, but when he heard you were gone, he said that you should stop by and see him in person. Claimed you'd understand."

Crane nodded. Rafe Skinner, the proprietor of the Acme Saloon, was just one of many who paid him under the table to look the other way when local gambling laws were broken. "I'll hunt him up later tonight. If that's all, you can go grab a bite to eat while I hold down the fort."

"Much obliged, Marshal," Deputy Weaver said and patted his stomach. "I am feelin' a mite hollow."

He made for the door, but after taking only a few steps, he stopped dead in his tracks and spun. "Tarnation! I almost plumb forgot!" Coming around the desk, he opened a side drawer and took out an envelope. "This came for you on the afternoon stage."

Crane's pulse quickened when he recognized the handwriting. Tearing the envelope open, he took out a letter. "It's from my daughter."

"You have a sprout?" Weaver said. "Hellfire, I never even knew you were hitched."

"I was for a short while a long time ago," Crane said and let the subject go at that. "As for Tessa, she's no sprout. She'll be nineteen in a few months." Eagerly Crane began reading. Finishing the first paragraph, he glanced at the date at the top of the page, then swore lustily.

"What's the matter?" Weaver asked. "Bad news?"

"My daughter is coming for a visit."

"Really? When is she due in?"

Tom Crane frowned. The mail service to Tucson was deplorable. It was a standing joke among the good citizens of the whole territory that letters sent from points back east might as well go by the way of the moon because they would get there sooner. The date on Tessa's letter showed Crane she had written it nearly six weeks earlier, yet it had only just arrived. "In two days."

The skinny deputy beamed like an idiot. "I bet you can't wait! When was the last time you saw her?"

Tom Crane had half a mind to grab Weaver and

hurl him through the front window. But he swallowed his anger and answered honestly. "I never have."

"Never?" Weaver made for the door, shaking his head. "Well, then, I reckon her visit will be downright interestin'."

"To say the least," Crane said half to himself. "To say the very least."

Chapter Two

The fragrant aroma of brewing coffee brought Clay Taggart out of a deep sleep. He didn't open his eyes right away. Instead, he lay under his blanket, savoring the warmth.

Moments of peace and tranquility were all too rare in Clay's life of late. Ever since he had been forced into hiding after being falsely accused of having his way with Lily Gillett, he had suffered one nightmare after another. He had been lynched by vigilantes and taken prisoner by Apache renegades. He had barely escaped being slain when the Apache camp was raided by vicious scalp hunters from south of the border. He had been hunted by the army, by bounty hunters, and by rogue Apaches. It was a miracle he was still alive—a miracle Clay had no intention of taking for granted.

So on that particular morning, his nostrils tingled by the delicious scent of the perking coffee,

HANGED!

Clay listened to the crackling of the low fire and the soft humming of the woman who shared his wickiup.

Clay had little fear that he and the renegade Apaches he had befriended would be attacked. At the moment, they were camped high up in the Dragoons, in a small hidden valley known only to the Apaches, a lush paradise watered by a sparkling spring.

Cracking his eyelids, Clay secretly admired the beautiful woman who was on her knees over by the fire, weaving a large basket in which she would store food. Her raven tresses seemed to shimmer in the firelight. Her smooth features were almost angelic. He noticed how her full breasts filled out the top of her beaded buckskin dress, and it kindled anew the exquisite sensations he had felt the night before during their passionate lovemaking.

Marista was a Pima. Her people were peaceful farmers who lived in seven villages along the Gila River. They grew squash, beans, corn, and tobacco. Never warlike, they only took up arms when raided. Unfortunately for them, their villages were in close proximity to the Chiricahua homeland; so they were raided often.

Marista had been raised as a member of the White Ant Clan. Like Clay, she had been unjustly accused of a crime she had not committed. Like him, she was an outcast.

It seemed that her former husband, a famous Pima by the name of Culozul, had decided he wanted a new, younger wife. But since Pimas were only allowed one woman by custom, and since divorce was unknown among them, wily Culozul had

21

resorted to lying in order to have his way. He had accused Marista of the one crime Pimas never tolerated: adultery. Women accused of adultery were either stoned to death or shunned.

So Marista and her young son Colletto had become outcasts. They had wandered the desert and mountains, barely scraping by, living in dread that each new day might be their last. Then they had stumbled on Clay when he was in dire need, and they saved his life. Out of gratitude, Clay had taken them under his wing. Much to Marista's surprise, Clay's gratitude had blossomed into love.

Clay's love surprised even him because, not all that long ago, he had looked down his nose on all Indians and their ways, branding them as scum that should be exterminated. Nor had he been alone in his belief. Most whites in Arizona felt the same way. Newspapers railed against the red nuisance. Preachers gave sermons decrying the heathen menace. Politicians, always quick to exploit the popular tide, went on and on about the need to solve the Indian problem, but they failed to offer workable ideas.

To the white settlers, Indians were the scum of the earth. They deserved to be wiped out or crammed onto remote preserves where the frontiersmen would not come into contact with them.

Recently, the fiercest of all the Apache bands, the widely feared Chiricahuas, had been herded onto a reservation named in their honor. Their revered leader Cochise had been largely responsible for the founding of the reservation. Always wise, Cochise had foreseen that, unless his people did as the whites wanted, they would be ruthlessly wiped out.

HANGED!

The Chiricahuas were luckier than most tribes in that the land assigned as their reservation included the Chiricahua and Dragoon Mountains, the region in which they had lived for more generations than any of them could remember. They were allowed to hunt and roam there as they pleased, but they were not permitted to leave the reservation for any reason. Nor could they raid into Mexico, as their fathers and their fathers' fathers had.

The majority of Chiricahuas agreed to the white terms, but not all. Bands of renegades, refusing to be told how they could live, waged relentless war against whites and Mexicans alike. Foremost among them was the tiny group led by a warrior once described as the Scourge of the Southwest. His name was Delgadito, and if not for him, Clay's neck would have been stretched by a hemp noose months earlier. But Clay still lived, and that morning, he was lucky enough to enjoy some rest as he watched the woman he loved.

Suddenly a shadow filled the entrance of the wickiup, and Colletto came in. The boy beamed proudly. From his right hand dangled a rabbit he had slain with a sling. He spoke to his mother in the Pima tongue and she answered, smiling sweetly.

Clay did not quite catch what they said. He was trying to learn their language, just as he had mastered the Chiricahua tongue. But he had a long way to go before he would be able to hold an intelligent conversation. Reverting to English, he said, "Let the boy know he did a good job, Marista. Rabbit stew will make a fine supper."

Marista turned, her smile widening. "I not know

23

you awake," she said in a clipped, heavily accented voice.

She knew enough English to get by, thanks to Dr. David Wooster of San Francisco. The good doctor had lived among her people for quite some time, tending the sick and helping out in other ways, such as holding classes to teach the white man's tongue.

Clay sat up and stretched. "It's about time I got my lazy carcass out of the sack." He was pleased when Marista ran her dark eyes over his bronzed chest and rippling muscles.

"I make breakfast while you be bear," Marista said, indicating a flat rock on which rested six circular cakes.

"Be bear?" Clay repeated, unsure of her meaning.

Marista closed her eyes, placed her cheek in her hand, then did a remarkable imitation of him snoring. Clay laughed uproariously, and Marista sidled over to him to place her warm hands on his shoulders. "My heart is your heart, Lickoyee-shis-inday," she said, using his Chiricahua name. "As long as sun and moon last, I be yours. Savvy?"

Clay brazenly scooped her into his arms and planted a lingering kiss on her full lips. "I understand," he said, "and the same holds true for me." Glancing up, he noticed her son gaping at him. "What's gotten into the boy? Why is he trying to catch flies with his mouth?"

Marista chuckled. "Him not used to way you laugh, to how kind you be. Culozul never laugh. Culozuil hit him a lot, not say him do good as you do. You much different, White Apache. You happy man."

The simple statement gave Clay pause. The hell

of it was she was absolutely right. He was happier than he had ever been in his entire life, even though his happiness made no sense. Taggart was, after all, the most wanted man in Arizona, with a huge bounty on his head. He was sought by the entire Fifth Cavalry and every law officer in the territory, not to mention every soldier in Mexico. He'd lost everything he ever owned: his ranch, his livestock, his personal belongings. He was despised by every white, distrusted by every reservation Apache, and loathed by the Nakai-hay below the border. By all rights, he should have been miserable.

Yet there Taggart sat, laughing and joking. Indeed, he was happier than he'd ever been in the old days. His lot in life was so ridiculous, he threw back his head and cackled.

After his mirth subsided, Clay dressed swiftly, donning leggings, a shirt, and a headband. A breechcloth went over his leggings, hanging down low in front and back. Last he pulled on knee-high moccasins, the style favored by Apaches. When he was done, he was the spitting image of a full-blooded Chiricahua warrior, right down to his sun-browned skin and his long black hair. The only giveaway that he was white were his deep blue eyes.

Marista held out a tin cup brimming with scalding hot coffee. Clay accepted it and sipped, relishing the warmth that spread down his throat into his stomach. Then he helped himself to a corn cake.

Suddenly, another shadow blocked the entrance. That one was made by a pair of legs. Whoever was outside had the courtesy not to look in unless invited. "Lickoyee-shis-inday, you are needed."

White Apache stuffed the last of the corn cake into his mouth and rose. He grabbed his Winchester and exited the wickiup to find Cuchillo Negro waiting for him.

Of the four renegades in the band, the man known to the Mexicans as Black Knife had always been the friendliest to Clay. Cuchillo Negro was a rarity among Apaches, and for that matter, a rarity anywhere because he did not judge others by the color of their skin. "Greetings, my brother. Delgadito holds a council."

White Apache did not need to be told where the meeting would be held. All their councils took place at the spring. Bending his steps in that direction, he asked, "Do you know why?"

"He would not say." Cuchillo Negro gazed toward his own wickiup and saw Florencia, the Mexican woman he had kidnapped to be his wife. She liked to sit out in the sun early in the morning; at the moment, she was busy mending a torn shirt of his.

"Things go well with you and your new woman," White Apache said. He was pleased to see them getting along so well since it had been his idea for the band to attack a *conducta* and make off with women for each of the Chiricahuas.

Necessity had demanded they take action. The four warriors had lost all their loved ones when scalp hunters had nearly wiped out the band. Since none of the Chiricahua women on the reservation would have anything to do with them for fear of suffering a similar fate, the renegades had done as Apaches had been doing since the dawn of time: They had ventured south to the state of Chihuahua and helped themselves to the first women they saw.

HANGED!

Now each of them had a wife, except the youngest warrior, Ponce, whose woman had managed to escape. Just days earlier, though, Clay had learned that Ponce was slipping off to pay a certain young Chiricahua girl on the reservation regular visits; so perhaps all of them would have women soon.

Clay hoped so. The band needed females in order to thrive. If they wanted to attract more warriors to their cause, they had to convince others that it would be safe for them to bring their families along.

Rounding Cuchillo Negro's wickiup, the two men saw a sparkling pool of water. Beside it hunkered three warriors. White Apache cradled his Winchester in his left arm and raised his right hand, palm outward, in greeting.

"Lickoyee-shis-inday," young Ponce said. A robust, handsome warrior, he took great pride in his appearance. His clothing was always clean, his hair always neatly parted and combed. He was also partial to wearing wide beaded bracelets. Across his legs rested a carbine.

A few feet from Ponce sat a powerfully built hulk who disdained wearing shirts. Fiero was his name, and he had a temperament to match. His features had the hawkish contours of a natural-born predator. His eyes, true to his name, always blazed with inner light. On his brow was a long scar in the shape of a lightning bolt. He had a polished rifle at his side, a pistol and a Bowie strapped around his waist. As was his habit, he merely grunted in greeting.

The last warrior was older than Ponce by two decades and less muscular than Fiero. He had,

27

however, a more commanding presence than either of the other warriors. That forceful appearance had nothing to do with his red shirt or the twin Colts at his side. His posture, his bearing, and his every gesture were ample testimony to why over a score of seasoned warriors had left the reservation to throw in with him on his ill-fated attempt to seek sanctuary deep in Mexico.

Once, Delgadito had been a highly respected Chiricahua leader. Once, many had believed that he would become head of the entire tribe. Then fate had reared its serpentine head. He had suffered one setback after another. The Mexicans had driven him north of the border. He had been forced to hide out in rugged, arid country where even Apaches found it hard to survive. His band ran so low on food, they had to eat nearly all their horses.

Then Delgadito thought he had a stroke of luck. He witnessed the lynching of Clay Taggart. As the whites who had hanged Taggart rode off, he had ordered Taggart cut down, but not because he cared one way or the other whether Taggart lived. He had rescued Taggart because he planned to have Taggart go to the army and arrange for the bloodless surrender of his band.

An attack by scalp hunters had spoiled everything. Delgadito had seen the slaughter of those he cared for most. His wife, his relatives, and his closest friends had fallen before the guns and knives of the merciless fiends who dabbled in the commerce of human lives for profit. Only four warriors, counting Delgadito, had lived through the attack. And one other: Lickoyee-shis-inday.

Through a quirk of fate, White Apache was well

respected by the other surviving warriors. White Apache was the one who had saved them from *federales* on a foray into Mexico. White Apache was the one who had led them on several successful raids near Tucson. White Apache was the one who had gotten them women. White Apache's good fortune was enough to make Delgadito gnash his teeth in outrage.

But the seasoned warrior knew better than to let his true feelings show. As he always did when around White Apache, he acted as if Taggart were his best friend. "Amigo," he said. "*Nejeunee, pinday lickoyee, nuestche shee.*"

Easing cross-legged to the ground, Clay placed the Winchester at his side. "Why have you called us together, my friend? Do you want to go on another raid?"

"*To-dah*. No. Soon enough, but not this day," Delgadito said. He pointed to the southeast. "I thought it best to let you know that before the sun is straight overhead I will leave for Palacio's village."

Clay did not know what to make of the news. Palacio was the current leader of the Chiricahuas, and he hated Delgadito. Even worse, Palacio's village was close to Fort Bowie. Delgadito was taking an enormous risk venturing there.

"Are you eager to pass on to the other side?" Clay asked. "If Palacio should learn you are there, he will send for the white-eyes to come and seize you."

"It must be done," Delgadito said. "Late yesterday I was hunting deer on the high ridge east of here, and I saw a lone warrior running in this direction. I slipped down to see who it was. Corn Flower, my nephew, sent a messenger with word that he and several other warriors are thinking of joining us. He asked me to go speak to them."

On the one hand, Clay was elated by the news. Increasing the size of the band was crucial. In order for the Apaches to carry the fight to the whites who had usurped their land, they needed to be stronger.

But on the other hand, Clay was wary of a trap. Palacio was as crafty a devil as had ever lived, and Clay would not put it past him to cook up a scheme to lure Delgadito to his doom. He said as much, adding, "Did you know this messenger? Is he someone you can trust?"

"His name is Klo-sen. Hair Rope, in your tongue," Delgadito said. "I have known him many winters, even before I broke away from Palacio and led my band into Mexico. Yes, I believe he can be trusted."

"I hope you are right for your sake."

Ponce picked that moment to cut in. "If Delgadito is going to the village, I will go with him."

Although no one responded, Delgadito thought that it would be safer if he went alone. Yet he did not have the right to refuse permission. No warrior did. Any Shis-Inday, as the Apaches called themselves, was free to do as he pleased at all times.

Clay knew that the young warrior wanted to see the maiden he had been courting. He racked his brain for some way of persuading Ponce to stay, but to no avail.

Just then feet pattered toward them. Up rushed a tall, skinny Mexican woman in a buckskin dress she had made with her own hands. Her name was Delores, and she was one of those taken from the *conducta*.

Fiero, of all people, had claimed her as his own.

HANGED!

At the time, he had done so in the hope she would die before they reached their sanctuary. He had not wanted a wife, no matter what White Apache said about taking one being important to the future of his people. He had figured that a woman so thin and frail would never last long. But she had proven him wrong.

Deep in his heart, Fiero was proud of her. He would never admit as much to her, much less the other warriors, but he had been pleased to find she was so tough, so adaptable. Of all the women, she had taken to Apache ways the quickest. Not once had she given Fiero the slightest trouble. Not once had he any reason to regret his decision.

Fixing her with a glare, Fiero said, "What are you doing here, woman? This is man talk. I have told you not to pester me when I am in council."

Delores Garcia knew her man well. Bowing her head before him and dropping to one knee, she said contritely, "I am sorry to disturb you, but it is important."

Pleased by her deference, Fiero motioned. "Say what you have to say."

Holding up a handful of flowers, Delores said, "I was near the entrance to our valley, picking these so our lodge would look nice for you—"

"I do not care about such things," Fiero said gruffly, embarrassed that she would even hint that he did in front of his companions.

"I ask your forgiveness again," Delores said. "But it is well that I was there because I heard horses at a distance. I climbed partway up the cliff and saw riders approaching. They wear blue uniforms."

Fiero gripped his woman by the arm. "No mistake, *neh*? You are sure of this?"

"Have I ever lied to you?" Delores said.

Clay spun and hastened to his wickiup. Tethered behind it were the nine horses that belonged to him. Vaulting onto a black stallion he favored, he lashed the reins and galloped bareback to the south. Delgadito and Cuchillo Negro were ahead of him; Fiero and Ponce trailed.

It upset Clay immensely that the army might have located their refuge. Once before, that had happened, and they had been lucky to escape with their lives.

The valley was an ideal place to hide, but it had a serious drawback: There was only one way in or out. If the cavalry blocked the entrance, the band would be trapped.

High peaks rimmed the valley on all sides. To the south, a cliff towered. Only the Chiricahuas knew that there was a gap in the cliff, a winding path no wider than a horse through which the Apaches gained entrance to the verdant oasis.

Clay came to the base of the cliff and reined up. He was off the stallion and bounding up the slope next to the rock wall before the black stopped moving. Careful not to dislodge loose stones and dirt, he reached a narrow shelf near the top and crouched next to Delgadito and Cuchillo Negro. Warily, he peeked over the top.

Delores had told the truth. Over a hundred yards out were seven riders. Six of them were white men, soldiers in uniforms. The seventh was an Indian, but not an Apache, judging by his clothes and the way he wore his hair.

"A Maricopa," Delgadito whispered in contempt.

HANGED!

Clay recollected that the Chiricahuas held the Maricopas in low esteem. Apparently the one below was more skilled than most, because he was leading the troopers straight for the gap in the cliff.

Chapter Three

Pvt. James Calhoun, Detachment G, Fifth Cavalry, keenly wished he was anywhere other than where he happened to be. Gripping his carbine in both sweaty hands, he gulped as he stared at a towering rampart of stone that reared ahead. He had a bad feeling about what they were doing—a very bad feeling.

Staring hard at the top of the cliff, Calhoun could have sworn unseen eyes were looking back. How was it then, he wondered, that none of the others seemed to feel the same way, not even the Maricopa or the sergeant?

Calhoun wanted to call out, to warn them that they were making the biggest blunder of their lives, that they should ride back to fetch the captain and the rest of the patrol. But he held his tongue. He was fresh to the territory, only assigned to Fort Bowie two weeks earlier, and the older, seasoned soldiers regarded him as a rank greenhorn. If he started hollering, he'd never hear the end of it. And the sergeant would probably put him on report and punish him but good when the unit got back to the post.

No, Calhoun decided, it would be better to keep his mouth shut. Besides, for all he knew, his unease was spawned by a simple case of raw nerves. He had never been in combat, and the mere idea of tangling with a pack of savage Apaches was enough to make any sane man queasy.

It was just one of those days when everything went wrong. The morning had started off on a sour note and gotten worse as time went by. Shortly before daybreak, when the corporal had gone around rousing everyone out of the sack, Calhoun had sat up and shook himself, trying to stir life into his listless veins. Without thinking, he had picked up his right boot and started to slide his foot in. His toes had brushed something that wriggled, and there had been a sharp stinging sensation.

Yelping loud enough to raise the dead, Calhoun had shot erect. He had thrown the boot to the ground and jumped up and down on his left leg while clutching his right foot. A lot of the men had burst into laughter. Then a brawny hand had clamped on Calhoun's shoulder, and he had found himself looking up at the ruddy complexion of Sgt. Paddy O'Shaughnessy.

"And what appears to be the trouble, boyo?" the burly soldier asked in a deceptively mild tone. "Bit by a rattler, were you?"

The suggestion terrified Calhoun. "I might have been, Sergeant!"

Showing his big, uneven teeth, O'Shaughnessy helped Calhoun sit. "Here then, take a seat, laddie, and we'll see what all the fuss is about." The sergeant picked up the boot and upended it.

Before Calhoun's horrified eyes, out tumbled a large reddish-brown scorpion. He nearly fainted then and there. "Oh, Lord!" he wailed. "I was stung by one of those!"

O'Shaughnessy lifted a leg and smashed his boot heel down on the scorpion, squashing it to a pulp. Then he squatted to examine Calhoun's foot. Under the big toe he found a thin red line. "The fates smiled on you, boyo."

"They did?" Calhoun asked, gritting his teeth against the agony, certain his leg was going to swell up and turn several shades of black and blue. The surgeon at the post would likely have to amputate, he reasoned, and he would spend the rest of his days hobbling around on a crutch.

"You weren't stung, lad," the sergeant said.

"I wasn't?" Calhoun asked doubtfully.

O'Shaughnessy touched the red line. "No, the critter pinched you with one of those nasty pincers of his. That's all."

Calhoun gawked at his foot, relief washing over him in waves. "Thank God!" Only then did he realize the men around him were laughing at him.

Sgt. O'Shaughnessy leaned toward him and gripped him by the shirt. His next words were uttered in an icy calm that made them all the more chilling. "Now you listen to me, boyo, and you listen well. If you ever pull a jackass stunt like that again, I will personally see to it that you spend the next year peeling potatoes and cleaning the privy."

HANGED!

"But—" Calhoun said, and O'Shaughnessy gave him a shake that rattled him to the bone.

"I'm not done," the sergeant said. "Time and again I've told you new recruits to shake your boots and such out first thing in the morning when we're in the field. Haven't I, lad?"

Gulping, Calhoun meekly replied, "Yes, Sergeant."

"Time and again I've also warned you not to make a lot of noise since we never know when the heathens might be about. Isn't that true?"

"Yes, Sergeant."

O'Shaughnessy patted Calhoun on the cheek. "Then be a good lad and get your kit together and be ready to move out with the rest of the patrol. If I hear another peep out of you, I will take you out behind the barracks when we get back and pound some sense into that silly wee head of yours just for the hell of it."

Calhoun had counted himself lucky that he had gotten off with a tongue-lashing. Sgt. O'Shaughnessy was not notorious for having a sweet disposition. The sergeant's favorite form of punishment was to have troopers bound and gagged and left out under the hot sun for eight to ten hours, or to make them jog around the parade ground for five or six hours toting a knapsack crammed with heavy rocks.

After his run in with O'Shaughnessy, Calhoun had dressed, made up his bedroll, and fallen in for roll call. Then, the men were required to water, groom and feed their mounts. Breakfast came last. As Calhoun was sitting in the shade of a boulder chewing on hardtack, O'Shaughnessy appeared at his side.

"Enjoying your meal, are you, boyo?" O'Shaughnessy said, and Calhoun was too shocked to answer. "Well, eat hearty, lad, because in fifteen minutes you are joining me for a little foray to the north."

"I am?"

"The Injun claims he found some sign. Capt. Eldritch doesn't want the whole patrol to go traipsing off on a possible wild-goose chase. So he's sending me to investigate. And I get to pick the five men who will go along. You came to mind right away, what with us being such good friends after our little heart-to-heart talk earlier."

Calhoun had wanted to pound his forehead against the boulder. One of the first lessons any army recruit learned was to never draw attention to himself. There was no surer way to earn extra duty.

And there Calhoun was, an hour out from camp, his nerves stretched as tight as violin strings, bringing up the rear as the Indian led the soldiers ever deeper into a terrible maze of canyons and gorges the likes of which the inexperienced private had never imagined existed. In Calhoun's estimation, they were wasting their time. Nothing could live in that godforsaken country. There was little water for miles around and scant vegetation, save for dry, withered brush. He couldn't understand why O'Shaughnessy didn't turn them around and head for the spot where they would rendezvous with the main patrol.

Calhoun raised an arm to mop his sweaty brow

with his sleeve. As he began to lower it, he glimpsed a bright flash of light near the top of the cliff. A strange pinpoint glare for which he had no logical explanation.

Suddenly Sgt. O'Shaughnessy stiffened, his gazed fixed on the same spot. Seconds before a rifle boomed loud and clear, he bawled out, "Scatter, boyos! Scatter! The heathens have us in their sights!"

Moments earlier, high up on the shelf, young Ponce had leapt to his feet and taken a hasty bead on one of the bluecoats. In his eagerness to draw first blood, he failed to take into account that the sun might reflect off his rifle and give him away.

Clay Taggart realized it, though, and a fraction too late, he whispered, "Ponce! No!"

Taggart and the warriors would have been better off if they'd allowed the Maricopa and the soldiers to come on through the gap. Then they could have jumped their enemies one by one. Since the element of surprise had been lost, the only effective plan was to wipe out every last trooper quickly.

Rising, Clay saw that a lanky soldier was already down, bleeding profusely from a side wound but still alive. The rest were turning to flee. Several snapped their carbines up to return fire. Clay aimed at a large man wearing the yellow stripes of a sergeant. As Taggart stroked the trigger, the man's horse plunged, spooked by the gunfire. The slug intended for the soldier's chest cored his shoulder instead.

Down below, Pvt. Calhoun, rigid with fear, saw Sgt. O'Shaughnessy sway as blood spurted from his broad back. Calhoun's first impulse was to dash to the sergeant's side. But everyone else was retreating, and the sergeant himself continued to roar that they should get the hell out of there.

Figuring that the experienced soldier knew best, Calhoun flailed his mount with his legs as he turned it to race off. He saw Sgt. O'Shaughnessy ride over to Pvt. Webber, who was on his knees with a side wound. O'Shaughnessy leaned down to haul Webber up behind him.

"Hee-yah!" Calhoun cried, urging his sorrel into a gallop. He glanced back just in time to see O'Shaughnessy arch his back and shudder as if cold. Aghast, Calhoun watched the sergeant let go of Webber, slump forward, and go limp.

Pvt. Webber, cursing a blue streak, had tottered backward. In a panic, he flung his carbine down and leapt, grabbing hold of the sergeant.

Calhoun was stupefied to see Webber yank O'Shaughnessy from the saddle. He slowed, thinking he would go to the sergeant's aid, when it occurred to him that O'Shaughnessy was dead and that Webber was only trying to get out of there alive. He saw Webber grip the saddle horn with both hands. Then Webber began to pull himself up. Suddenly, the other private's head jerked back as if to a heavy blow, and he toppled.

Calhoun fled for dear life. Everything had gone so wrong so fast. Two good men dead, and they hadn't even seen their attackers!

Looking around, Calhoun discovered his fellow troopers were speeding rapidly southward. Prine and Baker had veered off to the left. Grissom was off to the right. Calhoun faced front and spied the Maricopa a dozen yards ahead. Since it made sense that the scout would be able to find his way back

to the column without any problem, Calhoun stuck
with the Indian.

The private counted himself fortunate to be alive.
In less than an hour he would be back with Capt.
Eldritch and the others, and all would be well.
Thrilled by his narrow escape, he glanced over a
shoulder for one last look at Sgt. O'Shaughnessy.

Calhoun's heart skipped a beat. From out of the
cliff wall, as if by magic, three riders appeared. He
didn't know a lot about Indians, but he knew
enough to recognize the trio for what they were:
Apaches.

Clay Taggart and the Chiricahuas had gone down
the slope on the fly the second they saw that some
of the troopers were getting away. Springing onto
the black stallion, Clay paused long enough to
shout, "We cannot all go! Some of us should stay
to protect the women in case other soldiers show
up."

The Chiricahuas stopped. Ponce and Fiero commenced to argue over which one of them should
remain.

Even though Clay was the acknowledged leader
of the band, he had no right to tell the others what
to do. All he could do was suggest and hope the
others went along with his suggestion.

"Ponce, you and Cuchillo Negro should stay
here!" Clay shouted, then took the lead, speeding
through the gap as swiftly as the winding passage
allowed. Once in the open, he gave the stallion its
head.

Delgadito and Fiero were right behind him. Delgadito saw a trooper bearing to the southwest. Yipping like a coyote, he was off in pursuit. Fiero,

spying a pair of white-eyes in flight to the southeast, whooped and peeled off to chase them down.

That left Clay with a young trooper and the Maricopa. It was plain that he would not be able to overtake them within a short amount of time. So he held the stallion to a brisk trot, conserving its energy for when the mounts of the soldier and the warrior tired.

Swirls of dust kicked from under the hooves of the trooper's sorrel and the Maricopa's pinto. The former looked back, saw Clay, and went as white as a sheet.

Calhoun was petrified. He had only been at Fort Bowie a short while, but in that time he had heard scores of gory stories about Apaches and the atrocities they committed on whites they caught. A grizzled veteran had told him of finding a prospector whose heart had been carved out while the prospector was still alive. A lieutenant had mentioned finding a trader who had been tied to a wagon wheel and turned upside down over a roaring fire.

Calhoun's mouth went dry. His imagination got the better of him. In his mind's eye, he saw himself being hacked to bits. Then he envisioned being tied to an anthill and having red ants poured down his throat and over his eyes and nose.

"No!" Calhoun spurred the sorrel to go faster even though the animal was already running flat out. He realized he was still holding his carbine. Twisting, he tried to settle his sights on the Apache, but the bobbing motion of his mount threw his aim off. Behind him, the Apache grinned.

"Damn you to hell!" Calhoun returned to the business of getting away with his hide intact. He had hard riding to do. The scout had gained some ground, and Calhoun was not about to lose the man. That Maricopa was his sole hope of rejoining the patrol and returning to Fort Bowie safely. Sooner or later the Apache would grow tired of following them and give up. A long chase would not hold his interest.

According to the older troopers Calhoun had talked to, Apaches were masters of the lightning raid. They liked to attack like a bolt out of the blue, then melt into the wilderness before anyone was the wiser. Calhoun had only heard of one instance where Apaches had pursued a man for any length of time, and that had been a fellow riding a magnificent horse that the Apaches wanted to get their hands on.

Minutes dragged by. A half hour. Then an hour. Calhoun narrowed the gap between himself and the Maricopa, who was holding his horse to a trot. Every so often, Calhoun would look back. The Apache was always there. Presently, the Apache fell a little farther behind. Calhoun hoped the Apache's lagging behind was a good sign. The savage's horse had to be tiring.

In reality, however, the black stallion was barely winded. Clay had slowed down because he was in no rush. He had all the time in the world.

The three riders gradually descended the Dragoons. Soon they passed through a belt of ponderosa pine. Below that was woodland, mainly pinons and junipers. Still lower, and they were in chaparral.

The general direction in which the Maricopa and the young trooper were heading perplexed Clay. Initially, it had been to the southwest. But ever so gradually, the Maricopa had swung almost due west and started on a beeline for the far horizon.

So far as Clay knew, there was nothing but mile after mile of rugged, wild terrain ahead of them clear to the Gila River. And even though the Gila River country was home to the Maricopas, it made no sense for the Indian scout to head there. The Maricopa had a duty to report to his superiors at Fort Bowie. Clay shrugged. Wherever the other men were going, he would stick with them until his chance came to close in.

Another hour elapsed. Two. Then three. Pvt. Calhoun was so sore he could barely sit in the saddle. He was still not used to spending the greater part of every day on horseback. He was a city boy, born and reared in Albany, New York. The only occasions he had ridden had been on rare visits to a cousin who lived in the country on a farm.

Reminiscing about his cousin made Calhoun scowl. He should have listened to her. Marcy warned him that he was making a fool of himself by enlisting and going west to find adventure. But Calhoun had refused to pay her any mind. It was his life. He knew what he was doing.

Life in Albany had been so damn dull. Calhoun had worked as a clerk in a mercantile, more boring work was hard to imagine. Day in and day out, he had either stood behind a counter making change, stacked shelves, or marked prices on merchandise. The same three tasks over and over and over again until he dreaded going to work.

Calhoun had needed something different, something exciting. One day he had been strolling along a downtown street and seen a poster advertising the wonderful careers being offered by the army. He had stood in front of the poster; fascinated by the artist's depiction of a noble cavalryman charging across a plain, his saber extended, a horde of red devils fleeing from his wrath.

That was the life! Calhoun had decided on the spot. He would get to travel, to meet new people, to do new things. Best of all, he would be issued a revolver, a saber, and a rifle. He would spend his days making the frontier safe for lonely widows and pretty girls, who would be ever so grateful.

He daydreamed that he single-handedly decimated the Sioux nation and was rewarded for his gallantry with a parade in New York City. The daughter of the governor pinned on his medal and fell in love with him instantly. That fantasy had always ended with the two of them walking hand in hand into the sunset.

Calhoun shook his head at his own idiocy. There he was, the mighty slayer of Sioux by the hundreds, running from a single Apache! It was enough to make him laugh, and he did, bitterly.

Marcy had been right. Army life was not as Calhoun had expected it to be. In its own way, army life was as much of a drag as the mercantile business. Back at the post, his days were spent drilling on the parade ground, tending his horse, drilling some more, sweeping out the stable, then even more drilling. Two weeks of such drudgery had been enough to make Calhoun scream. He had actually been happy when picked to go on patrol with Capt. Eldritch. And look at where that assignment had gotten him!

Up ahead, the Maricopa entered a wide canyon. He slowed and looked back, surprised to see Calhoun following him. Angling to a low rocky knoll, the warrior reined up at the top to wait for the private to catch up.

Calhoun thought the man insane. Coming to a stop halfway up the slope, he gestured behind him and said, "Do you want to die, Injun? That damned Apache is right behind us!"

"You mistake, white-eye," the Maricopa said in English so atrocious the words were almost foreign. "Him not there now."

"What?" Calhoun shifted in the saddle. Sure enough, the Apache was nowhere in sight. "But that can't be! He was there just a few minutes ago! I saw him with my own eyes!"

"Apaches clever. Never know what they do," the Maricopa said. He was a robust man, his skin a lot like tanned leather, his long hair worn in massive plaits except for his bangs, which were cut even with the eyebrows. Cocking his head at the private, he asked, "Why you follow me, white-eye?"

Calhoun snorted. "What a stupid question! How else am I to find Capt. Eldritch? Now lead on and get us to the place where we're supposed to meet him without delay!"

A hint of a smile touched the Maricopa's mouth. "You think I go to patrol?"

"Of course! Where else would you be—" Calhoun stopped as a disturbing insight dawned. "Wait a minute! Do you mean to say that you're not on your way to rejoin the captain?"

"No, Eldritch that way." The Maricopa pointed

HANGED!

off in an entirely different direction from the one they had been taking.

Bewildered, Calhoun nudged his mount higher. "Then you must be heading for Fort Bowie!"

"No, Bowie that way." Again the scout pointed.

Almost beside himself with rising anger, Calhoun said, "Then where in the hell are you going, Injun?"

"Home."

"Where?" Calhoun asked, suspecting he had not heard correctly.

"My village. My people," the Maricopa said. "I no be scout. I no work for white-eyes anymore."

Unbidden, a few snatches of conversation Calhoun had overheard before leaving the post came back to him. Sgt. O'Shaughnessy had been talking to an officer named Forester, complaining that he didn't like the scout chosen for the patrol. The Maricopa was new, untested, O'Shaughnessy had said. The sergeant would much rather have had one of the Tontos. But Forester had told him that the colonel's decision was final. The commanding officer wanted to give the Maricopa a chance to prove himself.

"Why, you rotten coward!" Calhoun said. "The first fight you're in, and you tuck your tail between your legs and run off! I have half a mind to pull you off that pinto and thrash you."

"I think not," the Maricopa said. Smirking, he leveled the carbine supplied to him by the Fifth Cavalry at Calhoun's head. "I think maybe you talk too much, white-eye."

Calhoun recoiled just as a shot rang out.

Chapter Four

Marshal Tom Crane was in a sour mood. When that happened, he had a habit of stalking the streets of Tucson in search of anyone foolish enough to cross him so he could vent his spleen in the manner he liked best.

On this particular day, as Crane was passing Leatherwood's stable, he heard angry voices rise inside. Without breaking stride, he angled to the open double door to find out what the fuss was all about.

Leatherwood and a man Crane had never seen before were nose to nose. Both were red in the face. The proprietor picked that moment to jab a finger into the other's chest and say, "You'll pay the damn bill, or you'll never get your horse back, mister! And that's final!"

"Like hell!" the stranger said. Wearing a rumpled suit and a dusty bowler, he carried a black bag. Some people might have mistaken him for a doctor, but Marshal Crane knew the man for what he really was: a drummer. "You're trying to gouge me, you slimy weasel! You figure that, just because I'm only passing through, you can get away with fleecing me!"

Leatherwood held out a callused hand. "That'll be four dollars. Pay up or get out of here before I toss you out on your ear."

Fuming, the drummer reached into a vest pocket and produced a handful of coins. Counting them, he replaced two, then said, "Here's two dollars. That's the going rate. Take it."

"Like hell," Leatherwood said. "I won't accept a cent less than four."

"Why, you—" the drummer growled and balled his fist.

Marshal Crane entered, the thumb of his right hand tucked under his gun belt, inches from his Colt. "Gentlemen!" he said. "I would suggest the two of you hold down the ruckus or you'll answer to me."

The owner of the stable took a step back, a hand rising to his throat. "Marshal! We're just having a little disagreement. There's no need for you to get involved."

The drummer thought otherwise. Facing the law-man, he said, "Thank goodness, you're here. I want to file a complaint. This man thinks he can over-charge me and get away with it! Out and out rob-bery, that's what it is! I demand that you do something about it! I demand that he be called to account!"

Crane halted in front of the stranger. "You do, do you?"

"That's right!" the drummer said. "And I won't take no for an answer! I know my rights!"

Crane's draw was a blur. In a smooth motion, he slammed the barrel of his pistol across the man's temple, and the drummer staggered back against a stall, losing his bowler and dropping his bag of wares. "That's for disturbing the peace," Crane said. Closing in, he raised the Colt.

The drummer grasped at the lawman's shirt. "Please, no!" he cried. "I didn't mean—"

Crane slashed the barrel downward. It caught the man above the right eye and opened a two-inch gash from which blood spurted. "That's for resisting arrest."

Tottering, the drummer tried to run out into the street, but he only managed to take several wobbly steps before he collapsed onto his knees. "No more! I beg you! No more!"

Tom Crane paid him no heed. Striding up, he said coldly, "And this is for being a stupid son of a bitch who doesn't know when to keep his mouth shut." His right leg shot out, his boot ramming into the man's gut.

Sputtering and gasping, the drummer doubled over. He was still conscious, but barely.

Leatherwood, frozen in place until that moment, found his voice. "Marshal, for the love of God! There's no need for this! We could have settled it ourselves!"

Crane glared, and the stable owner shriveled against a post. "How would you like me to haul you in for interfering with a law officer in the performance of his duties?"

Licking his thin lips, Leatherwood vigorously

shook his head. "That won't be necessary. Do what you have to."

Marshal Crane twirled his Colt into its holster with a flourish. Picking up the bowler and the valise, he grabbed the drummer by the back of the collar and proceeded to drag the man from the livery. A low chuckle drew his gaze to a man leaning against the door. "What the hell are you laughing at?"

Rafe Skinner was tall, lean, and whipcord tough. The owner of the Acme always wore the finest of clothes, from his wide-brimmed gray felt hat down to his shiny black boots. It was common knowledge that the women of Tucson considered him the handsomest man in town. Rumor had it that Skinner carried a mirror in a jacket pocket just so he could admire himself when he got the hankering. "My, my," he said, falling into step with the lawman, "aren't you in a fine fettle this bright and sunny day?"

"Go jump off a building," Crane said.

A few passersby stopped to gawk as the drummer was hauled down the middle of the street. An elderly matron in a bonnet shook a bony finger at the lawman in reproach.

Rafe Skinner laughed. "The good people of Tucson sure do think highly of you, don't they? Any day now they should get around to erecting a statue in your honor."

Had anyone else spoken to Crane with such contempt, he would have kicked in his teeth. But Rafe Skinner was a rarity, one of the few genuine friends Crane had. They were a lot alike in that both of them pretended to make their living legally while milking the shady side of the law for all it was worth.

"Don't you have something better to do than give me a hard time?" Crane said.

"Yes, but it wouldn't be half as much fun." Rafe clapped Crane on the shoulder. "You really should learn to relax more. One of these days you'll give yourself an ulcer."

The drummer started to struggle. Halting, Crane turned and kicked him in the back of the head. "Be still, you, or I'll bust your skull wide open." Going on, Crane ignored the hard stares of the townsfolk on the boardwalks.

Skinner laughed. "Maybe you should come by my place later. I'll fix you up with Ethel. You like her, as I recollect. An hour or two with her will drain all the spite out of your system."

"You talk too much."

Unruffled, Skinner smiled at a pair of pretty young women and raised a finger to his hat brim. "Howdy, ladies," he said suavely. "Nice day for a stroll."

When the women coyly averted their faces, Skinner sniffed like a bloodhound on a hot scent. "Women! How they do delight and dazzle! They're proof, if any were needed, that God exists. Imagine how miserable our existence would be without their fair, luscious forms!"

"Don't you ever get tired of flapping your gums?" Crane asked testily. "The next thing I know, you'll be quoting more of that rotten poetry you like so much."

Skinner pursed his lips. "It wouldn't hurt you, Thomas, to acquire a little culture. It impresses the ladies no end, and I hear tell that a very special lady is coming to pay you a visit."

Crane halted so abruptly that the drummer bumped into his legs. "Let me guess. Weaver."

"He was in my place last night and had a few drinks too many," Rafe said. "Don't hold it against him though. I was the only person he told."

Crane had specifically asked his deputy not to breathe a word of Tessa's visit to anyone, and Weaver had given his word that he would. Somehow or other Crane was going to pay the jackass back. Maybe he'd come up with an excuse to dock Weaver a week's pay.

"So tell me," Skinner said, "how is it that you never mentioned having a daughter? Hell, you never even let me know you were married before."

"A man's personal life is his own affair," Crane said. "My marriage to Maggie was a mistake. She was a dove at the time, the first woman I ever bedded. I was young at the time. I thought I was in love. So we got hitched two nights after we met. About three months later, Maggie left. Later, I got a letter from her claiming she'd had a daughter by me. Now you know everything. Satisfied?"

"Have you been in touch with the daughter over the years?"

"Now and then, she'd write, mostly kid stuff," Crane said. "As she got older, the letters stopped coming as often. I'd about given up on ever hearing from her again. Now she's coming to see me. Who would have thought it?"

Rafe Skinner had been a gambler before he'd bought the Acme. To be successful in his line of work, a man had to be able to read people as well as he read cards. "Why is it I get the notion that you're not very happy about her visit?"

The jail appeared around the next corner. Marshal Crane jerked the drummer to his feet and spun him around. "Get walking, pilgrim. And don't trip or I'll boot you the rest of the way." Throwing open the door, he practically threw the hapless man inside, then propelled him to a cell and locked him in. "What's your name, anyhow?"

"Jones. Arthur Jones," the morose man said meekly.

"Make yourself comfortable, Mr. Jones," Crane said. "I'll write up the papers and take you over to see the judge later on. He'll set your fine."

Jones swallowed. "What if I don't have enough money to pay it?"

Tom Crane grinned. "Then you get to stick around a while and have the pleasure of my company." Hanging the keys on a peg, he went to his desk and eased into the chair. He looked at Skinner, who stood at the window watching several women go by. "Are you still here?"

"You never answered me," Rafe said.

"No, I didn't. A smart man like you should take that as a hint."

Disregarding the comment, the Acme's owner said, "If I had a daughter, I'd be plumb pleased to have her stay a spell. Think of it, Tom. She's your own flesh and blood."

"I haven't thought of anything else since I got her letter." Propping his elbows on his desk, he scowled and placed his forehead in his hands. "Damn it all, Rafe, the last thing I need is for her to waltz around Tucson letting everybody know she's my kin. You know as well as I do that most of the people in this town rate me as high as a sidewinder. The only reason I wear a tin star is because Miles Gillett wants me to."

Skinner sat and braced his boots on the edge of the desk. "You're fretting over nothing. I doubt anyone will come right out and tell her."

"Maybe so, but I still wish to hell she wasn't coming," Crane said. Leaning back, he sighed. "I'd sell my soul to the devil if it would stop her from showing up."

Clay Taggart, the White Apache, couldn't rightly say what had made him do what he did. He had the trooper squarely in his sights. He could have dropped the soldier, then slain the warrior with two swift shots. It was certainly his intention to kill them both.

But when Clay unexpectedly saw the Maricopa point a carbine at the young soldier he acted without thinking. Clearly, the warrior was going to shoot the private. Clay had no idea why.

Shifting, Clay aligned the sights of his Winchester on the center of the scout's chest and stroked the trigger. The .44 bucked and boomed.

Over 150 yards off, Pvt. James Calhoun was shocked to see the top of the Maricopa's head explode in a shower of gore. The impact smashed the scout head over heels past the rump of the pinto. The animal promptly took off at a terror-stricken gallop.

Almost as terrified as the horse, Calhoun turned and spied a puff of gunsmoke on the north rim of the canyon. The Apache was up there, trying to pick them off! Snapping his carbine to his shoulder, Calhoun did as he had been taught and fired at the smoke. Then, applying his heels to the sorrel and bending low to present a smaller target, he fled on down the canyon as if a demon from hell were nipping at his heels.

Clay Taggart could have easily dropped the young man. He went so far as to track the trooper for a few seconds with the Winchester, but he never touched the trigger. Lowering the rifle, he frowned, annoyed at himself.

If any of the Chiricahuas had been there, they would have slain the soldier without a second thought. And they would have chided Clay for being so weak.

But Clay couldn't help himself. It was as plain as the nose on his face that the private was green. Shooting the trooper would have been like stomping a kitten to death or strangling a puppy.

The revelation was upsetting. Clay had prided himself on being every bit as ruthless as the Chiricahuas had to be in order to survive, yet his sudden failure was ample proof he had a long way to go before he could claim to be their equal. It was also proof that part of him still clung to the past he had forsaken, that the years he had spent as a white man could not be erased in the blink of an eye.

So what was he going to do now? Clay asked himself as he rose and descended a game trail to where the black stallion was ground hitched. Would he go back to the hidden valley and tell the Chiricahuas that he had taken care of the two he was after? No, that wouldn't do. He wasn't about to lie to the warriors, not after all they had done for him.

HANGED!

Clay swung onto the black stallion. It occurred to him that, if he let the greenhorn blunder on off across the wasteland, nature would do what he couldn't. His problem would be solved. Yet he would still have the young soldier's life on his conscience. So what was he going to do?

Hundreds of yards distant, Calhoun was asking himself the very same thing as he fled past boulders the size of log cabins. Without the scout to guide him, he didn't stand a prayer of finding Capt. Eldritch again or of reaching Fort Bowie.

Repeatedly Calhoun glanced behind him, but there was no trace of pursuit. By the time he came to the end of the canyon, he began to relax a little. Evidently the Apache had been satisfied with killing the Maricopa.

Once out on the open arid plain, Calhoun was blistered by the intense heat. He paused after traveling less than 500 yards to shove the carbine into the boot and help himself to a swig from his canteen. It was nearly full, which was encouraging. He made up his mind to ration every drop from that moment on.

Goading the sorrel forward, Calhoun unbuttoned the top of his wool uniform. No officers or other soldiers were on hand to upbraid him, and he was sweating a river. The sorrel bobbed its head, apparently disliking the heat as much as he did.

As Calhoun's racing pulse slowed and he could think clearly again, he took note of the position of the sun. Since it was not yet noon, the sun had to be in the eastern half of the sky. So judging from the sun's position, he had to be heading due west. If that was the case, then, based on the directions in which the Maricopa had pointed earlier, the patrol had to be somewhere to the north and the post somewhere far to the southeast.

Calhoun had only one choice. The patrol was closer than the fort, perhaps only a few hours away. If he turned north and pushed the sorrel, he just might rejoin Capt. Eldritch before the afternoon ended.

His hope rekindled, the private cut the sorrel to the right and made off across the parched landscape. His gaze drifted frequently toward the canyon. Not so much as a bird stirred, convincing him that he had given the Apache the slip.

Pleased with himself, Calhoun smiled. One day he would regale his grandchildren with the tale of the time he had eluded a fierce Apache. He just hoped they would believe him. It was hard for him to accept himself.

The blazing sun continued to arc overhead. When it was straight above him, Calhoun halted to give his horse a breather. One fact Sgt. O'Shaughnessy had impressed on him during all that drilling was that a cavalryman had to take good care of his mount if he was to last long in the wilderness.

Calhoun limited himself to a single swallow of water. Dabbing his handkerchief, he liberally wet the sorrel's muzzle. The poor horse was so thirsty that it tried to draw the handkerchief into its mouth, but Calhoun hung on tight.

Once in the saddle again, Calhoun bore to the northeast to keep the mountains in sight. If he drained the canteen, he would have to find water quickly, or both he and his mount would soon perish. In the mountains, there were streams and lakes; in the desert, water was as scarce as hen's teeth.

The temperature had to be over 90 degrees, probably higher. Calhoun wiped his brow so many times he lost track. He was careful to avoid cactus plants and the wicked shindagger agave, which another trooper had pointed out to him shortly after the patrol left Fort Bowie.

After a while Calhoun began to notice things about the desert he had not noticed before, such as the wealth of plant life. There wasn't just one kind of cactus; there were dozens: tall ones, short ones, skinny ones, fat ones. Some were home to wild creatures, as he learned when a small bird emerged from a hole in a saquaro and flitted off.

Tracts of brilliant flowers were a stark contrast to the mesquite and other dry brush. He saw a little purple variety, as beautiful as any rose in any garden back east. Later, he came on over an acre of the most striking yellow and orange flowers, wondrous to behold.

Calhoun couldn't understand why there were so many different types in bloom. Then he remembered a heavy rain several days earlier, and he speculated that the downpour might have something to do with the abundance of flowers.

About the middle of the afternoon, Calhoun skirted a stand of manzanitas. He had taken to dozing for short spells, leaving the sorrel plod along as it liked. Abruptly, the animal nickered and shied so violently that Calhoun was nearly unhorsed.

Calhoun grabbed the reins tighter and said, "Whoa, boy! Whoa!"

The sorrel wouldn't listen. Exactly why became

obvious the next moment when a loud, harsh rattling sound erupted almost under the animal's hooves. Glancing down, Calhoun was horrified to find a enormous coiled rattler. The serpent's tail vibrated wildly as it eyed the sorrel.

"Go, big fella, go!" Calhoun cried, raking the horse's flanks. The animal took off as if shot from a cannon. Calhoun lashed the reins in a frenzy, glancing back to see the reptile go slithering off into the thicket.

"We did it!" The private gave the sorrel several pats on the neck. He pulled on the reins, but the horse was not about to stop. Worried that the animal would run itself into the ground, Calhoun tried again, hauling harder.

None of the many hours spent drilling under the boiling sun at Fort Bowie prepared James Calhoun for what happened next. The sorrel suddenly dug in its hooves, bent low, and slid to a stop in a swirl of dust. There was no warning whatsoever. Before Calhoun could grasp hold of the saddle horn, he found himself sailing through the air like an ungainly, oversize bird, and his landing left much to be desired.

Calhoun's jaw cracked hard. Stunned, he struggled to clear his head as fireflies danced before his eyes. The earth drummed under his cheek, and for a few moments, he could not comprehend why. When he did, he pushed to his feet and stood gaping in consternation as the sorrel sped madly eastward. "No!" he frantically shouted. "Come back here!"

When the horse didn't slow down, Calhoun broke into a run, hoping against hope the animal would come to its senses soon and stop. He tried not to think of the consequences if he wound up stranded afoot, with no canteen, no hardtack, and no carbine.

Anxious minutes went by. The sorrel dwindled in the distance, eventually, the animal was swallowed up by the clouds of dust it raised.

Panting heavily, his legs leaden, Calhoun shuffled to a halt and sagged. "This can't be!" the private said to himself. He squinted up at the blinding sun, swore under his breath, and started walking, paralleling the tracks left by his mount.

If it wasn't one thing, it was another! the trooper mused. He couldn't believe how awful his day had turned out. That scorpion in his boot had been an omen of things to come!

The sun baked him. The hot, dry wind was like the blast of a furnace. Calhoun unbuttoned his uniform from top to bottom to get some relief from the stifling heat.

Half an hour after the sorrel ran off, Calhoun neared the foothills. His eyes were blurry from motes of dust, his hair plastered to his head under his hat, his clothes soaked with perspiration. His body was so hot he felt as if he were on fire. To his overwhelming relief, a nicker fluttered on the breeze. He raised his head, thinking he had caught up with the sorrel, but it was nowhere in sight.

Feeling his mind was playing tricks on him, Calhoun looked to both sides, then over his shoulder. He nearly choked on his next breath. Sixty yards out was an Apache.

Chapter Five

Many miles to the east, a rosy-faced young woman with luxurious auburn hair and lips the color of ripe cherries peered out the window of the stage-coach she was in. She wondered for the umpteenth time if she were making the biggest mistake of her life.

Tessa Heritage sat primly in her seat, her neatly manicured hands resting in her lap. She was all too aware of the brazenly lecherous stares directed her way by the uncouth man across from her. Despite the heat and the dust, she was glad she wore a dress that covered her from throat to ankles.

Fanning her courage, Tessa looked the character in the eye and said crisply, "Sir, I would appreciate it if you would quit staring at me that way."

The only word to describe the man was slovenly. His clothes were filthy, his boots scuffed from toe to heel. His hat drooped as if about to fall apart at the seams, and grime caked every square inch of exposed skin. A thick wad of chewing tobacco made his left cheek bulge. Squinting at her, he laughed and said, "Are you talkin' to me, you pretty little thing?"

Tessa's temper flared. "How dare you address me in that tone! I resent being treated with such familiarity."

"Do you now?" The man leaned out the window to spit tobacco juice. Wiping a smear of saliva from his mouth with the back of his hand, he leaned toward her and winked. "Don't get your britches in an uproar, sister. It's not as if I'm tryin' to take liberties. And you can't fault a man for lookin', can you?"

"You, sir, are an unspeakable lout!" Tessa snapped.

The man laughed lustily. "Well, now, I've been called a lot of things in my time, but never that." Tipping his hat, he said, "The handle is Ira Kent. Maybe I'll look you up when we get to Tucson and the two of us can go out on the town. How would that be?"

Tessa was going to give him a verbal blister he would never forget, but an unexpected defender spoke before she could. To her left sat a quiet young man in homespun clothes. He had cast a few shy glances at her ever since getting on, but had not uttered a single word. He reminded her of typical young men back home in Ohio, except that they did not go around with a big revolver strapped to their waist.

"That's enough, mister," the young man said.

"You're being downright rude to this lady and I won't stand for it."

Ira Kent's dark eyes lit with amusement. "You don't say, sonny? And what are you fixin' to do—draw on me?" Kent patted an old Dragoon pistol on his hip. "Go right ahead if you're of a mind, but I'll put a hole in you the size of a melon before you get off a shot."

The younger man's lip stretched into a thin line, and Kent asked, "What's your name, sonny?"

"Harvey Wilkinson."

Kent had not taken his hand off the Dragoon. Rubbing the trigger with his thumb, he said, "Well, Harvey, your ma should have learned you some manners. It ain't polite to go pokin' your nose in the affairs of others. I have half a mind to pound on you a few times to teach you a lesson."

The young man's Adam's apple bobbed, but he said bravely, "I'd like to see you try!"

It was then that the fourth passenger in the stage stirred, the one who sat next to Kent. A tall, well-built man, he wore a fine black suit, a white shirt, and a string tie. A wide-brimmed black hat crowned his handsome head. It had been tilted down over his face for over an hour, and he had appeared to be sleeping. Now he pushed the brim up, exposing a pair of gray eyes that glinted like quartz. Fixing them on Ira Kent, he said in a soft voice, "Better yet, try me."

Tessa saw Ira Kent go as stiff as an ironing board. His thick tongue darted out and flicked across his pudgy lower lip, dripping tobacco juice. Slowly, exaggerating every movement, he took his hand off the Dragoon and set it on his thigh. "I don't want no trouble with you, Gallagher. I was just havin' me a little fun. That's all."

Gallagher shifted, seemingly to make himself more comfortable. As he did, his jacket parted enough to reveal a pair of pearl-handled Colts wedged under his wide leather belt, butts forward. His next words were as cold as ice, as hard as steel. "Don't pester the lady again or you'll answer to me."

"I won't open my mouth again." Kent lapsed into sullen silence.

The man with the pearl-handled pistols began to pull his hat down. Tessa, on an impulse, said, "I want to thank you, sir, for defending me. You and Mr. Wilkinson both."

Gallagher paused and regarded her intently. "You're welcome, ma'am," he said politely. Again he started to settle back.

Tessa did not want him to go to sleep. She welcomed the opportunity for a little conversation to relieve the monotony of the journey. "Might I ask if you are also bound for Tucson, sir?"

The man in black straightened up and rested his right hand on his hip, close to one of the expensive Colts. "Yes, ma'am. I am. You too?"

Tessa nodded, then smiled. "I'm on my way to visit someone," she said. "You?"

"A friend of mine wired me to come work for him at the Acme," Gallagher said, as if that explanation was sufficient.

"The Acme?" Tessa repeated. "I'm afraid I don't know of it."

"I should hope not," Gallagher said. "It's a gambling hall, ma'am. I make my living at cards."

The news delighted Tessa. She had never met a

professional gambler before. And she found Gallagher quite dashing, and possessed of an iron nerve few men had. "How marvelous. I would be in your debt if you would tell me some about your line of work. This is my first trip west and I have so much to learn."

"There's not much to tell, ma'am," Gallagher said. "I deal cards. I win sometimes. I lose sometimes. But not too often, or I'd be plumb broke."

Tessa laughed. "It must be an exciting way to make a living to hold the interest of a man like you."

The gambler did not say anything for quite some time. At length, his face softened and he replied, "That's an awful nice compliment, ma'am. Yes, it does have its moments."

Harvey Wilkinson cleared his throat. "Is it true, Mr. Gallagher, that you've killed fourteen men?"

Tessa had never seen a transformation like the one she suddenly witnessed. The gambler turned to granite right before her eyes. He was no longer mild and kind. Every fiber of him radiated raw violence. He looked at Wilkinson, and she got the impression that, if the young man was not extremely careful, he would be shot dead before her eyes.

"I don't mean to pry, sir," Wilkinson said. "It's just that I've heard so many stories about you. And I was in Albuquerque the night you shot those two card sharps. It made the headlines, remember?"

Gallagher visibly relaxed and sighed. "They tried to cheat me, son," he said. "When I called them on it, they went for their hardware. Their mistake." He did not act comfortable talking about himself. Turning to Tessa, he said, "You mentioned visiting someone in Tucson. Would that be a relative?"

"My father," Tessa said.

"Oh? Perhaps I know him. I meet a lot of men in my travels. What would his name be?"

"Thomas Crane."

The gambler cocked his head. "Tom Crane? Marshal Tom Crane?"

Tessa nodded. She was afraid to say more for fear he might quiz her further and learn the embarrassing truth about her family. She noticed that the slovenly lecher across from her looked as if he had just been shot.

"Dear, sweet, merciful heaven!" Ira Kent said. Lunging, he grabbed her by the wrist and squeezed so hard that it hurt. "Tell me it can't be true, missy! Tell me that you're only tryin' to give me a scare! Tell me that you're really not Crane's kin!"

Shocked by the man's outburst, Tessa pulled away from him and tried to wrench her wrist free. "Let go of me, sir! You have no right to manhandle me!"

A wild gleam came into Kent's eyes. "Tell me you're lyin', damn it! You can't be his kin! You can't be!"

Before Tessa could confirm the truth, the gambler was in motion. In all her life, she had never seen anyone move so fast. Gallagher seized hold of Ira Kent and slammed him back. Kent made as if to fight back when from out of thin air one of those pearl-handled pistols appeared, the muzzle pressed against Kent's temple. Kent froze, his mouth wide, his eyes wider.

"Not another peep out of you," Gallagher said.

"No, sir. No, sir,." Kent said. "I'm sorry. I'm honestly and truly sorry. I wasn't thinkin'. That's all."

Gallagher slowly, almost reluctantly, lowered the gleaming Colt. "If it wasn't for the lady, I'd blow your brains all over the inside of this coach." His hand gave a deft flip and the Colt disappeared.

Kent was breathing rapidly. "How can you blame me, damn it? Didn't you hear her? She's Tom Crane's daughter!" Closing his eyes, he trembled. "I'm a dead man, Gallagher. We both know it."

Tessa was at a loss to explain the man's strange behavior. "Now see here," she said, intending to assure him that he was getting overwrought for nothing.

To her astonishment, Kent flung himself onto the floor in front of her. On bended knee, he raised his clasped hands. "I'm beggin' you, missy! Please, for the love of God, don't tell your pa what I done!"

"Mr. Kent, really—" Tessa said incredulously.

"If I'd known who you were, I never would have poked fun at you. Give me your promise that you won't say a word to him. Swear on the Bible."

Tessa glanced at Harvey. His expression showed that he was just as bewildered as she. Facing the lecher, she said mildly, "You're being silly, Mr. Kent. There is no need to make a spectacle of yourself. I'm sure my father would not shoot you over a few loose remarks. He's a lawman, after all."

Kent did something that stunned Tessa even more. He tossed back his head and cackled like someone not in their right mind. "A lawman? That's a good one, missy! Did you hear her, Gallagher? She thinks her pa lives by that badge he totes. Don't she know that he's the slimiest, back-stabbin', murderin' son of a—"

Kent never finished his statement. The gambler

moved again, and that time, the barrel of his Colt caught Ira Kent above the right ear and felled him. Kent wound up on his side in the narrow space between the seats, curled up with his hands between his legs, looking for all the world like a bearded baby taking a nap.

"Some gents talk too much," Gallagher said, tucking away the Colt. Adjusting his jacket, he sat and stared out the window at the barren terrain surrounding them. "If I were you, ma'am, I'd pay him no mind."

But Tessa couldn't let the matter drop. "Why is he so afraid of my father, Mr. Gallagher? What did he mean by those comments he made?"

For a while, Tessa thought the gambler was not going to answer. When he did, he was plainly troubled at having to broach the subject.

"Pardon my prying, ma'am, but how well do you know your father?"

Tessa had to tell the truth. "To be perfectly candid, I've never met him before."

Gallagher swung toward her, his surprise self-evident. "That explains a lot." He removed his hat and ran a hand through his shock of sandy hair. "I don't rightly know how to put this without hurting your feelings. The truth is, ma'am, that your father has a reputation for being a mite mean tempered." The hat went back on. "You heard the boy here mention that I'm supposed to have gunned down fourteen men. Well, that's not quite accurate. It's fewer than that. But it's safe to say that your pa has made wolf meat of twice as many as I have, maybe a lot more."

"All in the performance of his duty?"

"Some might see it that way."

Tessa was growing more confused. "I'm sorry. I don't follow you. Can you be more specific?"

The gambler frowned. "Maybe it would best if you found out on your own. Do some asking around when you get to Tucson. It won't take long for you to learn the truth."

"I'd rather hear it from someone I trust. Like you."

Gallagher dipped his chin, preventing her from seeing his face. "Keep up with these compliments, ma'am, and I'm liable to blush myself to death. The best way I know how to put it is to point out that there are good lawmen and there are bad lawmen. Your father has a reputation for being one of the very worst."

"Oh, my!" Tessa said. She did not feel comfortable prying any deeper. She had learned more in the past two minutes than she had in the previous 18 years. "I had no idea. In his letters to me, he never talked a lot about his job. And my mother would never say much about him."

Suddenly Tessa realized the stage was creaking to a stop. She could hear the driver muttering to the team. There was a loud thud and the crunch of boots.

A grizzled face was framed by the door window. "Are you folks all right back here? I heard a bunch of hollerin'." said Curly Decker, the driver. His bloodshot eyes dropped to the limp form of Ira Kent, then automatically darted to the gambler. "Dang it, Jess. Don't tell me you bedded him down permanent? The front office will raise a stink, and I'll be the one has to sit and listen to Grimes jaw on

70

half the night about my duty to the passengers."

Tessa half expected the gambler to take offense at the driver's remarks. Instead, he grinned good-naturedly. "Sheath your horns, you ornery cuss. I didn't put lead into him. He was mistreating the lady; so I gave him a little tap on the noggin."

"You don't say." Curly pivoted toward Tessa. "Are you okay, ma'am? No harm done?"

"I'm fine." Tessa displayed her red wrist. "All he did was grab me."

"Kent did that to you? Then he's earned himself the right to ride topside with the shotgun and me." Cupping a hand to his mouth, Curly said, "Will! Get down here! We have us another idiot!"

Tessa heard Kent groan. "There's no need to put yourselves out on my account."

"T'ain't no bother at all, ma'am," Curly said, flinging the door wide. "It's standard policy, you might say. Any passenger who acts up has to ride on top until I say otherwise. Believe you me, four or five hours of being baked by the sun and swallowin' enough dust to fill a tub makes a man mighty sorry he ever misbehaved. Next time this buzzard takes my stage, you can bet he'll act civilized."

It took hardly any time at all for Curly and the shotgun messenger—a stocky man who never said a word—to haul Kent from the coach and hoist him on top. They were not the least bit gentle while doing so.

Curly clambered back down to close the door, saying as he did, "In a few more hours, we'll be at Horner's home station, ma'am. You can take it easy and chat with Mrs. Horner. She's a real sweet woman, and she makes some of the tastiest corn dodgers you're ever likely to eat. Usually she has cold tea, which I'd guzzle by the gallon if she'd let me." He wiped a finger along the side of the coach, and it came up coated thick with alkali dust. "We'll spend the night there and head out at first light. By tomorrow evening, you'll be in Tucson."

"I can hardly wait," Tessa said, although inwardly she had grave reservations.

The driver left. Within moments, the stage lurched into motion, bouncing and swaying across the bleak landscape.

Tessa had to grip the window to keep from being tossed forward. Once the rocking motion slackened, she made herself as comfortable as she could, retying her bonnet so it wouldn't be blown off. She studiously avoided meeting the eyes of her traveling companions, fearful they would bring up the subject of her father again.

The auburn-haired beauty did not want them to know that secretly she had been scared to death at the prospect of meeting Tom Crane. And that now she was more scared than ever.

Capt. Vincent Eldritch, Fifth Cavalry, was fit to be tied. He had nearly worn a rut in the ground with his tireless pacing. Taking his watch from his pocket, he saw he'd had been pacing the better part of an hour. Then he slapped the watch case shut and swore under his breath.

"Sir?" said Cpl. Tinsdale, who stood nearby ready to carry out any orders that might be given.

"I don't like it, Corporal," Capt. Eldritch said. "I don't like it one bit. Sgt. O'Shaughnessy and his men should have rejoined us hours ago."

HANGED!

"Do we go looking for them, sir?"

Eldritch had been debating that very question. The truth was that without their scout they were severely hampered. He could get the patrol back to Fort Bowie if he had to, but scouring the Dragoons was a whole different proposition. Wending through the canyons, gorges, and ravines was like trying to navigate a maze. Yet they could not just ride off and abandon their own.

Slapping his gauntlet against his sleeve, Eldritch nodded. "We do, Corporal. Have the men break camp and be ready to ride in three minutes."

"Yes, sir!" Tinsdale offered a snappy salute and was off to do his duty.

Capt. Eldritch slid the gauntlet on and thoughtfully surveyed nearby peaks. The Maricopa had given him a fair idea of where the tracks had been; so with diligence, he might be able to pick up O'Shaughnessy's trail. If not, he would keep on searching for as long as their rations held out.

Eldritch was military to the core, a West Point graduate who aspired to be a ranking general one day. He loved everything about the army, from the uniforms to the arms to the parades. He had always been an orderly, methodical person, and a life based on perfect precision appealed to him vastly.

Reveille at the crack of dawn? Eldritch didn't care. He liked getting up with the birds. The army's notoriously poor food? Eldritch wolfed it down without complaint. The long hours? The grueling patrols? The constant danger from hostiles? Eldritch relished them as a measure of his manhood.

No, the only problem with Capt. Vincent Eldritch's current assignment was Arizona itself. For

73

the life of him, Eldritch could not think of a more inhospitable spot on the face of the planet. The relentless heat, the parched soil, the months and months that went by without a drop of rain—Eldritch hated it all. In his more whimsical moments, he imagined that Arizona was really hell, and the prophets had forgotten to mention the fact in the Bible.

Eldritch had been in the Arizona Territory over a year. In another ten months, he could put in for transfer, and he couldn't wait. In the meantime, he had to do his best to stay alive and perform the duties required of him with the utmost efficiency.

"Ready when you are, sir!"

Cpl. Tinsdale's comment shook Eldritch out of his deep reverie. He was startled to see all 24 troopers mounted in a column of twos, awaiting his command. Stepping to his horse, he swung onto the McClellan, hiked his arm, and said, "Move them out, Corporal."

At Tinsdale's bellow, the entire patrol moved like the cogs in a well-oiled machine. Capt. Eldritch glanced back and nodded in approval. They were good boys, the troopers of the Fifth Cavalry. Every last one of them was as dependable as the day was long. He would gladly lead them into battle anywhere, anytime.

That thought brought to mind Sgt. O'Shaughnessy. Where the men of the Fifth might be compared to stout oaks, the massive sergeant was a giant redwood. O'Shaughnessy had over a decade of Indian fighting under his belt, and he was widely regarded as one of the best soldiers in the army. So what could have happened to him? Eldritch wondered.

The officer recalled his superior's warning prior to leaving Fort Bowie. "Watch that Maricopa like a hawk," Col. Reynolds had said. "We don't usually employ them as scouts because they have a tendency to head for the hills at the first sign of Apaches. I'm giving Chivari the benefit of the doubt because he comes highly recommended by Brewster, one of our civilian scouts."

Was that the answer? Captain Eldritch wondered. Was the Maricopa to blame for O'Shaughnessy's failure to return? If so, the captain made a vow that he would make sure the wretched heathen spent the rest of his miserable days in a federal prison.

Giving his head a toss to derail his gloomy train of thought, Capt. Eldritch rode deeper into the heart of the land he loathed so much.

Chapter Six

After a few moments, Pvt. Calhoun realized that the Apache sitting there watching him was the very same warrior who had chased him after the bloody clash high up in the mountains.

"I thought I'd lost you!" the young trooper said. Then he clawed at the flap of his holster. In his haste, he nearly dropped the pistol. Getting a better grip, he elevated his arm and sighted down the barrel to take precise aim, but the Apache was gone.

Calhoun blinked a few times. He scoured the brush, dumbfounded. "It can't be! Where in the world did the red devil go?"

Shuffling forward to investigate, he abruptly caught himself and shook his head. It would be a mistake to stumble on in his condition. If the Apache had not been just a figment of his overheated brain, he'd be asking to have his throat slit. In the condition he was in, he couldn't tussle with a five year old, let alone a fierce savage.

Calhoun let down the hammer on his pistol, but didn't slip it back into his holster. Holding the gun at his side where he could bring it into instant use, he continued on into the foothills, glancing back often to see if the Apache reappeared. When over half an hour had elapsed and all he'd seen were a few birds and a lizard that darted under a flat rock at his approach, he replaced the weapon.

Soon the sun rested on the brink of the western horizon. Calhoun knew that he could not possibly catch the horse before dark fell unless it had stopped close by. He searched for a spot to spend the night, a sheltered nook where he would be safe from beasts and hostiles.

A gorge opened before him. Hoping that he could locate a fissure or perhaps even a small cave, Calhoun entered. Here the shadows deepened. He was alert for rattlesnakes.

Another soldier had once told Calhoun that while rattlers liked to sun themselves during the heat of the day, the unpredictable reptiles did their hunting in the cool night. Once the sun began to sink, they would emerge from their dens and slither off to find food. A number of people had made the mistake of stepping on one in the dark and paid a fearful price.

Calhoun spied a crack in the north wall. Going over, he discovered it was a gap wide enough to sit in, but not lie down. Undecided whether to stay there or not, he gnawed on his lower lip and turned to gaze farther into the gorge.

Above him, a pebble clattered.

Calhoun did not attach much significance to the noise. Loose dirt and stones frequently fell when the wind gusted. But suddenly it hit him that the wind was deathly still. There was no reason for that pebble to have dislodged. Curious, he tilted his head back.

Like a great bird of prey, the Apache swooped toward him! Calhoun stabbed his right hand to his holster, but he hardly touched the flap this time when the Apache's rifle butt slammed into the side of his head. Calhoun thought that his skull had burst. The last sensation he felt was that of his body falling.

Clay Taggart stood over the unconscious trooper and grinned. It had been ridiculously easy to shadow the man undetected and await an opportune moment. Taking the soldier's Colt, he slid it under his belt.

The trooper's hat had fallen off, revealing his youthful features. Clay marveled that the army would send such boys to do a job only the most experienced men could handle. The average soldier had no more business being in Arizona than on an iceberg.

Squatting, Clay slowly drew his Bowie. The blade was so sharp that in short order he had cut three wide strips from the bottom of the trooper's jacket. With those strips, he securely tied the trooper's wrist. Squatting Apache fashion, he waited.

The sun was long gone when Calhoun felt himself floating upward through a murky well of dank water. With a start, he remembered the last sight he had seen before unconsciousness claimed him. His eyes snapped wide, and he went to sit up.

As he did, he found that he couldn't move his arms and he pitched onto his side. Then, a keg of black powder went off inside his skull, nearly causing him to pass out a second time. Everything spun. His stomach flipped and flopped, and for a few seconds, he feared he'd be sick. When the feeling went away, he looked up and stiffened in undisguised terror.

"You!"

Clay Taggart said nothing. The white part of him wanted to respond, to tell the trooper that he had no business being there, that he was lucky to be alive. But the Apache part of him did as an Apache would do in front of a mortal enemy and stayed grimly silent.

Calhoun tucked his knees under him and rose onto them. His mouth had gone as dry as sand, and he had a hard time swallowing. It was foolish to expect the Apache to say anything, but he spoke anyway.

"I'm Pvt. James Calhoun, Fifth Calvary. If you know what's good for you, Injun, you'll let me go. Harm me, and the entire might of the United States Army will be brought to bear against you. You'll be hunted down and exterminated."

Clay kept his face as impassive as the rock wall behind him. Inside, though, he smiled at the young man's show of bravado. The trooper had the brains of a turnip, but he wasn't a coward.

"Savvy English, Injun?" Calhoun asked when he got no response. It was spooky the way that the savage just squatted there watching him. He couldn't see the Apache's eyes clearly in the dark, but he imagined they were filled with hate and bloodlust.

"What do you intend to do with me?" Calhoun asked. The many lurid tales he'd heard of Apache atrocities came back to him again in a rush. He had to make a special effort to resist a tidal wave of panic that threatened to engulf him. He was a soldier, damn it! It would be unbecoming to show fear in the face of the enemy.

Clay studied the trooper closely. The man's inner struggle was plainly reflected by his shifting features. Clay was pleased to see that the younger man did not give in to the fear, and he almost chuckled when Calhoun set his jaw firmly and regarded him defiantly.

"Well, whatever you have planned, do your worst," Calhoun said. "I refuse to give you the satisfaction of seeing me grovel. Cut my heart out, skin me alive, stake me to an anthill—it won't make any difference. I'll die as a man should!"

Once again Calhoun's captor did not react. Calhoun squared his shoulders, determined not to betray a lick of weakness. His sudden resolve in the face of certain death surprised him.

Being a soldier meant that Calhoun faced the prospect of dying daily. Many a night he had lain awake wondering how and when his end would come and, if it were in battle, whether he would die with dignity.

Calhoun could not say why, but that was important to him. Some of the other troopers scoffed when he brought dying up, saying the only important thing was to get through his tour of duty with his hide intact. He didn't agree.

A man had little control over most aspects of his life. How he died was one he did have a say in, provided it wasn't in a blinding instant thanks to a bullet in the heart or some such calamity. Calhoun would rather go to meet his Maker with some semblance of honor.

Clay Taggart glanced up at the sky. A sliver of moon promised enough illumination to see by. Standing, he leveled the Winchester at the soldier.

Calhoun thought that the savage was about to shoot him. He closed his eyes, then changed his mind. He would look death in the face, not cringe in craven fright. "Go ahead! Do it!"

The trooper's eagerness to die was amusing. Clay jabbed him in the ribs with the barrel and motioned at the mouth of the gorge.

"You're taking me somewhere? Is that it?" Calhoun asked. "Probably to your village, I'll bet, so you and your friends can torture me to your heart's delight. What if I refuse? What will you do?"

For an answer, Clay stalked around behind the soldier, gripped Calhoun by the hair, and yanked him erect. The trooper let out a yelp as Clay applied the sole of his right moccasin to Calhoun's backside.

Calhoun stumbled forward. Catching himself, he twisted to give the warrior a piece of his mind. An iron hand gasped his shoulder and shoved, propelling him to go on whether he wanted to or not. Again he tried to turn, and that time, the rifle barrel poked him in the spine, flaring pain high and low.

"All right! All right!" Calhoun said. "I'll do as you want! But first chance I get I'm taking that Winchester from you and making you eat your own lead!"

Clay was tempted to thank the trooper for the warning. Smiling, he guided Calhoun out of the gorge and up onto the north rim to where he had left the black stallion ground hitched. Mounting, he swung the horse to the northwest, then gestured for the soldier to walk ahead of him.

Calhoun complied. He was puzzled though. According to the reports he'd heard, the renegades had their lairs deep in the Dragoon and Chiricahau Mountains. Yet there that red devil was, taking him back out onto the open plain and heading in a northerly direction. Why?

As time went by, Calhoun's strength flagged. He had been on the go since shortly after dawn and his body was not accustomed to being pushed so hard. More than anything, he craved rest. A few hours of sleep would tide him over, but he might as well have asked the Apache to let him ride double. He had to keep going whether he liked it or not.

Clay held the stallion to a slow walk in order not to tire the soldier out too soon. He listened to the night sounds to gauge whether they were alone in the vast chaparral.

To the south, a coyote yipped, and the cry was promptly answered by another. To the east, high up among the peaks, a wolf howled. The sound echoed and reechoed, giving the illusion of an entire pack voicing their cries all at once. After the howl faded on the wind, an owl hooted. Much closer, scales scuttled across the ground. A snake was abroad, but it did not come near them.

Calhoun mechanically lifted one foot after another. It taxed him to keep his eyes open, and presently, he started to talk about anything and everything that popped into his head just to stay awake.

"I don't see what you Injuns are making such a

stink about. I've heard that the government takes real good care of your people. You get all the food you can eat and clothes too. Your kids get to go to school just like every white kid does. Seems to me that you should be thankful for all the whites have done for you, not trying to plant us all six feet under."

Clay wondered if every trooper believed the same. Didn't they know that the government gave the Apaches a weekly ration of flour and beef that seldom lasted longer than three or four days? Or that the agents often skimped on the beef ration to line their own pockets with money by selling cows meant for the Indians to whites?

To make matters worse, the government would not let the warriors go off to hunt whenever their families were in need. A warrior had to get permission first, and nine times out of ten, such consent would be denied on one flimsy pretext or another.

Even gathering firewood was strictly monitored. The women were only allowed to gather a basketful of cottonwood and mesquite at a time. No one was allowed to stockpile any during the colder months; as a result, it was not uncommon for a family to be shivering in their fireless wickiup with the outside temperature down near zero.

Further aggravating the Apaches, many of their old ways were no longer allowed. Brewing tiswin, a potent beer made from corn, was an offense that could land them in the guardhouse. Even time-honored customs, such as cutting off the nose of a wife who slept with another man, were frowned on. And formal combat between warriors was out of the question.

Small wonder the Apaches hated the white man's policies. Smaller wonder that the tribes disobeyed them every chance they got.

The whites could only punish those they caught breaking the rules, and Apaches were masters at deceit. Tiswin was brewed where the fumes would not give it away and consumed only when the soldiers were nowhere around. Formal combat was held in remote spots, and the bodies of the losers were quickly taken and buried. Wives who were unfaithful were punished in a less obvious manner.

The trooper was speaking again. Clay listened with half an ear. "It's too bad you can't understand a word I'm saying, Injun. If you could, I'd make you see I'm not here because I hate your people or anything like that. I'm not one of those who thinks the only good Injun is a dead Injun just because your skin is a different color than mine. Believe it or not, I came west for the thrill of it all. I wanted to put a little excitement in my life." Wagging his bound hands, he gave vent to a sharp laugh. "Looks as if I found it, wouldn't you say?"

Clay didn't bother to reveal that he understood every word Calhoun spoke. When he offered no response, the young trooper lapsed into somber silence and did not speak again for over an hour and a half.

Calhoun had been plodding along for what seemed like an eternity, fatigue eating at him like a saw into wood. He was so tired he could barely keep his eyes open. Coming over a low rise, he beheld a long, flat expanse ahead. Wearily, he let his eyelids droop and headed down the slope. His right foot snagged on an obstacle. Before he could right himself, he toppled, smacking onto his shoulder. Gravity took over and he rolled to the bottom.

Clay spurred forward but there was nothing he could do.

"Damn it all!" Calhoun said, spitting dirt as he wriggled up onto his knees. "I can't go on! I'm worn out! Do you savvy me, Injun? I need sleep, or I'm liable to pass out right at your feet."

They had a long way to go in a relatively short time, or Clay would have obliged the man. Prodding the trooper with the Winchester, he indicated Calhoun should march on.

Exasperated, the Fifth Cavalry recruit said, "Don't say I didn't warn you when the time comes."

The night had grown steadily cooler. A brisk breeze from the northeast relieved the lingering heat of the day. It invigorated Calhoun until his fatigue mounted to the point where he dozed off and on while he hiked.

About three o'clock in the morning, Clay heard the private groan. The next moment Calhoun melted to the earth and lay there breathing heavily. Clay moved closer to give the solider a poke in the ribs. Calhoun never so much as twitched. Instead, he broke out in loud snoring.

Sighing, Clay Taggart climbed from the black stallion. He knew a lost cause when he saw one. The trooper had been pushed to the point of exhaustion. Forcing him to go on at that point would defeat Clay's whole purpose.

Making a circuit of the immediate area, Clay located a wide patch of grass where the stallion could graze. He returned to the slumbering soldier and sank down facing Calhoun. The Winchester in his lap, he let his chin droop onto his chest and soon drifted off himself, sleeping lightly the whole night through. Twice he was awakened, once by the whinny of a horse far to the east, another time by the faint crack of a rifle to the south.

As dawn painted the eastern sky a vivid pink, White Apache roused himself, stretched, and thoughtfully considered his captive. Rising, he nudged Calhoun. When that failed to wake the trooper, Clay hunkered down, scooped up a handful of dirt, and held it over Calhoun's open mouth.

The man still snored loud enough to be mistaken for a bear. Turning his wrist so the dirt could trickle out, Clay smiled when Calhoun sputtered a few times. The trooper shifted, muttering, and Clay lowered his hand closer. By craning his neck, he could see Calhoun's tongue. Impishly, he dribbled grains onto it.

A racking fit caused Calhoun to snap up off the ground. Coughing and choking, red in the face, he bent over to spit out the dirt.

"Damn you, you savage!" Calhoun said when he could speak. "What kind of way is that to wake someone up? Or did you intend to start your day by having me choke to death?"

Rising, Clay motioned for the soldier to do the same. At gunpoint, Clay steered him over to the black stallion. Mounting, Clay pointed due north.

Calhoun got the message. Striving to clear the cobwebs that impaired his faculties, he shook himself from head to toe. The chill morning air brought goose bumps to his skin. A bitter taste lingered in his mouth from the dirt, and he kept spitting to get rid of it.

HANGED!

White Apache kneed the stallion into a brisk walk. He deliberately bumped into Calhoun to spur the private to go faster and got a glare for his trouble. But Calhoun obeyed.

Once the sun rose, the temperature soared. Not a cloud marred the perfect blue of the sky. A few buzzards appeared, circling awhile before they soared off.

Calhoun's feet hurt with every step he took. His army boots did not fit all that well. They were about half a size too small. As a result, the many hours of tramping across the rugged terrain had chafed his left ankle to the point where it bled and hurt like the dickens. The toes on his right foot also ached to the point where he placed most of his weight on the heel of his boot to keep from lancing his leg with agony.

Clay Taggart noticed the trooper was limping, but there was nothing he could do to ease his pain. They had to cover ten miles before early afternoon.

Clay was upset that he couldn't simply shoot the soldier and be done with him. That was what Delgadito would have done. And Fiero. And Ponce. There was no mercy in their souls for those who had conquered their people and taken their land.

Cuchillo Negro was another story. Clay couldn't say whether Black Knife would have slain Calhoun outright or not. Of all the warriors, Cuchillo Negro was the hardest to figure out. He hated whites-eyes, but there was an abiding sense of compassion in him rare for an Apache or a white man.

Idle thoughts continued to occupy Clay until almost noon. By then, Calhoun dragged one foot behind him and winced a lot. They were passing mesquite. At a shaded spot, Clay forgot himself and said, "Stop and rest, Calhoun. We have a long way to go yet."

Clay realized his mistake when the astonished trooper whirled and gaped.

"What the hell? You speak English! You've understood every word I've said all along!"

Sliding off the horse, Clay said, "I should. I was born a white man, just like you."

Calhoun scrutinized the other man closely, unable to come to grips with that new revelation. His captor looked every inch an Apache, just like those Calhoun had seen in the vicinity of Fort Bowie. Then he realized the man had blue eyes. A shiver rippled down his spine. There was only one person in the entire territory who dressed like an Indian and had eyes the color of a mountain lake. "You're him! You're Taggart, the one they call the White Apache!"

No confirmation was needed. Clay squatted and leaned the Winchester against his leg. "You'd better rest. We'll stay put a spell."

Calhoun didn't know what to say. There in front of him was the most wanted man in Arizona, the bloodthirsty fiend his commanding officer had declared must be brought to bay at all costs.

"I've heard all the tales they tell about you," Calhoun said. "Tell me. What kind of man are you? How could you have done all the vile things they say you have?"

"When a man has nothing left to lose, it doesn't matter to him if he loses everything else."

"You're talking in riddles."

"And you talk too much," Clay said.

HANGED!

That remark shut Calhoun up. Clay plucked at a dry blade of grass and stuck it between his teeth. He was content to stay another five to ten minutes until he glanced to the east and saw a large cloud of dust in the distance. "Damn. On your feet, Private. We have to move out right away."

"I thought you just told me we could rest a while? What's your big hurry all of a sudden?" Calhoun asked grumpily, not really expecting a reply. He got one though, and it was the last thing he expected to hear.

"You have a stage to catch."

Chapter Seven

It was Curly Decker, the stagecoach driver, who first spotted someone lying in the middle of the rutted track of a road. Will, the guard, was wiping dust from his shotgun, while behind him, atop the creaking stage, Ira Kent sulked.

They had just crested a low rise. Curly was in the act of lowering his whip after goading the sweaty team up the east grade. The figure was several hundred yards away on its side.

Curly's eyesight had always been extremely keen. It served him in good stead in his line of work. Frequently, he spotted trouble coming from a long way off.

In this instance, Curly noticed that the figure wore a blue uniform. So either it was an army trooper, which he very much doubted, or a wily ruse by Apaches. He wouldn't put it past the red vermin to have one of their own dress in a stolen uniform and then lie out in the road to help ambush the stage.

Curly wasn't falling for any Indian tricks. Lashing the whip, he cried out, "Redskins ahead!" The stage barreled forward, gaining speed every second. Curly couldn't wait to feel the savage's bones crunch under its big wheels.

Inside the bouncing coach, Tessa Heritage gripped the edge of her seat to keep from being pitched from her perch. "My word! What did Mr. Decker shout just now?"

"Something about Injuns," Harvey Wilkinson said nervously.

Gallagher shifted toward his door and brushed the flaps of his black jacket back to expose his pearl-handled pistols. "If we're attacked, ma'am, I'd advise you to get down low and stay down until we're out of danger. Sometimes the arrows and the lead fly thick and fast."

"Mercy me!" Tessa said.

The station manager at Mesilla had assured her there would be no danger, that the stage would get clear through to Tucson without mishap. "Don't fret your pretty self about the hostiles, Miss," he had said suavely. "The tame bucks are holed up on reservations, and the army has the wild ones corraled way up in the mountains. You'll be as safe as if you were taking a stage from Kansas City to Denver."

Only then did Tessa remember that a few months earlier the stage from Kansas City to Denver had been waylaid by Arapaho or Sioux and every last person massacred.

Tessa heard the crack of the driver's whip. She

fervently prayed that Curly Decker would get them out of whatever tight situation they were in. It would be a calamity if she died after traveling so far to see the father she had never met.

Hundreds of yards ahead, someone else heard the pop of the rawhide and whooped for joy. Pvt. James Calhoun was bound hand and foot, but he had not been gagged. Swiveling so he could see the nearest bend, his every nerve aflame with excitement, he waited for the first sight of his salvation.

Calhoun was at a loss to explain why the White Apache had spared him. The renegade had not said another word after telling him that he had a stage to catch. At rifle point, Calhoun had been hustled to the road and made to lie down while his ankles were tied with strips from his uniform. He had come right out and asked Taggart why the man was letting him live, but Taggart had not answered.

Maybe, Calhoun reflected, the renegade wasn't as vicious as everyone claimed. Maybe there was more to Taggart's story than anyone knew. The man had to have a shred of decency left deep down.

At that moment, the stagecoach swept around the bend. Calhoun smiled broadly. Suddenly, it hit him that the stage was not slowing down. Indeed, the driver was cracking his long whip with a frenzy, driving the team to go faster.

"What the hell?" Calhoun said. The driver must not have seen him yet! Hooking his legs under him, he sat up and hollered at the top of his lungs, "Stop! Stop! For the love of God, I need your help!"

Curly Decker was about to swing his whip again when he saw the figure sit up. Since no Apache ever had sandy hair, he knew right away that it really was a white man. "Tarnation!" he thundered and hauled on the reins while simultaneously applying the brake. It was sheer desperation on his part. The stage was going like a bat out of hell, and there wasn't enough space between it and the man in the road to stop in time. But Curly had to try.

Inside the coach, Tessa cried out as it abruptly sloughed to one side and teetered as if it were about to topple over. She stifled a scream and glanced at her companions. Harvey Wilkinson had his eyes shut tightly and he was holding onto the frame of the window for dear life. Gallagher also had a firm grip, but he did not appear flustered. How he could sit there so calmly was beyond Tessa.

Up ahead, Pvt. Calhoun blanched as the huge stagecoach hurtled toward him. It could not possibly come to a halt before it was too late. His body would be ground to pulp beneath the flailing hooves of the horses, then run over by the coach itself.

"No!" Calhoun flung himself to the right and rolled as he had never rolled before. He flipped over and over and over, heedless of the stones that gouged him and a tiny cactus that tore at his cheek. He had to get out of the way or he would die.

Neither the frantic trooper nor the people on the stage were aware that the entire tableau was being viewed by a pair of steely lake-blue eyes. Clay Taggart was as astounded as anyone by the turn of events.

It was common knowledge that the stage from Mesilla passed along that particular stretch of road every afternoon about the same time. Sometimes it was accompanied by cavalry; sometimes it wasn't.

Clay had figured that leaving the greenhorn in the middle of the road was the surest way of returning Calhoun to where he belonged. He hadn't counted on the stage running the private over. And he dared not show himself to help. The shotgun messenger or the man who rode up on the luggage rack were bound to open fire the moment he did.

Calhoun was close to the edge of the road. A glance showed the stage to be almost upon him. The horses seemed enormous at that angle, their nostrils flaring, their eyes wide, their hooves hammering the ground like giant hammers. In his panic, they resembled fire-breathing beasts out of some mythological nightmare rather than ordinary horses.

The earth rumbled and shook. Calhoun rolled into the brush and winced when a sharp branch lanced into his arm. He was engulfed by dust so thick that he couldn't see the end of his own nose, so heavy that he choked and sputtered and couldn't take a decent breath.

On the driver's box, Curly Decker used every curse word he knew and a lot of them twice as the coach skewed wildly from side to side. The clattering, the rattling, and the whinnies of the horses drowned out his curses. All the muscles on his forearms stood out in stark relief as he fought to keep the stage under control. It lurched violently to the right, nearly spilling Ira Kent, who squawked in fright. But at the very last instant, when Curly was certain the stage was going over, it righted itself and finally came to a halt a dozen yards past where the soldier in the road had been.

Kent scooted to the rear of the luggage rack.

Swiping at the dust, he called out, "I see the jackass! He got out of the way! What in the hell was he doing in the middle of the road?"

Tessa heard the cry and opened her door to step out and see what was going on.

"I'd stay in here, were I you," Gallagher said. "There's no telling what might happen."

Hesitating with one foot part of the way out the door, Tessa leaned to the left to peer out Wilkinson's window. "Who is out there? What is this all about?"

"I don't have the foggiest notion, ma'am" the young man said.

Outside, Calhoun struggled to his knees as the dust settled around him. The driver swang to the ground. The shotgun messenger climbed onto the luggage rack beside another man who looked as if he were in dire need of a bath. Several faces peered at him from the windows. One was female. It had been so long since Calhoun had last seen a white woman that the sight shocked him.

Curly Decker could not help but notice the soldier's dazed expression and jumped to the wrong conclusion. "That was a close shave, I'll agree, but you're fine now, son. No harm done." He was only a yard away when he discovered the bounds. "Say, what are you doing trussed up like a hog for the slaughter?"

Calhoun tore his gaze from the vision of loveliness in the stage and told the driver who he was, adding, "Apaches bushwhacked the patrol I was with. I think I was the only one to get out alive."

Drawing a Green River knife that hung on his left hip, Curly cut the loops of fabric. "But who left you here in the road, Private? No Apache I know of would do such a thing."

"It was a man named Taggart. The one they call the White Apache."

About to slide the knife into its sheath, Curly Decker froze. "The devil you say! Taggart let you live?"

Up on the stage, Ira Kent jerked out his big revolver. "Don't dawdle, Curly! Get the soldier boy inside so we can get the hell out of here! That traitor Taggart might have left him there as bait."

With the driver's help, Calhoun slowly stood. His arms and legs tingled terribly from having the circulation cut off for so long. He tried to stand on his own, but his legs began to buckle and Curly had to grab him. "Give me a minute."

Ira Kent beckoned impatiently. "We don't have a minute to spare, boy! In case you haven't heard, Clay Taggart is murderin' scum. He sold out his own kind to go live with a bunch of filthy heathens. They say he's killed dozens of whites—men, women, and sprouts alike. He deserves to be strung up by the neck—or better yet to have his stomach cut open and his innards pulled out for the vultures to feast on."

Less than 15 feet away, concealed in the mesquite, the White Apache had been about to turn and go his own way. On hearing the unkempt man's words, he stopped, his face acquiring a flinty cast.

"That's enough out of you," Curly told Kent, nodding at the coach to remind him there was a woman present. But naturally, Kent didn't take the hint.

"Apaches aren't human like us," Ira said. "They're nothing but dirty, worthless animals who deserve to be hunted down and wiped out. It wouldn't be any great loss. More like squashing a bunch of fleas."

Curly made for the coach, the private leaning on him for support. "Not all Injuns are as bad as you make them out to be. I've known a few good ones in my time."

Kent snorted. "The hell, you say! I never took you for an Injun lover. There's not one of them worth a damn, Decker, not even the squaws and the sprouts. Fact is, the world would be better off if we dug a huge pit and buried every last one of them alive."

A single shot rang out. Ira Kent was snapped to his feet by the impact of a heavy-caliber slug that cored his forehead and burst out the back of his cranium. Arms flung outward, he pivoted and toppled off the rear of the stage, smashing face down into the dirt.

For a few moments, no one else moved. Then Will swiveled his shotgun and unleashed a barrel at the mesquite, even as Curly let go of the soldier, drew his revolver, and turned to shoot.

White Apache flattened himself in the nick of time. Buckshot blistered the limbs above him, breaking a large one clean in half. Pumping onto his elbows, he settled a bead on the shotgun messenger and fired just as the man was about to cut loose a second time. The guard's chest spurted blood, and he flew backward, disappearing over the far side of the coach.

Shifting, White Apache saw the driver taking aim. The buckskin-clad man had spotted him.

White Apache fired first, his shot striking the driver squarely in the sternum.

Pvt. Calhoun threw his hands before his face as blood and bits of flesh spattered him. Unarmed, there was nothing he could do except dive for cover under the stage. Above him, pistols blazed.

One of the shooters in the stage was uncannily accurate. White Apache flinched as lead whizzed by his face so close that it seemed as if he were being swarmed by angry bees.

Two heads were framed by the stage windows, and from the left-hand one poked a pair of glistening Colts. The man firing them was a gunman of uncommon skill. So White Apache shot him first. Centering the Winchester on the door, he sent a slug smashing through the wood. The gunman was flung from sight, leaving White Apache free to concentrate on the last white-eye.

In the stage, Tessa Heritage was glued in place by the horror of the sudden carnage. A body had toppled from the top and crashed down on her side, and she had looked out to find the shotgun guard sprawled on his back, convulsing violently. Aghast, she saw a scarlet geyser bubble from a hole in his chest.

Then Gallagher grunted and was flung to the seat. Tessa turned toward the gambler, appalled to see a red stain low on his white shirt. She reached out, but before she could help him, two things happened at the very same moment.

Harvey Wilkinson was slammed from the window as if by a giant mallet. Tessa glimpsed him flying toward her and tried to get out of the way, but failed. His shoulder collided with hers. The next thing she knew, she was sailing through the door she had opened as the stagecoach rolled into motion and went rattling off down the road, the team in a panic.

Tessa landed on her elbow and hip. Jarred but otherwise unharmed, she sat up. Will, the guard, was an arm's length away, breathing in raspy gasps. She extended her arm to comfort him, but the second her fingers made contact, the shotgun messenger commenced flopping like a fish out of water and making the most horrible gurgling sounds. Suddenly, his right hand came up holding his Colt. It went off into the air, not once but three times.

Tessa wished there were something she could do for him. It didn't occur to her that she might be in danger until the pistol unexpectedly swung toward her. His thumb curled around the hammer. In another heartbeat, he was going to fire. She tried to spring out of harm's way, but knew she would never be able to make it.

A pair of strong arms looped around Tessa's waist. Without ceremony, she was yanked to one side just as the six-shooter discharged. Startled, she looked up into the handsome face of the young soldier. Their eyes met, and something electric coursed through her from head to toe.

At that moment, another shot boomed. That one was much louder and came from across the road.

Tessa spun and immediately recoiled against the trooper. "Dear Lord in heaven!"

A warrior with a smoking rifle in his bronzed hands stalked toward them. White Apache paid the unarmed pair little attention. Striding straight to the shotgun messenger, he made sure the man was dead. Next, he walked to the stage driver, whose face was a mask of amazement. Many looked like him at the point of dying, Clay mused. The simple truth was that people figured it would always happen to others, but never to themselves.

Calhoun was in a whirl. So much had happened so fast. He could not quite accept the fact that one minute ago he had been about to board a stage to safety. Now, however, the same stage was racing westward without him, while to his right and left lay bodies pumping blood, and in his arms was one of the most beautiful women he had ever seen. The fragrance of her scented hair was enough to make him dizzy.

Tessa ordinarily would not let a strange man hold her close, but she was so stunned by the slaughter and the death of the kindly driver and the other two that she completely forgot the arm around her slender waist.

White Apache looked at them. In a moment of fury, he had saddled himself not only with the greenhorn, but a woman as well. A true Chiricahua would shoot the trooper and take the woman back to his lodge. But he still couldn't bring himself to slay the greenhorn. And he already had a woman.

Calhoun found that his vocal chords worked. "You bastard! You deliberately used me to get the drop on the people on the stage! You're a murdering fiend, just like everyone says you are!"

White Apache could feel the fury drain from him like water from a sieve. He saw no point in explaining himself to the trooper. Calhoun would never believe him. Covering the two of them, he walked to the still form of the man who had been on the luggage rack, the man who had wanted to dig a big pit and bury all Apaches alive. "What was this one's name?"

Bewildered by the question, Calhoun said, "I don't have any idea."

Clay glanced at the woman. She was attractive in a frail sort of way. "Do you know it?"

Astounded that the Apache spoke flawless English, Tessa answered, "Ira Kent. I have no idea where he lived or what he did for a living."

"It doesn't much matter. He was a waste of flesh," Clay said. Lifting his right foot, he stamped down with all his might. Kent's nose crunched. A surge of rekindled fury sparked Clay into stamping again and again until the dead man's face looked more like battered dough than skin and bone. The nose was shattered, the lips ground into the teeth, half the teeth broken, and both cheeks split wide.

Glancing up, Clay could not help but note the utter horror and loathing mirrored by the young couple. Again he elected not to say why he had done what he did. He couldn't. He didn't truly understand himself. Clay walked toward them.

Calhoun stepped in front of the woman. "I don't know what you have in mind, Taggart, but I'm telling you right now that I won't let you harm a hair on her head. You'll have to kill me first."

Tessa looked at her defender and felt a knot of warmth deep in the pit of her stomach.

Clay shrugged. "You keep saying that you want to die, trooper. Maybe it's high time I obliged you, after all." He leveled the Winchester.

To everyone's surprise, Tessa darted around in front of the trooper to shield him with her own body. "No! How could you? He's not even armed!"

"You're wasting your breath," Calhoun said. "This is the White Apache. He likes nothing better than to kill our kind. He's gone totally Injun."

Not until that moment did Tessa realize that the man she had mistaken for a full-blooded Apache was in truth white. Tessa gulped, convinced they were about to be slain in the most gory way imaginable.

Had the auburn beauty but known it, Clay Taggart had no plans to harm her or the soldier. His strongest desire was to be shed of both of them. He looked after the fleeing stage, well out of sight beyond the next bend, debating whether he could catch it and bring it back so that Calhoun and the woman could go on into Tucson, leaving him free to get on with his own affairs.

Calhoun followed the renegade's gaze and leapt to the wrong conclusion. "That's right, killer. You should be worried. Once that stage rolls into Tucson, every man in the territory will be out looking for the lady here. You can't harm a white woman and get away with it. Even you should know that."

Clay studied the woman. She might be frail by Apache standards, but there was fire in her eyes. If he were any judge, she had more grit than was apparent. "What's your name, lady?"

"Tessa Heritage."

"Meet Pvt. Calhoun," Clay said, nodding at the trooper. "The two of you seem to have taken a shine to one another. I reckon the two of you will go far together."

Tessa bristled. "I resent any man besmirching my reputation!"

102

HANGED!

Clay didn't doubt her. Women like her would rather die than suffer the shame of a fate worse than death. "That's not what I meant, lady," he said not unkindly and pointed westward. "It's a long walk, but I think the two of you can make it if you stick to the road and travel only at night."

"I don't understand," Tessa said, since obviously, he wasn't about to simply let them go.

Calhoun realized otherwise. As anxious as he was to get out of there, he couldn't resist asking one last question, the same one that had plagued him ever since it became apparent that Taggart did not intend to murder him. "Why, mister? Just tell me that."

"Go," Clay said and moved off.

Tessa faced her protector. "What's he up to? Is he going to shoot us in the back when we walk away?" Rotating toward the White Apache, she said, "You'd better not!" Fresh in her mind was the raw fear the mention of her father had instilled in Ira Kent. Perhaps, she reflected, it would have the same effect on the butcher. "Harm us and my father will never rest until he tracks you down. He's not a man to be trifled with."

Pausing at the road's edge, Clay regarded her as he might a boastful child. "I'm trembling in my moccasins. What's your father's name, lady?"

Tessa straightened. "Perhaps you've heard of him," she declared. "Marshal Tom Crane of Tucson."

Calhoun sensed that Tessa had made a grave blunder. He saw anger in the flaring flames in the White Apache's eyes and the clenching of the renegade's hands.

Jake McMasters

"Know him, do you?" Tessa gloated, flattering herself that she saw fear where there was none.

The next words Taggart uttered were torn from the depths of his ravaged soul. They slashed into Tessa Heritage like daggers, chilling her to the core.

"I'll never forget your father, girl." Clay Taggart paused to do battle with his roiling emotions. "The son of a bitch hanged me!"

Chapter Eight

Close to sunset, Marshal Tom Crane was talking to Rafe Skinner on a corner near the jail. A commotion up the street made both men turn. A team in harness and the rush of wheels gave the lawman an inkling of the nature of the disturbance.

"About damn time," Crane said. "The stage is over two hours late."

Skinner grinned. "Don't tell me that you were worried? I thought you didn't care about her."

"Be mighty careful, friend," Marshal Crane said. "I won't be prodded."

The owner of the Acme chuckled and held his hands up, palms out, to show he meant no insult. "The least you could have done was bought her some flowers. After all, the poor girl has come a long way to see you."

"I won't warn—" Crane stiffened as excited shouts broke out, spreading along the street like wildfire. He stepped to the end of the boardwalk, cocking his head to hear better. Loud and clear above the bedlam rose a bellow for someone to fetch the doctor.

Crane sprinted to the center of the street. A thickset man who seemed vaguely familiar was bringing the stage to a stop. Up on the box beside him was a thin man wearing jeans and a wool shirt. Crane recognized Slim Reece, a prospector. The thick set man was Reece's partner. A few months earlier, Crane had arrested them both for being drunk and disorderly.

People were converging from all over. The marshal had to shoulder through a babbling pack to reach the stage. Reece saw him and jabbed a bony finger at the coach.

"It's just awful, Marshal! We've got a dead one inside and one bad wounded." The prospector jabbered on while climbing down. "Bob and me were headin' east along the Tucson-Mesilla road when the stage came roarin' toward us. Right away we knew somethin' was wrong. There was no sign of Curly or the shotgun. We was able to bring it to a stop, and once we saw what was inside, we lit a shuck for town."

Crane shoved aside a citizen who stood on tiptoe trying to peer inside. The man complained, but Crane didn't give a damn. Yanking the door open, he looked in. The rank odor of blood and urine made him gag. Taking a shallow breath, he pulled down the folding steps and climbed up.

Lying crumpled on the floor was a young cowboy or rancher, a sizable chunk of his face gone. Flies crawled over the wound; a few buzzed into the air when Crane entered.

Curled up on the right-hand seat was a tall man in black, his eyes closed. Tucked under a red sash around his waist were a pair of expensive Colts, butts forward. The front of his white shirt bore a wide scarlet stain and he was grimacing in torment.

"It's Gallagher!" Rafe Skinner said from behind the lawman. "I sent for him a couple of weeks ago to come work for me."

Crane had met the gunman before. Crane would never admit as much, but Gallagher was one of the few men he made it a point never to cross. The gun shark had few equals, and Crane wasn't one of them. On top of that, Gallagher was as gritty as fish eggs rolled in sand.

Bending a knee, Crane placed a hand on the gambler's shoulder. "Gallagher? Can you hear me?"

The gunman's eyelids fluttered, then snapped opened. The instant he saw the lawman, his right hand closed on a Colt. "Crane? Where?" he said hoarsely.

"Tucson," Crane said. "I need to know what happened? Where's Curly and the guard? And what about the rest of the passengers? There was supposed to be a woman on board."

"Your daughter," Gallagher said, wetting his lips. "We talked some." He attempted to sit up, but would not have made it without a boost from the marshal. "Much obliged."

Crane waited for the man to compose himself. He was mildly surprised that he wasn't more upset about Tessa. He was concerned, but not overly worried, not as he would be if his horse were to be stolen or his pistol were to be lost. But then why should he be? he asked himself. Except for a handful of letters, he hardly knew the girl. She meant little more to him than any other casual acquaintance.

Out the windows on both sides, a sea of faces peered in at the gunman. Not a soul spoke. They were straining to catch every word.

Gallagher took a deep breath. "About five or six hours out, Curly stopped for a soldier lying in the road."

"A soldier?" Rafe Skinner said. "What was he doing there in the middle of nowhere? Had he been shot?"

Crane twisted and glared. "Keep quiet and let him speak his piece, you jackass."

The gambler sagged, but caught himself. Gritting his teeth, he pressed a hand to his side. "Hurts like hell. I need a sawbones."

"The doc should be here any minute," Marshal Crane said. "Go on with your story. I need to know what happened before I organize a posse."

Nodding once, Gallagher said, "It was no accident the trooper was there. He had been tied up and left there for us to find. Curly got down to cut him loose. That's when the firing commenced. I saw Curly take lead and drop. The rest is a mite fuzzy." The gunman paused, his head drooping. "I think the shotgun was picked off too. Oh, and Ira Kent."

"Kent?" Rafe Skinner said. "That worthless sack of manure is no great loss."

"How many were there?" Crane said.

"One man with a rifle."

"Just one?" Crane said skeptically. Everyone in

Tucson knew that Curly Decker was a handy gent with a six-gun, and Will, the shotgun messenger, had once dropped three outlaws before any of them could get off a single shot.

Gallagher's next words were almost a whisper. "It was the White Apache."

A hot coal seared Marshal Tom Crane's gut. Without thinking, he grabbed the gambler by the front of the shirt and yanked Gallagher toward him. "The White Apache? You're sure?" Suddenly he felt something else in his gut, a searing pang caused by a gun barrel jammed against his abdomen.

The gambler's head snapped up, his eyes clear and cold. Gallagher spoke so softly that only Crane could hear. "No one manhandles me, lawman. The only reason I don't blow out your lamp here and now is that I figure you're mighty upset about your girl."

Raw fury gripped Tom Crane. He let no man talk to him like that, but he was hardly in a position to do anything about Gallagher doing so. One wrong twitch and the gambler would carry out the threat. Crane could draw when Gallagher replaced the Colt, but it wouldn't do for the fine people of Tucson to see their law officer gun down a wounded man. Relaxing his fingers, he said evenly, "Sorry. Tell me why you blame the White Apache."

"The soldier told Curly that it was Taggart who tied him up and left him there."

Murmuring broke out among the crowd, and Crane said, "You still haven't told me about my daughter."

Gallagher leaned back, the pistol once again tucked under his sash. "The last I saw, she was thrown from the stage when the team bolted. I reckon Taggart has her now."

Loud, angry voices filled the street as the information was imparted by those in front of the throng to those in back. Through them waded a portly man carrying a black bag. "Let me pass, please!"

"It's Doc Pinkley," Skinner said.

Crane barely heard him. Thunderstruck at the development, he climbed down and leaned against the door. An elderly woman nearby said something about the poor marshal, which was rapidly passed along to others. A hand clapped him on the shoulder and Rafe Skinner leaned close.

"I guess I was wrong about you, pard. I've never seen you this upset before. You really do care about the girl, don't you?"

No, Crane wanted to shout, I don't! None of them understood a damn thing! It wasn't Tessa's fate that disturbed him so much. She had gotten what she deserved for not staying back in Ohio where she belonged.

Crane wiped his brow with the back of a sleeve. The real reason he was in turmoil could be summed up in two words: Clay Taggart. It seemed like only yesterday that Miles Gillett had asked him to rustle up a posse without anyone being the wiser to hunt Taggart down. And he had done it too. Crane could still remember the wild look in Taggart's eyes as the noose had been slipped over his head.

Crane nearly laughed at the memory. Of all those involved in the lynching, only Taggart and he had known that Taggart was innocent of the charges Miles Gillett had leveled. Clay Taggart never tried to rape Gillett's wife. The truth was that Gillett's woman had led Taggart on until the fool had been in so deep he'd been unwittingly snared in Gillett's net.

Crane had thought that hanging Taggart would be the end of the whole business. As the posse rode off that day, he had glanced back and seen Taggart kicking and thrashing at the end of the rope. But somehow Taggart had survived. Somehow, Taggart had taken up with Delgadito's band of renegade Apaches.

Taggart and the Chiricahuas had been raiding and plundering from one end of the territory to the other, even down into Mexico on occasion. No one knew where they would strike next. There was no pattern to their rampage, no rhyme or reason to the victims they picked—or so most everyone believed.

Tom Crane knew better. In addition to all the soldiers, miners, and traders who had been waylaid, several members of the lynch party had also been slain. Their deaths had not been chance accidents either. Taggart had sought them out and murdered them in their homes in the middle of the night.

One by one by one, Clay Taggart was killing off those responsible for stringing him up. To make matters worse, he was taking his sweet time about it, as if he were prolonging the suspense to make the rest of the guilty men sweat in their boots.

Crane hated to admit that Taggart's little scheme was working. Most of the posse members were terrified. None knew but that they might be next on the rabid butcher's list.

The lawman had figured that he would be one of the last Taggart went after. He seldom left town except in the company of deputies or others, and as

111

loco as Taggart had become, the man wasn't about to lead a raid on Tucson itself.

But the attack on the stage couldn't be a coincidence. Somehow, Taggart had learned that his daughter was going to be on board, and he had taken a trooper captive to use as bait, then gunned down everyone else to get his hands on Tessa. That was the only possible explanation.

Marshal Crane placed a hand over his mouth to hide a fleeting grin. Clay Taggart had outsmarted himself at last. The renegade probably figured on either carving Tessa up or using her to lure Crane into a trap. Either way, Taggart undoubtedly believed he was paying Crane back for the lynching.

Crane would have the last laugh. Little did the fool realize that Tessa meant next to nothing to him. Crane didn't care one bit whether the White Apache chopped her to pieces. Nor was he about to ride into a trap on her account.

"We're ready to ride out when you are, Marshal."

Crane looked up. While he had been pondering his situation, over 20 men had gathered in front of him. Half or so were dependable enough to be part of a posse. The rest were shiftless no-accounts who spent their days lounging in saloons. They'd be about as worthless as a four-card flush. Yet the no-accounts were the ones Crane pointed to, saying, "I'll take you, you, and you."

A few of the townspeople the lawman did not select glanced at one another, mystified by his selections. Crane wasn't about to tell them that he had picked the shiftless bunch because he had no intention of making a determined effort to catch Taggart. He'd go as far as the spot where the stage had been waylaid, and maybe a bit beyond, but that was it. He only wished that he could see the look on the White Apache's face when he realized the scheme had failed.

Rafe Skinner leaned toward him again. "What the hell are you doing, Tom? The bunch you've picked couldn't find their own hind ends without help."

Crane saw that it might be best not to be too obvious. Jerking a thumb at a lanky frontiersman in buckskins who lounged against a hitch rack, he asked, "What about you, Baxter? Curly Decker was a friend of yours, wasn't he?"

Clell Baxter had a salt-and-pepper beard and gray strands in his mane of brown hair. A scar from a knife fight pinched the corner of his left eye, lending him a perpetual squint. He studied the men that the lawman had already pointed out, then said, "I reckon I'll tag along. You'll need someone who can tell a track from a piss mark."

"We leave in fifteen minutes," Crane said. "I want every man to bring a rifle and at least twenty-five rounds of ammunition, plus enough grub to last a week."

The posse members dispersed to collect their effects just as Dr. Pinkley filled the doorway of the coach. "I'll need something to carry this wounded man to my office for surgery. A board would do if it's wide enough."

Several men dashed off, and Skinner moved to the steps. "What's the verdict, Doc? Will Gallagher pull through?"

The portly physician nodded. "His prognosis is excellent. The bullet missed his vitals. Give him two weeks to rest up and he'll be as fit as a fiddle." Pinkley climbed down. "He's a very fortunate man."

"That's Gallagher, sure enough," Rake Skinner said. "He's one hombre who was sure enough born under a lucky star."

Marshal Crane headed for the jail. He wanted to be alone with his thoughts, but the owner of the Acme fell into step beside him.

"So what was that all about back there?"

"I don't know what you're talking about," Crane said, playing the innocent.

"Like hell you don't," Skinner said. "Either you ought to be playing with a string of spools, or you're up to something and I'd like to be let in on what it is."

"Don't you ever do any work?" Crane asked. "In case you weren't listening, I have a posse to lead out in a quarter of an hour. That barely gives me enough time to give orders to my deputy and saddle up."

Skinner wouldn't let the subject drop. "Why'd you pick Gritz and Thorson and those others? You know as well as I do that they'll skedaddle with their tails dragging if the White Apache so much as jumps out at them!"

"They volunteered," Crane said.

"So did a lot of men worth taking." Rafe Skinner stared at the lawman a few moments, then said, "Why is it that I get the notion you're never going to answer me? Fair enough. If that's the way you want to be, it's your business."

Crane was almost to the jail. Over his shoulder, he said, "I'll see you when I get back and fill you in."

"No need. I'm going along."

Taken aback, Crane drew up short. "I appreciate the offer, Rafe, but I don't need your help. Baxter is one of the best trackers around. If anyone can sniff Taggart out, Clell is the man."

"It's not the turncoat I'm thinking of," Skinner said bluntly. "It's your daughter. Someone has to have her best interests at heart since you sure as hell don't."

The slur rankled Crane, but he refused to make an issue of it. As usual, his friend had seen right through him. "Suit yourself, but don't make trouble. And what I say goes."

Skinner went to leave. The marshal let the handsomest man in Tucson take three steps before curiosity got the better of him. "Rafe?"

"What?"

"Why? You don't know her. You don't owe her a thing."

"Yes, I do."

"How so?"

"I'm her father's best friend."

Pvt. James Calhoun tripped over a loose rock and almost fell. His legs were sore from hours of hard hiking and his stomach so empty that it growled constantly, but at least this time his wrists had not been bound.

Calhoun had made it a point to keep close to Tessa Heritage in case she should stumble, yet so far she had not needed his help. She marched along with her slender shoulders squared and her pretty head held high. The sight of her set his breath to fluttering, his pulse to racing. She was the kind of woman a man would gladly die for. And Calhoun almost had.

Back at the road, Clay Taggart had turned livid on learning Tessa was the marshal's daughter. Calhoun had never seen anyone undergo such a startling transformation. One moment the man had been standing there as calmly as could be, the next Taggart had stormed up to Tessa and gripped her arm so tightly she had cried out.

That was when Calhoun had nearly died. He had leapt to Tessa's defense, grabbing at Taggart's arm to pull it off. Taggart had whirled and rammed the butt of the Winchester into Calhoun's belly, folding Calhoun like paper.

There had been a click, and the private had looked up into the feral eyes of a man driven to the brink of madness. Calhoun had not moved, had barely dared breathe.

Once again Taggart had done the exact opposite of what Calhoun had anticipated. The rifle's muzzle lowered. The renegade grew calm once again. Afterward, though, Taggart was different: rougher, curt, not at all inclined to be friendly. Holding Tessa and Calhoun at gunpoint, the White Apache had gone to the stallion. Once he was mounted, he forced them to tramp eastward.

Evening had descended and still the White Apache showed no sign of stopping. Calhoun fanned his courage and said, "We can't keep on like this all night. Miss Heritage needs to rest sooner or later."

"It'll be later," Clay said. It was crucial that they put as much distance between themselves and the site of the stage attack as they could before midnight. Once he was positive no one was on their trail, he would let his captives rest, but not before.

Clay inhaled deeply, invigorated by the thought that within a day or two he would have one of the men he held most responsible for his lynching in his rifle's sights. Tom Crane, that lapdog of a lawman who licked Miles Gillett's boots day in and day out. Tom Crane, the tin star who had strung Clay up, knowing full well that Clay had never laid a finger on Gillett's wife. Tom Crane, the man Clay had dreamed about throttling with his bare hands. Tom Crane, the pathetic excuse for a human being who ran roughshod over the people of Tucson and got away with it only because he was backed by the wealthiest rancher in Arizona. Everyone knew Crane was a surly wolf, but no one lifted a finger against him for fear of the consequences.

Clay stared at Tessa Heritage, secretly astonished by the quirk of fate that had delivered her into his hands. He didn't see much of her father in her. Maybe around the eyes a little, certainly not in her character or personality. She was every inch a lady.

At that moment, the object of Clay Taggart's attention was also thinking about her father. Tessa knew that their captor expected Tom Crane to come after her. But would he? she wondered. Crane and she had never been close. Their letters, initiated by her, had always been cordial, but short. The man was under little obligation to dash to her rescue. Were blood ties enough to make Crane risk his life on her behalf? After the things Gallagher had told her, she sincerely doubted he would.

Clearing her throat, Tessa said, "You're wasting your time, you know, Mr. Taggart. My father and I have never met. He has no reason to care about me."

Clay avoided a prickly pear. "A while ago you told me that he wouldn't rest until he'd hunted me down. Which is it, lady?"

"I exaggerated to make you let us go," Tessa said.

"Maybe so," Clay said. "But it doesn't really matter whether your father and you are as close as two peas in a pod or as far apart as the earth and the moon. He'll come for you."

"How can you be so certain?"

"He won't have any choice."

Tessa was at a loss. For the life of her, she could not conceive of why the White Apache was so confident, unless his certainty had something to do with the four times he had dropped back a dozen yards and fiddled with large rocks.

"Let's suppose the marshal does come," Calhoun said. "He won't be alone. You'll be up against a small army, Taggart."

"The more the merrier."

Calhoun scowled in annoyance. "If you ask me, Taggart, you're as crazy as they come."

"The whole world is crazy, boy," Clay said. "And those of us who know it are crazier than most." He sniffed loudly a few times. "Do you smell it on the wind, trooper? Before I'm done, a river of it will flow across Arizona."

The private looked back, at a loss to understand the renegade's meaning. "A river of what?"

"What else, greenhorn?" Clay sniffed once more. "Blood."

Chapter Nine

Darkness forced the posse to call a halt when they were only three hours out of Tucson. There was no moon, and Marshal Tom Crane did not care to risk riding right past the bodies and then have to back-track later on, losing precious time in the process.

Or so Crane claimed. The real reason he stopped for the night was to foil Clay Taggart. By giving the White Apache more time to get away, Crane made doubly sure that the posse would neither overtake the renegade nor ride into whatever trap Taggart had planned for them.

Hunkered by the fire, Marshal Crane sipped at a cup of black coffee and idly listened to the six no-accounts complain about everything under the sun. The dust, the long ride, the threat of Apaches—all gave the saloon crowd plenty to gripe about.

Two small fires had been lit. Around one were the six no-accounts. At the other were Crane, Rafe

Skinner, and Clell Baxter. The frontiersman had not said two words since leaving town. At the moment, he was tamping tobacco into a pipe while regarding the lawman intently.

"Something on your mind, Baxter?" Crane asked.

"If there is, it's my mind, and I'll keep it to myself," Baxter said.

Crane took another sip, ignoring Skinner's grin at his expense. The old buffalo hunter was notorious for having a stinging wit and an acid tongue.

The lawman wondered if Baxter had guessed what he was up to and thought less of him because of it. Not that he cared one way or the other how the old man felt. But he didn't want the suspicion to spread. All it would take was a few words from Baxter, in passing, to any prominent townsman, and rumors would spread like the plague.

"If you have a complaint, I'd like to hear it," Crane said to spur the old man into revealing the truth.

Baxter glanced in contempt at the saloon crowd. "I should think you'd have a belly full of complaining by this time. To hear those men whine, you'd think they were just out of diapers."

The six no-accounts overheard Baxter's comment. Thorson, a beefy man with a bristling red beard and unkempt red hair, swiveled. "I'd be mighty careful who I poke fun at were I you, old-timer."

The frontiersman lowered a hand to the big Sharps rifle at his side. "I'm always careful, polecat," he said evenly. "Ask the folks back in Tucson. They'll tell you just how careful I can be."

Everyone knew what he was alluding to. Over a year ago, a pair of drifters had accused Baxter of cheating at cards. He had calmly sat in his chair while they called him every vile name there was, calmly sat there while one of them covered him with a pistol, calmly sat there as the other man started to rake in the pot, and then, just as calmly, he had knocked over the table, produced his Sharps, and shot the hard case through the heart with the pistol. The other drifter had gone for his iron, but he had not even cleared leather when Baxter's Bowie thudded into his chest.

No trial had been necessary. The other men had drawn first and threatened the frontiersman at gunpoint. It had been a clear-cut case of self-defense and a stupid stunt on the part of the drifters. Whatever else might be said about Clell Baxter, he was no cheat. The man was honest, one of the rare breed whose word was his bond.

Thorson decided he didn't want to risk rousing the old-timer's wrath. But a weasel with oily hair and a pockmarked face did not know when to leave well enough alone.

"You don't scare us, you old buzzard. There are six of us and only one of you. Give us any more guff and we're liable to take you over our knee and spank you until you beg for mercy."

Some of the no-accounts started to laugh, their mirth choking off when Clell Baxter rose, the Sharps held in both gnarled hands. "On your feet, you son of a bitch, and die like a man."

The man named Gritz had been about to take a bite of jerky. He went rigid, his eyes imitating saucers.

"I'm waiting," Baxter said calmly.

"You hold on, old-timer!" Gritz said. "I didn't mean no insult."

"Then you shouldn't have opened your mouth."

Sighing, Crane put down his cup and stood. "That's enough out of both of you."

Baxter did not even look at the lawman. "This doesn't concern you, Marshal. It's between me and that slimy son of a bitch who thinks he can treat others like dirt and get away with it."

Gritz was no gunman. He wore a Colt, but he was usually too drunk to be able to draw it, let alone fire. Blinking like a bird trapped by a cat, he swallowed and looked to the lawman for support. "You ain't just going to stand there and let him put a window in my skull, are you?"

"No one is going to shoot anyone else," Crane said.

The frontiersman took a step to the left, giving him a clearer view of Gritz. "That remains to be seen, lawman. I haven't heard no apology yet."

Crane nodded at Gritz. "You heard the man."

Flushing with anger, the weasel seemed about to make an even bigger mistake and insult Baxter again. At the last instant, he caught himself, then said, "I told you that I didn't mean no insult, old-timer. What more do you want?"

"Apologize for calling me a buzzard."

"Like hell I will!"

Baxter shrugged and hefted the Sharps. "Your choice."

Crane was ready to move in if it appeared the frontiersman was really going to fire. That eventuality didn't seem likely, since Baxter's finger wasn't even on the trigger. But the saloon crowd couldn't see that from where they sat.

Gritz flapped his hands in front of his face as if to ward off a horde of bees or a hail of flying lead. "All right, damn it! I'm sorry! I'm sorry! Are you happy now?"

"Tickled silly," Baxter said and sat back down. The Sharps went back to his side as he bent to help himself to a cup of coffee.

Rafe Skinner wore a Remington on his right hip, and he had traded in his white shirt and black jacket for a brown shirt open at the collar and a blue bandanna. He had not spoken a word during the clash. Yawning, he indicated the Big Fifty and inquired, "Is it true, Clell, that you once dropped a Comanche at twelve hundred yards?"

Baxter arched his good eye at the saloon owner. "Are you saying I'd lie? I credited you with more common sense than that."

"Then how can you even ask?" Rafe said, holding his own. "Besides, you know as well as I do how tales grow in the telling. Remember that time some drummer reported seeing a couple of Injuns south of town? By the time that story made the rounds, half the folks in Tucson believed over two hundred Apaches were set to swoop down on us."

"Yep, I recollect it well." Fondly, Baxter patted the rifle, then stroked the barrel as other men might a woman's leg. "Old Bess has been saving my hide for more years than you've lived, Mr. Skinner. And, yes, the story is true. Eight of us buffalo hunters were surrounded by a passel of Comanches. I picked off Chief Broken Ear. Billy Pike measured off the range after the Injuns skedaddled."

"That was some shot," Skinner said.

Crane had to agree. Twelve hundred yards was well over half a mile. A Winchester was only reliable at ranges out to three hundred yards, maybe a little farther in the hands of a competent marksman.

"If we see that White Apache feller," Baxter said, "I'm of a mind to earn me that reward money being offered by the government. How much is it now?"

"Ten thousand dollars, I think," Crane said. "It keeps going up after every raid."

"You don't sound very pleased about that," Skinner said.

"I'm not," the lawman said. "The higher the bounty, the more bounty hunters flock to the area to try to claim it."

Crane didn't object to the professionals who went gunning for Taggart; they knew what they were doing and never gave a lawman any headaches. It was the damned amateurs—the ones who didn't know one end of a gun from the other and who figured on making easy money—who were forever getting into hot water. They trespassed on private property, shot at shadows, and often mistook innocent citizens for the outlaws they were after.

In this case, three times in the past few months, so-called bounty hunters had shown up at his office crowing that they had killed the White Apache. Twice their victims had been harmless Pima warriors, the third time an elderly wrinkled Navajo too scrawny to lift a war club.

Crane had let them off with a stern warning never to show their miserable faces in Tucson again. In his estimation, killing Indians hardly rated a trial. It was the same as stamping out bothersome bugs.

HANGED!

At that moment Thorson stopped stuffing baked beans into his gullet long enough to inquire, "Marshal, how do you figure your girl is holding up through all this?"

"I can't rightly say," Crane said, resenting the mention of Tessa. He was doing his utmost to avoid thinking about her.

Gritz had to throw in his two bits' worth. "If that turncoat has laid a hand on her, we'll carve him up but proper, Marshal. No renegade can violate a white woman and get away with it."

Rafe Skinner fixed the weasel with a flinty stare. "Were you born stupid or did a bull stomp on your head somewhere along the line?"

"What did I do?" Gritz said, genuinely puzzled. "Why the hell is everyone picking on me?"

On that friendly note, conversation lapsed. It wasn't long before all of them had turned in except the man Crane selected to stand guard. They took turns throughout the night, each posse member working for two hours.

Crane was up before first light. He had slept remarkably well under the circumstances. As he pulled on his boots, he saw Baxter stroll out of the brush and nodded in greeting.

"Morning," the frontiersman said. "Today we should save that girl of yours, unless, of course, all the horses go lame."

"All of them at the same time? Never happen," Crane said.

Baxter smiled. "With this outfit, a gent never knows. Things ain't what they seem."

Crane did not rise to the bait. Starting the day being accused of not doing his best to rescue Tessa

125

put him in a sour frame of mind, and he barked at the others to wake them. In short order the posse had downed cups of coffee, and every last man was in the saddle, riding briskly toward the rising sun.

Baxter assumed the lead. The Sharps resting across his thighs, he rode alertly, scouring the vegetation on either side. If there were any sign to read, he would spot it.

In due course the frontiersman slowed and extended his rifle toward the sky. "I reckon we're closer than we thought," he said.

Vultures circled half a mile ahead, over a dozen of the large black birds, wheeling and dipping gracefully, like aerial dancers.

Crane spurred his dun into a gallop. After rounding a series of bends, he came to a straight stretch and spied three bodies sprawled in the road or near it. All three were covered with buzzards. Palming his Colt, he bore down on them. His first shot took the head off a bird nibbling at an eye socket. His second nailed a buzzard striving to take wing.

In a flurry, the rest of the vultures hastily rose into the air. Thorson, Gritz, and a few of their friends opened fire, cackling in glee as they blazed away. Over 30 shots were fired, yet the men only downed one bird.

Marshal Crane reined up and dismounted. The nearest body was that of Will Allen, the shotgun messenger. Close to it lay Ira Kent. On the south side of the road was Curly Decker. All three swarmed with flies.

For some reason, the buzzards had done more damage to Kent than either of the other two. His eyes, nose, and lips were gone, and a jagged hole had been torn in the soft part of his throat.

"There's no sign of your daughter or the soldier," Rafe Skinner said.

Crane absently nodded. His hunch had proven right. Clay Taggart was using Tessa as bait. But little did the bastard know that Crane was not going to go one step farther than he already had. "We'll bury these three, then head on back to town."

"Head on back?" Skinner said in surprise. "You can't be serious. What about Tessa and the trooper?"

Putting a hurt expression on his face, Crane said, "No one wants to go on more than I do. But we have to face facts. Taggart has learned Apache ways real well. He never leaves tracks. I doubt even Baxter will be able to trail him."

"We have to at least try," Skinner said.

Clell Baxter stood at the south edge of the road. Bestowing a wry smile on the lawman, he said, "I wouldn't fret about how hard it will be, not when Taggart has obliged us with an engraved invite." He pointed at the ground.

Intuition filled Crane with fleeting unease. "What are you talking about?"

Abe Thorson got there first. "Well, I'll be! Take a gander at this, boys! Seems as how the White Apache is hankerin' for a showdown."

A six-foot stone arrow pointed due south. Crane looked at it and wanted to rage, to kick, to punch. Taggart, that clever coyote, had outfoxed him again. Or had he? Crane saw a loophole.

"It must be a trick to take us off the scent. And if it's not, we'd be riding right into an ambush."

It was Gritz, of all people, who summed up the

attitude of the rest of the posse and shamed the lawman in the bargain. "What's more important to you, mister—your skin or your own flesh and blood?"

No one other than Baxter appeared to notice that Crane didn't answer. They busied themselves burying the dead men, while the frontiersman looked at Crane and shook his head. Then he walked off into the mesquite.

Although it was only the middle of the morning, the temperature soared. They were a hot, parched, tired bunch by the time the bodies were planted. Rafe Skinner tamped down the dirt on Curly Decker's grave and said, "Someone should say a few words over them. Decker and Will were decent men. They deserve it."

"I'm a lawman, not a parson," Crane said.

"Count me out too," Thorson said. "I ain't been to church since my ma died, and I was six when she took sick and gave up the ghost."

The matter was solved by Baxter, who glided out of the vegation to report. "I found another arrow a short way into the brush, near where Taggart had his horse picketed while he waited for the stage. This one points east."

"Toward the mountains," one of the men said.

"Toward Chiricahua country," another said.

Soberly, the posse mounted. The frontiersman led them to the second stone arrow. In a compact group they headed out, the majority of them holding rifles.

Marshal Tom Crane was at the forefront most of the time, but his heart wasn't in the pursuit. Despite himself, he was being forced ever deeper into the wilderness, ever closer to the snare Clay Taggart had set for him. He found his situation so damned frustrating. It was akin to being a steer led to slaughter. No matter what he did, no matter how clever he thought he was being, circumstances foiled him again and again.

In under an hour, the posse came to a third stone arrow.

"Don't this beat all?" Thorson said. "The mangy varmint is doin' everything but drawing us a map."

"He's not moving all that fast either," Clell Baxter said as he bent low to read the prints. "The woman and the soldier boy are on foot, walking in front of his horse."

Rafe Skinner glanced at Crane. "At least she's still alive. That counts for something."

Tom Crane begged to differ. If Tessa were dead, the posse would have no reason whatsoever to go on. The others would do as he wanted and turn around. "It sure does."

"I wonder what they're doing right this minute," Gritz said.

It was Skinner who responded. "Who can say? If I were in their boots, I'd just be glad to be alive."

Miles ahead, Pvt. James Calhoun was consoling himself with those very sentiments. His feet were so sore every step hurt. His legs felt as if he had run 50 miles without stopping. His throat had become a desert, his mouth a sand dune. When he licked his dry, cracked lips, no spittle formed.

"I'm dying of thirst! We need water, Taggart, and we need it soon, or you'll have two more bodies on your hands."

Since sunrise, Clay Taggart had been pushing the pair just as hard as the day before. They were well into the foothills, picking their way up a talus slope to a high ridge that would afford him a panoramic vista of the countryside.

White Apache studied the trooper, annoyed by his weakness. It reminded him too much of his own when he had first taken up with the Chiricahuas. The warriors had been able to do everything better than he had. They could run twice as fast, travel ten times as far without tiring, and last days longer without food or water.

"You'll get to drink about noon," Clay said. Beyond the ridge lay a valley watered by a creek that was dry during the summer months, but should still have water in it at that time of the year.

"How are you holding up, woman?" Clay said.

Tessa Heritage was on the brink of exhaustion. How she kept going she would never know. Her limbs were leaden. Her stomach was shriveled to the size of a peach pit, and her throat was as raw as red meat. But she refused to give her abductor the satisfaction of seeing her collapse or crawl. She would forge on for as long as she could hold out. "I'm fine."

"You're a lot tougher than you seem," Clay said. "You'd make a fine wife for an Apache. Most white women don't last very long."

Tessa twisted. "How can you talk like that? Don't you feel any guilt at all over what you've done? Over what you've become?"

"Not a lick," Clay said.

He honestly didn't. What he had become, as she phrased it, had been forced on him by his own kind.

HANGED!

It was a white man who had accused him of a crime he had not done, a white man who had stolen his land out from under him. It had been white men who had chased him down and made him the guest of honor at a necktie social. White men had placed a price on his head. And it was white men who would not give him a moment's rest until he was six feet under.

White Apache frowned. The woman was typical of Easterners, most of whom branded all Indians as wicked savages.

"I don't see how you can't be," Tessa said earnestly.

A white man going Indian was unthinkable to her. Yet Taggart wasn't the raving lunatic she had dreaded he might be. Every so often, she detected a spark of humanity under his gruff surface, and it made her wonder.

Suddenly, a loose rock slid out from under Tessa's heel. Taken completely unawares, she tottered and would have gone down if not for James Calhoun, who always seemed to be there when she needed him.

"Got you, miss!" the young trooper said.

Tessa met his gaze and he looked away shyly. The pressure of his arm around her waist brought warmth and comfort. "You can call me by my first name, kind sir."

"Whatever you want," Calhoun said, his fatigue and the severe heat momentarily forgotten. As he helped her straighten up, he marveled that her hair was still as fragrant as it had been the day before.

Tessa made no move to break his hold. She rather fancied being close to him and harbored a secret desire to get to know him better if they survived their ordeal.

"The two of you can make cow eyes at one another later," Clay Taggart said.

Blushing, Tessa pushed free and smoothed her dress. "You, sir, are no gentleman."

"Never claimed to be," Taggart said. "But to show you I'm not the heartless lobo you make me out to be, I'll turn my back so the two of you can kiss and get it out of your systems."

Tessa's cheeks burned. "I have no idea what you are talking about."

"Me neither," Calhoun said.

"If you say so. But you're making a mistake. You're a perfect match for each other."

"We are?" Tessa asked.

"Yep. Both of you are rotten liars."

The soldier and the young woman resumed their climb, mocking laughter wafting over them.

Near the top the slope steepened. Clay had to dismount and lead the black stallion. Dirt and pebbles rattled down from under the animal's hooves, raising swirls of dust.

Once on the crest, Clay faced westward and smiled. In the distance rose a lot of dust. "It looks like your father cares about you after all, ma'am."

Bent over with her hands on her knees so she could catch her breath, Tessa glanced up and saw the dust cloud. "Dear Lord! Is that who I think it is?"

"Sure enough," Clay said. "Before nightfall you'll get a rare privilege."

"What would that be?"

"You'll get to see your own father gunned down right before your eyes."

Chapter Ten

The posse came to the base of a ridge. Marshal Tom Crane scanned the talus slope above and fidgeted in his saddle. He didn't like being there, not one bit. His mind screamed at him to get the hell out before it was too late, but he couldn't just head on back to Tucson by himself. The others would brand him a coward or worse. And once word spread, not even the influence of Miles Gillett would keep him in office very long.

Crane rubbed the stubble on his chin. It galled him that Taggart's ruse was working in spite of all he had done. He was trapped, sure enough, not only by the damnable White Apache, but by his own kin, who he had never even met, and by his tin star. Lord, how it galled him!

"I don't like this," one of the men said. "That bastard could be up there right this moment setting his sights on us."

"He's not," Clell Baxter said.

Thorson glanced at the old frontiersman. "How can you be so sure?"

"I'd feel him if he were."

With that, Baxter kneed his bay on up the slope. Thorson looked at Gritz and rolled his eyes. The latter chuckled softly. Spreading out, rifles at the ready, the men climbed.

Crane rode near the middle. He was inclined to agree with the buffalo hunter. Taggart would pick a better spot, a place where he could box them in. Still, his eyes never left the rim, and he kept a finger on the trigger of his Winchester at all times. So it was that he didn't notice when the owner of the Acme slanted alongside him.

"I've been doing some thinking, pard," Rafe Skinner said.

"Don't strain yourself."

Skinner absently swatted at a fly, then pulled his hat brim lower against the blinding sun. "It's mighty peculiar if you ask me."

"What is?" Crane asked without lowering his eyes from the crest. His friend had a knack for picking the strangest times to be talkative.

"This whole business. Doesn't it strike you as odd how Taggart happened to hit the exact stage carrying your daughter? Stages use that road all the time, and it's been months since any of them had any trouble. Yet the one stage that your girl is in, Taggart stops."

Crane didn't like where Skinner's trail of logic was leading. "Coincidence is all."

"I suppose it could be. But Taggart seems to have had the whole thing planned out well in advance, even going so far as to take a soldier captive just so he could force the stage to stop. And then there are all these stone arrows. He's making certain we don't lose his trail—or at least one of us doesn't."

"You're saying he's out to get me?"

"Don't you think he is?"

Crane composed himself before answering. His friend was much too close to the truth for comfort. No one other than the men who had taken part in the lynching, and Miles Gillett, of course, knew about what had been done to Taggart, and Crane wanted to keep it that way. "You may have a point. But for the life of me, I can't see why Taggart would have it in for me. I hardly knew the man. I doubt we spoke ten words to each other before he went bad and turned Injun."

The lawman climbed half-a-dozen yards before he grew aware of the penetrating stare his friend was giving him. "Something the matter?"

"How long have we been pards, Tom?"

Crane had to think a moment. "About eleven years or so. Why? What does that have to do with anything?"

"Have I ever lied to you in all that time?"

"No."

"Have you ever lied to me?"

The last thing Crane wanted to do was hesitate, yet he did. There had been a few times, minor affairs hardly worth the mention. "No."

Rafe Skinner stared at the lawman a while longer yet, then flicked his reins and moved off, saying, "When we get back to town, Tom, I'd be obliged if you'd do your drinking and whoring somewhere other than the Acme."

"Rafe!" Crane said, but it was no use. His friend paid him no heed.

By that time, the posse was over halfway up the slope. Baxter was even higher. "Your daughter slipped here, Marshal," he said. "She would have taken a nasty spill but the soldier boy caught her."

Gritz, who was on Crane's left, could not leave well enough alone. "Did you hear that, boys? Sounds to me like true love is in the air. Wouldn't it be something if the marshal goes back to Tucson with not just his daughter but a new son-in-law?"

Anger gushed up from deep within Tom Crane. Given his relationship with Tessa or, more aptly, the lack of one, he had no call to act the part of a typical outraged father. Yet before he could stop himself, he growled, "Shut your foul mouth, mister! And the next man who acts as if my daughter is street trash will end up going back strapped to his horse, toes down! So help me God!"

Cringing in fright, as if trying to crawl into a hole that wasn't there, Gritz said, "I didn't mean nothing by it, Marshal! Honest!"

Crane spurred on ahead. At the top, Baxter waited next to yet another stone arrow.

"Taggart does like to rub our noses in it, doesn't he?" the old-timer said.

"I'll rub his in his own blood before long," Crane said angrily. He was near the end of his patience, and he didn't care who knew it. "How far behind them would you say we are?"

"No more than an hour or so," Baxter said, scratching his beard. "He's not letting them rest very often, but he's not prodding them as viciously as a full-blooded buck would either." He scratched harder, as if he had fleas. "Take Delgadito, for instance. I did some scouting for the army a while ago and saw his handiwork for myself. That devil would make captives run until they dropped, then poke them with his knife to get them to run some more."

Rising in the stirrups, Crane surveyed the countryside to the east. "How much longer does Taggart aim to keep this up?"

"Not much longer at all," Baxter said confidently.

"Do you know where he's headed?"

"I can make a good guess." Baxter gestured at the valley below the ridge. "On the other side is the best place in the whole territory to bushwhack someone. Odds are you've heard of the place."

Crane delved into his memory. A vague recollection pricked him, but that was all. "Where would that be?"

"Devil's Canyon."

Calhoun had been holding Tessa Heritage's hand for the last half an hour, and neither of them had given it a second thought. As they crossed a second low hill after leaving the valley, a vast canyon unfolded before them. Calhoun halted to scrutinize the foreboding stone ramparts and the maze of enormous boulders and barren knolls that dotted the canyon floor. "You're taking us in there?"

Clay Taggart brought the black stallion up close to the pair, then drew rein. He tingled at the thought of soon taking revenge on the man he despised almost as much as he loathed Miles Gillett.

Tom Crane was rotten to the core, a bad apple of a lawman who had no business wearing a badge.

Killing him would not only help to quell the raging flames that burned in Clay's soul; it would be doing the Arizona Territory a favor. But to succeed, Clay had to rely on every skill the Chiricahuas had taught him. It would not be as Clay Taggart, rancher, that he carried out his vengeance. It would be as White Apache.

Crane would not go down easy. Nor were the other posse members likely to stand around doing nothing—unless they had no other option.

"Only the woman goes with me," White Apache said.

Calhoun felt Tessa's grip tighten. Sliding in front of her, he glowered at the renegade. "I don't know what you have in mind, murderer, but she's not going anywhere without me."

"That's where you're wrong."

Tessa cried out as their captor lashed out with the speed of a striking rattler. The butt of the Winchester slammed into the trooper's skull, and he buckled, groaning as he slumped at her feet. With no regard for her own safety, she knelt to cradle Calhoun's head in her lap. A nasty welt marred his brow. "You fiend! How could you?"

White Apache did not mince words. Climbing down, he yanked out his Bowie, reversed his grip, and held the hilt toward her. "Cut two long strips off the bottom of your dress. Quickly."

"I will not!"

A glance across the valley showed stick figures moving on the crest of the ridge. White Apache pressed the muzzle of his rifle to the soldier's ear. "I have no time to argue. Do it or he dies."

Tessa had a sharp retort on the tip of her tongue,

138

but she did not voice it. The butcher wasn't bluffing. Unless she complied, she stood to lose someone who had become very important to her.

Grasping the hilt, Tessa diligently cut at the fabric an inch above the hem. The blade was a razor. It sawed through the material as a hot knife would through butter. In short order, she had the two strips required.

White Apache snatched the knife and replaced it in the beaded sheath. Motioning for her to move back, he squatted and quickly bound the trooper's arms and legs. He also wadded a short strip and crammed it into the private's mouth. Satisfied, he lightly slapped the soldier a few times.

Calhoun jerked up out of a gray haze. His first thoughts were of Tessa. Seeing that she was unharmed, he started to relax, then realized he was tied again.

"Listen to me carefully," White Apache said. "When the posse gets here, you will tell them that only Crane can go on from this point. If anyone other than the marshal enters Devil's Canyon, the woman dies. If you join him, the woman dies. Try any tricks at all, and she is the one who will suffer. Savvy?"

After Calhoun reluctantly nodded, White Apache vaulted smoothly onto the stallion. Bending, he hooked a finger at Tessa. "Up behind me."

To dispute him invited swift retribution. Tessa stepped up close and allowed herself to be hoisted behind him. His muscles rippled like cords. She looked at James and saw mingled despair and longing in his eyes. "I'll be fine. Don't worry."

Calhoun choked down an impulse to shriek in

outrage. It was almost more than he could bear to sit there helpless while the woman he cared for was taken away by a coldhearted fiend. He watched until they disappeared around a knoll. Tessa gave him a lingering look just before she vanished.

In a fury, Calhoun strained at his bounds. He heaved, wrenched, and yanked. He tugged and clawed at the knots. But Taggart had done too thorough a job. Calhoun gained a fraction of slack, no more.

Resigned, Calhoun rotated on his knees so he could spot the posse that much sooner. Nervously gnawing on his lower lip, he yearned for them to hurry up and get there. Time dragged by as if weighted by an millstone. Each second was a minute, each minute an hour.

Just when Calhoun began to think that the posse had lost the trail and would never come, tendrils of dust rose above the hill. The rumble of hooves confirmed the men were near, and he burst into a broad smile when a lanky man in buckskins reached the crown. The man shouted over a shoulder, then barreled down the slope and reined up in a cloud of dust.

"Hold on there, sonny," Clell Baxter said. "I'll have you free in two shakes of a lamb's tail."

The posse converged at a gallop. Tom Crane scoured the canyon floor in dread of a bullet in the brisket. He tried not to dwell on the fact that Taggart might be fixing a bead on him at that very moment. As he dropped to the ground, the soldier stood.

"Marshal!" In his anxiety over Tessa, Calhoun dashed to the lawman and gripped Crane by the shirt. "You have to listen! That madman will kill her if you don't do exactly as he says!"

Crane pried the younger man's fingers loose. "Calm down, boy."

Calhoun couldn't quiet his pounding pulse if his life depended on it. "You have to listen! Clay Taggart, the man called the White Apache, has taken your daughter into the canyon. He wants you to go on by yourself. If anyone else tags along, he says that he'll kill her."

"We know who took her, boy," Calhoun said, studying the maze of boulders and knolls. An entire army could hide in there. What chance would he have going in alone?

Rafe Skinner placed a friendly hand on the cavalryman's shoulder. "How is the girl, Private? Has Taggart harmed her?"

"No, he hasn't laid a finger on her," Calhoun said. "He never really tried to hurt either of us. I have no idea why."

"We do," Clell Baxter said, glancing at the lawman.

Crane needed to think. He advanced a dozen feet to be by himself as the trooper and the members of the posse swapped names. It appeared that Clay Taggart had him over a barrel.

The lawman was no fool. Going on by his lonesome was bound to get him killed. As good as he was with a six-shooter, he'd be no match for a man taught by Apaches.

There was only one thing to do. Early on in Crane's checkered career as a lawman, he had learned a secret essential to the survival of every tin star west of the mighty Mississippi. The lawmen who lasted the longest were the smart ones, the ones who never went into a fight without an edge. It might be a sawed-off shotgun hidden under a coat or a pistol with a shortened barrel concealed in a pocket or a holster that could be tipped up to fire so the lawman did not have to waste precious instants drawing.

All that mattered in the end was that whatever the lawman picked worked. Given the fix Crane was in, he could think of only one thing that might save his bacon. "Baxter?"

The frontiersman ambled over. Pushing his floppy hat back on his head, he asked, "What do you need?"

"Your rifle."

Clell Baxter's scarred eye twitched. "I'd say you must be drunk, but none of us thought to bring a flask along." He patted the Sharps. "Nobody puts a hand on Old Bess but me."

Crane was not about to take no for an answer. Nor would he risk gunplay to get what he wanted. "Hear me out, Clell. Taggart always uses a Winchester. Everyone knows that. And a Winchester doesn't have the range of a Sharps. With your rifle, it would be a cinch to pick him off."

"For me, maybe," Baxter said. "I've been using Old Bess for pretty nigh on twenty-five years. At five hundred yards, I drop antelope and deer all the time. At two hundred yards, I can knock a squirrel out of a tree. And at one hundred yards, I can put a bullet through a bull's-eye ten times out of ten."

Baxter's claims were not idle boasting. Crane had seen the old-timer take part in a marksmanship competition a few years back and win by the highest score ever. He stared at the breech loader, and another inspiration took root. "You mentioned once that you might be interested in collecting the bounty on Taggart. How would you like a chance given to you on a silver platter?"

Baxter pursed his lips. "I'm listening."

"I doubt Taggart will kill me the second he sets eyes on me. My guess is that he wants me to sweat a spell first. So it shouldn't be hard for me to draw him out of hiding to give you a clear shot. What do you say? Will you shadow me into the canyon? We'll split the bounty fifty-fifty."

The frontiersman took all of two seconds to mull it over. "Seventy-thirty and it's a deal."

"Fifty-fifty," Crane said. "I'm the one whose life will be hanging by a thread."

A grin curled Baxter's seamed face. "But I'm the jasper who has to make the shot. Without enough incentive, I might just miss. I do, you know, once every blue moon."

Crane knew not to buck a stacked deck. "Seventy-thirty then. Let's shake on it."

As they did, Calhoun stormed over. He had caught the last part of their exchange, and he was infuriated. "What the hell do you use for brains, Crane? Didn't you hear a word I told you? Taggart will kill your daughter if you don't go on to meet him alone."

"Calm down, boy," the lawman said. "Baxter knows what he's doing. Taggart will never get so much as a glimpse of him."

"But what if he slips up?" Calhoun said. "No, it's too risky. I won't allow it."

Marshal Crane straightened. "You won't allow it?

And just who do you think you are, Private, to be giving orders to me? I'm wearing the badge here. I can do as I damn well please." He started toward the horses.

Calhoun could never say exactly what made him snap. Maybe it was the lawman's callous disregard for the welfare of a woman who had traveled a third of the way across the country to see him. Maybe it was being treated as if he were a child instead of a grown man. Or maybe it was simply love.

Taking a stride, Calhoun threw his entire weight into a solid right to the jaw. It should have knocked Crane down, or at the very least, staggered him. But Calhoun had been without food for days. Lack of sleep and tramping mile after miles across the blistering landscape had further weakened him. His blow merely caused Crane to break stride, no more.

"Why, you young whelp!" the lawman snarled, and he closed in with his fists flailing.

Calhoun blocked the first few punches. Then one clipped him on the cheek and another sank into the pit of his stomach. His knees kissed the ground. His head swam. He barely felt more blows that rained on his shoulders and chest.

Feet pounded. Someone shouted, but Crane couldn't distinguish the words. It was Rafe Skinner. He had grabbed Crane by the shoulders and torn the lawman off the soldier before he could beat the young man half to death. "Simmer down, Tom!"

"Let go of me!" The lawman's pent-up frustrations and simmering hatred of Clay Taggart had found a release, and he wanted nothing more than to pound the trooper into the ground, to grind Cal-

144

houn under his bootheels until his wrath evaporated.

Skinner spun the marshal away and crouched, his right hand hovering near his Remington. Over the years, he had lost track of the number of times he had seen Crane go nearly berserk with fury. The most recent incident had been ten months ago when Crane had pistol-whipped an unruly cowboy nearly into a coma. "I won't let you cripple him or worse. He's just doing what he thinks is right."

No one there expected Tom Crane to draw. The lawman and the saloon owner had always been the best of friends. Skinner himself, despite all that had happened, believed they had been pards for too long for Crane to throw down on him. Every last man there was wrong.

Crane's Colt leapt and boomed, and Rafe Skinner was jolted backward by a jarring smash to his right shoulder.

Swaying, he looked at the bullet hole and said in amazement, "Damn, Tom! You shot me!"

The tableau froze. No one was more shocked than Tom Crane. Until that morning, Rafe Skinner had been his best—some might say his only— friend. Crane had counted on patching up their misunderstanding later on. But Crane's temper had ridden roughshod over his willpower. In a blind rage he had put a slug into the only person in the entire world who gave a hoot if he lived or died.

"Rafe, I—" Crane stepped forward, but Skinner made a sound like a riled cougar and pushed him back.

"Don't you dare, Tom! Not after what you just did!" Skinner teetered. His legs wobbled.

Jake McMasters

Calhoun had recovered enough to loop an arm around the man who had helped him, repaying the favor by slowly lowering Skinner to the ground. Not much blood flowed, which surprised Calhoun. He had always been under the impression that, when someone was shot, he spouted blood.

Crane automatically shed the spent cartridge and inserted a new one. Holstering his revolver, he marched to his horse and forked leather. "Do what you can for Rafe," he said to Thorson and Gritz. Then, raking his spurs, he trotted off into Devil's Canyon.

Calhoun almost sprang in front of the lawman. A groan from Skinner brought him to his senses. Quivering with hatred, he had to stand there and watch in impotent indignation as the lawman and the old man in buckskins departed.

Marshal Crane and Clell Baxter went around the far side of a knoll and were gone. And all Calhoun could do was say the one word that had come to mean the world to him, "Tessa!"

Chapter Eleven

Tessa Heritage gave the young soldier a last longing look as the black stallion swept around a knoll. Calhoun's expression was ample proof that he felt the same way about her that she felt about him. She was going to wave, but the knoll blocked him from view before she could lift an arm.

It took some doing, but Tessa shut Calhoun from her thoughts for the time being. A more immediate concern demanded her attention. "What do you intend to do with me, Mr. Taggart?"

White Apache was studying the lay of the canyon, seeking the ideal spot to carry out his vengeance. He did not like being distracted. "Keep your mouth closed, woman, unless I say otherwise."

Tessa resented being treated so callously, but her abductor's tone left little doubt that he was in no frame of mind to be bothered. She could sense that a change of some sort had come over him. He was

147

colder, harder, more abrupt. He even sat his horse differently: straighter, his head held high, an almost savage air about him.

White Apache slowed down to examine a cluster of boulders that might do for his purpose. It soon became apparent, though, that none were quite broad enough to completely screen the stallion from random gunshots, so he went on. He would not let any harm befall his mount.

Devil's Canyon owed its name to the Spanish, who had called it *Canon del Diablo* long before the arrival of the white man. Their reason for so naming the region was shrouded in mystery. Some claimed it had to do with a priest who had been part of a wagon train. The wagon train had stopped in the canyon for the night, and at some point, the priest had supposedly seen a vision of the devil. Another tale claimed the name was derived from ancient Indian sources that said the very first Indians to settle in the region had believed the canyon was home to evil spirits or demons.

The old stories were of no consequence to White Apache. No devils or demons were going to prevent him from doing what had to be done.

A dark opening at the base of the right-hand wall attracted White Apache's attention. It turned out to be a shallow pit worn down by erosion, the opening was neither deep enough nor wide enough to suit him. He went on.

Another quarter of a mile fell behind them. White Apache was growing vexed. He didn't like to think that he had gone to so much trouble for nothing.

Then a high earthen bank appeared on the left. White Apache veered over, his interest piqued by a cleft in the center of the bank, a cleft wide enough for the big stallion to pass through with ease. On the other side was an open space bordered by a field of jumbled boulders. If he had to make a hasty retreat, the boulders would shield him nicely. The bank's facing slope was gradual, not steep.

That would do, White Apache grimly reflected. Swinging a leg over the stallion's neck, he slid off. He ordered his captive to get down. Not waiting to confirm if she obeyed, he dashed to the top. There, he had a clear line of fire in all directions. No one could get anywhere near him without being spotted. The closest cover had to be well over 500 yards off, well beyond the range of a Winchester or Henry.

Tessa stood meekly by the horse, waiting for Taggart to come down. She knew better than to attempt to ride off. The renegade would drop her in a heartbeat.

Warily watching him descend, Tessa was startled to see a strange gleam animating his deep blue eyes. It reminded her of dancing flames or the flicker of candles. When he looked at her, he seemed to gaze right through her.

"Turn around," White Apache said. She hesitated too long to suit him, prompting him to seize her arm and spin her around. "Stand still," he said, kneeling.

The Bowie made short shrift of the hem of her dress. Using two strips, White Apache bound Tessa's wrist and ankles. As an afterthought, he gagged her, saying, "I can't have you warning your father."

Moving the stallion away from the gap where it would be safe, White Apache let the reins dangle.

He checked his rifle and pistol. Both were fully loaded. As ready as he would ever be, he climbed to the top, stretching out on his stomach just below the rim. The gap was a few feet away to his left.

Since there was no sign yet of the lawman, White Apache set down his rifle and cast about the slope for a long, thin rock. Finding one that resembled a spike, he crouched near the top and rapidly dug a groove about two inches deep and three feet long. In it, he laid the Winchester, then sprinkled dust over the barrel.

The trick was as old as the hills. The dust prevented sunlight from glinting off the metal and giving his position away. Lying flat once more, White Apache focused on the spot where he expected Tom Crane to appear. He was so eager to get revenge that he quivered with excitement.

Below, lying on her right side, Tessa Heritage had to tilt her head far back to see the crest 20 feet above. Taggart was so intent on killing her father that he was paying absolutely no attention whatsoever to her.

Tessa had a decision to make. Was she going to lie there helplessly while her own flesh and blood was murdered? So what if she had never met Crane? So what if he had neglected her over the years? And what did it really matter if he had a reputation as the worst law officer in Arizona? Thomas Crane was still her father. She owed it to him to try to warn him of the White Apache's trap, even if doing so cost her life.

Slowly hiking her knees to her chest, Tessa used her elbow for leverage and pumped herself a few inches closer to the gap. She was careful not to make any noise that might alert her captor. Freezing for a few seconds in case he glanced down, she bunched her shoulder and stomach muscles, then pitched forward.

Inch by gradual inch, Tessa neared the gap. She could not help scraping against the ground occasionally, but never loud enough to be heard. The swish of her dress was a mere whisper.

The whole time, Clay Taggart peered off over the rim, as immobile as a boulder. The Apaches had taught him well.

It took a lifetime, or that was how Tessa felt when at long last she crawled into the gap and was promptly shrouded in shadow. Making bold to go faster, she pushed up onto her knees and hunched along like an oversize snail, her knees wriggling back and forth.

The gap ran eight feet from end to end. Tessa covered half of that distance and cracked a grin in anticipation of thwarting Taggart's scheme.

Then a darker shadow fell across her. Shifting, Tessa was horrified to find the butcher in midair, his features as feral as those of a rabid wolf.

White Apache was incensed. He had shown the woman every consideration, going out of his way to avoid harming her. Where Fiero would have beaten her into submission, he had merely been firm. Where Delgadito would have made her grovel and obey every whim, he had accorded her a measure of dignity.

Not anymore! Few things riled him like having a kindness thrown back in his face. Landing next to her, White Apache gripped her by the hair and yanked her face up close to his. "You've brought this on yourself!"

Tessa squealed as she was roughly dragged back, the gag muffled her outcry. She lashed out with both legs, but the angle was all wrong for her to connect. Twisting her head only made the pain worse, so she let herself be hauled to where the stallion stood. Without ceremony, she was dumped on her back.

"Try that again and you'll lose some teeth," White Apache said. Quickly taking his place near the top, he surveyed the west end of the canyon and was overjoyed to detect wisps of smoke drawing nearer. It wouldn't be long.

Marshal Tom Crane was thinking the same thing. His right hand resting on his Colt, he probed every nook and cranny. Beads of sweat trickled down his spine, and every so often, he would catch himself holding his breath.

Crane was scared. He'd never admit as much to a living soul, but he was deathly afraid of dying. Worse, he couldn't stand the idea of being slain by the likes of Clay Taggart.

The lawman had not held anything personal against the rancher that day Miles Gillett had come to town and told him to organize a lynch party. The request had just been the latest in an endless string of jobs he had done for Gillett.

It had embarrassed Crane tremendously when he had learned Taggart had somehow survived and taken up with a pack of renegade Apaches. Gillett had been livid. Crane couldn't blame the man since he had paid good money to make sure things were done properly. For the first time ever, Crane had failed.

That was when the situation with Taggart had become personal. Crane not only had a score to settle, he had to redeem himself in Gillett's eyes. The rich man never tolerated fools, and he certainly did not abide incompetents. If Miles Gillett were to think that Crane was no longer able to get the work done, he was not above removing the marshal from office and replacing him with someone who could.

Crane wouldn't let that happen. He depended on the money Gillett lavished on him to be able to retire one day with enough to tide him over until he was planted in a grave.

Passing a knoll, Crane came to an open tract. Immediately a sixth sense he had honed over the years flared up. A tiny voice screamed in his head that he should wheel his horse and get the hell out of there while he could. But he rode on, studying a high earthen bank to the north. Nothing moved along the crest, nor was there any telltale gleam of sunlight off a rifle barrel. Still, something told him that was where Taggart must be.

Someone else shared those sentiments. Clell Baxter had been through Devil's Canyon before. As was typical of any frontiersman worthy of the name, he had a phenomenal memory for landmarks and the lay of the land in general. So it was that, when the lawman had passed two likely spots for an ambush and not been attacked, Baxter had become convinced that the White Apache lay in wait on the earthen bank.

Veering to the north, Baxter paralleled the lawman instead of trailing behind. He held his horse to a slow walk to avoid raising dust. On reaching the last knoll, Baxter dismounted and crept to the rim. Leery of exposing himself to the turncoat, he hiked an eyeball high enough to peek over.

At that moment, Marshal Tom Crane was 50 yards out. He searched for tracks, but the earth was so rocky that none were evident. Going another 50 yards, he noticed a gap in the bank. Shaded by the high wall of dirt, the gap was as likely a place for Taggart to be as any other.

The clomp of his mount's hooves echoed dully off the towering canyon walls. No other sounds could be heard, not even the wind that whipped Crane's hat and plucked at his shirt.

Two hundred yards of open ground were covered without incident. Then 300. Crane wondered if maybe he had been mistaken.

But White Apache had the marshal of Tucson dead in the sights of his Winchester. All Clay Taggart had to do was stroke the trigger when Crane came a little closer. The corners of his mouth curled as his finger did likewise around the trigger. He held his breath to steady his aim. Pivoting on his heels, he tracked Crane as the man came steadily closer.

The lawman was less than 100 yards out when a strange thing happened. White Apache suddenly dipped the barrel of his rifle over an inch. Without hesitation, he fired.

Tom Crane heard the sickening fleshy smack of hot lead as it ripped into the side of his horse. Voicing a strident whinny, the animal staggered, shook, and fell. Crane pushed off from the saddle, seeking to leap clear, but his left spur snagged on the stirrup. Franticly, he tugged with all his strength. His boot popped free, but before he could spring, the horse toppled on top of his leg, pinning him.

Fully expecting another bullet to tear into him at any second, Crane shoved against the dead animal. He couldn't move it. In desperation, he threw himself backward, pulling at his trapped limb, which wouldn't move. Bending, he grabbed the saddle horn for extra leverage and heaved upward. It was then that he saw the bronzed figure stalking toward him.

White Apache had the Winchester wedged to his shoulder, the sights settled squarely on the lawman. He advanced cautiously, the barrel never wavering until he was 20 feet from the man who had strung him up and left him for the buzzards to feast on. Raw, bitter emotion almost overwhelmed him.

"Remember me, bastard?" Clay Taggart said.

Marshal Crane held himself perfectly still, his hands resting on the saddle horn. To make a stab for his pistol would earn him a round in the chest before he could hope to clear leather, so he made no abrupt moves. His hope was that Clell Baxter would come to his aid before Taggart got around to firing. Stalling, he said, "I never forget the face of someone I've hanged."

Clay's boiling core erupted. Storming forward, he stood poised to shoot. The Winchester's muzzle was mere inches from the lawman's brow. "You dare to rub my nose in it, sidewinder?"

Crane realized the statement had been a mistake the moment the words were out of his mouth. He braced for the searing pain of impact, but the turncoat didn't fire. "Take it as a compliment, mister.

All I meant is that you're a tough hombre to kill."

"A compliment?" Clay said, flabbergasted. "You helped Miles Gillett ruin my life, and I'm supposed to be flattered?" Overpowering hatred coursed through him. Taking another step, he kicked the lawman.

Crane tried to dodge, but pinned as he was, he caught a glancing blow to the shoulder that smashed him onto his back. He looked up at Taggart, his gut balling into a knot. Never had he seen anyone so close to the razor edge of going berserk.

Without being obvious, Crane glanced westward, seeking some sign of Clell Baxter. There had been plenty of time for the old-timer to catch up and discover his plight. So why hadn't the man done anything? What in the hell was Baxter waiting for?

At that instant, on top of the knoll, the frontiersman did indeed have his Sharps trained on the White Apache, but he held his fire because of the potential danger to the marshal. Even though Clell was confident the Sharps would drop Taggart where the man stood, there was a chance that Taggart's trigger finger might coil in automatic reflex. If that happened, the Winchester would go off and send a bullet into Crane.

Baxter gnawed on his lower lip, biding his time until Taggart either lowered the rifle or seemed about to shoot.

Clay was in no rush to do either. "Do you want to know why I shot your horse out from under you instead of shooting you?" he asked Crane while leaning down. "I wanted the pleasure of watching you die up close. I want to see the look in your eyes. I want to hear you gasp your last breath."

HANGED!

Again Crane glanced westward. Where are you, Baxter? he wanted to shout.

Clay slowly straightened up. Contempt replaced the hatred, and he let the Winchester drop a trifle. "It's a good thing your daughter won't see this. She doesn't deserve to have a polecat like you for a father."

"Tessa?" Crane had forgotten all about her since his clash with Rafe Skinner. "Where is she?"

Clay wagged an elbow at the earthen bank. "Over yonder, tied up good and proper." He was sorry that he had neglected to plug her ears so she wouldn't hear the screams.

"What do you aim to do with her?" Crane asked, continuing to stall. It didn't matter to him whether she was alive or dead.

"What do you care?" Clay said. The Winchester dropped lower as he reached for his Bowie knife.

A few minutes earlier, at the mouth of Devil's Canyon, Pvt. Calhoun applied a cloth soaked with water to the brow of Rafe Skinner, who was drenched with sweat and gritting his teeth.

"Maybe this will help some," Calhoun said.

"Much obliged, son," Skinner said.

Nearby, the men from Tucson huddled, whispering excitedly, as they had been doing ever since the lawman and the buffalo hunter had left. Thorson turned and came over, the others at his heels. "We've been thinking," he said.

"Did it give you a headache?" Skinner asked sarcastically despite his condition.

Thorson shrugged off the crack. "We figure the marshal is trying to cheat us out of any stake in the reward. Baxter and he likely figure on dividing it up between them and leaving us with empty pockets. Well, we're not about to let that happen. Which is why we're going after them."

"You can't go in there!" Calhoun said, clutching the bearded ruffian by the shoulders. "It's bad enough that Crane took Baxter with him. If all of you go, poor Tessa won't stand a prayer."

Batting the trooper's arms aside, Thorson said, "She doesn't mean a thing to us, boy. All we're interested in is the money."

"That's right," Gritz said.

In a body, the six men turned to go. Calhoun took a bound and grabbed Thorson again. "Please listen to me! Her life is in your hands!"

Bellowing an oath, Thorson waded into the cavalryman. Calhoun planted himself and blocked a flurry of fists. Cocking his right fist, he landed a solid right that rocked the bigger man. But then Gritz and two others pounced, and Calhoun went down under a hail of angry punches. Another pair unlimbered their hardware to cover Calhoun while the others mounted.

Dazed and tormented by the conviction Tessa Heritage would die, Calhoun stared blankly as they departed. It numbed him to think that fellow human beings could be so uncaring, that six grown men were willing to let a helpless innocent perish in order to line their pockets.

A cough reminded Calhoun that one posse member remained. Turning, he was surprised to behold Rafe Skinner struggling to sit up. "You should lie down." Calhoun said.

"Help me."

HANGED!

"You've been shot," Calhoun said.

Skinner snorted. "Think I don't know that, Private? Now help me, damn it." He indicated a waist-high boulder a few yards away. "I want you to prop me up over there."

Against his better judgment, Calhoun did as the tall man asked. "Satisfied?"

Rafe Skinner placed a hand on the soldier's wrist. "Take my horse and go after them before it's too late."

Calhoun glanced at the zebra dun. Part of him yearned to fly like the wind to Tessa's aid, but another part of him balked at leaving a wounded man alone. "I couldn't—"

"You love her, don't you?"

Calhoun gawked, at a loss to comprehend how this stranger could penetrate to the very depths of his soul.

Rafe Skinner grinned wryly. "Hell, Private, it's as plain as could be. Why else would you be so worried? Light a shuck. I'll be fine until you get back. I have my pistol." Skinner licked his dry lips, then motioned at his right foot. "Slip your fingers in there and take what you find."

It was a derringer sporting pearl grips, a two-shot model with a circular hammer and no trigger guard. Calhoun hefted it as he rose. "I'll never be able to thank you enough," he said, choked by the man's kindness.

"Just go, you dunderhead!" Skinner said.

Calhoun lost no time in running to the zebra dun. It shied, and it might have dashed off had he not caught the reins. Speaking softly to soothe its ruf-

159

fled nerves, Calhoun managed to calm the horse sufficiently to climb on.

"Be careful," Skinner said. "He's a mite frisky."

Hardly was Calhoun in the saddle before the horse streaked into Devil's Canyon. Calhoun tossed back his head to shout for joy, but thought better of the idea. Forewarning Thorson and Gritz that he was after them would be a mistake.

Raking the dun's flanks, Calhoun raced to save the woman he adored. On the tip of his tongue was a prayer that he wouldn't be too late, that he would reach Tessa's side before the shooting started. But just at that moment, in the distance, a rifle boomed.

A minute earlier, the Fifth Cavalry officer responsible for the young private's welfare, Capt. Vincent Eldritch, was approaching Devil's Canyon from the east. His patrol had scoured the northern Dragoons for some sign of Sgt. O'Shaughnessy and his men without result.

The day before, Eldritch had been about to call the search off and return to Fort Bowie when they had stumbled on an exhausted cavalry mount wandering aimlessly. Cpt. Tinsdale had recognized it as a sorrel issued to Pvt. James Calhoun, one of the men with O'Shaughnessy's detail. So Eldritch had pressed on.

Now the officer was ready to call the search off for good. There had been no trace of the missing men. It was as if the earth had opened up and swallowed them whole, except for the lone horse.

Capt. Eldritch glanced over a shoulder at the tired, dusty troopers strung out in his wake. He raised an arm to give the signal to halt. A short breather and they would head back.

As he did, a rifle shot rang out to the west.

Chapter Twelve

As Clay Taggart's fingers closed on the smooth hilt of his Bowie knife, Marshal Tom Crane clawed at his Colt. The revolver was wedged between the lawman's pinned leg and the soil. Crane tugged, but he could not get it out.

Grinning in triumph, Clay Taggart lunged, spearing the Bowie at Marshal Crane's throat. Suddenly it felt as if an invisible hammer had slammed into his left shoulder. He was flung over three feet and crashed onto his back next to the dead mount's head. Only then did he hear the boom of a distant rifle and realize he had been shot.

Crane wanted to howl for joy. The frontiersman had come through for him in the nick of time! Then he saw Taggart move. Twisting, he renewed his attempt to draw his pistol.

Clay rose onto an elbow, warding off dizziness and nausea. The slug had cored the fleshy part of his shoulder, sparing the bone and veins. It hurt like hell. But compared to the agony of being hanged, it was nothing. He started to rise. The impact had jarred the Winchester from his hands, but he still had the Bowie.

Up on the knoll, Clell Baxter's fingers worked feverishly as he fed another big cartridge into the Sharps. He knew that he had missed Taggart's heart. The renegade had moved just as he fired. It could happen to anyone.

Baxter sighted down the barrel once more. He could see the crown of Taggart's head, but little else thanks to the dead horse. Its rump blocked his view. Then his intended quarry reared up and Baxter swiveled his elbow to place the sights squarely on the White Apache's chest. He was a shade too slow. Before he could shoot, Taggart pounced on Tom Crane.

The lawman had finally pulled his pistol. He was leveling it when Clay slammed into his chest and they both went down, locked together, each with an iron grip on the other's wrist. Clay strived to bury his blade while Crane attempted to get off a shot.

Tom Crane knew that Baxter couldn't fire so long as Crane was on top of him. Grunting, he shifted and heaved, but Taggart clung to him as tenaciously as a panther.

Clay guessed what the lawman was up to. Hooking a leg around Crane's free leg and digging his knee into the ground for added purchase, he drove the Bowie steadily nearer. Already the gleaming tip was inches from Crane's throat.

Growing desperate, the marshal triggered a shot

that went wide. He strained his utmost to level the Colt and could not. A fraction at a time, the Bowie came inexorably ever closer. Crane broke out in a cold sweat. "Damn you! May you rot in hell!"

"You first!" Wrenching his whole body to one side to throw Crane off balance, Clay thrust down and in. The polished steel lanced into the lawman's throat to the hilt, shearing flesh, severing arteries. Warm blood spurted onto Clay's arm. Drops spattered his cheeks.

Above them, Clell Baxter raised his head. Even that far off, he could tell what had happened. The lawman was as good as dead, which didn't bother Baxter one bit since it meant he could keep all the bounty money for himself.

Tom Crane had gone abruptly weak. His limbs flopped to the ground and he had difficulty sucking in air. A pink haze seemed to envelop the world around him. He wanted to speak, to explain that the lynching had not been personal, that it had been a job, nothing more. Why that should be so important, he didn't rightly know. His mouth, though, wouldn't work.

A haze also enveloped Clay Taggart, a red, fiery haze, as the hatred he had pent up for so long found release. There was one of the men who had destroyed the life he had once known, who had made him an outcast, who was responsible for the loss of everything he once held dear! Yanking the bloody Bowie out, White Apache arced his arm on high. Then he stabbed the lawman in the chest, again and again and again. He stabbed until his arm was coated crimson from fingertips to elbow.

Watching from 500 yards off, Clell Baxter

laughed. "That boy is plumb loco." He fixed a bead on the turncoat's chest. "This time, I won't miss, mister."

In the midst of his torment, at the peak of his outrage, Clay Taggart suddenly remembered that Crane had not been alone. He did what any man would do: He threw himself to the ground and rolled. A bullet whizzed overhead, passing through the very space he had occupied a heartbeat before. On elbows and knees, he scrambled to his Winchester and scooped it up. Another slug thudded into the earth a hand's width from his head as he whipped around and pressed close to the horse.

Clell Baxter was in a funk. It was unthinkable that he had missed twice in a row. He worked the trigger guard of the Sharps, which acted much like the lever on a Winchester, and opened the breech so he could insert a new cartridge. Taggart had ducked from sight, but Baxter wasn't worried. The renegade had nowhere to go. It was too far to the knoll for the Winchester to reach. And the nearest cover, the earthen bank, was about 100 yards from the dead mount. Taggart couldn't possibly reach it.

Clay had pinpointed where the shots were coming from, thanks to puffs of gunsmoke above the knoll. He didn't waste lead returning fire. Instead, he stared at the gap in the bank, pondering. Odds were that the shooter had a Sharps, since no other rifle was as accurate at that range. If so, Clay had a slim chance, but it was worth taking.

The Sharps line of rifles had long been acknowledged to be the most powerful on the frontier. For years, they had been used by mountain men, fur trappers, and buffalo hunters alike. A Sharps could drop a bull buffalo with a single shot and bring down hostiles at 1,000 yards, or so many claimed. Its range was unequaled.

But the Sharps had a major flaw that explained why so many plainsmen, ranchers, and gunmen relied more on Winchesters, Henrys, and Remingtons. For all its power, the Sharps was a single-shot weapon. It only held one bullet. Unlike the Winchester, which could be loaded with 15 rounds and then fired just as fast as a man could pump the lever, the Sharps had to be loaded one cartridge at a time. Since the cartridges were so large, and the rifle itself heavy and cumbersome, the average rate of fire for even the most skilled of marksmen was only four or five shots a minute.

Clay calculated that it would take him much less than that to reach the bank. The man on the knoll might be able to get off two shots, certainly no more than three. It was crucial that Clay get out of there. The gunfire was bound to bring the rest of the posse on the run.

Girding his legs under him, Clay sucked in a breath and hurtled toward the gap, flying as if there were wings on his feet, weaving and winding to make a harder target.

Clell Baxter was taken by surprise. Cursing, he jammed the Sharps to his shoulder and jerked on the trigger instead of stroking it. Dust kicked up at the renegade's heels. Swearing fiercely, Baxter fed in another cartridge, then steadied his breathing and took deliberate aim, wanting to be sure.

Clay Taggart tensed for the next blast. He had been lucky the first one had missed, and he knew the shooter would be more careful with the second.

Zigzagging sharply, he never ran more than three steps in any given direction. He was halfway to the bank when he dived, hitting the ground on his shoulder and letting his momentum carry him back onto his feet.

The frontiersman had been about to shoot. At the last instant Baxter held his fire, waiting until Taggart was erect and barreling toward the bank. Quickly sighting, Clell smiled as his finger curved around the trigger. He had the turncoat dead to rights. The Sharps belched lead and smoke.

Clay Taggart was a dead man—or he would have been had his right foot not caught in a rut, throwing him off stride. He stumbled to one side just as the bullet whined past. Recovering, he raced forward, gaining the gap before another shot could ring out.

"Son of a bitch!" Never in all his born days had Baxter seen anyone so damned lucky! Lowering the Sharps, he slid down the knoll to his horse and swiftly mounted. As he wheeled westward, he saw the six no-accounts bearing down on him.

"Where's the marshal?" Thorson said. "What was all the shooting about?"

Baxter rested the Sharps across his pommel. "I did my best, boys, and it wasn't good enough. So long." He lifted the reins, but a cry from Gritz gave him pause.

"You're leaving? Just like that?"

"I haven't lived as long as I have by being a jack-ass," Baxter said. "Taggart's medicine is too strong for me. I know a lost cause when I see one." With that, he flew off at a gallop.

Thorson and Gritz exchanged looks and smiled. "That means we don't have to share the money with anyone else," the bearded man said.

"What are we waiting for? Let's get the turncoat!" another man said.

At that moment, Clay Taggart was bent over Tessa Heritage. He saw raw spite in her eyes, and he could guess what she was going to ask before he removed the gag. "Yes, he's dead." A slash of the Bowie severed the loop binding her wrists. Another freed her ankles.

Tessa drew back a hand to slap him, but paused, aware of something moist on her wrist. Looking, she discovered fresh drops of blood. Her father's blood. "Oh, Lord!" she said, her stomach churning.

Tessa had heard the shooting and hoped against hope that it meant Taggart's ambush had failed. But knowing the truth, the proof glistening on her skin, she felt something snap deep within her. "Murderer!" Rising, she flung herself at Taggart, seeking to claw his eyes out.

Clay had been about to climb on the stallion. Catching hold of her wrists, he held her at arm's length while she thrashed and kicked and fumed.

"Do you have any idea what you have done?" Tessa asked. "After everything I've been through! The years of wondering, of feeling like part of my life was missing! Now I'll never get to know my father! Never! Thanks to you!"

Dodging a kick that would have shattered his knee, Clay was content to stand there until she quieted. The clatter of hooves let him know he did not have that luxury. Shoving her so hard that she fell, he vaulted astride the black. "I can never make you understand, lady, so I won't even try."

Tessa glowered, every fiber of her being vibrating

with a fury such as she had never known. "Words won't change what you've done! If it's the last thing I ever do, I'll see that you pay for killing my father!"

Sadly shaking his head, the most wanted man in Arizona reined his horse into the gap. He stopped on spying the posse near the slain lawman. A posse had tracked Clay Taggart down, a posse had tossed a hemp noose over his head and left him gasping for breath at the end of a rope.

White Apache walked the stallion into the open. The stock of his rifle rested on his thigh. His shoulder ached, but he refused to give in to the pain. Throwing his head back, he voiced a Chiricahua war cry.

Thorson, Gritz, and the others with them swung around. Thorson jabbed his pistol at the dark-haired figure. "It's him, boys! Money on the hoof! Ours for the taking!"

Yipping and hollering, the men from Tucson charged. They commenced shooting even though they were too far away for their pistols to be effective. Greed made them careless. Stupidity made them reckless.

White Apache spurred the stallion to meet them. With the reins held loosely in his left hand, he snapped the Winchester up. Twice the rifle cracked, and at each crisp retort, a saddle emptied.

"Split up!" Thorson said. "Don't make it easy for him!"

Veering to the right with Gritz close behind, Thorson thumbed the hammer three times. He wasn't a good enough shot to drop the renegade, but he was sure he could bring the horse down. And once Taggart was on foot, they could close in and finish him off.

White Apache swiveled, tracked a white-eye, and cored the man's brain at 60 yards. Leaden hornets buzzed him thick and fast, but none came near enough to sting. The Winchester bucked again and a fourth townsman toppled.

Only Thorson and Gritz were left. Suddenly deciding that it was suicide to go up against the renegade by themselves, they looped to the west to flee.

White Apache had others ideas. Giving the black stallion its head, he gave chase. The pair sped past the knoll, lashing their steeds in stark fear, glancing back every now and again to see whether he was gaining. And he was. Yard by yard, bit by bit, the stallion overhauled them.

"Oh, God!" Gritz said. "We're done for!"

"Just ride, damn it! Ride!" Thorson said.

White Apache heard their yells. So did Pvt. Calhoun, who picked that moment to appear out of a maze of boulders. Seeing only the bearded man and the weasel, Calhoun reined up. "What are you—" He froze as the White Apache rounded a bend.

"Run for your life!" Thorson said.

Calhoun did no such thing. Staying right where he was, he calmly waited until Clay Taggart was almost on top of him. He held the derringer close to his thigh so Taggart would think he was unarmed. Then, suddenly brandishing the small gun, he barked, "Stop or you're a dead man!"

Clay Taggart reined up. "We meet again, soldier boy," he said with a smile.

Confused by the White Apache's friendly greeting, Calhoun took a few moments to marshal his wits and blurt in an official tone, "In the name of the United States Government, I take you into custody."

"No," Clay said softly.

"No?" Calhoun said, shocked that the man could sit there so casually with a derringer pointed at his head. "Nothing you can say or do will stop me."

"What about the filly you're so fond of?" Clay asked. "She's back up the canyon, unarmed, with no one to keep her company but her dead father. Adios, Private. Let's hope we never meet again."

"You're not going anywhere!" Calhoun extended the derringer farther. It was his duty to take the White Apache in or to kill him. Yet in spite of all that had happened, in spite of the ordeal Taggart had put them through, Calhoun found that he couldn't squeeze the trigger. Try as he might, he simply couldn't.

The trooper's inner conflict was etched on his face. Clay brought the stallion up next to the zebra dun. "You're no killer, Calhoun. You can't gun a man down unless he's trying to do the same to you. And you're not the kind to shoot someone in the back either. She needs you. Don't make a mistake you'll regret the rest of your born days. A woman like her only comes along once in a man's lifetime."

Calhoun, Fifth Cavalry, dutifully sworn to uphold the Constitution of the United States of America and to defend all its citizens, sat and watched as the scourge of the Arizona Territory galloped around the bend.

For a few seconds, Calhoun stared numbly into empty space. Then, with a toss of his head, he hastened eastward. It did not take long to find Tessa on her knees beside her father. Tears were streaming down her cheeks, and her hands were clutching her heaving bosom.

Calhoun was off the dun while it was still in motion. He ran to Tessa and knelt, draping an arm over her shoulders. "I'm here," he said, as if that would be enough to comfort her.

Tessa's gaze was glued to the lawman. "Did you kill him?" she asked in a voice so harsh that it seemed as if another person had spoken.

"Taggart?" Calhoun said, and he was terrified of her reaction should she learn the truth. "No, he—he got away."

"Good. I want the honor of killing him myself."

Horrified, Calhoun lowered his arm. "You can't mean that," he said. She wasn't the same kind, gentle woman he thought that he knew. She had become someone as cold as ice, as hard as flint.

At that moment, Devil's Canyon echoed with the drum of hooves in regular cadence. Calhoun spun, prepared to sell his life dearly to protect Tessa from the hostiles he was afraid were descending on them. The sight of a long column of blue uniforms of buttons and tack glinting in the sunlight, of seasoned soldiers sitting straight and proud filled him with boundless joy. "It's Capt. Eldritch!" he said, leaping to his feet and waving his arms. "We're safe now! Everything will be fine!

Tessa Heritage didn't answer. As far as she was concerned, her life would never be fine again until she stood over the lifeless husk of the butcher who had shattered her dream of getting to know the father she had always longed to have.

"We're safe!" Calhoun said again as the patrol drew near. He wondered if by some miracle the captain could overtake Clay Taggart before the killer got to the open country to the west, and he very much doubted it. Once Taggart reached the mouth of Devil's Canyon, he could melt into the wilderness without a trace.

The thought caused Calhoun to stiffen and pivot. In his anxiety over Tessa, he had forgotten the wounded man he had left at the canyon entrance.

Rafe Skinner was directly in the White Apache's path.

Heat blistered the owner of the Acme Saloon. His wound throbbed, and his mouth was parched. Skinner swallowed a few times to relieve dryness in his throat.

The shooting had stopped a couple of minutes earlier. Judging by the echoes of the gunfire, a regular battle had taken place.

Rafe suspected that Tom Crane's ruse had not worked out as intended and that he would never see his old pard again. Just a day earlier, he would have been saddened by the loss. But he wouldn't feel much sadness for Crane's passing since he'd learned that Crane thought so little of their friendship and even less of his own daughter.

Hoofbeats heralded the arrival of a pair of riders who thundered toward Skinner in a swirl of dust. Squinting in the bright sunshine, he reached for his pistol. In his condition, he doubted he could hit the broad side of a barn, but he was not about to have his lamp blown out without putting up a fight.

Thorson and Gritz came to a halt only feet away from Skinner, and the bearded bear beckoned. "No time for talk! The White Apache is after us! Get up and you can ride behind me."

Skinner had already tried to stand several times. "I can't. I've lost too much blood."

Gritz cast an anxious gaze into the dust cloud. "Hurry, damn it! I swear I heard him right behind us!"

Thorson did not need a lot of persuading. "Sorry, Skinner. We can't tote you clear back to Tucson. He'd catch us for sure." He touched his hat brim. "You can see how it is, can't you?"

Rafe Skinner never got to reply. Two shots spaced a second apart rang out. At the first blast, the front of Gritz's forehead exploded in a shower of gore, some of which rained on Skinner. The next shot blew a hole the size of an apple in Thorson's face. Both men thudded to the earth at the same time and lay twitching and quivering.

From out of the dust another figure appeared, riding slowly, a smoking Winchester propped on a muscular thigh. Rafe Skinner attempted to raise his arm, but it was so unsteady that he feared he would hit the black stallion instead of the renegade.

White Apache drew rein a dozen feet out. He pointed the Winchester. "Are you a member of the posse?"

"I am," Rafe said.

"Any last words?"

One thing was uppermost on Skinner's mind. "The girl?" he said. "Is she all right? Or did you butcher her like you have so many others?" On the sly, he firmed his hold on the Remington. He had no reason to expect an answer, and every reason to believe that in another few moments he would be sent to meet his Maker. But he didn't cringe, he didn't flinch.

To Rafe Skinner's astonishment, White Apache swung the Winchester barrel skyward again, then clucked to the stallion. The horse passed so close that Skinner could have reached out and touched it. Too dazed to shoot, he twisted and saw the rogue outlaw ride off into the haze.

"Why?" Rafe said to the solitary horsemen. "Why did you let me live?"

It was a question that would haunt Rafe Skinner for many days to come. And it was one to which he received no reply.

A moment later, the mesquite closed around White Apache. Once in deep cover, he bent the stallion's steps toward the high Dragoons and the secluded valley he called home.

WHITE APACHE

DOUBLE EDITION
They left him for dead, he'll see them in hell!
Jake McMasters

Hangman's Knot. Taggart is strung up and left out to die by a posse headed by the richest man in the territory. Choking and kicking, he is seconds away from death when he is cut down by a ragtag band of Apaches, not much better off than himself. Before long, the white desperado and the desperate Apaches have formed an unholy alliance that will turn the Arizona desert red with blood.

And in the same action-packed volume....

Warpath. Twelve S.O.B.s left him swinging from a rope, as good as dead. But it isn't Taggart's time to die. Together with his desperate renegade warriors he will hunt the yellowbellies down. One by one, he'll make them wish they'd never drawn a breath. One by one he'll leave their guts and bones scorching under the brutal desert sun.

_4185-5 $4.99 US/$5.99 CAN